The Price

of Life

By Brian Barnard

First published in the United Kingdom in 2023

ISBN

Main characters

Brian (Barney): Team leader
Jess (Baby Girl): Pilot
Danny (Little Fella): Mechanic/Driver
Karen Fletcher (Fletch): Tactical Operations Manager
Cassisdy Dawkins (Cass): FBI Special Agent
Jocelyn Harker (Joss): CIA analyst/Cyber crimes specialist
Charlotte Green (Charlie): Combat Surgeon
Catherine Muller (Katie): Interpol Major Crime's officer
Sean Miller: SBS/Royal Marine Weapons expert
Scott Dean: Navy Seal/Marine Sniper
Aleksandr Lyashev (Alek): FSB counter terror specialist
Levi Johnson: DEA agent
Christopher Dawson: British Intelligence
Nick Sanchez: CIA forensic specialist
Pierre Laurent (Pete): Canadian scientist and chemical specialist
Bruce: Barneys Dog, Retired explosives search dog
James Ramsey: Operations Manager CSM 3rd Battalion Rangers
George H Leverson: 3 star General based at the Pentagon
Harland Jones: British Intelligence

Stephen Goodbanks: Billionaire businessman
Damian Stevens: Assassin/Fixer
Miguel De La Cruz: Cartel Boss
Angie Saunders: Con artist/Fixer

Chapter 1

The explosion had knocked them both off their feet, Sean had been slightly luckier as he was ten foot behind Barney when the building went up. Neither of them could hear or see, their ears were ringing, and the air was full of brick dust and sand from the blast. Barney felt like he'd been hit with a sledgehammer, the sudden force had winded him, and he was fighting to breathe. He'd been working around explosives for years and had seen the effects numerous times, sometimes close up and sadly sometimes at the cost of a friends life. One thing he knew for certain was that he didn't want to be that bloody close ever again.

The assignment they were on couldn't be carried out by the military. A high-ranking Afghan businessmen had disagreed with his Brother-in-law and they had fallen out, the brother-in-law was so outraged he'd kidnapped the businessmen's two children. Not knowing how to even begin to get them back he called a friend in America who called a friend who had enough clout to get the team involved. It was yet another assignment that they'd carry out bridging the gap between civilian and military involvement.

Barney had been approached as he was coming to the end of a pretty hectic tour in Afghanistan. He was asked if he'd be prepared to head up a team created from various nationalities and skill sets that would work between governments and countries dealing with issues that, in all honesty, nobody wanted to acknowledge or own up to. Their assignments took them all over the world bridging the gap between agencies and cultures that just simply wouldn't deal with each other in the public eye. Often facilitating favours between governments under the radar, which is why Barney found himself back in Afghan, in the heat of the day and on the receiving end of a booby trap.

Sean had managed to get to his knees, the air was beginning to clear and he was looking for his headset. Not surprisingly it wasn't where it should have been. He saw it lying ten feet away and crawled over to it, it seemed to be okay and he put it back on his head connecting it back to the radio in one well rehearsed movement hoping that everything was still going to work. His breathing was still rather rapid as he spoke into the mic, "mobile one can you hear me?"

The response from Danny was instant "Mobile One go ahead."

Sean instantly relaxed a little, "come straight to us, we'll both be waiting."

Danny had known something wasn't right when he heard the explosion in the distance. It wasn't hard to guess that it was related to their assignment. This was going to be a simple job Barney had said, we go in, talk to the brother-in-Law and get the two kids back. No dramas, no problems. Well apart from the bloody great explosion it was all going to plan. The only problem was Danny wasn't sure just whose plan it was now. He was parked about ten minutes away and was driving as fast as he could without making himself stand out too much. Things were now far more complicated, and he didn't want to make himself a further complication. He'd spent a fair bit of time with Sean on familiarisation sessions on all the roads, good and bad. Danny had been amazed at just how poor the road network was the further you got away from civilisation and hadn't even been to some of the areas that the guys had experienced contact with the enemy. He certainly admired the military drivers doing this day in and day out. "Mobile two, this is one over."

"This is two, go ahead."

He could hear the concern in her voice and knew that she would be worried but sensible enough to remain thoroughly professional. "Meet at RV Bravo, I'll update you as soon as I know more," he hoped she'd be okay,

"Roger that."

He could tell from her voice that she was fine. Within five minutes of the blast the Defender and the Bell were on the move.

When Jess found out the Client had secured a Bell 249 for the assignment she was over the moon, she was like a child with a new toy.

5

To anyone watching though, now it seemed like she was trying her very best to break it, she was in the air as fast as the systems would allow. She kept to 200 feet and raced to the RV. It was less than ten minutes away, but she wanted to be there and ready as quickly as she could. She loved flying and spent every minute practicing with various trainers or on simulators that she'd managed to convince people to let her use. Not that they had much choice as she was rather persuasive when she wanted to be. She kept the helicopter as level as possible to allow Charlie to get everything ready, they both knew something had gone wrong because Bravo was the emergency pick up point and if everything had gone to plan they would be taking a leisurely flight to Alpha.

Charlie already had most of the kit she might need in place and was just making a few adjustments in case things were bad when they landed, she was used to bad, for the last five years she'd been a combat surgeon based in some of the busiest military bases in the world. "Okay Jess I'm ready, bring us down so we're facing south, that way they'll be driving straight to the side I need them."

Jess looked over her shoulder at Charlie and smiled, she was trying to hide the concern but wasn't doing a good job.

"They'll be fine, if they weren't we'd already know because one of them would have told us what they need, and we've heard nothing."

Jess just nodded and focussed on getting them there as quickly as possible. Her movements in the cockpit were smooth and precise, almost textbook. She was good at flying and never really showed off her skills, the only way you'd know just how good she was is if you were a pilot yourself. Then you'd appreciate the way she made everything look effortless.

While Danny and Jess were heading to their respective new locations Sean had already checked on Barney who was now up and about and in what could only be described as a foul mood. "Well they obviously knew someone was going to be coming but I didn't expect this." The two story building had almost been levelled. The two houses either side weren't looking that great either. Locals were beginning to make themselves known and although they were in casual clothes, they both knew that they stood out and were very aware that they needed to get away. "We need to know if the kids were in there Sean," Barney was looking at the rubble lying all around knowing what he'd just said was

6

almost completely irrelevant. If the kids had been in there, then there wouldn't be anything either of them could do about it.

Sean looked Barney in the eye and simply said "If they were they probably knew nothing about it, let's move, Danny will be waiting for us if we aren't careful." They both moved off down the alleyway as the noise of the locals grew louder and the first of many sirens could be heard heading their way. They got to the meeting point within five minutes and thankfully before their lift arrived.

Danny knew he was only a couple of minutes away and there were so many things rushing through his mind. The Defender was performing flawlessly which he knew would be the case, he'd spent more time working on this vehicle than any of the others the team used. He'd incorporated every conceivable option available as well as stripping the engine down and giving it a complete overhaul. As he turned off the highway, he took the safety off the Sig that was sat in the centre consol. He'd spent enough time under Sean's guidance to know what he needed to do as he pulled up. He was nervous, this was his first real experience of what he felt was clearly now a hostile situation. He pulled up in the yard making sure that he had the vehicle facing the exit should he need to get out of there fast. He opened the door and jumped out keeping his right hand well out of view so that the pistol couldn't really be seen. He kept most of his body behind the door to give himself as much protection as possible. Not that a Landrover door was going to offer much protection, but it was better than nothing at all.

"Put the safety back on Little Fella."

Danny did as Sean instructed knowing that there's no way Sean would have told him to do it unless it was totally safe to do so. Danny was the youngest member of the team and almost from day one the majority of them had referred to him as 'Little Fella'. There wasn't actually anything little about him really. He was 5' 10" which wasn't short at all and could bench press more than anyone else, if he wasn't working on a vehicle or playing on his X-box he would be in the gym. It was more of an affectionate term and he actually liked it. He put the Sig in his jacket pocket and stepped out from behind the door. He noticed the heat for the first time, the aircon in the Defender had been doing its job. Barney and Sean didn't look at all good although Danny noticed it was made worse as a result of the sweat mixing with the brick dust and sand that they were both covered in.

Barney smiled "Let's get moving to the RV and meet up with the chopper, they'll be worried."

They all went to the back of the Defender and Danny opened the back up knowing exactly what the guys were after. Their M4s were exactly where they had left them, and they both grabbed their respective guns. Despite the fact that they hadn't been apart from them for long they both checked they were ready for use. They all jumped in the Defender and Danny started the short drive to the RV. Sean had already been thinking long and hard about what happened and started the conversation after a few seconds "They knew someone would be there and rigged the building, the only thing I don't understand is why blow it early?"

Barney turned himself slightly so that he could look back at Sean, "I guess they either got it wrong or didn't really want to kill anyone, thankfully for us it doesn't matter which," they both knew that they'd had a lucky escape. Barney picked up a sat phone and hit the speed dial, it was answered on the first ring.

"What have you done this time?" the female voice said. The tone sounded like Barney had disturbed her during something important, but he knew otherwise. Fletch was the Operations Manager, she kept everything working like clockwork and on the odd occasion that it wasn't she'd move heaven and earth to get things back on track.

"Can you call the client and ask him to check with his source to see where the kids are? My guess is they've been moved, and we've just been subjected to some rather nasty scare tactics. Don't tell him what's happened just get him to update you on their whereabouts."

Fletch kept silent for a second, "I would never have thought of doing that," she said with a hint of sarcasm.

Barney looked at Sean and rolled his eyes, "okay, so how long before he comes back to you?"

"He'll be back to me within the hour, I'll know before you all get back and I'll start working on a revised plan."

Barney thought for a second "I'll come back in the chopper and the boys will drive back," he looked across at Danny who simply nodded and looked rather relived that he wasn't going to be asked to leave the Defender in the middle of nowhere. "Fletch, put a call through to the General, we may need some help getting the kids back."

Danny and Sean both knew what was going to happen next and started grinning, suddenly they could hear her as clear as anything.

"WHAT ON EARTH DO YOU THINK I DO WHEN YOU'RE NOT AROUND?" The line went dead.

Barney sat there looking at the phone, "well I guess we've finished that conversation."

Sean laughed, "you asked for that, I don't believe you sometimes. You know how good she is. She's always been at least one step ahead of us at all times and yet you still make dumb mistakes like that."

As they arrived at Bravo, Charlie was ready and waiting. She gave Sean and Barney a thorough check and agreed that they were both okay, just a few superficial cuts and some bruising, which by now was already turning a rather nice shade of 'ouch that hurts'. She agreed that Sean was okay to travel back with Danny in the Landrover and the boys were grinning as they climbed back in. She knew that once Sean had debriefed Danny they'd stick whatever their current favourite album of the moment is and be singing away. They had very similar tastes in music and would always be pushing the boundaries. The flavour of the month at the moment was Against The Current, which Charlie had to agree was a pretty good group and boy could the lead singer belt out a tune. Although Charlie had a distinct feeling that Danny was more interested in the fact the lead singer Chrissy Costanza was in his words 'mighty fine'. Danny called out, "see you back at the airport," and before anyone could reply was already moving off. They were about five miles out of Jalriz so had about a 60 kilometre drive back to the airfield at Kabul.

Jess got the Bell ready for take-off and motioned for Charlie and Barney to get in. She took off and headed straight for the airport, calling the tower well in advance to let them know she'd be going straight to the hanger as she had an injured passenger. They gave her clearance, and she settled in for the short flight. The flight gave Jess a chance to enjoy flying the GlobalRanger which she knew she was going to miss as she had to give it back soon. She left Charlie to give Barney a more thorough check over, knowing full well that he'd be arguing with her and losing. She approached Hamid Karzai International Airport at just over 200 ft and flew straight over to the far corner where a bleak looking hanger stood almost on its own. She dropped the Bell down and landed without even the slightest of bumps. She sighed as she went through the shutdown procedure and Charlie and Barney jumped out.

A US Marine suddenly appeared out of nowhere and opened the small side door. They walked through the door into a noisy bustling environment, not what you'd expect from the exterior looks of the hanger. It was staffed and run by the US military and was used to plan and monitor some of the less formal operations.

A second floor had been erected housing numerous offices and work areas. The ground floor had a huge area set up as an armoury with what seemed like enough weapons to facilitate a rather substantial conflict. There was an open plan area that was assigned to triage and this led to a state of the art operating room that was better equipped than most hospitals in the area. In the middle the operations area had been laid out in such a way that the senior officer could see exactly what was going on during the dozen or so operations currently being executed. Around the edges were more offices varying in size. No matter where you looked there was something going on and it was hard to believe that from the outside it almost looked deserted.

Back outside the hanger as Jess was grabbing her flight bag she heard the now familiar drawl of one of her ex-instructors.

"So did you enjoy your little sightseeing tour?" Mitch had a huge grin on his face showing off his almost perfect white teeth. He was a textbook stereotypical American Pilot, mirrored shades, tan, leather jacket and a smile that could melt a girls heart. Mitch was from Texas and was an instructor pilot with the 160th Special Operations Aviation Regiment out of Fort Campbell and had taken her through countless hours of flight time on the Blackhawk. A present to her from the US Government for her part in a previous job that had seen the team rescue a Senators Daughter from a holiday in Europe that had gone horribly wrong. None of the team had asked for anything but Jess had jokingly said she'd love to qualify on a Blackhawk and before she knew it she was embedded with the Night Stalkers spending hours and hours moving Marines from one place to another.

"It was lovely Mitch. Right up to the point the Boss got blown on his backside," she knew there was no point in trying to keep things a secret as everyone in the hanger knew full well what was going on.

Mitch smiled again, "well let's go and get some food while the grownups decide what to do next," Mitch had taken good care of Jess while he was instructing her, in fact she'd stayed with him and his wife for a few weeks during her training. His kids looked at her as though she was their big sister and she visited as often as she could, which wasn't as often as she'd like. Her boyfriend was a drummer for a swing band and when she had spare time, she'd often find herself at a Swing Zazou gig loosing herself in the relaxing sound as they played their set. If she wasn't doing that, she was looking for any chance to get in the air flying anything at all.

"Come on then Mr Instructor you can treat me to dinner, well treat me to whatever they have available in the mess at the moment," she linked her arm though his and he led the way.

Barney made his way towards the office that Fletch and James occupied, he could see through the window that she was already on a video call with someone and as he got closer, he could see General Leverson on the screen sat at his desk with his usual coffee in his hand. As he got closer to the door the General beckoned him in, for someone close to retiring he didn't miss a thing. Even when looking at a screen he was tuned in to what was happening in the background. Barney sat down and the General continued.

"I know things aren't going to plan Karen but we really need you to wrap this up quickly, you see we have another assignment for you to handle and it needs to take priority," the General didn't do nicknames, he was old fashioned and always referred to you by your first name or if things were really bad your surname, which meant things were still okay otherwise it would have been Miss Fletcher instead of Karen. "You're going to get a call from your client and he's going to give you a new location for his Brother-in-law. I can assure you that the kids will be there this time and he will be more than accommodating. I can't tell you how I know that or why the change of heart but suffice to say your job should be a walk in the park," the General looked straight at Barney expecting some comeback, but Barney merely smiled. This conversation belonged to Fletch and wasn't his to hijack. "I'm going to send you a file that the three of you need to read but before you do wrap things up and get on the transporter home. Your pilot has already been given a present, but we want it back with all its associated kit and equipment, so go and find her and get squared away smartish," the screen went blank before Fletch could say a word.

Fletch stood up, "let's go and find Jess and see what she's been up to," without waiting for a reply she walked towards the door. James was working his way through a pile of paperwork and without even looking up said "I'll catch you both in a bit, I want to finish this," before Fletch could even reach out for the door handle her phone started ringing "I'll meet you out there, it's the client."

Barney nodded and left her too it. As he got outside the hanger, he could see Jess standing by a Blackhawk laughing with Mitch while Sean and Scott were on the ground attempting what seemed like the world record for press ups. They were always challenging each other, Sean an ex SBS/Royal Marine, Scott an ex-Seal/US Marine constantly trying to prove who was the best. Barney laughed to himself because in all the time he'd known them Sean had never lost a challenge and he did admire Scott's persistence. "Okay Jess the General informs me that you know what's going on."

Jess smiled, "well, this," she gave the chopper an affectionate pat, "has had some work done on it and needs a test flight, he," she nodded toward Mitch "is going to be conveniently having a nap in the front, and they," she nodded at Sean and Scott who had given up on the press up challenge "fancy a bit of exercise and want to go for a walk with a couple of mates, which is handy because during the test flight we have to carry out a take-off and landing just to be sure everything is okay," she smiled, "So in short, we take off, fly for a bit, then land. These gentlemen go for a wander, then we wait for them to come back to us, and we then come back here. Simple."

He looked at her and grinned, "will they be bringing any presents back with them?"

She laughed, "I think there are a couple of things they want to bring back as souvenirs."

He could see the excitement in her eyes, "okay but Charlie and Danny go with you, I can't trust these two idiots with valuable presents," Barney looked over towards Sean and Scott who were already busy getting their kit sorted out. He heard a hanger door bang shut and turned to see Charlie and Danny walking towards him with four fully kitted eager looking bodyguards. Well, almost bodyguards. They were in fact armed to the teeth with a variety of weapons and kit. Even the untrained eye could tell these weren't just ordinary soldiers. The General isn't messing about with this Barney thought. He vaguely knew the four guys and acknowledged them as they arrived. "Guys, keep it simple and any problems you know what to do."

Sean stepped forward. "Don't worry, we're just off on a little wander, it'll be fine."

Barney looked at him, "yes, that's just what we said a few hours ago and look how that turned out. I'll be with Fletch, Danny I want a running commentary, Jess" he looked at the Blackhawk, "don't damage it. If you do, the General won't be happy," he looked at them all one by one stopping at Jess, "bring all of this equipment back in one piece as well."

She grinned, "of course I will, let's go boys unless you want to walk all the way there and back."

He left them to check each other over and went back to find Fletch. He grabbed a couple of coffees and made his way back to the office. Fletch was sat in one of the chairs at the end of the big desk and he dropped down into the seat next to her. She briefly looked at him, smiled and took the coffee from his outstretched hand. She had a thick file in her hand and was speed-reading her way through each page. He could see from her face she was deep in thought and decided to leave her to it. As he started to get up out of the seat she looked at him "I can see why the General wants us to move onto the next assignment."

"I'm guessing it's big or he wouldn't have given us the help he has. I've just left Jess prepping a Blackhawk for take-off with a spec ops team as the cargo."

"I can say without a doubt this is going to be the toughest assignment yet and we're going to need everyone and everything to even begin to make a start. I've already given the others the heads up and they'll meet us in four days."

"Okay, I'll read the file on the plane but I want to keep an eye on what's going on right now so I'll leave you to it," she didn't even look up as he left the office she was far too engrossed in the brief she was holding.

Jess knew exactly what she was doing, she'd done it countless times before. The only slight difference this time was she was on an active assignment rather than a training exercise. She looked across at Mitch who gave a slight nod of his head indicating that she was good to go. "Everyone ready in the back?" There was a slight pause and then she heard Scott's voice

"We're all good Baby Girl, let's go."

Jess was the second youngest member of the team and Danny was her brother. She'd inherited the 'Baby Girl' title within minutes of Danny being awarded 'Little Fella', it was the teams' way of showing their affection towards them both. Every member of the team was fiercely protective towards them, which often amused them both. In truth they weren't that much younger than some of the team, but it was nice to know that they always had someone watching out for them. Scott always made sure she was safe, Jess reminded him of his little sister back home, Jess had met her a few times, Scott's wife was always kind enough to involve Jess in family parties whenever she was stateside.

The flight time was a little over 20 minutes and before she really knew it she was going through the initial preparations for landing. She didn't need to say anything at all to the guys in the back. She knew they'd be ready to exit the second the wheels touched the ground.

"Jess it's Charlie, I've already told the boys that we're going to drop them and move to a standby location. I want to play safe and Sean agrees that after the last episode we should just be a little cautious."

"Roger that," Jess didn't need to say anything else. She turned in her seat and could see Danny talking, obviously updating Barney on what was happening. She grinned at him and he winked back, despite their constant arguments and fallings-out when they were on assignment they performed perfectly together and every argument and disagreement was forgotten. Until they got back home and then it all started up again, but they loved each other and more often than not it was harmless sibling rivalry. Her thoughts were broken by the sound of Mitch in her headset.

"Okay let's take off and fly east for two miles, there's an area there we can set down and leave the bird turning rather than shut down, that way we can be back here almost straight away when Scott calls in."

With a second "Roger that." within seconds she had them back in the air moving east. They hadn't been on the ground for more than fifteen minutes when the sound of a voice filled her headset.

"Mobile one, we're at the extraction point with two souvenirs awaiting collection."

It couldn't have gone any better, they'd split into three groups of two. Taking no chances, they had advanced to the location tactically, covering each other as they moved. They weren't going to get caught out a second time. Sean took the lead, there wasn't a debate or discussion, they all simply knew that he had more experience in this sort of situation and he was without doubt the right person to take charge. Coming in from different angles they had the whole area covered with the house right at the centre. As soon as they were in the assigned position, they all stopped and went down on one knee in such a way that their arcs of fire overlapped perfectly. Nobody could sneak up on them. Sean got ready to move off "Okay here we go."

He moved forward crouching down so as to present the smallest target possible "We're here," he called out, just loud enough for anyone in the house to hear. He didn't want the whole area to know they were there. He heard a movement from inside the house and then feet shuffling, two children appeared, being ushered out by a middle-aged man.

"No trouble, no trouble." his voice was trembling, and he was clearly distressed.

Sean looked him in the eye, he didn't need to look down the sight of his M4, he knew that if he needed to pull the trigger the shot would be fatal. "Send the children over to me," they moved forward without any intervention at all. They were desperate to get away from the man. They moved so quickly Sean wasn't able to move his weapon and suddenly found that he was compromised as they moved between him and the man. Sean needn't have worried, two of the team could see what was about to happen and had moved forward slightly so that they came into view. The man could see that he was now in the sights of two rather nasty looking individuals who clearly weren't messing about or taking any chances. He slowly raised his hands and stepped back slowly into the house.

Sean asked the children if they were ok and they nodded. Without them really noticing he checked them out for booby traps. As soon as he was satisfied that they were clear he smiled at them "Do you know who sent us?" They nodded eagerly, "okay well let's get out of here shall we?" They were moving before he was, they wanted to be as far away from the house as they could. They changed their formation as they made their way the extraction point. They were moving far slower and with even greater care now that they had the children in the middle of them.

Once they were on board the chopper Charlie checked them both over, they didn't object once. Mainly because Danny had suddenly produced a bag full of sweets that he'd got off the Marines before they'd left the hanger. She confirmed that they were both okay and showed no signs of any physical abuse. There were obviously going to be mental scars but there wasn't anything she could do about that on the chopper. She'd make sure that some professional help was provided down the line.

Jess flew straight into Kabul. There was a helipad that had been cleared for them and the client was waiting. Charlie had already briefed the team and asked them all to stay in the chopper, where they were landing was safe and she didn't want to create a scene when six heavily armed soldiers suddenly appear without warning. Charlie waited until Jess had the chopper firmly on the ground before she opened the door. The children seemed reluctant to get out until they saw their father and then they suddenly forgot about being cautious and rushed over to him. Charlie just waved to him and climbed back aboard. She didn't need to say anything that wasn't her job, after all this was simply a favour from one government to another.

Scott's voice filled everyone's headphones "Let's go Baby Girl, I'm hungry."

The flight back to the airport was short. They all jumped out leaving Jess to hand the chopper back to Mitch. When they got into the hanger Charlie and Danny went to find Barney while the others went to get some food. Everyone was happy, despite the initial setback everything had gone to plan.

Several hours later, having said their goodbyes, they were all strapped into the military transport taking them back to the UK.

Chapter 2

The screen was blank. Just a curser blinking.

The deal was complete. The three months of planning and preparation had paid off. He was even richer. His companies' turnover now exceeded $950 million a year, allowing him to clear a salary of almost $10 million a year and with this latest acquisition it wouldn't be long before he hit his target of a million dollars a month. Things were looking good, and he smiled to himself.

The screen was still blank. The curser still blinking. Just waiting for him.

It was simple, he just put down what he wanted, and it would be delivered, no questions, no fuss. He deserved something special after all the hard work, this was certainly going to be something special. He'd shopped here before. In fact, this was his fourth time and each and every time he'd been given a loyalty discount. A nice touch, not something he agreed with and certainly didn't encourage in any of his businesses, but a nice touch none the less.

He looked around his office. His various companies owned the top three floors of the tower block and he'd made sure that every office was always kept smart and clean, image was everything. He'd had the maintenance team knock six offices into one to give him the space he wanted to create the sumptuous, opulent surroundings that he spent the majority of his time in. Everything in the office was just right and met his exacting standards in every way.

He thought long and hard and had already changed his mind several times in the last half an hour. The last time he'd been on here he'd chosen well, and the goods lasted just over six months. The first two times had been a disaster and within two weeks he'd had to call them to take them back. That was all part of the service, not only did they deliver but they took the goods away once you no longer wanted them. No questions, no fuss, that's one of the things he enjoyed, the simple and straightforward service. He knew that he ultimately paid for that service, but it was still worth every dollar.

The screen was still blank. The curser still waiting.

He knew that somewhere the supplier was just waiting for him to complete the order, the deposit already paid the balance on delivery. He smiled to himself and let his fingers rest loosely on the keyboard. He knew the routine, no boxes to fill in, just type and hit return. Be exact and clear.

Brunette

Green eyes

23

5' 10"

Californian

Deep tan

34DD natural

Slim

No piercings

There were options for intelligence and character traits but this time he'd decided to keep it simple. After all, he wasn't really looking to engage in any meaningful conversation. He hit the enter key.

The screen went blank. The order had gone through. He closed his eyes and let his mind paint a picture. This was the life. Successful business deal warranting a decent reward for all the hard work, not a cheap reward at two million dollars but well worth every single bit of hard work. Now he'd wait for the message giving him the delivery date.

He thought about the last girl. She had been good and very quickly realised that he rewarded good behaviour. She'd been eager to please and lasted five months before she'd started to ask too many questions and in the end he realised that he'd had enough. She was no match for him strength wise and wasn't able to put up much of a fight as he'd strangled her. She'd tried to use her legs to stand up but her feet kept slipping on the polished tiles. He'd looked into her pleading eyes as the life left them, eyes that he'd looked into many times as he'd satisfied himself. Her lifeless body hadn't been on the floor for more than five minutes before he'd put the request through to have her removed. Within 24 hours there wasn't a single shred of evidence that she'd ever been there.

The first girl hadn't stopped screaming and crying. In the end he had got so annoyed with her that he had punched her in the face with such brutal force that it had snapped her neck. The second girl didn't fare any better although she didn't scream quite as much but had still riled him enough for him to hit her and as she fell her head had hit the basin with such force it had killed her instantly.

He hadn't shown any remorse, he didn't feel that he needed to. They were just expensive toys for him to do with as he pleased. That was the whole idea of the service, they didn't care what you did with the merchandise. After all, once you'd paid for it and they'd delivered they didn't care at all what you did. Apart from talk about the service, they'd made that very clear. Under no circumstances would they tolerate you discussing the services they provide with anyone. They'd stressed upon him that if he did the repercussions would be swift and very brutal.

He stood and looked out of the window, the sun was setting and, the numerous windows of the tower blocks around his had a lovely orange tint to them. He let his eyes refocus on his own reflection in the window. He allowed himself to smile again. He still looked good, his daily exercise routine saw to that. All of his clothes were handmade and he had a refit every six months to ensure that everything was exactly as it should be. He'd been described in a recent interview as a power dresser. It was nothing to do with power, he just wanted to look right. In the same interview he'd also been described as a powerful businessman, he wasn't, he was a good businessman.

All the business deals, the consistent growth of his companies, the continual upward trend of his profit margin, none of these things had anything to do with power. They were all a result of good business decisions and planning. He'd experienced power though, the only true power that he believed in. The power over life and death, he closed his eyes and relived that feeling as he decided if he should release the grip he had on her throat or continue to apply pressure. In those seconds he had the power to grant life or death, he had chosen death. Not because he disliked her but simply because he could. That, in his eyes, is what real power is all about.

He closed his eyes. He could still feel her pulse through his fingers. As they tightened the pulse slowly got weaker and weaker. He had shut everything else out. The noise she was making as she fought to breathe, the sound of her feet and arms doing their best to resists the inevitable, the weight of her body as she lost strength. He opened his eyes expecting to see her now lifeless eyes staring back at him but they weren't. He smiled. He could still feel the surge of power that had swept through his whole body as he'd taken her life and he was eager to feel that again.

Thousands of miles away on another continent a meeting had just started, there were only three people present but for this meeting they were the three most powerful people within the whole organisation and this was a behind closed doors executive meeting. Goodbanks stood up "Coffee?" He didn't wait for an answer before moving towards the refreshments that had been delivered just five minutes ago. He knew they'd both want one but he always asked none the less. The coffee was a special roast that was supplied to him alone. The company had agreed to never sell it to anyone else, and for that they were paid a small fortune. The publicity from that deal alone netted more business each year than their annual advertising. Everyone wanted to be part of the Goodbanks experience, even if it was only the fact they used the same coffee supplier.

Stephen Goodbanks was an incredibly successful businessman and was a billionaire several times over. He had offices in virtually every capital city in the world. It was rumoured that he owned a substantial business holding in just about every industry there was. Globally he was a success story no matter where you looked although you wouldn't see him very often. He was a very private person, actively choosing to stand very much in the shadow of his brands. He had numerous ambassadors to act as the face of his companies and this allowed him the freedom and privacy that he relished. He picked up the two cups of coffee that he had just poured and took them back over to the boardroom table "Damian, yours white with two sugars and Angie yours black no sugar." They both said "thank you." At the same time which caused them all to laugh. He wasn't what you'd expect. In fact at times he didn't come across as one of the wealthiest people on earth. He almost appeared as one of the staff as opposed to being the owner. On the surface this would appear to anyone looking in from the outside as a casual meeting but the truth was that this was a very important and crucial meeting. It was in fact probably the most significant meeting of the business year so far.

Damian was the Chief Operations Officer and Angie was the Chief Finance Officer and they were here to discuss the way forward for the business, well at least that's what it said on paper. Now any normal strategy meeting for a business the size of Goodbanks empire would have at least a dozen suits sat round the table with numerous project plans and presentations to go through. But this wasn't a normal meeting and it didn't relate to his normal business empire. The size of the Goodbank empire was breath-taking, everyone knew that. What they didn't realise was that the profit margins released every year to the masses were insurmountable compared to the profit of his other business interests. The interests that remain hidden under the surface and are very rarely discussed. Except at special meetings like the one today. His business transactions carried out via the dark web could be described as colossal and were controlled by the two people sat at the table with him.

He relaxed in his chair and allowed it to tilt back slightly, his elbows sinking into the leather armrests "so Damian, down to business, how are we doing?"

Damian put his cup down gently, the coffee was, as always, absolutely perfect, "well, we've seen a steady upward trend in most areas of the business which isn't a problem at all and exactly what we expected to see. Every safeguard we have in place to ensure secrecy is still in place and we have no real concerns," he looked across at Angie "we can go through the financials if needed, Angie has them all."

"No I don't think there's much need for that. I know the pair of you will warn me if we have a real problem."

Angie lent forward slightly, "there is a problem. Actually, more of a slight issue which could very easily become a problem. The volume of orders in one particular area has risen quicker than expected. In fact this week alone we've received fourteen new orders. We can fulfil them as they're all relatively straight forward, especially the females as every request is for an American under 25."

He let his chair return to the upright position, "should that really be a problem? We always knew that this particular service would become very popular."

Damian joined in, "it won't be a problem, we can still meet every delivery deadline but the volume has tripled within four months and although we considered an increase this is significantly faster than we anticipated."

Goodbanks didn't respond, he put his elbows down on the boardroom table and put his hands together, fingers touching opposing fingers. The table seated fourteen. Each seat handmade and easily at home in the first class section of an airliner, the leather soft and inviting almost begging you to sit down. In front of every chair was a leather bound jotter, hand stitched with unique and luxurious paper just waiting to be written on. A hand carved pen holder, the wood highly polished cradled a Mont Blanc pen. Each pen around the table a slightly different shade. The coasters were also hand carved, inlayed with such intricate designs that it just didn't seem possible that they hadn't been machined. The table itself had such a deep sheen that it almost appeared that the varnish was still wet. In fact, if it was your first time in the office you probably wouldn't be able to resist touching it to find out.

"I don't really want to slow anything down. I'd like the pair of you to work on a strategy that allows for similar growth in the coming months." He sat back again, the leather almost sighing as the seat tilted back.

Angie relaxed, "we've already started to do that and we should have something for you within 48 hours," she looked across at Damian who nodded.

"Stephen, we're okay even if this does double, however our delivery time would increase simply as a result of the precautionary steps we have in place to ensure that the whole process is flawless. The only way to reduce the delivery time would be to create a second sourcing team and that's not really an option." Damian smiled, "that should always be controlled by the pair of us to maintain the integrity of the whole operation."

Damian and Angie were the only two people that were allowed to call him Stephen. To everyone else he was Mr Goodbanks. But the nature of the relationship the three of them shared allowed for a more personal approach. Having said that though there were still times when even in private, they were professional enough to call him Mr Goodbanks.

"I agree. It's important that you are in full control but I'd like you both to seriously consider bringing in two people trustworthy enough to mirror what you do, only with regard to the sourcing, I don't want anyone to know anything about the rest of the business."

The sourcing was the hardest part. Hours of following potential targets, countless background checks, intense relationship building. It was something that Angie was born for. She was a gifted natural and so far it hadn't ever taken her more than three weeks to complete the clients order. She didn't really want to share that with anyone else, she loved her job and knew that she'd be insanely jealous if anyone else was working with her. She also knew in her heart that eventually she would have to work with someone else as she simply wouldn't have the time to deal with every single order. For now she was okay and was relishing the task ahead. Eight out of the fourteen new orders were women, she was going to be very busy in the coming weeks.

She looked at Stephen, "we'll work on it, I promise, but for now we need to run through the financial reports," she lifted the iPad and started to run through dozens and dozens of figures.

Chapter 3

Barney parked the car in Madeira Drive, leaving it unlocked while he walked to the pay and display machine. He always paid for two hours even though he had never been more than an hour. He'd arrived home after the drive from RAF Brize Norton just after midnight. The roads had been fairly clear even though it had been a Friday night. Well most of the roads had been clear until they got to the M25. That was the usual car park that everyone had grown to expect. Even though it was a Saturday, the team were due to meet later and he wanted to get his hair cut. It had been six weeks since the last one and he always went first thing on a Saturday, one of the few rituals he was able to stick to. He dropped the ticket on the dashboard, making sure that it was facing up the right way and locked the car. There were closer places to park but he always found that Madeira drive was easier to use as there was always a space at this time of day. He ran up the stairs to Marine Parade and crossed the road. It was just before 09:00 and the traffic on Brighton seafront was still fairly light.

O/S Barbers was in George Street, Brighton and he'd been going there for some time. He liked the way that Alex cut his hair and had once mentioned to a friend that whenever he left them he didn't ever feel like he'd just had his hair cut, it felt like he'd just had it styled. The attention to detail was incredible and he also enjoyed catching up with how Alex was getting on with his filming. As well as being a full-time barber and being in a band. Alex had a passion for filming and had recently started to develop his filming skills working towards creating his first short film. As always Barney was the first one there and Alex greeted him with the same friendly smile he always wore.

He'd been sat in the chair for no more than five minutes before he heard a commotion outside the shop. A Black Audi RS6 had come to a sudden stop and two suited men jumped out of the front. One of them walked to the door of the barbers opened it and stepped inside.

Lewis got up from his seat and said, "morning."

The man looked at him and smiled, "good Morning, sorry I'm not here for a haircut I'm afraid."

Barney turned his head "sorry Lewis he's with me."

Lewis sat back down.

Sean grinned, "morning Boss."

Barney turned to face forward so that Alex could carry on, "to what do I owe this pleasure?"

"The meeting has been moved forward and we need to move now. Pete is in the car if you give me your keys we'll drop him to your car and he'll move it." Sean held out his hand knowing that Barney wouldn't say no.

Barney got his keys out and handed them over, "how did you know where I'd be?"

"Cass told us exactly where to look, she's in the car with Bruce and quite frankly Boss, he seems a little annoyed that you haven't said hello yet."

"I was going to see him as soon as Alex had finished."

"Well don't worry, he couldn't wait for you to come to him so he's come to you." Sean walked back out of the shop. The two rear doors opened and a man and a woman got out, Sean handed the keys to the man who simply walked off with them. Barney didn't need to tell Sean where the car was parked, all of their cars had trackers on them so they already knew exactly where it was. The woman walked to the back of the car and opened the tail gate. A huge German Shepherd jumped down and immediately sat beside her. She closed the tail gate and walked towards the shop. As soon as she started walking the dog moved with her, pausing as she stopped to open the door.

She walked into the barbers and stopped, the dog stopped and within two seconds once again sat down beside her. She was 5' 9" and immaculately dressed, not a hair out of place. Her suit was fitted and made her even more imposing, "good morning Mr predictable," her soft American accent filled the shop.

Barney looked at Alex in the mirror "sorry, can you give me two seconds."

"Of course," Alex put the clippers down.

Barney turned round in his seat and looked straight at Cass, "can't I get a haircut in peace?"

"No Boss, you can't. The meeting has changed and you need to spend some time with Bruce," she looked down at the dog, who was looking at Barney with his head at a slight tilt.

"Come here boy." Bruce leapt forward and jumped up licking Barneys face, "okay, okay I'm sorry," almost instantly he sat back down at Barney's feet. "Cass I'll be ten minutes, take him down to the beach and I'll meet you there."

"You got it, come on boy," Bruce instantly went to her and followed her out of the shop. The Audi moved off with her as she walked down the road towards Brighton beach.

"Sorry about that guys, Alex I'm all yours." Barney turned his seat round to face the mirror once again. As soon as Alex had finished, Barney paid him and gave him a much larger than usual tip by way of an apology for the disruption the team had caused. He walked down to where his car had been, knowing that they would have parked the Audi close to where he had originally parked. He walked onto the beach to find Bruce chasing seagulls with Cass urging him on. Bruce caught sight of him and came charging over.

Cass followed but without the same sort of urgency "Sean has gone to Shoreham Airport to collect Harland and Pete has taken your car back to your house. Not sure who's collecting us but they'll be here any minute."

"If it's Harland that he's picking up then that explains why the meeting has changed and from the notes we read on the flight back I don't think this is going to be an enjoyable assignment."

"Boss I don't think we're here for the enjoyable stuff. The beauty of what we do is the fact that we can somehow manage to get whatever countries are involved to work together even though they don't want to be seen doing so."

"You've got that right Cass. When did you get in?"

"Arrived first thing yesterday, met up with Alek and Pete and caught up with all the briefing notes we have so far."

They were slowly walking along the beach enjoying the morning sun. Bruce was still chasing seagulls although he never actually caught any. He always stopped just short and allowed them to fly away, "how are things at home?"

"Oh they're the same as always, spend a few days helping around the ranch, catch up with a few friends, report in and get briefed on whatever they feel I need." Cass was born in Texas and raised on a ranch that was bigger than Sussex, the County Barney lived in. She went through school and college excelling at almost everything. She had a particular aptitude for sport and was a key member of almost every team the school and college had. At nineteen she was absorbing information so fast that she was finding it hard not to lose her Professors. Then the government stepped in and she was placed in a special program with twenty or so other students with her talents. After a year they were all sent to different organisations and she found herself on the bottom rung of the FBI. She took part in every training course going and very quickly advanced. Within two years she had been singled out for a special project and found herself working with a multi-national group dealing with assignments that took them all over the world. She loved her job.

The phone in her pocket pinged. She took it out and looked at it "Alek is waiting for us by the statue."

Barney nodded, "here Bruce."

Bruce was chasing yet another seagull but on hearing the command he somehow seemed to turn mid stride and head straight towards Barney. They walked back to the promenade making their way to the statue. It had been erected in honour of Steve Ovett who'd been a runner for Brighton and Hove Athletic Club who then went on to become quite a sensation is the world of Athletics. Barney had been a member of the athletics club as well but that seemed like a lifetime ago. Adjacent to the statue was a black Audi Q7 with a somewhat serious looking driver. As they approached he got out. Bruce went bounding towards him, Barney shook his head in mock surprise.

"No loyalty these days," he said.

Cass just laughed and the man stood up.

"He's fiercely loyal, he won't let anyone touch your vinyl collection. I just don't understand why anyone would want to go near it." Alek smiled and held out his hand, "nice to have you back Boss."

Barney shook his hand, smiling, "it's good to be back Alek, for however long that might be."

Alek had the back of the Q7 open and Bruce jumped in without even being asked. Cass got in the back and Alek got in the passenger seat, nobody else drove when they were in Brighton. It was Barneys town and he always drove. Besides he knew the fastest way around the City and none of them liked to be caught up in traffic. Barney turned the Q7 around and headed straight along the coast road, they were lucky the first three sets of traffic lights were green and they were passing what was left of the West Pier before they knew it. Barney turned down First Avenue and started to cut his way through the back streets of Hove and before long they were on the Old Shoreham Road almost within sight of the office, not that it looked at all like an office. A while ago a car dealership had closed and when another dealership stepped in they didn't want all the site. The team had stepped in and leased the remaining building which had originally been a workshop.

They had left the outside of the building as it was so that it still looked like a part of the new dealership but had completely modernised the inside. It was now a state of the art command centre with significant additions supplied by various governments to enable them to communicate securely. Each team member had their own office. That was important as they all spent a fair bit of time in them catching up on paperwork and research, there were always huge volumes of after assignment reports to complete and every government agency demanded thorough reports. It was something they couldn't ever get away from. They had several meeting rooms and a huge conference room that could seat 30 if needed. The kitchen area was almost a professional setup and the team between them always did all of the cooking. Having said that the local take aways always did very well when the team was in the office.

They had six rooms setup as bedrooms all en-suite so that the team members that weren't local didn't need to pay for hotels. The building had been laid out so that if need be they could work and rest without having to leave. That had been the case several times over the last couple of years and it had made all the difference. The workshop itself had been converted to a large parking area with a gym at the end. Every room or open space had wall mounted monitors enabling the team to be part of a video conference call no matter where they were in the building. The IT infrastructure was state of the art and it seemed was always in a state of being updated, usually to allow the addition of some new gadget that one of them had acquired.

Barney approached the roller shutter and the transmitter in the Q7 activated the shutter, he pulled in and parked up. Everyone got out and Bruce raced off to find something to eat, Cass went after him knowing that if he couldn't find anything he'd come and find her because he knew that she'd be the first to give in and feed him. Barney put the key for the Audi on the rack and walked towards stairs. "Conference room in ten people, Alek can you let the rest know please."

Alek already had his phone in his hand, "will do," he wasn't making a call he was checking the vehicle tracking software to see where the teams vehicles were. It was far easier than phoning around. Suddenly the monitors came alive and a map appeared, Alek smiled, "you've got to love technology."

Barney knew that there were only three team members missing and he could see from the screen that Fletch and Charlie were less than five minutes away and Sean was showing as being no more than ten minutes behind them. He had time for a coffee so he went straight to the kitchen. Once he'd made it he went straight to the conference room to see who else was there. He could hear laughter as he approached, he loved hearing that sound knowing that more often than not indicated the team were at ease and relaxed. Apart from the three team members not quite there yet everyone else was already seated. Including Bruce who was curled up in Barney's seat watching what was going on.

Barney looked round the table, "morning people, which one of you is responsible for telling him to get in my chair?" There was a chorus of "not me." none of them sounding at all convincing. Barney looked at Bruce "who was it boy?"

Bruce looked at Scott and barked, everyone burst out laughing except Scott who looked at Bruce with a look of disgust and said "snake." Bruce barked at him again which caused even more laughter. Barney heard the roller shutter open and two cars pulled in "Okay, that's Fletch and Charlie arriving so now we only need Sean and Harland. You've all read the briefing notes so I guess this is a meeting to bring us all up to speed with any new developments and everybody else's thoughts."

Within ten minutes everyone was sat down, they all had the same set of briefing notes in front of them except Harland who had two folders.

One identical to the team and one slightly larger. Harland Jones looked every bit like an Intelligence Officer should, he was dressed in a three-piece suit, tailored to perfection. Everything about him was, as always, immaculate. Even when he spoke it was with an air of authority and generally when he spoke nobody else did. He always seemed to command the room whenever he was in it, the team liked that about him even though whenever he was briefing them it was always related to a high level assignment that was never easy.

"I'll keep this as short as I can. We have a situation that several governments want investigated and as usual they don't want to be seen investigating anything." Harland looked round the conference table and he could see that without doubt he already had their attention. "We have been approached to investigate a claim that within the dark web is a site that is currently being used for trafficking. Now normally we wouldn't even entertain investigating this and we'd pass it off to some government agency to deal with but this relates to the trafficking of people."

He looked around the room, nobody looked at all surprised or shocked by his statement. He had worked with the team before and knew that they were all professional and wouldn't ask any questions until he invited them to.

"It seems that you can place quite a detailed description of the type of person you want and within a short space of time the order is delivered, no questions and no fuss. The service isn't cheap and is extremely thorough, we have been given evidence to show that you really do get exactly what you ask for," he opened the larger and took out several smaller folders, passing one to each of the team, "this shows you just what I mean, on the first page you'll see a very precise list of features and on the reverse you'll see a photo that is an exact representation of the list. The second page is a statement given detailing how the site works. You can read that once I've left and I think you'll find that it's rather frightening."

The room was silent, if the clock on the wall hadn't been digital you could have heard the second hand moving. Fletch stood up and went over to the coffee machine. She selected a Latte and let the machine do its thing. Nobody spoke, they all started to read the statement, they knew the drill, the sooner they were up to speed the sooner they could get started. The machine finished the latte and Fletch put it down in front of her seat, she went back to the machine and selected an Earl

Grey tea. Harland never drank coffee and she knew that he'd never make one himself unless he was invited to and Fletch very much doubted he'd know how to use the machine so it was far easier for her to just make him one. Once the machine had finished she took it across to him. He smiled thanked her as he always did demonstrating his always faultless manners.

"While you all get your drinks I'll explain the next step. We need you to meet with the source. It's going to be difficult as he is very reluctant to give any further details however he has been diagnosed with a terminal illness and has a matter of months to live which is why he's come forward. He's very religious and wants to atone for his sins. I don't know what you'll be able to get out of him but every little bit of information at this stage is going to be invaluable. We need to get to him quick, he's not going to be charged or investigated at this stage because there'd be little point." Everyone was back in their seats and Harland looked round the table "Questions?"

Alek looked up from the statement "I'm guessing he's not coming to us so where do we need to go to meet him?"

Harland leant forward resting his elbows on the table. "We don't know just yet, we're waiting to hear back. Having said that we're hoping to find out tomorrow. As soon as we do we'll need you to move straight away as usual. We'll make the necessary hotel bookings and you'll need to tell us if you're flying commercial or on you own. Whichever you choose we will again make the necessary arrangements."

Harland looked around the table and stopped when he got to Barney, he instinctively knew that it would be him that spoke next. Barney didn't disappoint. "We'll fly commercial, it'll reduce our exposure and we'll send a couple which will make it look more like a weekend break. I know that we aren't necessarily being watched but even at this stage I'd rather take a cautious approach. Cass and Alek you'll take the lead on this. The rest of us will stay back and do some of the basic research that we're going to need."

Harland sat back. "Excellent, we'll prepare everything and send you the details. Now unless anyone else has any questions I'll be making my way back to London." The room was silent, "okay then ladies and gentleman I'll be off. Who has the enviable task of taking me back to the airport?"

31

Sean stood up "I'll take you, that way I can make sure you actually do go back to London." Everyone burst out laughing, almost from day one Sean and Harland had always had a love hate relationship. It was completely unfounded, their fathers had served together in the military and although they didn't socialise there was and always had been a strong friendship between them.

Harland looked at him, "come on then driver take me to the airport."

Sean looked at him and sighed, "roger that."

Chapter 4

Angie opened the door to Starbucks. It was just as busy as she had hoped. She'd already checked it out twice before in order to work out the busiest times. It wasn't about the number of people but about the type. Which is why she'd had two previous visits.

Half an hour earlier she'd been in her hotel room picking out what to wear. Every time she'd done this she'd spent hours making sure she looked just right. Meticulously checking every single detail to ensure everything was perfect. This time was no different. She'd chosen a pair of black jeans with black converse, no belt as she didn't need one. The jeans were always a perfect fit. She went for a simple white blouse, almost see through, the top three buttons undone and no bra. She'd used the same outfit before, she was fishing and using herself as bait. So far she'd never failed to land the fish she wanted.

The door closed behind her and she found herself behind six other people which was perfect. That gave her about three minutes to casually look around and she worked her way forward. At first glance she saw two people that met the profile, she made a mental note of where they were and moved a few steps closer. It was just as she'd hoped and full of students from the local university. The girl in front ordered an Americano, Angie smiled inwardly as that was a quick drink and it'll be her turn next. The Barista smiled and asked her what she'd like.

"I'll have a skinny latte please."

The baristas nametag said Sam, and Sam appeared to meet every single criteria. For once this could be easy Angie thought.

Sam smiled again and said, "that'll be four dollars," as she said it she picked up the takeaway cup and the pen ready to add the name on the side of the cup.

"It's Amy," Angie said with a smile and with a practiced move she bent slightly at the waist to get the money out of her front pocket, this allowed her blouse to open up which gave Sam a front row seat to Angie's perfectly formed right breast. She delayed a few seconds making it appear that she was struggling and then straightened up. When she looked at Sam her eyes were still focused on her breast and at that point Angie had a feeling that this really was going to be surprisingly easy. Having said that it was still going to take a lot more than one trip to Starbucks, the hard bit was yet to come.

Angie stood to one side and waited for her drink. She didn't have to wait long, she saw Sam pick up her cup and she saw her smile before calling out "Amy."

Angie stepped forward quickly so that she had the time to brush her fingers against Sam's before she fully let go of the cup. Rather than linger to see Sam's reaction Angie picked up the coffee and left making her way back to the hotel. She'd already researched the shift patterns and knew that Sam had another four hours left before she finished so plenty of time to relax and call in to report how things were going.

Three hours later she was ready to take the next step. She picked up the three shopping bags she had obtained the day before and took a circular route back to the coffee shop to waste some time. More importantly she wanted to have the sort of look that gave the impression she had actually been shopping and was happily making her way home. The traffic wasn't heavy and that's how Angie liked it because it made it easier to strike up a casual conversation when there was less road noise. This was all a gamble, she didn't know how long it would take Sam to actually leave work and she'd added ten minutes hoping that would be enough, she was 100 yards from the door when she saw Sam come out and walk off in the other direction.

This wasn't a problem at all. It would have been too good to be true if Sam had walked towards her. Anyway Angie always had a plan B. In fact she always had several plans at any given time, in this line of work she had to. She decided to follow Sam for a while so that she could give herself some alternative options for that all import accidental meeting. Angie followed for three blocks and then let Sam go. She wasn't really in a position to carry out a covert follow and she definitely didn't want to be seen. She took a left and made her way back to the hotel, this was only day one after all and tomorrow was another day.

Three days later and Angie opened her eyes to the early morning sun streaming through her hotel window. From the rhythmic breathing she could tell that Sam was still asleep, the smell of sex still lingered in the air. It had been different this time, Angie had never felt as sexually alive as she did with Sam. Although she would probably never admit it, she had never experienced an orgasm with the level of intensity as she had a few hours earlier. She had a high sex drive, which was always far higher when she was working, it had always been that way. Her job simply made her more aware of her feelings, perhaps because for the last five years or so she'd been using her body to lure people into her trap.

She managed to get out of bed without waking Sam and went into the bathroom and turned the shower on. She tested the water to make sure that it wasn't too hot and then stepped in. She wasn't sure how long she'd been stood under the deluge of water before she heard the soft footsteps on the bathroom floor. An arm moved round her waist and she felt a wave of pleasure as Sam kissed her shoulder. She knew that this wasn't going to be a quick shower as she felt Sam's hand move slowly up to her breast.

Two hours later and they were saying goodbye as Sam left to go and start her shift. Angie called room service and ordered a large coffee and a fruit salad. She had some serious thinking to do as she was in unfamiliar territory, never before had she felt anything towards any of the people she'd targeted, but this time it was different. She looked round the hotel room, up until now they had all looked the same, different chain maybe but in essence all very similar. She thought logically and decisively. After all, at the end of the day she had a job to do and nothing could ever get in the way of that. The answer was glaringly obvious, over 50% of the people that went into that particular Starbucks were students and about another 30% were out of work actors. Angie could simply visit Sam at work and select an alternative target from the hundreds of people that came through the door each and every day.

Angie arrived at the coffee shop an hour before the end of Sam's shift. She ordered a skinny latte and sat at one of the four person tables. Knowing that before long, someone would ask if they could sit down and join her. Within twenty minutes she had three college students sat at her table, ten minutes later she had their names and knew what classes they took. She'd always been good at getting people to open up and it was extremely rare for her not to be able to engage someone in a deep and meaningful personal conversation. It was very busy and Angie had already spotted two new potential targets. One of them had returned Angie's smile instantly and in a stroke of luck had said hello to one of the girls sat at the table. Within minutes Angie knew that the girls name was Phoebe and that she was studying at the local college.

Angie realised that she now had a problem. She couldn't hunt Phoebe in the normal way, she would have to make sure that any interactions happened away from the coffee shop. In truth that wouldn't really be a problem but it was a complication that she'd never had to consider before. Having said that she'd dealt with far more complicated situations before and had always managed to succeed. The noise level had increased and the coffee shop was now filling up as classes ended for the day and all of the students turned their attention to their homework and social lives. Within half an hour Angie had managed to find not only Phoebe's Facebook profile but also her Instagram and Twitter accounts. She followed her straight away and began her research.

Sam came across as soon as her shift finished and they got up and left, Sam had convinced Angie to let her cook dinner and they were heading over to Sam's apartment for the evening. This really was unfamiliar territory for Angie but she felt surprisingly comfortable with the concept. The traffic was heavy but it didn't matter as Sam only lived three blocks from the coffee shop so they most definitely didn't need to drive. The traffic was mainly made up of cabs, endless numbers of them as they fought to get to their destinations. They didn't say much, to be fair the road noise didn't make talking easy. It didn't matter too much as they arrived at the apartment quite quickly. Sam opened the door and they both made their way up to the first floor. Sam looked at Angie and seemed quite embarrassed as she said "it's not much but it is mine."

Angie was surprised. It was very clean and tidy, everything seemed to have its place. She hadn't expected it to look anything like this. It was almost as if the room had been set up as a showroom. Sam had gone straight through to the kitchen, Angie heard the cork being pulled out of a bottle of wine and Sam returned with two large glasses of red.

"I'm doing steak and salad so a red seemed like the right choice," she smiled as she handed Angie one of the glasses.

"I'd say red is the perfect choice." Angie took the glass, she took a sip, "this is definitely the perfect choice." The wine had a rich fruity flavour to it and probably cost a fortune. Angie suddenly realised that Sam had obviously pulled out all the stops to make sure the evening went well.

"Dinner will be about twenty minutes so make yourself at home, put the TV on or stick some music on."

Angie walked over to the iPod dock. There wasn't a password and the Spotify App was already open. She flicked through Sam's music library and was quite surprised at some of the albums. Lots of Norah Jones and Alicia Keys, which wasn't a surprise, David Bowie, Fallout Boy and Mayday Parade was what caught Angie out. She selected a Best of Bowie album and set the volume so that it was at a nice background level.

"Good choice," Sam shouted from the kitchen.

Angie went to the kitchen to see if Sam needed any help, she was amazed to find that Sam had changed, she was now wearing a pair of shorts and a loose-fitting gym vest. Angie suddenly realised that her feelings for Sam were real and far stronger than she had acknowledged. At some point in the very near future she was going to have to come clean about some aspects of her life if she wanted to continue her relationship. That was the near future though and right now she didn't need to worry about it, she just needed to relax and enjoy herself.

Angie woke up early, Sam was fast asleep so she carefully got out of bed and got in the shower. She didn't bother to dry her hair as she wanted to leave Sam sleeping, once she'd dressed, she wrote a note and left it on the pillow. She had a busy day ahead and wanted to get everything done which is why she'd decided not to wake Sam, although deep down she wanted to, so that she could explore her body once again. They'd lost track of time last night before they'd both collapsed exhausted and thoroughly satisfied.

Angie made her way to the block that Phoebe lived in. Whilst she'd been going through Phoebe's tweets she had found out that she went for a run every so often with two girlfriends so Angie had decided to get there early in order to do some much needed surveillance. Not that it really mattered but now that Sam was no longer a viable target she needed to try to gain a bit of time back. In the past she had always made sure that she was as efficient as possible and she wanted to get back on track. It was a gorgeous day, just the odd wispy cloud every now and then in the clear blue sky. Angie looked around. It was starting to get busy which was exactly what she needed. It would make it so much easier to follow Phoebe without having to worry too much about being spotted. The objective today was to simply make some sort of contact, hopefully a coffee shop or library. Angie had noticed that every other photo on Phoebe's Instagram had been taken either in a coffee shop or when she was studying in a library. Angie knew that either of those locations was a perfect place to make the all-important initial contact.

Phoebe was waiting outside as the other two jogged down the road towards her. They set off at a really leisurely pace slowing down to cross each intersection. Once they reached the park they upped their pace a little but it was still a very easy going pace and Angie had to actually slow herself down. Her normal pace was considerably faster but she needed to stay behind them for a bit in order to gather some much needed information. If she was too friendly with her running mates it would make things difficult as she'd be missed too quickly, Angie needed to find the loners, the ones that had moved to escape their parents or the grip that the dead end town had on them. They were the ones that nobody would realise had moved on again. Sure, they'd be missed at college but the assumption would be that things had got to difficult and they'd given up on another chapter of their life. They weren't talking too much while they were running which was a good thing. They clearly weren't girly girls catching up on every little detail of each other's lives, and although not great because she clearly had regular contact it was good that they clearly weren't that close. Angie had enough for what she needed and she changed her pace and ran three more laps of the park before heading back to Sam's to shower.

Sam was up and getting ready for work when Angie got back, she gave her a quick kiss and then jumped in the shower, as usual she set the water temperature to a nice comfortable level for a few minutes and then turned it up a little. She often used her time on the shower to think but every time she tried an image of Sam appeared and started washing her back. She gave up and turned the temperature down to give herself a bit of cold water to shake off the thoughts, not that she really wanted to but she knew deep down that she had a job to do and it needed doing quickly. For the first time she had been distracted from the task at hand as she knew full well that she'd have to leave Sam behind, she simply couldn't be part of her life but the unexpected had happened and she actually found that she had feelings for someone. When she went into the bedroom Sam was almost ready to leave.

Chapter 5

Danny accelerated hard coming out of the bend, the RS6 responded instantly just as Danny expected it to. He knew just how hard he could push the car, particularly on the roads he was using as he'd travelled them countless times. The bend from the A27 onto the A23 was clear so he was able to go much faster that he would've been able to in a couple of hours' time. At rush hour the traffic backed right up and he'd be taking the bend at a snail's pace but that wasn't the case right now and he was up through the gearbox in no time at all. He was heading to Gatwick airport to drop Alek and Cass off. They were heading to Ljubljana to meet up with a businessman that had made contact with the authorities stating that he had some information that would be useful to them. Danny had plenty of time but still drove the car hard. Ensuring that he stayed within the speed limits, but only just. The trip to the airport took no time at all and before they all knew it Danny was pulling up at the drop off point at the North Terminal. Alek and Cass were travelling light so they only had hand luggage. It was more for show than anything else as they could easily have gone there and back same day but to keep up appearances they were staying overnight to make it look as though they were on a city break together.

They moved swiftly through security at Gatwick due to only having cabin luggage and they were so used to airport protocol it amused them both to watch as countless passengers failed to put their liquids in bags despite all the notices. While waiting for his bag to emerge from the X-ray machine, Alek could hear raised voices and turned to see a middle-aged woman arguing with the security staff. They were trying to explain why she couldn't keep her expensive perfume bottle. They weren't getting anywhere despite pointing out that it was over the limit for liquids. The passenger's voice was getting louder and louder and she was beginning to go red in the face. He smiled to himself and turned back to find his bag had already gone past him on the conveyer. He grabbed the tray and moved to the side. Cass was already there putting her watch on and judging by the smile on her face she was just as amused by the commotion.

"Let's go and get something to eat before I go over there and get involved."

Alek laughed. Knowing that if Cass did get involved the passenger would probably find herself wishing she'd never said a word.

"Where do you want to eat?" he asked.

"I don't really mind as you're paying, remember we have to keep up appearances and you need to be seen to be keeping me in the manner I've become accustomed to."

With a big grin on his face he responded with "Oh, but honey, there isn't a McDonalds here."

"You'll pay for that you jerk, now move and let's find a table somewhere," with that she moved off into the main part of the terminal.

It was always busy at the North Terminal but they found a table straight away and ordered some food. They'd already slipped into their roles and although the chance of anyone actually paying attention to them was very slim they still made the right noises and discussed what they were looking forward to on their mini break. They'd booked two nights away but probably only needed one. As they didn't know how the meeting was going to go they booked an extra night just in case. They always paid for any drinks or food in cash so if they needed to they could leave after one night without any problems. The whole team operated this way. They'd found that it gave them far more flexibility especially this early on when they didn't actually know what direction they were going.

Their food finished, they made their way towards the screen to check which gate they needed. They were still too early. It wasn't due to update with the gate number for another twenty minutes so Alek suggested a quick bit of window shopping. They made their way to the Superdry shop and Cass tried a jacket on.

Alek looked at her. "It suits you, I think you should get it."

"Oh no I couldn't, but I think you should."

Alek rolled his eyes knowing that this was a battle he was clearly going to lose and took the jacket off her and made his way to the till. Once he'd paid they went over to get a book each. Partly because they both liked to read but more importantly books were a great prop to use when you wanted to blend in. They both knew that they could be waiting around for quite a while and a book allowed you the ability to stay in one place for a while without attracting too much attention. Alek went straight to the top twenty and picked up the latest Lee Child book.

"Think I'll see what Jack Reacher is up to now, what are you going for?"

"I picked up a book a couple of months ago that was the first in a trilogy so I'm going to see if they've got the second one," with that she moved further into the shop.

Alek grabbed some sweets that he knew she liked and turned to go and find her only to see her moving towards him with a big smile on her face.

"They've got it so I'm happy, let's go and pay as they must have announced the gate by now."

Once they'd paid they made their way back to the screens showing the departure details, their gate had been assigned so they made their way towards it. The North Terminal at Gatwick was really easy to navigate and within five minutes they were at the gate. They could see the plane was on the stand and the ground crew were already loading the hold luggage. They didn't even get a chance to sit down before the 'Speedy boarders' were told they could make their way forward.

The team always used speedy boarding and booked the seats by the wing exits, the extra legroom was nice and it didn't worry them at all that they had to assume some responsibility for operating the emergency exit should it be needed. Their boarding passes were on their phones and they were putting their cabin bags in the overhead lockers in what seemed record time. The plane was an Airbus A320 and as usual was clean and tidy and ready to go. It always amazed Cass that during the turnaround it was the cabin crew that cleaned the plane and not a team of contract cleaners.

They sat down and strapped themselves in. Their phones already in airplane mode and books in the pocket in front of them. The whole team made a point of paying attention during the safety brief. Something that not many passengers appeared to do, the assumption being that nothing is going to happen to them. The Cabin Manager introduced the cabin crew and started the briefing. Once completed the cabin crew made their way down the rows of seat ensuring that the passengers had their seatbelts fastened. The First Officer introduced himself and told everyone that they were about to push back from the stand and make their way to the runway, the winds were in their favour and the flight time should be slightly shorter than expected.

Alek and Cass were both experienced fliers and they were totally relaxed. The same couldn't be said for the lady sat next to Alek. She was already gripping the armrest and they were only taxiing. The weather forecast was for clear skies so thankfully less chance for turbulence. They were in the air quickly and before everyone knew it the cabin crew were in the aisle offering food and drink. Despite eating at the terminal they both ordered food and drink. This was partly through habit as they didn't always know when they would next eat due to the nature of what they do when on assignment and partly because they were aware that the cabin crew got a small commission from what they sell during the flight and they both wanted to do their small bit to help. They both started to read their books occasionally chatting about what they wanted to do during their stay. Cass genuinely wanted to go up into the mountains, she loved the snow. Depending on how things went they'd already agreed that if they had the time they would visit Velika Planina, Cass wanted a coffee from the cafe which was accessible firstly via cable car and then ski lift and was definitely on her list of places to go.

The flight went without a hitch and they had managed to get through arrivals without any issues at all. They'd booked a transfer to the hotel and not surprisingly the driver was waiting for them holding a placard with their names on it. The driver spoke English with hardly any accent at all and on the journey to the hotel gave them a free and rather enjoyable history lesson about Slovenia and the key things they should do while they were here. Bordered by Austria, Hungary, Italy and Croatia and with a population of just under two million, covering just over twenty thousand square kilometres it's what can be best described as a hidden gem. The traffic was light and they got to the hotel in good time. They had booked into the Intercontinental as they'd managed to get a pretty good last minute deal and Alek enjoyed the creature comforts that a five star hotel offers.

They checked in and were given a room on the fifteenth floor overlooking the city. They didn't bother unpacking and went straight up to the rooftop bar to get a drink. The meeting wasn't until ten the following morning and they had time to relax so they ordered a dink each and went out onto the terrace. The city spread out below them and they could see the dark shape of the mountains in the distance. They had already studied the layout of the city in detail so that if needed they could find their way around unaided, something that had paid off countless times before and was now something they did now without even thinking about it. They knew the key routes in and out, the main tourist attractions and the key buildings. It always made things so much easier.

Cass finished her drink. "Right, we need to eat so I suggest a nice walk along the river and then we stop at Pops Place for a burger."

Alek smiled "do you ever stop thinking about food?"

"Nope, so get your arse out of that chair and let's go."

Alek got up and they made their way out of the hotel, they were only about fifteen minutes away from Pops and as they weren't under any time restraints they took a slow walk along the river passing Dragon Bridge and then crossing at the Triple Bridge. It was quite busy with plenty of tourists taking in the sights and when they got to Pops there was only one table left. They ordered two beers, a local brew which, according to the reviews online, was definitely worth trying and a burger and chips each. Despite the fact that the food is cooked to order it arrived quicker than they expected, and just as they hoped it was absolutely delicious. After finishing the burgers they ordered another beer and whiled away a bit of time chatting almost as if they were actually a couple.

Alek and Cass has spent countless hours together on assignments and although they didn't have any feelings for each other knew that their cover would be far more believable if they were relaxed and acted naturally as a normal couple out together would, they would laugh and joke about things they'd done always using real examples which made it so much easier.

"Come on you, let's walk along the river. It'll do you some good and get rid of some of the calories you've just eaten."

Alek just looked at Cass and rolled his eyes, she had a metabolism that seemed to defy nature and could eat almost anything she wanted without putting on any weight whereas Alek had to work hard in the gym to keep his weight down. Although it was made easier as he kept himself in the gym for hours on end practicing various martial arts so was always in pretty good shape.

They linked arms as they walked and joined the numerous other couples enjoying the evening stroll along the river. They eventually made their way back to the hotel and went back to the rooftop bar for one last drink.

They were at breakfast first thing as they wanted to be at the meeting place as early as possible. They were meeting at the main cafe in the castle which overlooked the capital. Rebuilt in the twelfth century the medieval fortress offers breath-taking views of the surrounding area, the viewing tower allows anyone with a camera to get some incredible shots of the town below and the snow-capped mountains in the distance. The castle grounds open at ten and they wanted to be able to check the area out before they met the source, all they knew was that his name was Josef Pichler and that he was the CEO of an investment bank and had some information for them. On the way to the castle they had tried to call Fletch to see if she had any updates but rather strangely she hadn't answered which had them worried at first till they called Barney and he explained that General Leverson had sent her back to Afghan. They were stepping up operations and every country wanted their spec ops team to be given priority and it was all beginning to fall apart so the Americans had declared that operational control would be handled by a central team that wasn't controlled by any one country. Fletch was heading that team and would be for some time.

Although a bit of a setback from a morale perspective it didn't affect the team operationally as James took over. To look at him you'd think he'd spent his life working behind a desk for a corporate company in the city but in this case looks could be deceiving. He was always dressed immaculately, trousers, shirt and tie and was one of the most polite people you could ever wish to meet. His soft mid-western American accent gave the impression that he was one of those people that you wouldn't really notice at a party. The sort of shy retiring man that was always off to one side. In truth he was and still is a Command Sergeant Major with the 75th Ranger Regiment out of Fort Benning. General Leverson had signed off on a secondment from the

45

Regimental Reconnaissance Company and James suddenly found himself taking on the role of Tactical Operations Manager within the team. A role he enjoyed and excelled at but secretly wished for more time in the field. This didn't really change anything for Alek and Cass so they waited for the gates to open, they were three couples back from the front of the queue when the gates opened. Even though they'd studied the layout online they still had a quick walk around to familiarise themselves with exits and escape routes should they need them.

They made their way to the cafe and selected a table outside. It allowed Alek and Cass to sit with their backs to the cafe window so they could easily keep an eye on the crowd. They weren't expecting any trouble at all but it paid to be prepared and they didn't want to take any chances. Alek ordered two large lattes and made his way back to the table. He'd hardly sat down as an elderly looking gentleman approached them.

"I'm Josef," he said holding out his hand

Alek stood up. "I'm Alek and this is Cass."

Cass went to stand up. "No no, please stay seated, it's a pleasure to meet you."

Alek stayed on his feet, "can I get you a drink Josef?"

"Yes please, could I have a black coffee with sugar."

"Take a seat and I'll be right back."

While they were waiting Cass and Josef chatted about the trivial everyday things people discuss when they first meet. They both wanted to wait till Alek was back before discussing anything important. The cafe was still fairly empty and Alek returned quite quickly, he placed the coffee in front of Josef and sat back down.

Josef put his hand in his pocket and took out a small flash drive. He passed it over to Alek. "All the information I have is on here but I would like to explain everything to you and I'm hoping you won't judge me."

Cass smiled at Josef, "we aren't here to judge Josef, we're simply here to listen."

"Thank you, that's makes all the difference. I've been diagnosed with terminal cancer and I have less than six months to live. During my life I've done some wonderful things and had many amazing experiences. I've created an incredibly successful investment bank and leave my two children a wonderful legacy. There is however one very dark deed that I am utterly ashamed of and I must atone for my behaviour before it's too late."

Josef took a sip of his coffee before continuing. "Just under two years ago I was at a business conference with an old friend and we'd had too much to drink. It was late in the evening and we were having an open and honest conversation about triumphs and regrets. He told me his greatest thrill was having the power to decide over life and death, I asked him to explain and he told me that he had ordered a girl through a secret website. A girl that was his to do with however he saw fit. He told me that he'd sexually abused the girl for several weeks and then killed her. I thought he was joking at first but as soon as he started to tell me in detail what he'd done I realised he was telling the truth. He saw it as being a member of an exclusive club and membership was by invitation only. I have to be honest and say that when he asked if I wanted him to put me forward I was excited by the idea and said yes."

He took another sip of coffee and took a deep breath before continuing. "I'm ashamed to say that when I received an email stating that I'd been vetted and was being offered the opportunity of a unique and very private service I instantly replied without hesitation saying that I'd like to be considered. The emails are on the drive. What I've done is appalling and this is only the second time I have ever mentioned it to anyone, the first being my contact who, it seems, has quite a bit of power considering I only spoke to him a few days ago. I was asked what I was looking for and told to describe who I wanted in detail. I sent an email with my requirements on it and almost instantly was given account details and told to deposit two million US dollars, I did that almost straight away, I didn't even hesitate."

Cass was worried, Josef was clearly getting emotional, she could hear it in his voice and see it on his face. "Josef, you don't need to continue, we can take the drive away and investigate the information that's on it."

Alek had been keeping an eye on everything around him and he couldn't see anything at all to cause any concern. "Would you like another coffee Josef?"

"No thank you but I would like to continue. I must. It may not seem that important to you but for me I must do everything I can to put things right although I cannot change what I've done."

"That's fine Josef, please continue."

"You must believe me when I tell you that my actions from that point don't reflect on the rest of my life or my family. Within seven days I had taken delivery of a girl that was exactly what I had asked for. I have a summer house in the country and had told my wife I needed to go away on business for two weeks, a normal thing with my job. My behaviour was shocking, I was like an animal. I'm appalled and highly ashamed of my actions, that poor girl."

"Josef, stop there, we'll get the rest from the drive."

"I killed her you see, just because I could. They took the body away, it was as if she'd never been there," there were tears in his eyes and it seemed as though he was beginning to fall apart. Cass stood up.

"Come on, let's explore the castle." She didn't give him an opportunity to refuse, she took his arm and almost lifted him out of the chair, "we'll leave Alek here while we take a little tour."

Alek called James straight away and gave him a very quick overview of the conversation. "Cass has taken him for a quick walk to hopefully take his mind off things as we could do without him having a breakdown here. Can you get us on the quickest flight out of here, doesn't matter when but we need to explore this drive and get things moving. This seems far worse than I thought."

"I'll talk to Barney, He'll probably call the General to pull some strings." James paused for a second "how quickly can you be at the airport Alek?"

"Probably within three hours, maybe two if things go our way."

"Get there as quick as you can and I'll call you back shortly."

"Thanks James, this isn't good. It's not at all good."

Alek cut the call and saw Cass heading towards him. "I've called James and asked him to get us out of here ASAP, we need to get to the airport as fast as we can."

"I put him in a taxi, he pulled himself together a bit but kept saying sorry he couldn't do more to help."

"He's done enough already, let's get out of here."

They hurried back to the hotel and were packed and ready to go within ten minutes of getting back to the room. The roads were clear and the journey to the airport was remarkably quick. They grabbed their bags out of the boot of the taxi, gave the driver his fare with a tip and headed into the airport. All of a sudden things changed. The airport was packed, a problem with the baggage system had created a huge backlog and they were now faced with a sea of people trying to get through passport control.

They realised that there was nothing at all they could do so they patiently joined the mass of people that were gradually organising themselves into several semi organised lines.

Alek looked around and sighed, "this is nuts."

Cass looked at him and smiled, "there's nothing we can do, we don't have any authority at all here and even if we talk to a member of staff they'll just tell us to join the queue."

Alek was looking around in an attempt to while away the time when he noticed a side door open and man emerged flanked by two armed policeman. The man was immaculately dressed and seemed to be heading straight for him.

"Cass, I think we've got company," he nodded in the direction of the newcomers.

The lines of people parted to allow the trio through and the noise level noticeably dropped all around them, the trio stopped just before Alek and Cass. The two officers holding back slightly in order to enable themselves to keep a close eye on the surrounding passengers.

"Terribly sorry to bother you but would both of you mind coming with me please."

Without even waiting for a response he turned and started walking back towards the door that he'd just emerged from.

Alek looked at Cass, "he's fairly confident that we're going to follow him isn't he?"

"Come on, let's go and see what this is all about," with that she picked up her bag and made her way towards the door. The passengers had still left a clear path and the two policemen fell in behind Alek and Cass and as they passed them Cass could hear several making remarks about what was probably happening. Drugs seemed to be the most common guess.

Once through the door they were taken down two corridors and down a flight of stairs. A security door was opened by a member of staff and they went through to find themselves airside. A people carrier was waiting for them with the rear door open, their guide turned to them, "well, nice to meet you, he'll take you to where you need to go," with that he turned and went back inside.

49

Alek and Cass got into the people carrier and the door automatically closed behind them. The driver manoeuvred his way around the various ground crew going about their business and followed a road that seemed to follow the perimeter of the airfield. On the far side of the airfield a jet sat on its own and as Alek got close he could see that it was a Gulfstream G550. He looked at Cass, she smiled, "guess that's where we're heading then." The driver stopped just short of the jet and the side door opened. Alek and Cass got out and before they could say thank you the door was closing and the people carrier was driving off.

Before either of them could say anything a voice called out from inside the jet "Get your arses up here we haven't got all day, we've already been cleared for take-off," they both looked up to find Danny smiling at them both.

Cass smiled, "a please would be nice."

"Oh I don't think so," he said, "you're the passengers and I'm the crew so get up here, sit down buckle up and enjoy the flight."

Cass sighed, "kids of today, no manners."

As soon as Cass and Alek were in Danny closed the door. "We're in," he called out. Before he'd even sat down the plane was moving.

"Hello Ladies and Gentleman, welcome to Baby Girl airlines. We've been cleared for priority take off so will be in the air shortly, we'll be cruising at a height of 39,000 feet and will be travelling as fast as I can get this thing to go. I hope you enjoy the flight and unfortunately for you I have to leave you in the not so capable hands of my colleague, who quite frankly drove me nuts on the flight over wanting to play with all the switches and dials so under no circumstances are you to allow him to come back in here."

Cass laughed and looked at Danny who shrugged his shoulders and grinned.

"What? It's real life GTA. What do you expect me to do?"

They were in the air quickly and climbing fast, Alek looked out of the window,

"She's not hanging around is she?"

Danny suddenly looked serious, "no she isn't." he leaned forward in his seat to save himself having to raise his voice. Due to the rate of climb and the fact that they were at full throttle the noise was greater than normal. They weren't conducting a standard take off that was for sure. "The team is already at Gatwick waiting for us to get back, the

General wants to know exactly what we're dealing with and wants to put things in motion as soon as he can. This has got more than a few people worrying already. After James spoke to Alek he briefed the General, who picked up on the fact that James seemed concerned. As you well know if the General thinks James is concerned then things happen and they usually happen fast."

James had been under the Generals' direct and indirect command for a number of years and during that time the General had learnt to pay attention to him. His instincts and intuition had kept more than a few missions on track in the past and had helped to avoid some embarrassing and costly mistakes. James had realised that as soon as Alek has requested an immediate pick up that this was serious and had conveyed that during his briefing with the General.

Which was why they currently found themselves at 39,000 feet travelling as fast as the G550 would go which, with a slight tailwind, was currently 495 knots. They really weren't hanging around.

Cass unbuckled her seatbelt and stood up. "I'm going to check on Jess."

Danny stood up as well, "ask her if she wants a drink."

He went to the back of the plane to get a few drinks out of the fridge.

Cass moved into the cockpit. Jess was completely relaxed at the controls and Cass picked up the headset from the co-pilots seat and sat down, "hey honey, how're you doing?"

"Well to be honest I'm a little frustrated. No matter what I do I can't get this bucket of bolts to hit Mach 1." She looked across at Cass with a twinkle in her eye, "doesn't matter how much I tweak the controls it just won't get there."

Cass laughed, "well that's a good thing. You probably need to give it back in one piece, especially as it isn't ours."

Jess rolled her eyes. "I guess so."

Cass was qualified to fly the jet but she always felt a little inferior when she was sat next to Jess as she made everything look so effortless. She had quite a few hours under her belt but compared to Jess it was nothing at all and she often sat in awe of her abilities.

Suddenly two cans of Pepsi max appeared between them. Cass took them from Danny, "so have you managed it yet?" he asked.

Jess sighed, "no and we're running out of time."

"You could always just stick us in a dive, I'm sure that would do it."

Cass whipped her head round, "get out of here you damn idiot, don't give her any ideas."

Danny laughed as he walked back into the cabin.

Jess smiled, "don't worry Cass, as much as I'd love to break the sound barrier I don't need the attention it would attract from the General, especially as I don't even know who he's borrowed this jet from. We'll start our descent soon, not a surprise I guess but we've been given priority clearance for landing and are going straight to a hanger on the south side of Gatwick, the team are already in a meeting room waiting for us. I have a distinct feeling that the information you guys have is going to create a few waves."

"You're not wrong there, it's not good at all. Human trafficking at its worst I would say just about describes it."

Jess looked across, "really?"

"Yes, from what we've heard so far money really can buy you anything, including the ability to take a life without any incrimination at all."

They landed without incident and Jess taxied the plane straight to the hanger. She was expecting to stop the plane outside the hanger doors but as she approached they opened and she was marshalled inside. She followed the directions given and when the Marshall crossed his arms she stopped and starred the shutdown procedure. The doors to the hanger had already been closed and Danny opened the plane door.

A uniformed RAF Sergeant made his way up the stairs and turned into the Cockpit. "I'll finish shutting the plane down Ma'am."

Jess smiled "Nick I work for a living, don't ever call me Ma'am."

"Just get your butt out of the seat so I can do my job. I've got better things to do than follow a bunch of overpaid civvies around doing their jobs for them."

Jess laughed, Nick Crawford was an RAF Sergeant assigned to a small team that the General used. The team was made up of members from various units of the UK and US armed forces which always gave the General the edge because he always had someone that knew someone on his staff.

Jess left Nick to it and joined the others as they made their way towards the main office. They'd used this hanger a couple of times before so knew where to go. When they got to the office they suddenly realised why they'd been given priority clearance for the flight. Almost every seat around the table was occupied. The whole team was there as well as the General himself with his senior members of staff. The room fell silent as they walked in, Alek walked straight to the General and gave him the flash drive "I guess this is what you're after Sir."

The General nodded with a grave face, "sadly, yes it is, and thank you Alek, grab a coffee and take a seat with the others."

He passed the drive to a Major who inserted it into secure laptop. The General sat down, he looked around the table and took a deep breath, "okay people, this isn't great and you're about to watch a video diary which at best can be described as disturbing. At the end we'll need to formulate a plan and get things moving as soon as possible. I can't stress how important this is and you can be sure that every single government involved is going to want this dealt with swiftly and quietly so we'd better make sure that's exactly what we do. Right let's make a start."

Chapter Six

It only took Angie a week and a half to seduce Phoebe and for the first time ever she didn't enjoy it a bit. There wasn't any of the usual excitement as she ensnared her victim. Almost all of the time she was around Phoebe she kept thinking of Sam and that wasn't something she'd ever had to deal with before. As a result she was conscious that she wasn't always acting as she normally would. She looked at Phoebe lying on the bed, the drugs keeping her in a deep sleep. Angie had already called in for a pick up and the team were on their way now. She got up out of the chair and started to clean the apartment to remove as much evidence as possible that would show that she had been there. She hadn't been to the apartment that often so it wasn't going to be too hard although Angie was very aware that she wouldn't be able to remove every single trace. Even though her fingerprints and DNA weren't in the system she still carried out a thorough clean up.

Phoebe was from out of state and Angie had checked her call history and she didn't have much contact with her family so it would be a while before they realised she was missing. There weren't too many friends from college and Angie knew that Phoebe had already told everyone she did know there that she'd met someone special and was going to spend some time with them so Angie knew that she had a couple of weeks at least before anyone thought to look. Angie looked around the room. It was clean and tidy. Everything was where it should be and to a casual observer it would look as if Phoebe had simply gone away for a few days.

To assist with that illusion as always Angie packed a bag of her victims' clothes and obvious belongings that they'd take with them if they actually did go away. This was always with them when they travelled and was given to the client. The idea being that the sight of familiar items might in some way reduce the stress and anguish they may feel when they find themselves in strange surroundings. Angie didn't dwell on that thought for long, it wasn't something she ever really worried about. Her job was simply to find the right person and call the pickup team.

Her phone vibrated. It was at text from the team they were five minutes out. Angie had one last look around to make sure she was happy. The apartment was clearly lived in by a single college girl. All the photos and paraphernalia dotted around supported that. College books on the shelves and half written essays and projects all over the place. Angie had packed Phoebes Mac and her cell phone to help build the illusion that Phoebe had simply gone away for a few days.

There was a gentle knock at the door, Angie opened it and two men walked in. She had met them a couple of times before. The organisation used a number of teams but every so often Angie would see the same pair. They were both dressed in black combat boots, blue jeans a T-shirt and a jacket with a huge embroidered logo on the back advertising the local college football team. They were carrying a kit bag between them which already seemed to be full as it looked as though they were struggling with it. As soon as the door was closed they relaxed and dropped the bag on the floor. It was obviously empty but to anyone watching them arrive it would have seemed as though it was full of sports kit. All part of the illusion carefully crafted over months and months till it was now almost a work of art.

"She's out for the count, you've got about three hours before it starts to wear off."

One of the men grunted and started to open the bag, no names were ever exchanged and there weren't any pleasantries, this was a job pure and simple.

"We'll be on the road for about two hours and then we'll sedate her again," this time the partner had spoken. He was standing beside Phoebe getting ready to lift her up so that the kit bag could be placed underneath her.

Angie stood out of the way, this was their job now and all she had to do was make sure they didn't damage Phoebe when they put her into the bag.

He lifted Phoebe almost effortlessly while the first man placed the opened bag under her. Once the bag was in place he lowered Phoebe down. Angie had already put the travel bag that she had packed for Phoebe at the end of the bed. That was placed in the kit bag as well and without a word the man that had grunted zipped the bag up and took hold of his handle ready to lift.

The talker looked at Angie "anything else we need?"

"No that's everything. You can get going, I'll finish up here."

"Cool," he took hold of the other handle and they lifted the bag between them, it looked no different as to when they had walked in the room and the bag was empty. They'd obviously perfected the move over time, they made their way to the door and Angie opened it. They walked out and Angie shut the door, as simple as that another assignment completed.

Angie didn't need to let anyone know that Phoebe had been collected. Over the years they'd realised that the less they communicated the smaller the chance of anything being intercepted or used against them. All communication with Stephen was face to face. All she ever got was a seemingly dull spam email that was in fact coded and told her where to be and when. She went about her business for another five minutes and decided the apartment looked just as it should so she turned off the light and shut the door behind her.

The men carefully lifted the bag into the back of the car. They'd chosen an average people carrier, identical to the one that most of the local 'soccer mums' would be driving. Although a van would have been easier they didn't want to stand out at all and it was far easier to blend in at this time of night with a car rather than a van. They made sure that the kit bag was secure and that if for some reason the girl should move she wouldn't hurt herself.

They had done this enough times to know that their payment was completely reliant on the package arriving to the plane without any damage at all, that had been made perfectly clear, there wasn't any room for error and they knew they would pay dearly if they failed. They closed the rear door and got in the front, although the airfield was only three hours away they had agreed to split the driving. Within twenty minutes they were on the interstate and cruising at 55 mph, everything was going to plan. After an hour and a half they stopped to administer the next dose of sedative. This had to be injected as the girl wasn't awake so they couldn't use pills or a drink.

They were always very careful to ensure that the injection left almost no mark at all, the girl would be checked thoroughly when they got to the airport and they wouldn't get paid if she wasn't in perfect condition. In fact, they both knew that they probably wouldn't survive if she wasn't which is why they always took extreme precautions to make sure that they didn't do anything that would ruin their chance of payment for a job well done. They had no idea who they were working for and had both agreed that they didn't ever want to know.

They each got $5k upon completion, by the time they'd taken out expenses they still cleared over $4k each which wasn't bad for a couple of days work. The airport always changed. This made their job slightly harder as they had to make sure they had an alternative vehicle to swap into nearby, which is why the job always took a couple of days. Most of that was spent acquiring the two vehicles they needed and making sure they were in the right place. The second vehicle was always a rental which they always got from the closest large airport, they'd then return it and get on separate planes and go back to leading their normal lives waiting for the next email.

They arrived at the municipal airport slightly ahead of time, the guard at the gate simply pointed to a hanger and they drove over to it. As they pulled up the hanger door opened slightly and they could see a small jet inside with medical insignia on the side. Two men came out, very similar to themselves. No words were exchanged; everyone knew exactly what they had to do. The kit bag was removed from the back and they both watched it being carried into the hanger. From the angle they had they could see a medical trolley with IV drips already in place sitting to one side of the plane. The girl was lifted out and suddenly two people in white coats appeared. They checked the girl out, looking for any damage and then checked her vitals. The female nodded to one of the men and he picked up the now empty kit bag, they could see the back of an SUV in the hanger and the rear door was open. The bag was thrown into the back, as usual the disposal of the bag was down to the next team in the chain.

One of the men appeared from the hanger carrying two small sports bags. The routine was always the same. Inside would be a change of clothes and an envelope containing their money. They would change there and then putting their old clothes bag in the bag and handing it back. Not a word was spoken as they changed, none of the men knew who each other were and didn't even know if everyone spoke the same language. It was all part of the strict security process created to minimise the risk of leaks or exposure. They handed the bags back and simply drove away. Another job completed flawlessly. If it hadn't been they were both very aware that they wouldn't have been driving anywhere. In fact they probably wouldn't be breathing anymore.

The doctor gave the all clear for the girl to be loaded onto the plane, they didn't know her name, and in fact they didn't care. Their job was simple get her from A to B ensuring that she was delivered in pristine condition. The doctor and nurse had been working together for some time now and were in fact the only consistent team used again and again, they had the whole procedure down to a fine art and hadn't ever failed to deliver the patient in perfect condition. It took the pair of them less than twenty minutes to have everything ready and the doctor gave the pilot the go ahead to take-off.

The flight plan was genuine. The medical company the jet was registered to was totally legitimate and this was one of ten jets the company owned. The slight difference was that this jet didn't always fly legitimate patients, it was always on standby for the special patients and the crew was always the same. After take-off they'd always fly straight to a major airport to refuel and stock up. This kept up the appearance that this was just another regular medical flight repatriating a patient. This time they had a two hour flight before getting to the airport so they settled down and relaxed. They checked on the girl a couple of times before they landed. They knew it wasn't really necessary but they liked to make sure everything was okay and they'd agreed from the start it was far better to be safe than sorry.

Before they knew it they'd landed and as always were directed to a hard standing close to the airports medical centre. The pilot and co-pilot disembarked and went into the centre. This was always to keep up appearances and they'd spend some time while the plane was being refuelled talking to other pilots to give the appearance that this was just another straight forward no nonsense flight. The doctor and nurse never got off together. One of them would always stay with the patient just in case the unexpected happened. Like the pilots one of them would go in and chat with the medical staff on site giving the illusion that they were catching up with the gossip and touching base with colleagues. It was an act they just wanted to keep everything above board and make sure that everything went to plan.

Within an hour they'd been refuelled and the food and drink has been restocked. The plane was always very well stocked and they had plenty of food and drink to make the flight more enjoyable. They were flying far more frequently now and as a result spent far more time on the plane than ever before. Business was booming. They were back in the air with the minimum of fuss, it helped with the fact that they were a medical flight and they were always given a certain level of priority which was nice. The flight was uneventful, the patient didn't need any attention at all. They updated their charts and records in accordance with protocol so that if anyone looked it did genuinely appear as if this was a routine patient repatriation. The facade was complete as the plane was equipped for medical repatriation; it had every single piece of equipment and kit that would be needed for doing just that.

They landed without any issues and once again taxied straight to the medical centre. They carried out the last checks and updated the charts while the pilot was shutting the plane down. The plane would remain here while they went to a hotel for the night and returned the following morning to fly back to the states. They nearly always went back empty but every so often would take on a genuine patient for the return trip, partly because it made financial sense and partly to keep the pretence even more realistic. An ambulance pulled up next to the plane its blue lights flashing. They helped the two-man crew to transfer the patient, once more the whole process was very slick.

As soon as the back doors of the ambulance were closed the crew on the plane were relieved of their duty of care. They then could afford to relax. The pilots completed all their checks and once done they left the plane and went into the medical centre to organise a taxi to their hotel. The doctor and nurse were already in a taxi and almost at their hotel. They all stayed in local hotels and made sure that they kept their behaviour and spending within the limits of the other crews so that they kept themselves well under the radar. With the money they made with each trip they could easily afford to stay in far more luxurious surroundings but that would look odd so they kept everything looking normal. Like the original team that picked the girl up they were paid cash on their return stateside and they paid their own expenses so on average they were each making $8k per trip. Not bad work at all.

Chapter Seven

It had been three days since they'd sat through the meeting with the General and none of them had stopped at all. They had research notes and scraps of paper littered over every desk. Every assignment was the same, meticulous investigation always preceded getting boots on the ground. This time it was slightly different, the information they had to go on was sketchy at best and they were already having to fill in too many gaps. The video diary they had all watched hadn't really given them a great deal to go on. It did clearly show that there was an incredible sophisticated operation under way that allowed you to simply buy a life, and once you'd paid you could do whatever you wanted with that life. In a nutshell they were selling the power of life over death. The basic premise was simple. You put a request in for a certain type of person and that's exactly what was delivered. They did know that the girl had been an American and she was 22. She'd mentioned a couple of times that she was a student at a university in Seattle but hadn't been specific. It had at least given them somewhere to start.

Cass and Jocelyn had reached out to their contacts and had a list of missing persons that fitted the description but they'd had to expand the search to the entire state of Washington as an initial starting point as they couldn't be sure she was actually from Seattle. They then moved out slowly state by state until they had a horrifyingly long list of missing 22 year olds. As it was so close to the border they'd even contacted the Canadian authorities. Her accent was American rather than Canadian but in order to cover every avenue they'd got the figures to play safe. They had then worked through the list and managed to narrow it down the just under twenty that had been reported missing from college or university and three of those were from the Seattle area. They had a place to start although it still wasn't much to go on. For the last 72 hours they'd begged, teased and bullied information from their contacts. It had been a series of conference calls, video links and facetime sessions trying to squeeze every little piece of information out of the FBI and CIA that they could. They were exhausted and moved their working day so that they were awake at the same time as their colleagues in the states.

Cass had spent quite a bit of time working with the FBI field office in Seattle whilst Jocelyn had been working half a dozen different sources at Langley to see if any unknown American women had turned up dead or alive throughout the rest of the world. It wasn't an easy task and the workspace looked a mess, the four whiteboards surrounding them though didn't. They contained precise information laid out in a logical manner and each time they found something new the boards were updated.

Every so often food would appear beside them and they'd eat without thinking. At this stage of most assignments the support staff take the lead and the team that's usually at the sharp end works the support role. Sean, Scott, Alek and Barney worked a shift pattern to ensure that food and drink was available around the clock for whoever was awake. They knew exactly what everyone liked and made sure that they were eating and drinking regularly. During the investigation stage you can easily lose track of time so the guys always kept regular snacks and meals on the go. They knew all too well the importance of a good sustained calorie intake and whilst sitting at a desk doesn't require the same physical energy the guys expended in the field it was vital that the research team were functioning at their best. Especially at this stage when they had so little information to go on. While they weren't Michelin star chefs they did know how to create some stunning dishes and would often be cooking two or three different meals at once to cater for the different tastes of those on duty. That said they did regularly fall back to the staple diet of egg and bacon sandwiches, something that Danny always enjoyed.

He was busy down in the main part of the building giving every vehicle a thorough check. Although they were obviously going to be working on foreign shores for the majority of this assignment, a key part of their standard operating procedures was to check and double check every piece of kit and equipment. So he was always going through the vehicles and comms equipment to make sure everything was working perfectly. All batteries charged, all leads and chargers working, spare sim cards and SD cards. They all had their own assigned phones but when they travelled they took spares and these were set up and placed into each individual's grab bag, along with their iPads and Macs. Each team had a camera kit as well and Danny would also check each one of those. During this stage of an assignment the comms room was a mass of chargers and leads with vast quantities of batteries and attachments on charge. Each camera body was cleaned and serviced as were the lenses, SD and CF cards were checked and formatted. Danny had everything arranged in kits and methodically worked his way through each of them. Once completed each kit went back into the assigned drawer so that the individual teams could just grab what they needed.

Once he'd finished with the cameras he would work his way through the iPads and Macs checking that they were fully charged and the software was up to date. He followed the same process in the same order every single time to ensure that he didn't miss anything. Every so often a sandwich and can of Pepsi Max would appear somewhere near him and as if by magic as soon as he'd finished, the empty plate and can would be gone. Once he'd completed the Macs he sent Nick an email to let him know.

Nick Sanchez dealt with everything IT, although if you went into his office you'd never know it. The desk was virtually empty apart from a Mac on a docking station, a screen, keyboard and magic mouse. It looked like an almost vacant room which was exactly how Nick liked it. The server room was equally as tidy. All the patch cables were routed neatly and it almost looked like a work of art. Nick was tapping away at his keyboard trying to work his way through the multitude of false trails that were stopping him from tracing the emails they'd recovered from the flash drive they'd been given. Whoever they were dealing with were very good and covered their tracks really well. Annoyingly he wasn't having much luck and had even resigned himself to having to ask for help from a friend that was still at MIT. Nick had been approached while he was there and was asked a simple question, do you fancy working for a team that frequently deals with impossible situations with little or no background information? He'd jumped at the chance and very quickly found out that little or no information was an incredibly accurate description. He'd often spend hours trying to piece together something tangible for everyone to work with and this assignment wasn't any different. He'd managed to trace the email through part of its journey even with the false trails but it was getting harder now and taking far longer than he wanted it to. Despite this, he kept going knowing that he'd do everything possible to give the team the start they needed.

Barney was sat with James in the boardroom trying to work out who was going to go where and when. Most assignments called for two teams, one would stay in the UK and coordinate things while the other was out in the field. This was different, they knew they'd need at least one team to cover Europe as they already had proof that one girl had been killed there.

James looked up from the screen, "okay so let's create two teams of three to cover Europe, we send one straight out to work through everything with Josef and hold the other here as backup. The lead team are Katie, Alek and Charlie and I'll put Chris, Sean and Levi as the backup team."

Barney thought for a second, "that makes sense, each team is fairly balanced with local knowledge, muscle and technical skills."

"That's the plan," James sat back in his chair, "the rest of you will make up the other team and I have a strong feeling you'll be heading stateside, at least some of you heading to Seattle as that is the only really firm bit of data we have so far. Nick and Jess will stay here with me and you'll take charge of the second team."

Barney couldn't see any reason to disagree as it made perfect sense. "We'll send Katie and her team off first thing tomorrow and put Chris on immediate standby."

"I'll make the necessary arrangements shortly. Boss, I'd split the second team before you go, even though you'll all travel out as one. I have a feeling you'll possibly need to go in several directions at once so I'd create two teams now to make things easier."

"I agree, your thoughts?"

"Well I'd have Cass pair with Scott and you with Joss. You take Danny with you as a driver and if things become complicated out there we pull Charlie, Levi and Jess from the European teams and send them straight over and if we need any more than that then I'm sure the General has plenty of bodies to fill the gaps."

"Okay let's brief everyone in thirty and let them know what the next step is. I'm going to grab a coffee and take Bruce out for a quick walk."

Barney was back within twenty minutes and when he walked into the boardroom everyone was already sat down and waiting, James had arranged the seating plan so they were all seated in their planned teams. Everyone already had a drink and all of them were working their way through three boxes of Krispey Creme donuts that had mysteriously appeared on the table, something he knew Jess and Cass were responsible for.

"You're all aware of what we know so far, I fear it's only the tip of the iceberg and we're going to need to attempt to deal with this quickly before it becomes a major problem. Katie, Alek and Charlie you'll be leaving first thing and you'll go and meet with Josef and get every single detail out of him you can. Chris you'll be on immediate standby to back them up and you'll have Sean and Levi with you. Cass, Joss, you'll be with Scott, Danny and myself and we'll be heading to Seattle," Barney paused for a second to pick up a glazed raspberry donut and in between mouthfuls he carried on. "I don't have to begin to tell you how politically complicated this is going to get. The FBI will want lead because an American was kidnapped and murdered, the CIA will want lead because it happened outside the states and to cap it all Interpol will want lead because it happened on their turf. You can also add into that every single intelligence agency wanting their share, so initially Cass you'll oversee the relationship with the FBI, Joss you'll handle the CIA and Katie you'll deal with Interpol. I'll work with the General to pull or push each of them in the right direction."

While he'd been talking Danny had put another glazed raspberry donut on a plate and pushed it in front of him. "What's that for?" Barney asked.

Without hesitation Danny replied "I'm saving time, we all know full well that you're not going to eat just one so to save time I thought I'd speed things up for you."

Everyone laughed and Barney rolled his eyes, "give me strength."

"I am," Danny said "now eat the donut, we all know you can't survive on just one."

James spoke up trying hard not to laugh, "to help I'll take over so you can focus on improving your donut eating skills. We may need to boost the team stateside so if need be Charlie, Levi, Sean and Jess will be pulled from the European teams and be sent over. Jess we'll have a plane on standby that you can use. It'll be faster than trying to sort out tickets etc and if need be we can get the General to backfill. I know that's slightly different to what we initially agreed Boss but it makes more sense."

"I agree, it's a good idea, has anybody got any questions?"

There was a pause and then Katie spoke "Boss, from what Alek and Cass have said Josef seems to be in a bit of a state. How far can we go with him? From the notes he was introduced by a friend and we could really do with knowing who that friend is so that we can talk to them."

"As far as you need to. We really need a break and anything we can get will help. I know your contacts at Interpol have declared him clean but get them to dig into his business contacts. These high flyers often associate with likeminded people so there's a good chance that his friend is a high level business contact so that is the first place I'd look." Barney looked down at the empty plate and with perfect precision a second later a half full box of donuts stopped in front of him. He looked straight at Danny.

"Just saving a little more time Boss," he had a huge grin on his face.

Barney picked up another donut, "so we start tomorrow morning, Katie, You and your team will leave first thing, Chris I want you and your team on immediate standby. Jess I need you to be ready to go so that you can get the backup team across to Katie as quickly as possible. James will go through a few more bits while I sit and eat these," he moved the box closer and selected another one.

"Jess, if we need to send you and the others stateside you'll be on a domestic flight. We'll want you ready to fly as soon as you land. Depending on where that is we'll make sure there's something waiting for you. I'll make sure the General has got that covered," James looked round the table, "as usual no matter how insignificant you think something is let Nick know, I want as much data coming in as possible, I'll arrange for some extra bodies in here if need be to assist with going through it all."

Barney put his half eaten donut down, "if nobody else has any questions let's start getting our shit together, check and double check your go bags. Make sure you've got what you need for when you arrive. I don't have any issues with James sourcing extra kit but I'm not going to be impressed if we have to get something you should already have."

The room suddenly exploded with noise as almost everyone got up and cleared the table of all the folders and pads they'd come in with.

They all had a job to do, those not leaving straight away assisted Katie and her team, that's the way they always worked, as a team.

Danny went straight down to the RS to give it a quick once over to make sure it was ready for an early morning airport run. Once he'd done that he'd head to the kit room to see who needed anything extra, or more importantly anything he'd forgotten to get ready.

The building was full of the sound of movement. Everyone knew what needed to be done and they got on with it making sure they all had everything they needed. As soon as the first team's kit was ready they all moved onto their own gear and before long there were bundles of kit bags in groups all ready to be loaded. They began to relax a little, ordered a mountain of takeaway food and had a relaxing evening together knowing full well that it could possibly be a while before they could do it again.

Chapter 8 (North America)

The plane landed at Seattle airport after a somewhat dull flight.
Although they had all been seated together they couldn't talk about the
case with so many people around so they slept for a bit, watched a film
or read a book. Danny had managed to find a stereotypical American
petrol head and had spent most of the flight discussing which engine
and drive train setup was the best. As the plane came to rest at the
stand Barney looked out of the window to see the rain coming down
with such force each drop seemed to bounce of the wing three or four
inches back into the air. They all stayed seated for a bit and allowed
everyone around them to get themselves sorted. They only had a small
cabin bag and once the initial commotion that accompanied every
flight that has just landed seemed to be over they all stood up and
joined the queue that was now making its way swiftly off the plane.
Their suitcases had already been sent over via military transport and
had been dropped off at their hotel so getting out of the airport was
going to be fairly easy as they didn't need to go to claim any hold
baggage. They made their way towards immigration along with all the
other passengers and before they knew it with very little fuss they were
in the main arrivals lounge at the airport.

They made their way over to Starbucks to get a coffee. They were
meeting an FBI and CIA contact and going their separate ways from
the airport so this was a quick last chance for the group to relax. Joss
and Cass both sent text to their respective contacts to let them know
where they were in the terminal and that they were having a quick
coffee. Almost as soon as they'd grabbed a table two well-dressed men
approached them. Cass got up and went straight over to the man on

the right, they embraced and she gave him a peck on the cheek. Turning back round she faced the others to see them all grinning.

"Everyone, this is Wilson Saunders. Will and I worked together on a somewhat lengthy operation a few years back."

Danny put his coffee down, "well you certainly don't look how I expected an FBI agent to look."

Will smiled, "that's because Jake here is the FBI agent and I'm CIA, they get a better clothing allowance than we do."

Danny burst out laughing and Jake stepped forward to introduce himself.

"Hi, I'm Jake Burns and the truth of the matter is that we actually just have better dress sense."

That caused everyone to laugh and they all introduced themselves, once the introductions were over they all made their way to the exit. The team was splitting straight away, Joss and Scott were going to a local CIA office and the others were going with Jake to the FBIs Seattle field office. As they came out of the terminal building they made their way towards two very similar government looking SUVs that were being watched over by two airport security guards. The two teams said a quick goodbye and got into their respective vehicles.

Barney got into the back with Danny. Normally he'd sit in the front but he felt that the correct etiquette for today would be to let Cass sit up the front as she was an actual FBI agent. Barney sat back and enjoyed the ride. Well enjoyed watching the torrential rain still bounce a couple of inches in the air when it landed. This was one hell of a storm. Barney shook his head and laughed to himself. If it wasn't for the fact that he was travelling on the wrong side of the road he'd happily think he was in Brighton on a miserable day like this.

"How long has the weather been like this Jake?"

"It's been raining like this on and off for the last two days Sir."

"No need to call me Sir Jake, my name's Barney."

"Sorry Barney, I've only been given a real quick briefing. The agent that was going to be your main point of contact has been pulled back to a task force he was working with a few months ago and I was only switched to this a few hours ago and I don't really know where you guys fit in to an FBI investigation so I assumed you're some high level State or Military team."

"That's alright Jake. We'll go through everything but we're actually a multinational team that work worldwide to bridge the gap between the Military and Government so we basically get the short end of the stick and have to perform miracles in order to achieve our objective. We're here working with the FBI and CIA to try to get to the bottom of a rather unpleasant human trafficking ring that we've so far managed to trace to this state. When we get to the office I'll give you a full update and bring you up to speed."

"We're almost there, the office is just around the corner. Your ID badges have been arranged and should be waiting for you at the gate when we get there. I'm sure I don't need to tell you to keep them on display at all times. Visitors don't normally get full clearance for the building and would get a restricted visitors badge but they've told me you've got the freedom of all facilities which is part of the reason I made the wrong assumption about who you are."

Cass laughed "Jake I'm sure they'll regret letting those two loose around the building, but they'll find that out for themselves quick enough I'm sure."

Jake smiled and had hardly finished straightening the wheel after turning the corner before he indicated and turned into a smart looking three story building with a heavily armed front gate sitting about fifty yards back from the entrance. The security guard clearly knew Jake but asked for his ID anyway. Jake showed it and the security guard scanned it. He smiled and asked Jake to drive through the gate and pull over. Jake had hardly stooped the vehicle when the security guard appeared at his window again with a small package.

"Here's their ID badges," he passed Jake an envelope, "please keep you ID on you at all times folks, it'll save us having to question you while you're here." The guard had turned round and walked off before Jake could say anything. He handed the envelope to Cass and pulled into the underground car park. He pulled into a space and they all got out.

"Your ID badge will grant you access to the lifts and will determine which areas you can get into but as I said you're cleared for all areas so the only bit to warn you about is if you want to use the range the best time is early morning. As the day goes on it gets busier in there and we do have one of the best set ups in the area so if you get the chance then I'd make the most of it."

Danny smiled, "oh we'll definitely do that."

They got to the lift and Jake touched his ID against the pad and the doors opened, they all got in and he hit the button for the third floor.

"They've set one of the conference rooms up for you. It has an office linked to it that's yours as well. There's also a laptop and three cell phones all setup and ready to go."

The lift stopped and the doors opened. There was a buzz in the air that you'd expect from a busy office. Jake stepped out of the lift and turned right, they were all greeted with a clean and open plan area. They followed Jake to the conference room, receiving a few glances from some of the agents that were busy at their desks. The conference room was big. A central table that seated twenty people, dry wipe boards, a couple of smart boards, four large screens on the wall, a floor to ceiling screen with projector, fridge and some would say most important of all, a coffee machine.

Jake turned to them, "take a seat guys and grab a coffee, there are a couple of people you need to meet and then we'll start." Without waiting for a reply he left the conference room. Barney put his bag on a chair and made his way to the coffee machine. He poured three cups and added two sugars for Danny. Cass and Danny had already sat down and had their Macs in front of them, Barney put their drinks down returned to get his and then sat down next to Danny. The three of them were sat together facing the main door to the room, Barney knew they'd have plenty of time to explore the room and the office at the end so for now they got ready to brief whoever it was that Jake came back with.

Jake returned a few minutes later with three people, a twenty something female who looked a little out of place, a man in his late twenties dressed in a similar fashion to Jake and a man in his late forties, maybe early fifties carrying an air of superiority that almost screamed out I'm the man in charge.

Before Jake could say anything the older man stepped forward "I'm Anthony Di'Angelo the agent in charge here, I'll keep this brief so that you can get on. I've been given an update on why you're here and I'll do everything I can to help. You've got a hell of a task ahead of you so I'm going to let you get on with it. My office is at the end of the hall and if you need anything at all please come straight to me. It's been made very clear to me that this is a priority and I have to be honest I already have a number of high priority cases but this seems to have come from the top so you'll get everything that we can give. I'll leave you with Agent Burns and he'll do the other introductions. Good luck people and remember come find me if you need me." With that he turned on his heel and left.

Jake smiled "Well that's the longest speech I've heard him give for a while. Guys, this is Agent Drew Evans and Tech Specialist Grace Halford."

Once all the introductions were over they all sat back down. Before Barney could start, Grace asked them for their Macs so that she could connect them all to the network to make things easier for them. Once she had all three she announced she'd be back shortly and took them away.

Barney looked at Jake, "so how much do you and Drew know about why we're here?"

"To be perfectly honest we don't know a great deal. We know it has to do with human trafficking and we know that you have a lead that's lead you to Seattle but other than that we're a little in the dark."

"Okay well here's what we know so far." Barney started to brief them.

Less than five miles away in an office not to dissimilar to the one Barney and the team were in Joss and Scott were going through a very similar briefing with two CIA specialists. From outside the building it wasn't obvious that it had anything to do with the CIA at all. In fact the first three floors belonged to an investment banking company. The fourth floor however was a different matter, the swipe cards for the investment bankers only gave them access to the first three floors in the lifts. The swipe cards the CIA used however took them straight to the fourth floor and the doors opened onto a series of offices of all different sizes. Several were set up as conference rooms and there was also a large open plan area with desks arranged in a haphazard way.

Saunders had quickly handed Joss and Scott over to two specialists that had previously worked a multinational smuggling ring that the CIA had been dealing with just under a year ago. They'd been assigned to the task force in the hope that they'd be able to join some dots and give the team a head start. Kelly Giles was a stereo typical twenty something IT geek and he both looked and sounded the part. Quite the opposite, Ed Dawson didn't have a stereo type at all. To look at him you'd never guess what he did. It's obviously one of the qualities that made him one of the up and coming members of the CIA. They'd both been briefed and had a series of thick files on the desks in front of them.

Ed was leading the briefing as he'd been the lead field agent on the last operation and Kelly had taken the lead on the technical side. Their previous op had initially appeared to be a straight forward smuggling operation until they found a side-line that involved people smuggling. That discovery had turned their investigation on its head and suddenly catapulted them into several countries. The hope was that some of the framework that they'd developed could be used to jump them forward a few steps with this investigation.

"I suggest we grab a coffee and sandwich and then start to work through what we know to see if there are any possible similarities in the two operations." Ed stood up "Kelly I'll get you your usual, do you both want to come with me, there's a food cart on the corner of the block."

Joss stood up but Scott stayed where he was, "Joss just get me any sandwich, a snack bar and a coffee and I'll stay here with Kelly and make a start."

"No worries. Come on then Ed lead the way," with that Joss and Ed left the room.

Scott looked around. The office was clean and tidy but lacked the lived in feel that most government offices had. Everything appeared functional and looked right but something was missing. He looked at Kelly who was busy tapping away at the keyboard on his Mac. "So tell me Kelly, why doesn't this office seem quite right? There's something missing and I can't quite put my finger on it."

Kelly looked up from his screen, "most probably because these are temporary offices. We move around every six to nine months. We have two or three sets of offices in most cities and use whichever one best suit our needs. To be fair we move around so much it becomes a way of life so we never really make any of the offices our home base."

Scott looked around again, "well I guess it works for you guys. So what are your thoughts on the case?"

"I've got to be brutally honest and say I don't think there's any link at all between what we dealt with and this. We were dealing with a drug cartel kidnapping illegal's and selling them. Nothing to order they just took advantage of the fact that there are just so many people trying to keep under the radar because they shouldn't be here. They were kidnapping whole families with no regard for anyone. They were sold en-masse for whatever money they could get. Their setup, once we got to grips with it, was incredibly crude but effective. What you're dealing with however seems highly sophisticated and well backed. From what I've read this isn't some quickly put together scheme. This is clever, calculated and so far very effective."

"I had an awful feeling you were going to say that, they seem to do their homework. They deliver exactly what the client wants down to the last detail and that takes some planning and a well-financed organisation."

Kelly nodded, "yes it does and that's why I don't think it has anything at all to do with what we uncovered."

Scott sighed, "so where do we start?"

"Well, you've got some good solid information to start with and we've managed to locate where your girl lived and the college she went to. She was an only child with no parents, from out of state so very few friends which is why nobody has really missed her. We've talked to a couple of people that shared a class with her but she really was a loner. We've pieced together some of her movements but to be frank too much time has passed and we're having to make too many assumptions."

"Well at least you've managed to identify her, even if she doesn't have any family of anyone that misses her."

"It's a small consolation but not nearly the breakthrough we need Scott. Whoever they are they're thorough. Reading through the brief we were supplied it's clear they aren't snatching people randomly off the street. I mean to deliver a person to order down to the last detail takes one hell of a lot of work and infrastructure."

"I was thinking that. Josef describes the girl down to the finest detail and when she was delivered to him she was, in his words, the picture of perfection. In other words she didn't have a mark on her, she was flawless so clearly not thrown in a container and shipped from one place to another. How did they get someone from the States to Europe? The speed at which she was delivered to him suggests they either have hundreds and hundreds of girls already locked up somewhere or they are that good that they can locate and deliver the exact girl without a single mark on her. It's almost as if she just got on a plane and flew there under her own steam."

"Maybe the team you have in Europe will find out a bit more, just a shame that your man didn't manage to get more information out of her before he killed her."

"He's not our man Kelly."

"Sorry Scott, poor choice of words."

Scott paused for a second already feeling this was going to be much harder than the team expected, "so what's our next move?"

Before Kelly could answer Joss and Ed returned with the food and drink. Joss passed Scott his and sat down next to him.

"So where are we?" She said as she removed her sandwich from the bag. She'd gone for a healthy cheese salad sandwich with brown bread which seemed like a good idea at the time but as she took the first mouthful she wished she'd gone for the sweet chilli chicken option that she'd got for Scott. As if he knew he grinned at her as he took the first mouthful of his sandwich, she shook her head in mock disgust and looked away.

Kelly talked while he ate, "so we started by speaking with the FBI and split the states in half. We then contacted each of the main colleges and universities in each state. As you can imagine there are hundreds so we've kept it to the larger ones for the moment as we simply don't have the manpower to contact each one. That being said we've already had a number of hits and we've started to investigate them as they come in."

Ed had finished his sandwich so he took over from Kelly, "we simply asked if they'd had any students drop out without any notice and completely disappear. I've got to say I'm quite shocked at how frequently this seems to happen. Of the sixteen instances we've had reported local Police departments have managed to clear nine of them so far. It turned out that almost all of them had simply had enough or couldn't cope and returned home. Two more at first glance appear to be the same but they are still to make contact to confirm that although from speaking to the parents it seems that it is a case of them giving up under the pressure. The other five, well, as yet the local PD haven't made any progress so we've declared those as possible victims."

Joss looked around the table, "well I guess that's our starting point. What do we know so far?"

Kelly quickly tapped away at his Mac and five images appeared on the large screen on the wall. "We have three girls and two boys, all aged between 18 and 20. They all seem to be smart kids doing well with no initial issues according to the staff at the schools. All of them just suddenly stopped turning up with no advance warning or indication that was going to happen."

Scott finished his coffee and put the cup down, "what about friends and family do any of them have any ideas as to why they might have stopped going? Or where they might be?"

Kelly paused for a second, "well that's the problem. The local PD don't have the manpower to investigate any further, to be honest I'm quite surprised they even got this far. They're way too understaffed to start an investigation of this sort especially as there's nothing solid to say they are actually missing or in danger."

Ed stood up and walked over to the bin and dropped his trash onto it. "The only way I see of being able to get to the next step is to split up and investigate it ourselves. Unfortunately all five missing people are in different states. We could split both groups up and look into the first four and whoever draws the first blank moves onto the last one."

Joss picked up her phone "I'll call Barney and let him know what we've got and he'll make some arrangements."

Ed picked up the file that was just to his left. He opened it to the second page, "okay so the five states are Florida, Texas, California, Arizona and New Mexico. We've made a blind guess that once they've selected someone they're moved across the border into Mexico and shipped out from there as it's far easier and cheaper."

Kelly Sighed "I don't think we have the budget to cover that kind of distance easily. I know that we've been tasked to assist you in any way possible but we do have restrictions and that's one hell of an area to cover by road."

Joss smiled, "let me worry about that, I'll check in with Barney and he can pull some strings. In the meantime let's create five folders with as much information as possible so that we're ready to go as soon as we get a green light."

Five blocks away Barney put his phone down on the table. "So Joss and her team have managed to find five people that are potentially missing that fit the brief we supplied. Unfortunately they're in five different states. She's suggested we split the teams and look into the first four. I think it's probably the best way forward. I'll make some calls and sort out some transport. They're creating a profile for each person so to be honest there isn't a great deal we can do so take a few hours off and be back here for nine tomorrow."

Cass picked up her phone, "if we've really got nothing to do till tomorrow I'm going to hit the range. Now I'm on home soil I can draw a weapon from the armoury here but as it's not going to be my own service pistol so I want to spend some time sighting it in." She looked at Danny who had a big grin on his face as he knew what was coming next. "I'll take Danny with me to keep him out of trouble unless you need him for something?"

Barney smiled and looked across at Danny, "no that's okay you can take him with you. To be honest I was wondering who I was going to get to babysit him so thanks for volunteering."

Danny shook his head, "no respect these days, just wait till we're looking for a home to put you in old man, then you'll wish you'd treated me differently."

Jake stood up "come on the pair of you I'll show you the way. It won't hurt for me to spend a bit of time down there."

Barney watched them all leave the office. He took a deep breath and closed his eyes. Like most assignments they undertook the information they had was sketchy at best and they were expected to produce amazing results in next to no time. He could hear the rain hitting the window, it seemed to be getting harder. He opened his eyes and picked up his phone. He scrolled down the contact list and selected the number he wanted.

"Hello James, I need you to speak to the General and arrange some transport. Ideally I need a pilot and a plane, something that can take at least ten passengers and I'll need him to sort out a point of contact on the ground here for flight plans fuel etc. It doesn't matter if it's military or civilian but it must be something that's at our disposal and can easily get around with the minimum of fuss." Barney listed for a few seconds, "tomorrow morning is great as the team will be back together and you can update us all at the same time, thank James."

Barney put the phone back down on the table and closed eyes again. The rain was still beating against the window and didn't appear to be slowing down at all. He opened his eyes again, picked up the phone and started calling the others to find out how they were getting on. As he was about to dial the next number on his list the phone rang in his hand. It was Katie. He spoke with her for about five minutes as she updated him on how their meeting had gone. He didn't need to even remotely suggest what she should do next as she'd already worked out the next step and he had to admit he would have done exactly the same.

Jake led Danny and Cass through the door of the armoury. He turned to Cass, "any preference? We have various Sig and Glock variants?"

"I'll take a Glock with four mags, some ammo and an extra 100 rounds for sighting."

Jake turned to Danny, "you can draw a weapon for use on the range but as you aren't cleared you can't take it out of the range. Do you have any preferences?"

Danny smiled "that's okay, I'll take a Glock, I wouldn't want to let Cass have the excuse of me using a different weapon when I do better than her."

Cass laughed, "okay bigshot, here's the deal. If you can get your score to within five of mine I'll pull some strings with a friend that works for Taran Butler and get you a day with the team at Taran Tactical."

Danny replaced his smile with a sly grin. "Absolutely! You're on, but being a gentleman please make sure that you arrange for us both to go as I'd hate for you to miss out on the opportunity."

Jake grinned "I'll score and will have the final say, no arguments, what I say goes. If the shot breaks the line the higher score counts."

Jake turned round to the armourer, "hi Steve, two Glocks please, one with four mags and a standard ammo package to be signed out for service, one with two mags. I'll also need an extra 300 rounds." He turned back round to face Cass and Danny, "that'll give you 50 rounds each to sight in and then 100 rounds each that I'll score. Ten targets, ten rounds at each. Sound okay?"

They both nodded and within five minutes were in booths next to each other loading their magazines. They'd been issues ballistic glasses and ear defenders which they were now wearing. Jake was stood behind them but slightly closer to Danny as he knew that as Cass was trained he didn't really need to keep an eye on her. He was surprised at how proficiently Danny was handling the weapon as he inserted the first loaded mag.

Jake took a step forward, "right guys, for sighting they'll be two targets set at five metres, you'll fire twenty five rounds at the first, we'll bring it back and you can check it, then another twenty five rounds at the next one. Once you've done that they'll be ten targets at different distances and you'll fire ten rounds at each and they'll be the ones I score."

"As soon as you're ready begin."

Danny took a deep breath pulled the slide back and released it putting the first round in the chamber. He relaxed himself and then moved his finger onto the trigger. He took his time not rushing it and after fifteen rounds changed mags and fired the remaining ten rounds down range. He ejected the empty mag and pulled the slide back locking it in place. He lifted the two empty mags and tilted the pistol over and called clear.

Jake was quite surprised and taken aback by this not expecting Danny to be that switched on. They both hit the buttons on the side of the booth and the targets came towards them. Cass had grouped hers quite well even though the pistol was new to her. Danny didn't have such a tight grouping but Jake was still quite impressed.

"Okay guys put up the new target and send it down range. As soon as you're ready take the next twenty five rounds."

They repeated the process again and when the targets came back Cass had managed to significantly improve her grouping. Danny had done better as well but Jake could see that Cass has easily scored higher than Danny.

"So now the real fun begins, I've put your names on ten targets each, you'll load a mag and then send the target down range. Each target will be at a different distance. When you've fired the ten rounds we'll bring the targets back in and send the next one down. I'll score them and then we'll see who's scored what. Sound okay?"

They both replied yes at the same time, Cass gave Danny one of her mags so that they could each load three mags with ten rounds. The first targets went down range and they began. Danny took his time and made sure that he didn't rush. He relaxed and ran through all of the things that Sean had taught him when they'd been on the range. Five targets in Danny was feeling much better and was now really into the swing of it. He'd been quickly checking his groupings as the targets came back towards him and he was pleased with how he'd done so far.

The last target went down range and Danny made a snap decision. He'd been really pleased with what he'd done so far and decided to double tap the last magazine. He took a few deep breaths and set himself up. Cass was already half way through her last mag when

Danny began. When he'd fired the last round he ejected the mag for the last time and cleared the pistol. He hit the button and the target came back towards him. As they were alone in the range they took their ear defenders off.

Jake had already scored the first nine targets and took the targets from each of them to tally up the final score.

Cass turned to Danny, "I'm surprised you went for a double tap on the last magazine as I took a sneaky peak at some of your targets as they were coming back in and I was really impressed."

Danny smiled "well I felt it only fair to give you a bit of a chance."

Cass laughed, "why thank you kind sir. You're such a gallant man."

Jake cleared his throat. "I've got the final scores and it pains me to say that there was a six point difference between the two of you."

Cass turned to Danny, "I've got to be honest Danny I didn't expect you to get that close, that's really impressive."

Jake cleared his throat once again. "Not so fast Cass, he beat you by six points."

Cass looked shocked, "what?!"

"I'm afraid so and I've got to say that I'm truly impressed especially as on the last target he scored two higher than you and he was double tapping."

The sly grin was back on Danny's face, "I really don't mind if you want to ask the guys at Taran Tactical if you can come along as well."

Cass shook her head, "how on earth did you manage that?"

"That's easy." Danny said. "I just followed my training."

She looked a bit blank and suddenly her facial expression changed, "shit, you've been working with Sean haven't you?"

"Why yes I have and I can't wait to describe the look on your face to him when Jake mentioned the score."

Jake was amused by the look that Cass now had on her face, "is Sean a member of your team."

Cass turned to him, "yes he is and he's rather good."

Jake looked impressed. "Well he certainly is good if this is what one of his students can do. Is he an ex Seal?"

Cass shook her head "No, He's ex SBS."

Danny grinned, "if you're going to be trained then be trained by the best, isn't that something you often quote Cass?"

Cass groaned, "oh god I'm never going to live this down, beaten by a child."

Jake laughed, "right let's clean up and go and get a drink."

Two hours later they were in a bar a few blocks from the office, both teams had met back up and were enjoying a drink and something to eat. Danny hadn't said a word to anyone. They'd just finished their food and had ordered another drink when Cass received a text message. She looked at her phone and exclaimed "You're such an arse." then looked at Danny.

Danny held both hands up. "What!"

"You couldn't help yourself could you?" The group had gone silent and everyone looked from Cass to Danny and back again, "it's a text from Sean" Her face was a picture. "You told him didn't you?"

Danny lowered his hands and adopted a serious look on his face, "I'm not sure what you mean, what does it say."

"It says" Cass shot Danny a look of disgust, "it says and I quote 'Oh dear, a trained professional shown up by a kid. How embarrassing' Now how did he know that?"

Danny smiled "whoops, I might have mentioned it to him."

Cass rolled her eyes, "you're such a dick."

Cass then spent the next ten minutes explaining what had happened and then the next two rounds being ridiculed by everyone.

Chapter 9 (North America)

The following morning they were all in the office for half eight, with coffees and various breakfast options they sat down and waited for Barney to update them. "Guys, we're going back to the airport. The General has secured a plane and a pilot so we'll go to each state in turn. We'll split into teams of two and work as quickly as we can. The first team that draws blank calls in and gets picked up and dropped off at the final State. When you're dropped at the airport hire a car, keep all receipts and everything gets billed to the team's cards. We only use FBI or CIA funds as a last resort. Anyone got any questions?"

There weren't any questions at all but to be fair Barney hadn't expected any. Everyone around the table had pretty much got the message last night when they were talking so the morning meeting was just a formality really. They made their way downstairs and out into the parking lot. Two people carriers were waiting and they split into two groups and got in. Two extra FBI agents joined them and Barney made the introductions Marcus and Boyd had both been working in an FBI gang taskforce for some time and had worked several cases that involved people smuggling so they had some useful contacts and knowledge. The journey to the airport was uneventful and most of the team spent time reading the files that had been prepared on the five individuals.

At the airport they were cleared airside almost straight away and the two people carriers drove over to the far corner of the airfield. There was a military looking plane sat on the tarmac with an air force crew member at the foot of the steps. They all got out and were greeted and advised to go straight up and strap in as they were already cleared for take-off. They all stowed their bags and sat down. The crew member shut the doors and called through to the cockpit to advice the flight deck that they were clear for take-off.

A dull tone came over the intercom and a voice started talking, "good morning Ladies and Gentlemen, I'm your Co-Pilot for this flight and I'd like to welcome you on board. As soon as we're airborne Steve will sort out any refreshments you may require. We'll keep the flight as brief as possible and we'll be on our way just as soon as the bitch next to me stops giving stupid commands."

Most of the team looked shocked and confused at the announcement but Scott and Danny both laughed as they'd recognised the voice and were pretty sure what was going to happen next.

The tone on the intercom sounded again, "I apologise for the prick in the co-pilot seat and welcome to Baby Girl airlines. As soon as he gets his shit together we'll be on our way although judging by the way he's currently performing I'm amazed that he's even certified to fly a kite. For those that don't know me I'm Jess and from what I understand, my baby brother has recently demonstrated to everyone that us kids shouldn't be underestimated. Hi Cass, how are you doing?"

With the exception of Cass everyone started laughing, at which point the door to the flight deck opened and Jess appeared. Danny got up out of his seat and moved forward to give her a hug, "when did you get in?"

"Late last night, Mitch met me at the airport and we were flown straight here to prep the plane."

Jess walked up to Cass and dropped down to her level, she put her hand on Cass's shoulder and sighed. "There there, don't worry. They'll have forgotten about it in a few years."

Cass rolled her eyes and stood up giving Jess her second hug of the day

Mitch called out from the flight deck, "Jess we've got the next slot."

Jess called over her shoulder, "roger that, be there in a sec. Okay we're going to California first and it's literally going to be a drop and go so if you can clear the plane as quickly as possible that would be great as we've got a fair distance to go and I want to get you on the ground as quickly as I can. Once we've dropped the last pair we'll refuel and fly back to an air force base somewhere centrally to wait your call. As soon as we're airborne I'll come back and catch up."

They were in the air with the minimum of fuss. Before long the door to the flight deck was opened again and Mitch stepped out. Scott got up and met him shaking his hand, "how did you manage to land this gig?"

"My whole squadron is back stateside and we aren't due to be deployed again for a few months. The general put a request in to my boss for me to be released. In truth the kid doesn't need me sat next to her, to be honest she can fly most things better than I can. James wanted a second pilot available in case we need to break the teams up and go in different directions. As I was stateside and have been with you on a few assignments I was the obvious choice and so here I am."

"Hey flyboy, get up here and do something useful."

Mitch shook his head, "bloody kids of today."

He made his way back to the cockpit and a few seconds later Jess appeared again "How is everyone and how are things going?" Over the next forty five minutes introductions were made and Barney updated Jess on how they were doing and what the plans were moving forward. The flight was smooth and faultless and before she knew it Jess was making her way back to the cockpit to prepare for landing. The landing was smooth and the first team were met airside by a standard black people carrier. They were whisked away and Jess got clearance to take off, they repeated this three more times and after the last team had left they made their way to Luke Airforce base in Arizona. It had been decided that this was the best location for Jess and Mitch to wait while the teams carried out their investigations. They had no way of knowing which team would call first so they fuelled the plane and went straight to the mess to get some food and drink.

Four hours later Jess got a call from Cass, she and Drew had drawn the first blank so were the team that needed to be collected and taken to the final drop off. Within 30 minutes Mitch and Jess were airborne again and heading towards the airfield that Cass and Drew were already waiting at. The flight to the final drop off was as flawless as all the other drops and they were on the ground with the minimum of fuss. It had been agreed that they'd wait at this airfield until the final team called it a day and then they'd work backwards collecting the rest of the teams as they went.

They'd only been on the ground for half an hour when Jess got a call from Barney letting her know that two more of the teams had drawn a blank. Joss had a strong lead and was staying locally overnight and he'd just received a call from Cass to say that she'd already confirmed that the lead she was working was worth investigating further. Barney had already contacted James to arrange for the teams to use Luke AFB as a temporary base of operations so Mitch got the plane back in the air to collect the two teams and headed for an overnight stop at Luke.

The team stayed on base even though Phoenix wasn't that far away. They had everything they needed and so decided to start to write up the reports on the first three, two of them had suddenly decided that college life wasn't for them and had gone travelling instead not bothering to notify their respective families. The third had developed a crush on another girl and the two of them had gone into hiding as they didn't want anyone to know that they'd fallen for each other.

While Barney had been talking Jake had taken two phone calls. It was the other two teams calling in with updates and as soon as Barney finished talking, Jake took over.

"Okay so Cass and Drew have managed to find out quite a bit. The girl they're investigating was seen with another woman and they seemed to be more than just friends. They've interviewed some of the staff at a local coffee shop who informed them that the two of them were seen a few times together and had a closeness about them that gave the impression that they were an item. They both suddenly disappeared and neither of them has been seen since." Jake paused as Barney had just received a text message. When Barney put the phone down he continued, "so when Cass and Drew went to the girls apartment everything seemed normal The local PD had initially thought they'd gone away on vacation but looking in the apartment there aren't enough things missing to collaborate the theory that they've gone away. They've got CSI there now going through the place room by room but it does seem rather odd. Her name is Phoebe Stiles, a 23 year old originally from California. She moved to New Mexico as the college offered her much better prospects than the one in her home town. They'll call us shortly to give us an update on their progress but I'd say at this stage that this is our first positive lead." Jake closed the file in front of him and looked at Barney who unlocked the iPad in front of him.

"Thanks Jake. So Joss has just sent an update. Their lead doesn't look quite so promising. A 22 year old lad called Conner Dawson has gone missing, possibly seen with two known gang members although they don't have a positive ID as yet so that's just an informed guess at the moment. The local PD now think it's drug related and doubt it's connected to our investigation but Joss is checking out some CCTV footage and will get back to us. For the moment I'd like us all to concentrate on finding out as much as possible about Phoebe. I want a full history as quickly as possible. I'll message Cass and get her to look into CCTV footage from local businesses etc."

"Barney, I think we should split the team into two groups." Jake looked around the table, "one group goes and gets something to eat and has a break while the others start digging. Then we swap over. That way if we have to split and send anyone to help Cass then at least we'll have a fresh team that can leave straight away. Once both teams have eaten I suggest we stand one team down so that they can get some sleep."

Barney nodded, "that's a good idea Jake, Jess can you and Mitch split and join a team each, that way we'll have one rested pilot who can fly straight away."

Jess grinned "I guess the old man should be the first to sleep, I'll go and prep the plane so that it's ready for an immediate take off." She was up and out of the room before Mitch even had a chance to respond.

The team split and they all went about their business, those getting food were treated to the normal variety of superbly cooked options, the variety of meals on offer was staggering and it seemed almost available 24 hours a day. The rest of the team split themselves in half one group researching Phoebe and the others searching for other clues from the statements that the local PD had supplied. They'd been emailed everything that was available and were busy digging out little clues here and there.

After an hour and a half they swapped over and within three hours they were all back in the office suitable feasted, although a couple of them had still managed to bring a few snacks along despite eating to what amounted to a three course feast. The information was beginning to mount up and they were now beginning to get some files from Joss. The team decided that before some of them went to get their heads down they'd spend a quick hour working on the stuff that Joss had sent through.

Jake had acquired four large whiteboards and Jess and Dan had assigned themselves to a team each and were busy writing up the important bits of information that had surfaced so far. Various blocks of information were starting to appear on the boards as the teams tried to piece together all of the clues found so far. Gradually a picture was building and it was beginning to look as though this was indeed a solid lead and Phoebe was slowly becoming the first true positive step forward they had so far.

They'd been sent some CCTV footage from a coffee shop just down from the college campus and they were all watching it on a large screen. There wasn't any sound but Phoebe could clearly be seen with a friend enjoying a coffee. Jake had sat down part of the way through and asked for it to be played again so he could see the beginning. He suddenly straightened up "Pause it there." Everyone looked round at him, without realising it he was taping a rhythm on the table with his pen, "has anyone noticed anything strange about the friend she's with?"

Danny smiled, "well other than she seems to look quite pretty and they get on well together nothing really."

Jess shook her head "Danny, really, all you can add is you think she looks quite pretty."

Before he could answer Jake cut in, "hang on Jess, Danny has hit the nail on the head, Danny you said she seems to look quite pretty. Why didn't you say she looks quite pretty?"

"Well I guess because I haven't really seen her face yet."

Jake grinned, "exactly, in every bit of footage I've watched so far you don't ever get a clear view of her face, even when she's leaving with Phoebe. Jess, can you get it to the point where the friend comes into the coffee shop please."

Jess picked the remote up, "yes, of course."

She quickly found the point and pressed play, they all watched with renewed interest. Just as it got to the point that they'd all started watching he asked Jess to pause it. Jake looked around at everyone and saw that they were waiting for him to speak, "so what did you all notice?"

Barney spoke first, "she's not an ordinary person, from the point she came in to the point she left she made sure that the cameras didn't get a full view of her face. She seems like a professional, as soon as she walked in she was casing the place, taking everything in and looking at everyone. I can tell from what I've seen that you'll be lucky to ID her with any facial recognition software as there isn't enough of a profile to go on."

"This could be a lucky break or a wild goose chase. Okay can someone ask Cass to get us all of the CCTV footage she can from before this."

Jess picked up her phone, "I'll call her now."

Grace was busy on her Mac. "I'll get the best possible stills printed off so that we have a least a partial idea of what she looks like. The quality isn't too bad but we won't be able to enlarge it by much."

Ed spoke up for the first time, "I was watching Jake but I was also looking at some of the stuff that Joss has sent through, it's nowhere near as comprehensive as what Cass and Drew have managed to compile but there's something that I think is worth investigating."

Jake turned in his seat, "okay Ed let's hear it."

"Well, the local PD told Joss that they felt that Connor had simply got mixed up with the wrong crowd as he'd been seen with some know dealers. That part is true but they've found some CCTV footage that I've looked at and the gang that the dealers are associated with have also been known to dabble in smuggling illegal's across the border from Mexico. Now what if they've diversified and are now smuggling people into Mexico as well as out?"

This seemed to interest Jake, "so that could easily be the case." He thought for a few seconds. "Barney I think we need to bolster the two teams we have on the ground. I'd like to send at least two extra bodies to Cass and Joss so that they can begin to investigate this further."

Barney nodded his head, "I agree Jake, we've possibly got two leads and as we don't have anything else at the moment let's throw some extra resources on the ground and see what we turn up. Okay everyone, grab yourselves a coffee and be back here in ten while I come up with a plan. I'll let James know what's happening so that he can update the General. I'm sure he's got plenty of people chasing him for an update."

On Barney's instruction Jess had woken all of the team except Mitch. It was decided to leave him asleep as he was needed to fly and wouldn't be on the ground so didn't need to be updated as yet. Jess got her head down as Barney had said it would be a few hours before they needed to leave.

Ten minutes later everyone was sat around the table. There were post it notes and bits of paper everywhere. Cups of coffee and snacks littered the table as well. The whiteboards had even more information on them now and the members of the team that had been resting were scanning the details on the boards.

Barney put his coffee mug down and looked around the table, "so after speaking to James the General wants as many boots on the ground as possible." Barney laughed, "I wonder if he sometimes forgets just how small this team is. In light of that here's what we're going to do. Grace you'll stay here with me and we'll collate everything that comes in and then relay it back to James as we need to. The rest of you will split up into two teams and join Cass and Joss, I don't mind who goes with who but just remember, as always, mix up the skill set. You'll be leaving in three hours so gather all the information you need, check your kit, grab some food and get a bit of rest. Jess and Mitch will have the plane ready in exactly three hours so make sure you're all on it. Anybody got any questions?" Barney knew the answer but asked anyway.

Nobody had any questions and they were already making notes and adding files to their Macs and tablets.

"Grace, go and get some rest, they can all handle everything from here. Our job will only really start once they are on the ground."

Grace nodded and closed her Mac. She grabbed a few bits of paper that she'd been writing on and left. Everyone else left the room and silence descended. Barney sat there for a few minutes simply looking at the boards and reading through the information they'd gathered so far, they'd been lucky. He picked up his empty mug and moved over to the coffee machine. Pouring himself a cup he stood there for a few seconds looking around. In the distance he heard a couple of jets take off, with everyone in the office the noise level covered up the usual noises associated with an air force base. He checked his phone to see that he had a message from Charlie letting him know that they were about to meet with the friend that Josef had put them in touch with. Everything seemed to be going their way and that was something Barney didn't expect. He sat back down and called James to update him and more importantly to get an update of the overall view of things as it was always quite easy to get taken in by everything that's going on around you and to lose sight of the bigger picture. James supplied that bigger picture and that was what Barney wanted right now.

Three hours later Jess was getting final clearance from the tower to take off. The team was strapped in and ready to go. Jake was leading one team and was meeting up with Cass and Ed was leading the other team. There was a little disappointment in Ed's team as they felt that on balance Cass had the stronger lead and was possibly chasing the best intel that they had. Having said that they all realised that as a team sometimes you had to chase the lead that lead to a dead end, it was just part of the job. They dropped Jake and his team off first and then Ed's team. Rather than fly straight back it had been agreed that Jess and Mitch would stay at the airport. They'd all decided that the information Joss had wasn't as solid as the other teams and the likelihood was that they'd arrive at the dead end fairly quickly so it made sense for the plane to wait locally.

Chapter 10 (Europe)

Alek was having a déjà-vu moment as he cleared security at Gatwick Airport. He was heading back to Slovenia to meet the new contact in the same place that they'd met Joseph. Frederik Karlstein had agreed to meet them and said that as he wanted to catch up with Joseph he'd meet them there and travel to see Joseph after they'd met. After grabbing something to eat they made their way to the gate and within twenty minutes were happily seated on the plane and ready to go. They'd managed to secure seats by the wing exits so had the benefit of a little extra leg room. The last passenger had boarded and the Cabin Crew had closed the doors.

"Good morning ladies and gentleman, welcome aboard this Easy Jet flight to Slovenia, my name's Saskia and I'm your Cabin Manager today. I'm joined at the front of the aircraft by Ellie and we have Helen and Amie at the back. Shortly we'll be taking you through a safety briefing during which we'd appreciate your attention." Saskia placed the handset into its slot and tapped the screen to begin the briefing. The team travelled extensively and whilst, when flying with Jess, they all adopted a somewhat cavalier attitude they knew what they needed to do should the need arise. On commercial flights even though they knew what to do they still had the decency to pay attention as the cabin crew took them through the briefing.

The flight was uneventful; the crew making it look effortless as they handled all of the passengers' requests. Alek was in the aisle seat and when they got to his row the three of them ordered drinks and snacks, he paid with his card and said thank you when Saskia handed it back to him, she replied with a smile and a "You're welcome." Alek noticed that her smile was genuine, he could see from her face that this was someone that thoroughly enjoyed her job and demonstrated absolute professionalism in everything she did.

Charlie hit him on the arm, "stop eying up the crew."

Alek turned his head to look at her, "I wasn't, I just noticed how much she clearly enjoys her job."

Charlie laughed, "rubbish, she's cute and you're a tart."

"She may well be cute and yes I may well be a tart as you put it. However the fact of the matter is that if you watch what she does she adopts a remarkably professional approach and that happens when you're looking at someone that thoroughly enjoys what they're doing."

"I had noticed that but you're still a tart."

Alek shook his head in despair, "there I was thinking travelling with Cass was a challenge. Boy was I wrong there."

"Shut up, it's you that's the challenge."

Alek laughed "oh I don't doubt that."

The rest of the flight went by quite quickly. Alek had grabbed a book at the airport and got lost in it and realised they were landing before he knew it. They'd already booked a transfer from the airport to the hotel. In fact they'd used the same service as last time. Once again the driver was waiting for them in arrivals with a plaque bearing their name. The trip to the hotel seemed to miss most of the traffic and they arrived at the hotel with plenty of time to book in before the meeting. As usual they'd travelled light and in no time at all they'd booked in and were ready to make their way to the cafe at the castle. Alek led the way as he knew where they were going. They'd decided that Alek and Charlie would meet with Frederik, Katie was going to arrive early and sit to one side so that she could check to see that they hadn't been followed. They weren't really that concerned but as they had three of them there it made sense to take the extra precautions.

Alek and Charlie stopped at a street vendor and grabbed two coffees to give Katie a bit of a head start so that she could get herself settled. Twenty five minutes later Alek got a text from Katie letting him know she was all sorted and at a table in the corner with a view allowing her to see everything that was going on.

They'd been stood on the Triple Bridge when the text arrived. "Katie's ready so let's make our way up to the café. We're still quite early but that won't hurt." They followed the same signs that he had followed with Cass and paid for two tickets to enter the castle. They went straight to the cafe and selected one of the empty tables outside that would give Katie a clear view. Alek went into the cafe and ordered two more coffees and some cake. He didn't need to wait as the Barista told him that she'd bring it all out shortly so he went back outside and sat down next to Charlie.

Alek sent a quick text to Katie to make sure everything was okay and when she responded that it was he let Charlie know. They sat there making small talk as they waited for the coffees to arrive. Ten minutes after they'd arrived Alek got another text. This time it was Frederik letting him know that he'd arrived and was walking through the castle entrance. Alek sent a message back letting him know where they were. A few minutes later a smartly dressed man in his fifties made his way over to their table.

"Hello, you must be Alek and this rather delightful lady must be Charlie." Frederik's English was almost perfect with only a very faint accent.

Alek nodded shaking the outstretched had that Frederik had offered, "yes, please take a seat, can I get you a coffee?"

"No no, I wouldn't hear of it, please allow me to get you both one." Without waiting for an answer Frederik went into the café. He returned a few minutes later and undoing the buttons on his suit jacket sat down. "Thank you for meeting me, I've had a long talk with Joseph and he said that you'd been very patient with him and allowed him to tell his story at his own pace."

"Yes we felt that the whole thing was clearly quite a traumatic experience and something that he was quite ashamed of."

"Well you'll be glad to know that my story doesn't have such an unhappy ending." Frederik paused for a second, "although I do often wonder what happened to her."

Charlie put her now empty coffee cup down, "if it's okay with you we'd like to record our conversation to save us taking notes."

"Yes that's absolutely fine my dear."

Charlie smiled, "would you like to start from the beginning?"

"It all started just over a year ago. I was having a business meeting with Joseph and one of his colleagues. Joseph and I go back a few years and after the meeting we decided to get a bite to eat. Well during the meal Joseph asked me if he could take me into his confidence and I of course told him that he could without hesitation."

The coffees arrived and Frederik passed one each to Charlie and Alek. "I asked the Barista what you'd ordered and told her I'd like to order the same again."

Charlie passed over her original now empty coffee cup and replaced it with a fresh full one, "thank you."

"My pleasure, where was I?"

"At dinner with Joseph." Alek reminded him

"Ah yes, dinner. Well Joseph told me about this service that he'd used to custom order a girl. At first I was shocked but then became intrigued. I must point out that until recently I had no idea that the girl had died. I assumed he'd done the same as me, anyway I digress. He told me how he'd filled out an order that fitted his requirements and after he'd made a payment she was delivered exactly as he'd specified. I thought it too good to be true. Now I'm not proud of what I did and like Joseph I would like to atone for my actions. You see, I've recently found God and realise that there are consequences for my actions and I must do whatever I can to undo them." He paused to take a sip of coffee.

Neither Charlie or Alek said anything during the pause they simply waited for Frederik to continue.

"So I asked Joseph to put my name forward as an interested party in the service. A short time later I received an email and a day later I found myself filling out a similar order to Joseph. I must point out before I go on that I didn't kill the girl. Once I'd finished with her I sent an email and she was collected but was in perfectly good health when she left me. I was intrigued and well I must admit that I'd used my wealth in the past to secure the services of a few escorts however the thought of having someone that was there at my beck and call to do whatever I wanted whenever I wanted was almost too good to be true."

The look on Charlie's face must have given away what she was thinking.

"I can see you don't approve my dear. Well I can't say I blame you. I may not sound as though I'm ashamed but believe me I am which is why we're now talking. The tone of my voice may appear to show that I'm almost proud of what I've done but believe me I'm not."

"I'm sorry, I didn't mean to judge but...."

"No need to apologise, I do understand. The day came and she arrived and just like the girl Joseph had requested she was exactly what I'd specified, right down to the deep southern accent. It took her a couple of days to settle in. I suppose looking back now that's not a surprise, she had after all been kidnapped and deposited in a foreign country only to be told that she was now mine to do with as I pleased. I was respectful and made sure she was comfortable with plenty to eat and drink, I'd had a builder make some adjustments to one of my properties that gave her the use of a bedroom and a living room. The bedroom had an ensuite bathroom and I'd made sure that there were suitable toiletries and clothes for her. After a rather rocky start she began to realise that I didn't want to hurt her and that I was just really after a sexual companion. We talked and well to cut the story a little short I used and abused her. Nothing violent and I didn't injure her at all."

He paused again for another mouthful of coffee, "well I now realise that I may not have physically injured her but mentally I know that I've done her great harm and understand that what I did is something that is unforgivable and sadly for her unforgettable. I do hope she's okay and that in time she'll be able to forget."

Alek leant forward in his seat, "we're not here to judge Frederik, can you tell me anything specific about her so that we might be able to identify her?"

"Well as they followed my requests she was nineteen, natural blonde, green eyes and five foot six with a natural all over tan and fit. I've got to say I believe that she was exactly as requested, I did ask her what her first name was and she said it was Sharne but that's all I asked her. I'm ashamed to say I wasn't really interested in where she was from as she was just a play thing. Someone for me to act out and share some fantasies with. After three weeks I sent an email letting them know that I'd finished with her. When she left me she really was in good health, I'd made sure that she was looked after and didn't want for anything whilst she was with me."

Alek was struggling to hide his emotions but knew that he had to keep them in check, "can you tell us anything about the people that dropped her off or picked her up?"

Frederik shook his head, "no I can't, you see when they dropped her off I was out. I'd left a key for them and when I got back to the property she was already in the room. It was the same on collection, I didn't tell her she was leaving I just went out for the day and when I came back the room was empty and completely spotless. It was as if she hadn't been there, every trace of her had been removed."

Knowing that Alek may say something Charlie jumped in, "so do you have any of the emails Frederik?"

"No, alas I'm not as thorough as Joseph. He told me that he'd copied all his emails and given them to you. I'm afraid I wasn't as organised. After she'd left I deleted everything and sold the property. You see I'd fulfilled my desires and had no need for any of it anymore. Now I look back I can see that my actions were wrong, so very wrong but I cannot change the past. I can change the future which is why I want to help and after speaking to Joseph I realise this is the right thing to do."

Charlie looked him in the eye, "it is the right thing to do and I want to say thank you for helping us. Do you have anything else at all that may assist in us being able to identify her?"

"All I have is the description that I sent on the original email," he reached inside his suit jacket and removed a piece of paper from a pocket. He placed it on the table and pushed it across to Charlie, "I don't know if it'll help but this is what I asked for and apart from this I don't have anything else at all."

Charlie forced a smile, "that's okay this gives us something to work with, thank you."

"No thank you for allowing me to cleanse this from my past, I know it doesn't wipe it clean but I feel that I've at least done something to help and now if there's nothing else I'll bid you good day, I have plenty more of the Lords work to do and sadly a lot of things to make up for." Frederik stood up and buttoned his suit jacket back up, "it was a pleasure to meet you both and I thank you for listening." Without waiting for a reply he turned around and walked off into the crowd.

"I was hoping that we'd get more." Charlie had picked up the piece of paper and was reading the description. She passed it over to Alek, "what do you think happened to her after they picked her up?"

"My guess is one of two things, they killed her and dumped the body somewhere or they take her somewhere and wait for someone else to place an order that matches her description. The thing I know for definite is they wouldn't have let her go, it would be too risky." Alek took a photo of the piece of paper and sent it to James.

95

Charlie picked up the digital recorder and turned it off, "let's go back to the hotel, listen to it all again and write it up."

They both stood up and walked out of the castle grounds making their way back to the hotel. Katie left it a good ten minutes before doing the same making sure that she took a different route back. Once back at the hotel she made her way back to her room and called Alek. "I'm back, they have a business suite her so I'll call down and book one of the offices so that we can listen to the recording without having to worry about people hearing." His response was short as Katie put the phone down almost instantly after she'd spoken. She called down to reception and booked one of the meeting rooms for the rest of the day. She sent a text to Charlie and Alek and grabbing the padded sleeve that contained her Mac she made her way down to the room.

She used the phone to call reception and ordered some drinks and snacks to be brought through. Charlie and Alek joined her a few moments later. Alek put his Mac on the table, "have you ordered any drinks?"

"Yes, just before you came in. I've also asked for some pens paper and post it notes." They'd found in the past that reviews like this one often raised lots of questions and they found that paper and post it notes was a quick way to get their thoughts down as they were talking. Alek looked round the room, there were no windows which was good as it meant they could work without having to worry about what someone may see, the desk was fairly large with twelve chairs round it. On one wall was a large white board with the usual pens etc, on another was a white screen with a ceiling mounted projector. The third wall had a smart board on it with instructions for its use in several languages next to it. The last wall containing the door was clear with two small units either side of the door.

He plugged his Mac into one of the floor sockets and fired it up, "I guess we should wait for them to bring the drinks in before we actually start." There was a soft knock at the door, Katie got up and opened it. A member of the hotel staff had a trolley with the drinks snack and stationary items they'd asked for. Katie stood to one side so that they could enter and with the minimum amount of fuss put the drinks and snacks onto one of the units and the stationary on the desk next to Alek. Katie said thank you and then closed the door after them as they wheeled the now empty trolley out of the room.

Katie looked at Charlie and Alek, "so any initial thoughts?"

Charlie started, "well annoyingly he hasn't given us anywhere near as much detail or information as Joseph."

Alek got up to get a drink, "I don't think he strikes me as the sort of person that would have held onto anything, if, like he says, he's found God then he'd want to erase as much of it as possible. Perhaps he wouldn't have told us anything if Joseph hadn't spoken to him. Deleting everything and wiping any reference to what he did would be enough."

"Maybe, he did seem a little blasé about the whole thing," Charlie looked at Alek.

"Sometimes people with money fail to appreciate the value and because they have enough to get whatever they want they don't always understand what they have. I think he's probably one of those people. A rich businessman with far too much money and no idea as to what to sensibly do with it."

"You could well be right. Let's listen to the recording and then go over any questions or thoughts."

Charlie picked up the digital recorder and pressed play. They actually listened to the conversation twice. They were all taking occasional notes as they went. Katie put her pen down. "Alek your thoughts first."

"Well now I've listened to it again something doesn't seem right. I get the finding God bit and wanting to make things right but there's almost something in his tone that doesn't really support that. I can't put my finger on it. His English is good but, like me, sometimes he doesn't always get the tone and mood of the wording to fit the situation. At times it almost seems as though he doesn't actually care about what he's done. He's very matter of fact about the whole thing."

Charlie was looking at what she'd written, she put her pen down, "do you think that's his upbringing? I mean he's German and has a typical no nonsense direct approach and I get what you're saying about his tone, the words of remorse were there but none of the feeling."

"So although I saw most of what was going on I wasn't watching all of the time, what about facial expressions?"

Charlie picked her pen up again and used it to scan down her notes, she stopped at one of the bullet points on her pad, "I'm no expert but I definitely didn't feel that he showed the level of regret that he described. I'm wondering if he's only talking to us as a favour or out of duty to Joseph. They've been friends for years and maybe talking to us was just a loyalty thing towards his friend."

Alek looked thoughtful, "that would explain why he had the sort of attitude he did, I mean he didn't come across in the same way Joseph did when we met him. You could see and hear the emotion in his voice as he described how ashamed he was, with Frederik there wasn't any of that emotion at all."

Katie nodded, "there's a difference though, Joseph killed the girl he had but according to Frederik he let his go, well had her taken away at least."

"I've got to be totally honest, of the two of them I would have expected it to have been Frederik that committed murder and not Joseph." Alek looked at Katie, "having spoken to both of them it's almost as if it should be the other way around."

They spent the next hour or so going over the conversation, breaking each bit down and comparing notes. They had another drink and started on the snacks as they went backwards and forwards discussing their notes. Katie looked up from her pad, "let's take a break and get some lunch. We'll collate everything and send a report over to James. I'll join you in a minute but first I'm going to make a call to get a search started on Frederik and get a profile created so that we can get a bit more background on him."

Charlie and Alek got up and made their way out to the hotel restaurant. As much as they'd liked to have gone out to sample some of the local cuisine from a time perspective it made more sense to eat in the hotel. They asked for a table for three and were seated, menus were given to them and they both started to have a look at what was on offer. Knowing that Katie wouldn't be long they waited before placing their order. Sure enough within a couple of minutes Katie joined them, "have you ordered?"

"No. We're waiting for you but we both know what we're having." They all ordered and were pleasantly surprised to find that the quality of the food was outstanding. The restaurant wasn't full but had a nice atmosphere about it. The staff were all very professional and rather than coming to the table waited until requested. They didn't rush their meal but knew that they had a lot to do so they finished up quite quickly and made their way back to the meeting room. As Katie passed the reception she asked them for fresh dinks to be organised for the room.

Back in the room they all sat down and fired up their Macs once more, just before they'd finished lunch Katie received an email on her phone. It was a preliminary profile for Frederik, and now back at her Mac she selected the email and opened the file. "So his parents lived just outside of Berlin. Father was a director for a large company in Berlin. Mother didn't work. He left school with an aptitude for maths and joined an accounting firm quickly rising up to senior management. He then branched out into property development and acquisition and that's where he made his money. A considerable amount by the look of things."

Alek put his elbows on the table and rested his chin on his hands, "anything in there that raises any concerns?"

Katie shook her head, "no, it seems as though he's quite highly regarded and moves in all of the right circles. Looking at this he initially appears all above board. I've asked for an in depth review of his businesses and properties as well as finances."

Alek was staring at the wall deep in thought, "anything back on the girl?"

Katie checked her inbox, "no nothing yet." After requesting the file on Frederik she'd also sent an enquiry regarding any unknown females that had been found dead or alive. The description had been a little vague as she'd used the details Frederik had given them, omitting the breast size and accent. The request had gone to Interpol HQ as she wanted the offices across several countries to check rather than just the local office in Germany.

They spent the next two hours creating a report relating to their meeting and giving brief details from the profile they'd been sent. Just as they were putting the finishing touches to it Katie got another email containing a brief outline of Frederik's business and finances. She forwarded the report to the others before scanning through it quickly, "well, he really isn't short of money. With all his incentives and bonuses he nets over a million Euros a year and that's without his salary."

"His salary will add at least another half a million on top that I expect." Alek was looking at the businesses and property part of the report "Says here he runs four main businesses and has several residential properties throughout Europe, which means that we might not be looking at a property in Germany that he modified to accommodate the girl."

Charlie had been reading through the report and hadn't made a comment yet. She stopped reading and looked up, "with his money and influence he could do anything he wants, which I guess is exactly why he did. On the surface he looks every bit like the successful businessman and after looking at this I wonder if he is telling the truth about finding God and wanting to make good on all his misgivings."

"Looks can be deceiving Charlie, look at how many times we've dug deeper and found a different story to what we see on the surface." Alek looked over at Katie, "if I were you Katie I'd send this to Nick and get him to dig a little deeper. It'll be easier for him and if you go back to Interpol asking them to do it they may want to know why and as it stands I don't think we'd have a good enough reason."

"With the interview and this report all we've got at the moment is the fact that somewhere out there is a girl called Sharne so I think you're right and it would be pointless requesting anything else at the moment. I'll send it all to Nick now and let him do his stuff."

Alek closed his Mac and looked up, "next steps for us?"

Katie paused for a second before answering, "I think that you and I Alek should head to Lyon and base ourselves there. We'll have more resources readily to hand. Charlie there's no point in all three of us going so you could head back until we know where we might need to go."

"Sounds good to me, I'll check to see what flights are available." Charlie started typing into the search bar.

Alek had a grin on his face, "so we're going to Lyon, Interpol are going to love having me wandering around."

"Don't worry I'll tell them that I'll have you on a short leash and won't let you out of my sight." Katie was trying her hardest to keep a serious look on her face.

"Oh boy this'll be fun, are you sure you two don't want to go for a girly trip together?"

Charlie shook her head, "no you're okay. It won't hurt you to have to be good for a while."

Alek held his hands up, "I can't believe I'm being bullied by the pair of you."

Katie tilted her head slightly, "if you think it's too much for you I could see if we can get you replaced."

Alek grinned, "good luck with finding someone that will put up with you."

"Okay children, pack it in." Charlie looked up from her screen, "the only flights will be in the morning. We won't get to the airport in time to fly out this evening."

"In that case we've got a little time to kill. I suggest we go out and get some dinner in a bit and then have an early night so that we can be at the airport first thing."

"Do you want me to book some hotel rooms in Lyon?" Alek asked

"No, that's okay we'll stay at my family home. It's just outside the city centre so we'll easily be able to commute back and forth."

"You're taking me to meet your mother?" There was a hint of surprise in Alek's voice

Katie looked Alek in the eye, "yes, is that a problem?"

"Erm well actually yes it is." Alek smiled, "I didn't realise we were at that stage in our relationship so I don't have anything smart enough to wear."

Katie smiled, "oh that's Okay. It wouldn't matter what you were wearing she'd know straight away that I wouldn't be dating someone like you."

Charlie laughed, "ouch that was a low blow, understandable, but low."

Alek chose to ignore them both, "seriously though, I'll have to stop somewhere to get some clothes. There's no point going shopping here as I don't have a big enough case to put them in."

"It's okay. There are plenty of shops on the way from the airport to the office so we'll go there before heading down to my parents. We'll get a car at the airport and then we can hit the shops and leave it all in the car."

Before they walked into town to eat they made a couple of calls. Katie called Barney to give him a quick update on their progress, or lack of it, and Alek call James to give him a brief rundown on what had happened and their next moves. As the food had been so good last time he was here Alek took the girls to Pops place. They elected to sit outside as it was a nice evening and enjoyed a relaxing meal with a few drinks. The atmosphere as always was great. The food was excellent and the music balanced everything nicely.

They didn't feel guilty for enjoying themselves. Quite often during their investigations they had periods of time where they simply couldn't do anything and had to wait patiently. This was a prime example. With Jess stateside, they had to rely on commercial flights and that frequently had time restraints. They could have possibly made part of the trip by train but would still have had to book into a hotel and in truth wouldn't arrive at their destinations any quicker. The team spent a great deal of time travelling and waiting, it was part of the job. Often frustrating and downright annoying they'd got used to the fact that some things were well out of their control. If there'd been a real sense of urgency then they would have called James and asked him to pull some strings but as they didn't have anything concrete to go on so far Katie didn't feel that she could justify making that call.

They finished up at Pops with a last drink and then made their way back to the hotel. Once again Alek was impressed with how clean the city was and vowed to himself that when he had the time he'd definitely come back to Ljubljana for a relaxing break. Probably during the winter so that he could enjoy the snow on the mountains. Several people had now told him he really needed to visit the Velika Planina cable car and the Skodla snack bar as in the winter they serve some great snacks and drinks and the views are breath-taking. He'd seen a few pictures and had instantly added it to his must visit list.

Chapter 11

Phoebe opened her eyes slowly. She felt groggy and her brain was working far slower than normal. Her eyes came into focus and she found herself staring at a plain white ceiling. She could see several small lights giving off a soft glow. Moving her eyes around she could see the ceiling was spotless, it was immaculate. Her brain suddenly engaged and she realised this wasn't her ceiling. Her body reacted and she sat bolt upright. Her head throbbed and she felt instantly sick. The room was spinning out of control. She laid back down, rubbing her temples trying to control her breathing. Questions filled her mind. She wasn't able to answer any of them, she started to panic. A voice inside her head told her to relax. She stopped thinking, tried to empty her mind, taking deep and slow breaths.

The nauseous feeling drifted away and she was left with a dull ache in her head. She gently moved her head to the side, a wall came into view, the paintwork as smart and clean as the ceiling. It was a subtle shade of pink, almost an off white colour. She looked up at the ceiling again and then after a few breaths looked to the other side. The wall was the same colour but she saw a drawer unit with a mirror attached and a chair, they went well together and looked good against the colour of the wall. She tilted her head back a fraction and looked up to see a wooden headboard. The same type of wood as the drawer unit and chair was made of.

With her breathing now under control she lifted her head and looked down. She saw that she was lying on a double bed, the sheets crisp and white. Against the remaining wall there was a wardrobe and another drawer unit. Both the same style and colour as the first one she'd seen. She laid her head back down. The bed felt soft and extremely comfortable. The pillow moulding nicely to the shape of her head. She tried to take everything in. Her mind was blank, she couldn't work out what was happening. She took a deep breath and slowly sat up.

This time she was able to without feeling dizzy or sick. She looked around. The room was quite big, immaculate, everything was pristine, spotless. She had her breathing fully under control and felt like her normal self again although her head still hurt. She slowly looked round the room and saw that on one side of the bed was a small bedside unit and on the other side a drawer unit smaller than the other two in the room. On it was a bottle of water and a strip of what looked like some sort of pill.

She swung her legs over the edge of the bed and placed her feet on the floor, they came into contact with a soft plush carpet and she realised her feet were bare. With a sharp intake of breath she felt herself to find that she was clothed. She looked down, they weren't her clothes though. She picked the bottle of water up and removed the top, taking a small mouthful she picked up the strip of pills. They were painkillers, a brand she recognised, she popped two out of the strip and swallowed them with along with a mouthful of water.

"Where am I?" she hadn't realised she'd spoken to herself and it startled her. She suddenly realised she couldn't hear a single thing. The room was completely silent, not a sound, not even an electrical hum that you can sometimes faintly hear. She looked around again, noticing for the first time that in the wall opposite there was a really faint outline of a door. No visible handle, it just seemed to blend seamlessly into the wall. She stood up, her legs felt a little shaky and she sat straight back down. She looked around the room again, this time slowly and carefully. She noticed another door on the opposite wall to the first, almost hidden just a faint almost imperceptible outline. Above the drawer unit next to the bed she could see that the colour of the wall was ever so slightly different. She slowly moved across to that side of the bed and swung her feet over again, her feet once more touching the soft carpet.

She reached out and touched the wall and jumped as a screen came to life. You'd never know it was there. It blended in exceptionally well with the wall. There were three icons on the screen, music, film and food. Phoebe touched the music icon and Spotify opened. She closed it and touched the movie icon. Several categories appeared along with a search option. She closed that and tried the food icon. A list of fast food logos appeared as well as a number of different cuisines. She closed the app staring at the screen for a few seconds, her mind racing.

She shook her head and reached over for the water bottle. She took a couple of gulps and put it back down. She stood up and walked over to the door in the wall. She ran her hand over the barely visible line, the texture of the wall and door were slightly different. With no handle to grip she pushed against the door, heard a click and the door sprang open slightly. She peered through the gap and was greeted with the familiar sights of a bathroom. She pulled the door open and looked inside. It had a similar stark cleanliness as the room she was currently standing in. She walked in, the walls were again painted a subtle off white colour, at the far end was a huge walk in shower with an integrated seat. She could see a huge shower head and numerous directional jets in the walls either side. There were two recessed shelves which contained various shampoos, conditioners and shower gels.

Above the sink was a huge mirror and off to one side was another almost invisible door the same size as the mirror. She pushed against it and it opened. Inside were various toiletries, medicines and other everyday items you'd find in a bathroom. She stood still for a second her brain trying to take it all in. She had a few friends that came from very well off families and what she was looking at seemed to be the bathroom of someone with a significant amount of money. Every product she could see was from a high end brand. Her mind drifted for a second. If she could design a bathroom this is what it would be like. Everything neat and tidy, everything tucked away making the room minimalistic and stunning.

She suddenly came back to reality. This wasn't a bathroom she'd designed and unless this was an incredibly realistic dream this certainly wasn't her apartment. She quickly walked to the other door and pushed against it. The door was solid, no movement at all. She tried again with the same result. Panic started to set in and she realised she was breathing much faster again. She hammered her hand against the door and it made a subdued sound, not the loud sound she expected. She moved back from the door and sat back on the bed. She reached over and picked up the bottle of water and took another mouthful, slowing her breathing down once more. The dull ache in her head had gone, clearly the tablets had started to work.

She realised she needed to use the toilet so went back into the bathroom. The seat was down so she lifted it and lowered her jogging bottoms and sat down. The seat wasn't cold as she had expected it to be, it was slightly warm which was something she hadn't been expecting, but then again she hadn't expected any of this. When she was finished she flushed and put the seat back down. As she put her hands under the tap the water came out at an almost perfect temperature. It all seemed too good to be true.

She dried her hands and went back into the main room closing the door behind her out of habit. Just what she would have done if she'd been in her apartment back home. She sat on the bed, pulled her knees up under her chin and just sat there, wondering what the hell was going on. She wasn't stupid, she knew this wasn't a dream and at the moment it didn't seem to be a nightmare either. The honest truth she admitted to herself was that she didn't have the faintest idea what was going on. Although she was confused she was thinking clearly and decided to test something out.

She stood in front of the screen and placed her finger against it. Once again the three icons appeared in front of her. She touched the music one and then touched the search option, she typed in Norah Jones and a list of her albums appeared. At the bottom of the list was a random playlist option and she pushed that. Nothing happened for a few seconds and then the familiar opening bars of 'Come away with me' filled the room. Phoebe noticed a volume slider and raised the volume slightly.

She couldn't answer any of the questions filling her mind and sat back down on the bed, confused with everything around her, unable to even begin to work out what was going on. Without realising it her foot was taping to the music as it always did, her body was doing its normal thing despite what was going on. She put her head in her hands for a few seconds and took a couple of deep breaths. She lifted her head and stood up again. She went back into the bathroom and rinsed her face, she dried it off and looked in the cabinet again. There was an electric toothbrush sat on its recharging dock, it was brand new and exactly the same as hers. Even the head was the identical firmness she used. She shrugged her shoulders and brushed her teeth. Once she finished she went back to sitting on the bed, nothing made sense.

After a few minutes she went back over to the screen, she minimised the music and tapped the food icon. She selected Chinese and a vast Chinese menu appeared before her. She looked down it and ordered some chicken noodles and sweet and sour chicken balls. She dropped down to the drinks and selected a diet coke and then touched the order icon. The screen went blank and after a second or two returned to the music display. She sat back down wondering what happens now. She reached over for the water bottle again and took another drink.

Phoebe was normally a very rational person, a bit of a loner and more than content with her own company. Right now though she was beginning to question herself, doubt was creeping in. Where was she and how on earth did she get here? Why was she here? The questions going through her head over and over again. She looked down to see that her fists were clenched tight and she realised her breathing was far more rapid than it should be. She took a few deep breaths and stood up. She walked round the room, carefully examining every bit to see if there were any compartments or screens she'd not yet noticed. There wasn't so she opened the bathroom door and did the same in there but found nothing new.

She sat back on the bed, looking round beginning to feel more than a little desperate. She needed answers, she needed to understand what was going on and despite her usual ability to remain calm and rational she was starting to panic. She was desperately trying to work out how she got here. She looked around the room once again with a blank expression on her face, just where the hell was she!!

She jumped as she heard a soft click behind her, she turned round and the door in the wall was now slightly ajar, she could feel her heart beating faster and for a few seconds could do nothing more than stare at the now open door, expecting something else to happen. Nothing did, she hesitantly got up and walked round the bed towards the door, once again taking deep breaths to try to calm herself down. She got to the door and peered through to see what was on the other side. She could see a table and chairs and on the table was a brown paper bag. She could suddenly smell the faint recognisable scent of food, she opened the door further, it moved without a sound.

She walked into a large room, the decor identical to the bedroom. There was an office desk, a bookcase, oddly empty. The table and chairs and she could see another almost hidden screen on the wall, three times the size of the one in the bedroom. Questions were racing through her head again, she sat down on one of the chairs, beginning to feel dizzy again.

She suddenly realised just how hungry she was and looked at the brown bag, she didn't need to open it to know what was inside, she could smell the distinctive aroma of Chinese food. She opened the bag and looked inside, there were two containers, and two bottles of diet Coke. She took everything out of the bag and found there were some serviettes and chopsticks at the very bottom of the bag. She opened the first container and tried the noodles, she was surprised by the taste and texture, she couldn't remember ever having tasted any as good as this. She opened the first bottle of Coke and took a sip, when she opened the second container she found a small tub of sweet and sour sauce surrounded by a number of almost perfect looking chicken balls. Whoever cooked this certainly knew what they were doing she thought.

The food was delicious and Phoebe had eaten the lot before she realised it, she'd been far hungrier than she thought. She stood up with the half-finished coke in her hand and walked around the room the same way shed done in the bedroom, looking for the less obvious things but couldn't find any. She stopped at the big screen and touched it, expecting the same results as the one in the bedroom but nothing happened, she stared blankly at it and touched it again. Still nothing, she finished the coke and went back to the table. Habit kicked in and she put the empty food containers, chopsticks and serviettes back in the bag and looked round for a bin to put it in. She wasn't surprised to find that there wasn't one, she picked up the unopened bottle of drink and walked around the room once more hoping to spot something she'd missed. She couldn't find anything and walked back into the bedroom and looked around again. Still nothing new, as she walked away from the door she heard a soft click and span around to find the door had closed behind her.

She just stood there and stared at the door, how did that happen? Why did that happen? She sat on the bed looking around and suddenly realised she hadn't even thought to look in the drawers or the wardrobe. She stood up and moved to the first drawer unit and opened the top drawer, it was full of new matching underwear. She looked closer, all her size and just the sort of thing she'd buy. She closed the drawer and opened the next one to be greeted with three neat piles of vest tops, again the same style and colour that she'd buy. All four drawers were full of perfects clothes, everything was perfect, almost as if she'd been shopping herself. The second drawer unit was the same, full of jogging bottoms, jeans, hoodies and night clothes. Even down to the type of tee shirt she'd wear to bed.

She moved to the wardrobe and opened both doors, she was met with a row of neat dresses and tops on hangers. Pristine and with that new smell that always accompanies clothes when you first get them. The two drawers at the bottom of the wardrobe had more clothes in them. She closed the wardrobe and sat back on the bed, she looked around desperately trying to work out just what was going on. She put her head in her hands, suddenly overwhelmed, her composure leaving her rapidly as tears began to roll down her cheeks, she began sobbing uncontrollably. She lifted her head tears streaming down her face and shouted, "where am I?" she was rewarded with complete silence, rational or not she was beginning to feel overwhelmed by the situation which made things worse and she screamed at the top of her voice "Help!"

She heard a soft beep and lifted her head to look at the door, it didn't appear to be open. She stood up and tried it only to find it was firmly closed. She looked around confused and suddenly the screen came to life. It wasn't displaying any icons, only a flashing cursor. She walked over to it and touched it hoping to bring up a keyboard to enable her to type a message but nothing happened. The cursor just kept flashing so she sat back down on the bed staring at the screen. Suddenly words started appearing.

"Hello Phoebe, please don't be alarmed, you're perfectly safe. I'll answer as many questions as I can but please speak clearly."

Phoebe looked at the screen for a few seconds her mind a blank. "What the hell's going on?"

"That's an easy one to answer, you're my guest and I will take care of you in the best way I can."

"What do you mean guest?"

"Well you're staying with me for a bit and if you need anything you only have to ask."

"I don't understand."

"It's quite simple Phoebe, you make me happy and I'll make you happy, good behaviour is rewarded, you show me how good you can be and I'll show you how good I can be." The words seemed to be somehow calming and not at all threatening.

Phoebe stared at the screen unsure what to say as her mind was full of questions that needed answers, she was totally confused and didn't understand what was happening. She looked round the room and that just added to the confusion as the room itself was neat and tidy, not only that it was warm and safe, well relatively safe. She looked at the screen unsure as to what she should say "I don't understand what's happening at all but okay. Though something tells me I don't have a choice."

"Good now relax and try to enjoy your stay."

A few seconds later the words disappeared and the screen was blank once again, leaning forward she taped it and the now familiar three icons appeared.

Chapter 12 (North America)

Joss met them outside the terminal building. She was leaning against the same sort of people carrier they'd been using for the past few days. She wasn't on her own. Standing with her was a smartly dressed man who, to anyone in the know, was clearly a member of law enforcement. Joss spotted Ed and smiled, "so you drew the short straw and got to join me?"

Ed laughed, "not at all, you're definitely the one to be with. The others have drawn the short straw."

"You're such a liar" Joss turned slightly, "okay everyone, this is Deputy US Marshall Clay Turner. He's been assigned to us as the Marshall service have had a couple of minor run ins with the same group of people we're now looking onto."

Everyone introduced themselves and they all got in the vehicle. Clay was driving and Joss was sat next to him. She was turned in her seat so that she could look at most of them as she was talking, "we're going to the Marshalls office as they've given us a conference room to use as a bit of a base of operations. I've got to be honest I don't think we'll be here long as they don't really seem to have the brains to be part of the operation we're looking at but we'll investigate them all the same."

Clay took over, "it's a short drive to the office and we're above the court house in the centre of town. Joss is right, they've only really dabbled in a bit of minor human trafficking and most of it has been from Mexico into the US, and low grade movements at that. What you're looking at appears to be a high end organisation and I really don't think they'd stoop as low as these guys."

Ed leant forward a little, "so you said most of the time it's Mexico into the US, what about the times it was the other way?"

Joss took over again, "I've looked at the case files. Every time they appear to have been involved in a US to Mexico movement it's been to get a convicted felon out of the country. They don't appear to have the type of connections needed to move the grade of people that we're looking at. Having said that though they do seem to have secure roots and most of their involvement is speculation. Gang members have been seen in the last rough location that several felons have been spotted."

Ed sat back in his seat, "so it's not a solid lead then?"

Clay sighed, "no it's not, but as it stands at the moment it is the best lead that we've got and Connor was seen with two of them and hasn't been seen since."

Joss took over once more, "we know that Connor hasn't been convicted of any crime. In fact, he seems whiter than white. From what we can get from a few college classmates he wasn't into drugs and during a couple of debates took quite a strong anti-drugs stance. Now that could have been a ruse but they seemed convinced that he was completely clean and wouldn't even consider touching any drugs. He had enough money not to be in any financial difficulty so we don't think he was looking to deal so the only conclusion we've come up with so far is that they either killed him during some sort of initiation ceremony or they smuggled him across the border."

"So looking at the report when you searched his apartment everything still seemed to be there, similar to the apartment of the girl that Cass is looking into?"

Joss turned round, "yes Marcus. In fact it's almost exactly the same. It's as if Connor had intended to return. The sort of things you'd normally take with you even if you were only going away for a couple of days are all still present. Virtually nothing is missing at all, and to be honest, that's what raised the concern and made us take the gangs involvement a little more seriously."

Clay slowed down and pulled into a large car park which ran the whole length of the rather smart building. He pulled into a space and switched off the engine. He turned in his seat to get a better look at everyone, "we haven't got formal ID badges for you so for the moment we'll just issue a standard visitors badge. We weren't sure which team members were going to be with us so though it safer to wait till you were here before getting the IDs sorted."

Joss opened her door and got out. Everyone followed suit and noticed for the first time how humid it was. They hadn't realised just what a good job the air conditioning in the vehicle was doing.

Clay led the way and entered through a side door. They all went through the security checks and collected their visitor ID. They followed Clay to the elevator and once inside he hit the button for the second floor. When the doors opened they were greeted with a large sign informing them that they were now stepping into the office of the US Marshall Service. Clay led them through a large open plan office. Several people were at their desks and from the noise you could tell that right at this moment it was a busy office. They arrived at a large conference room where along one wall was a full length worktop with what looked like filling cabinets underneath it. A coffee machine sat at the end along with numerous bottled drinks and a small desktop fridge.

"Guys grab a drink if you want one while I get set everything up for a briefing." Clay left the room and the team got themselves drinks and sat down. They all removed their pads, Macs tablets etc and even before they could start talking Clay had returned.

The office had windows on three sides and Clay drew all of the blinds. He picked up a remote control and pressed the top button. A white screen descended down from the ceiling one end of the conference room while a projector dropped down in the centre of the room. He then spent the next thirty minutes going through the gang members they knew about and their history. A large scale map appeared on the screen showing the town and a few neighbouring smaller towns with several buildings highlighted.

"So the highlighted buildings are known properties that the gang use on a regular basis. We've searched a couple of them in the past but from the reports there wasn't anything that would really support this investigation. We do know that they have helped several people cross into Mexico and we have some CCTV footage and witness statements to support those claims. We've tried to infiltrate the gang a couple of times but with no luck. To be fair they're such a low level gang that we didn't really get much support from other agencies and couldn't warrant using a big chunk of our annual budget on what was classed as a low level case."

The room went silent for a few seconds then Marcus looked up, "so where do we start?"

"Well there are two clubs they use regularly and as you're all from out of town you won't be recognised." Clay paused for a split second, "Scott and Marcus I'd suggest you hit the first club as it's predominantly a strip bar and where we think they do most of their meet and greets with clients. Joss you'll go with Ed to the other club. It's slightly more down to earth and they tend to use this for their downtime and for meeting the less influential customers. Danny you'll be with me. I'm not expecting trouble but as the others are all cleared to carry weapons and you're not I'd feel much better if you were with me."

Danny smiled, "that's absolutely fine with me. Although at some point I wouldn't mind getting myself cleared."

Clay grinned, "well I can't directly help you with that although once we're done here, I'll see if I can put in a good word and maybe get things moving for you."

They decided to deal with one club at a time, they were four blocks apart and as they were doing this with no technical backup all they had were earpieces. So to avoid any complications they felt that it would be far easier just to deal with one establishment at a time. Clay dropped Joss and Ed off just round the corner from the entrance to the club, he'd left the others in a quiet diner that was two streets away and within easy range of the earpieces they were all wearing.

Joss took Eds arm and they walked through the main door, it was fairly well lit inside and the music was at a half decent level. They looked around quickly to see that it wasn't that busy and there were only about twenty five people in the club. A few were obvious gang members but there were a few couples at the bar and three or four couples in the booths against the far wall. Ed made his way to the bar and Joss followed him, the bartender came over.

"What can I get you?"

"Two beers please."

They took their beers and made their way over to the end booth as it gave them a reasonable view of the majority of the club. The two booths next to that were empty so nobody would hear what they were saying. As there wasn't anyone within earshot they were able to simply talk to each other about what they could see. The rest of the team could listen in and to anyone that was watching it looked as though Ed and Joss were simply chatting.

"It all seems normal enough at first glance." Joss smiled at Ed and then looked around, "so far I've counted thirteen cameras and that's after a quick scan, I'd say there are probably a few more hidden ones."

Ed laughed, to the casual eye they would appear to be sharing a joke. "The bartender is keeping a real close eye on everyone and behind the bar are two fairly large mirrors that don't have anything in front of them. I'd say they're one way glass because they give quite a good unrestricted view of most of the club, add that to the CCTV coverage and you would be able to see almost everything that's going on."

They talked back and forth for another twenty minutes and ordered another beer each. Ed took a mouthful and paused for a second, "over in the far booth there's a group of three guys. The one that's facing me looks similar to one of the images pulled from the CCTV, I can't be 100% certain but I'd say he's a close enough match."

Joss nodded, "I don't think we're going to get much from here. One thing I have noticed though is that they are definitely dealing here. Not large quantities but it's quite a smooth operation."

Ed frowned, "how have you seen that?"

"Oh it's not easy to see and I only noticed by accident. Several of the couples have ordered food, when it comes out there's an extra napkin with the cutlery. Five booths down there's a couple, probably both at college. They've just paid for their meal and left what looks like a large cash tip. The guy just picked up the napkin and put it in his pocket. As he did it opened slightly and there's a plastic bag inside the napkin. If I hadn't been looking at him right at that moment I wouldn't have spotted it."

Ed raised an eyebrow, "this seems to be full of college kids and office workers and quite busy by the look of things. I wonder if this is how they got their hands on Connor?"

Joss shook her head, "I'm not sure, remember from the statements we have no one thought he had a drug habit or problem."

"Yes but what if he came in here with someone that did have a drug problem." Ed paused and looked around, "there are a fair few couples in here and if he's come in here they may have flagged him as a match for someone they were looking for. Remember the basis of this is they're given very precise criteria for a person. All they need to do is scan the clientele and when they get a match they move in."

"Okay that's quite plausible now I've seen this place. I suggest we go and write up what we've seen while Scott and Marcus go and check the other club out."

They got up, left a tip and made their way out of the club, they walked a block and a half before getting Clay to pick them up. Once they were in Clay pulled away from the curb, "so do you really think it could be that easy and simple."

Joss spoke first, "yes I think so. It's all really straight forward. They have quite a business going on in there and at some point you'll want to pass that over to the DEA because they should be able to set up a nice little operation to catch them in the act. The only downside is that they can't do that until we've completed what we're doing otherwise we'll possibly lose everything. Levi should be joining us soon as his assignments almost finished and he'll be able to handle that."

Ed nodded, "I agree, as much as I'd like to get them to move in now I think we should wait. They seem quite complacent so we'll write it up and submit a report and maybe the DEA can do the groundwork straight away and as Joss says move in once we're done."

Clay had a worried look on his face "In theory that's what I'd like to happen but in practice the DEA might want to move in straight away which would only give us 24-48 hours at the most."

They pulled up at the diner, Joss and Ed got out and went in. The others occupied a corner booth and Scott and Marcus got up and made their way out to the vehicle. Clay then repeated the same process at the other club.

Scott walked through the door first and they found themselves in an outer room with a cloakroom over to one side and two security desks each having three staff, two male and one female. Scott walked up to the left hand desk. One of the male staff stepped forward, "evening sir, this is a simple security sweep so if you could place all loose items from your pockets into the tray and then I'll quickly check you over."

Scott smiled, "sure, do you want me to take my watch off?"

"Yes please but don't worry about your belt or shoes."

Scott did as he was asked and noticed that Marcus was doing the same thing at the other desk.

The security guard used a wand to check Scott for any metallic objects and it beeped once as it passed over his belt buckle and once as it passed over his left thigh. The security guard stopped moving it and looked at Scott.

"Metal plate inserted after a disagreement with a roadside bomb. Plays havoc with airport security too."

The security guard smiled, "who did you serve with?"

"Marines," Scott replied.

The guard grinned, "Rangers myself but I guess I can let you in even though you're a Jarhead."

Scott laughed, "well that's mighty kind of you."

The guard smiled, "go to the bar on the left. Ask for Nikki and tell her Sam sent you. She'll give you your fist drink on the house and you have a good time buddy."

Scott thanked him and walked through the door into the club, he found himself at the start of a short corridor. The walls decorated with hundreds of photos of strippers and guests. Marcus joined him a few seconds later and after ten paces the walked through a second door. The noise him them instantly, loud music, people laughing, people whistling. Multiple strobe lights and lasers were carving through the dimly lit club to the beat of the music.

Scott leaned in towards Marcus, "let's go and get a drink," he led Marcus over to the left hand bar exactly as Sam had told him too. The bar had four members of staff working and as luck would have it the redhead that approached him had a nametag that read Nikki.

Scott smiled at her, "hi Nikki, Sam sent me to ask for you."

She smiled back, "another one of his Army buddies after a free drink."

"Not quite Nikki, I'm a Marine and more than happy to pay if you'd prefer."

"Hell no, I'd never hear the last of it if I made you pay for your fist drink. Don't worry though we'll rip you off later to cover the cost."

Scott laughed, "in that case two beers please and some advice as the best place to be in here"

As if by magic two beers suddenly appeared and Nikki lent forward so that she didn't have to shout so loud, "the booths over in the corner are best if your just here to see the view. The better dancers use that stage and they tend to deliver a more eye catching show. The waitresses that side are more physical as well. If you're a little more conservative then go to the right as it's a softer and less intrusive experience. My old man was a jarhead so taking that into account you need to be going go to the left"

Scott took the two beers and winked, "thank you Nikki," he passed one of the beers to Marcus and indicated a corner booth that was empty. The view wasn't great but it was the obvious one to head to as Nikki had suggested it. Scott and Marcus sat down, "okay so the view isn't great, and we can't see all the club but for the moment it'll do."

They both looked around and took in as much as they could without making it look too obvious that they were casing the place. Marcus spoke first, "so I count at least twenty cameras this side of the club. They'll have a clear view of just about everyone that comes in which would make it really easy for them to pick someone out, even in this light."

Scott looked around, "judging by the number of people that are in here this is clearly the place to be," he took another drink and put the empty bottle down on the table. A virtually naked dancer was going through her routine on the stage. She was engaging with as many people as she could that were seated along the three sides of the stage. Scott noticed quite a few couples seated and turned back to Marcus, "well they certainly seem to draw the crowds in," as he finished speaking a topless waitress came over with two more beers.

She had a big smile on her face as she put them both down on the table, she looked at Scott, "there you go sugar."

"How did you know we wanted two more beers?" he asked.

"Oh honey of course you want two more beers," she leant in towards him, "how else would you get to see my tits?"

She stood up, "do you want a tab or pay as you go?"

Marcus got his wallet out, "pay as you go if that's okay."

"Oh that's more than okay honey, that'll be twenty bucks."

Marcus gave her a twenty and a five. She bent down and whispered a thank you on his ear, her bare breast touching his arm as she did. She stood up again and all Marcus could think to say was "you're welcome."

Scott was laughing, "do me a favour and give her a twenty as a tip next tip I want to see what she does to you for that."

118

Marcus shook his head, "oh no, your round next so you can experience what that provides."

Three songs later the dancer had changed and they'd finished their beers, once again the waitress was there with two more drinks. This time Scott paid and he gave her an extra twenty knowing that Marcus would never let him forget it if he didn't. The waitress did nothing more than take the money smile and walk away. Marcus burst out laughing, "so for five dollars I get to feel her breast against my arm and for twenty you get a smile, that's hilarious."

Scott had a sly grin on his face, "maybe not."

The waitress was back but without the drinks tray. She expertly dropped onto Scott's lap and gave him a long kiss on the lips. As she stood up she made a point of leaning forward so that her breasts brushed against his face. She turned to face Marcus, "well the next round should be interesting and it's your turn to raise the stakes. If you think you can handle it." Without waiting for a reply she was gone.

"Well I wasn't exactly expecting that and unless you really want to stay I guess we'll finish this and leave."

Marcus shook his head, "no I think we've seen enough and we aren't going to learn anymore from sitting here. Anyway the barmaid has been trying to catch your eye. I think you've pulled."

Scott looked over at the bar but Nikki wasn't to be seen, "I very much doubt that, let's get out of here."

They both stood up and started to make their way over to the exit which wasn't via the same door they entered through. Once outside they walked a couple of blocks before being picked up by Clay, he took them straight back to the diner where they all sat around a table. By now the diner was virtually empty so they were able to relax a little as there wasn't anyone sitting anywhere near them.

Clay put his coffee mug down, "I need both teams to write up their reports and we'll go through them tomorrow morning to see what we've learnt. Anyone have any questions?"

Joss spoke first, "no questions but I've just received a text from Barney and we have a slight problem. The DEA already have the second club under surveillance and have an undercover agent inside. They're onto a large drugs operation being run by a Mexican cartel," she looked round the table and nobody seemed surprised. "Levi is joining us tomorrow to brief us on what he knows but this could be good or bad news for us."

Clay had finished his coffee, "let's get out of here and meet up at eight at the office. We'll debrief before Levi gets in."

They all got up and Clay dropped them off before heading home.

Chapter 13 (Europe)

The office in Hove was significantly quieter than it had been over the last few days, with half the team stateside and three of the others out of the country as well. Nick pretty much had the building to himself. Levi and Chris had gone up to London to meet with James and Sean was out taking Bruce for a long walk. The three of them would be back later but for now Nick had the place to himself. So time for the volume to go up on the music and to settle down and start the possible lengthy process of tracing the emails that Joseph had supplied on the flash drive. Nick enjoyed the depth and secrecy of the dark web whilst at the same time got frustrated by the multiple layers and ever increasing security. Something that the users really enjoyed and valued. After two hours he had to admit that this definitely wasn't the work of a novice. Whoever was sending these emails had the benefits of an IT professional and some serious money as Nick was going deeper and deeper without finding any clues or answers. As usual he was so lost in what he was doing he failed to notice that Sean had come back with Bruce and had dropped the volume down on the music.

Sean put some fresh water down for Bruce and headed down to the tech store to prep a set of cameras and the other items they may need if they were tasked to go and assist Katie. He worked his way through cleaning the cameras and lenses, checked and cleared the SD cards. He checked all the batteries were charged and then set everything to one side once he was happy. As soon as he finished he decided to go for a run. He left a message for Nick in the kitchen area as he didn't want to disturb him. At times like this Nick was best left alone to focus on what he was doing. He ran out onto the Old Shoreham Road not sure where or how far he was going. As he ran he decided a nice run along the seafront would be in order so he made his way down and joined the Esplanade at Hove Lagoon. He could see Brighton Marina to the east and started to run in that direction. He got into a nice flow and before he knew it he was at the roundabout by the entrance of Brighton Pier. He pushed onto the marina and turned round and started to run back. As he passed the pier once more he pushed up the pace. The esplanade was fairly busy and every now and then he'd have to dodge round a dog or cyclist but that was part and parcel of running along the esplanade.

Once back at the office he showered and got changed. He made his way to the kitchen to sort out some food and knocked up a couple of omelettes. Taking one through to Nick who was, by now, totally oblivious of the time and how hungry he was. After eating Sean found himself at a bit of a loose end, no requests or updates had come through from anyone so he decided to take Bruce for a walk over the downs. Barney had a spot that he would regularly use and Sean decided to head there. He told Nick what he was doing and went down to the garage and grabbed the keys to one of the cars. Bruce was already stood at the top of the stairs his head tilted slightly to one side. Sean ignored him at first and opened the back of the Audi, he looked round at Bruce and said "Come on then." which was all Bruce needed to hear. He expertly bounded down the stairs and jumped into the back of the car. The drive to Falmer road didn't take long and Sean pulled into the lay-by and parked. He opened the tailgate and grabbed the long lead. He probably wouldn't need it as the cows weren't in the field he was going to walk through but even though Bruce was highly trained they still took a lead with them. He locked the car and walked the short distance to the gate. Once through he let Bruce off the lead. The path along the edge of the field led them up to the South Downs Way. Sean took a leisurely stroll allowing Bruce the chance to explore as they went.

When they got to the end of the path Sean opened the gate for Bruce and they both went though. They were now on the South Downs Way and Sean walked forward till he got to the fence line. Behind him was a small wood, and looking ahead in the distance he could see Lewes. He looked to his left along the valley and saw the cottages nestled just below the railway line. Barney came up here because he had a lot of fond memories of the area. He'd spent quite a bit of time during his youth here as his grandparents had lived in one of the cottages and he'd spent many weekends and summer holidays at number two Littledown Cottages. His Grandfather would walk him and his cousins up to the woods regaling them with wonderful facts about nature and the surrounding countryside. Sean liked it here too. It was always peaceful with only the odd hiker or cyclist passing by. Sean walked along the crest of the hill towards Lewes with Bruce still sniffing and exploring. After a while he made his way back to the car and headed back to the office.

A few hours later Sean and Chris weren't having much luck at all, they'd split the business and property list between them and so far every avenue they'd explored came to a dead end in as much as everything was completely above board. It began to look as though Frederik was just a rich business man who had indulged his dark side and was just as he'd said trying to make amends. Despite this they kept going, knowing that until they had checked everything off the list they couldn't stop.

"Let's call it a day and get something to eat."

Sean shook his head, "do you know what, I'll cook something. You check in with the others and see how Nick is doing. We've got enough stuff in the kitchen for me to rustle something up."

Chris sat back in his chair, "that sounds like a plan," he picked up his phone and hit the speed dial and started making some calls.

Sean went into the kitchen to check on what they had, he grabbed some chicken, peppers and onions and started preparing it all. He started by making a black bean sauce. Which, once he was happy with he put to one side. He'd cut the chicken into thin strips and he added it to the wok. As soon as he was sure the chicken had cooked thoroughly he added the diced pepper and onion. He opened the cupboard to find some rice and saw that they had some noodles. They weren't fresh but they'd do for what he wanted, after all he wasn't trying to impress anyone he just wanted to feed the three of them.

Chris joined him, "anything I can do?"

"Yes, can you let Nick know he's got about five minutes unless he's really busy and wants to reheat it later?"

Chris was back a minute later, "he'll eat with us as he said he could do with a distraction."

123

Five minutes later the three of them were sat down, a big plate of food in front of each of them "So hypothetical question for both of you," Sean looked at them both as he spoke, "if you had the money would you pay to have someone delivered to you that you could do with how ever you pleased?"

Chris and Nick replied "No," almost at the same time.

Chris put his fork down, "so if I did have limitless funds then yes there are lots of things I'd buy and lots I'd do. But if I wanted to push the sexual boundaries with someone then I'd go to someone that specialised in that and was a willing participant."

Nick nodded, "me too."

"I agree but here's the thing. If I was power hungry and a control freak would I settle for someone that was willing to participate but had boundaries? Or would I want someone that wouldn't and more to the point couldn't question what I wanted?" Sean took another mouthful of food.

"Well if you put it like that then I guess no you wouldn't. If your moral compass was out of whack then you possibly wouldn't care." Nick looked at Sean holding up a fork loaded with food "this is good by the way. I might have to request you stay back for a while and act as the in house cook."

Sean laughed, "yes, well that's not going to happen so don't even try."

Chris sat back in his chair, "so we frequently deal with some very sick individuals and regularly question their judgement. This is clearly another case involving some really disturbed individuals. Does money and power really make you that warped?"

"I don't know if it's the money, power or a mental instability. Take Joseph, listening to the recordings and hearing from Cass and Alek he seems like a genuine person. Nothing about him would lead me to believe that he'd not only pay a large sum of money for someone but would take their life." Sean looked at them both, "although he confesses it was an accident he still killed her, he purchased the ability to take a life."

All three of them had stopped eating. They'd actually finished most of the meal but the conversation was getting a bit deep and none of them felt like to continuing to eat. Quite often during an assignment some of the team would get into conversations like this, they'd try to explore things and attempt to look at things from a different angle. It didn't always work though and sometimes they'd achieve nothing at all.

"If you're a high powered businessman demanding more and more with every success would the sadistic side of you emerge?" Sean leant forward and filed his glass up with iced water from the jug in the centre of the table.

"If I already had a sadistic streak it would certainly grow if I had money and power but I don't know if I had all that money I'd develop a sadistic streak."

Nick looked at Sean, "let me ask you this. Other than in a combat situation could you see yourself willingly taking someone's life?"

"Sitting here right now no I couldn't. Would money and power corrupt me? Well the answer is I'd like to think not but who knows what we'd all do with a few million in the bank."

"I'm sure if I wanted to act out some sexual fantasies I'd pay a high class hooker and be done with it." Nick stood up and put the three plates on top of each other and took them out to the kitchen. A few seconds later he came back in and sat down.

Sean looked at Nick, "that may be the case but what do you do when you've acted out the fantasies you can think of? Do you dream up some more, do you push a few boundaries?"

"Well I don't know, I suppose I could possibly want more and if I had the money I could get it"

"So if you're a middle aged man with more money than sense and you suddenly developed a lust for someone that couldn't say no to anything you wanted. No matter how wrong or perverted, would you tune to a service that could provide exactly that? Imagine a person delivered to your door and taken away again. Yours to do with as you please."

Nick hesitated, "well I really don't know."

"I do," Chris had a pained expression on his face, "you'd do exactly what Josef and Frederik did. You'd order your fantasy girl tailored to your exact specifications and then sit back and enjoy yourself. They wouldn't see what they're doing as wrong. They're drunk on power and money after all."

Nick had a look of displeasure on his face, "god that's warped and sick."

"Yes, it is," Sean said, "but that's exactly what both of them did, now thinking about it what's to stop them doing it again and again?"

"Money or the risks associated with it I imagine," Nicks face had returned to normal now.

"Are we saying that they've done it more than once?" Chris asked.

"No. There's nothing to say they did and if they've both come forward, as they have, then they've got nothing to hide. On the surface they both seem genuine and we haven't found anything so far to suggest they aren't."

Nick had a thoughtful look on his face now, "well none of us have found anything so far so I wonder if Josef or Frederik have any other associates they've shared their secrets with?"

"Damn good question," Sean thought for a second, looking at his watch "I'm going to see if I can get hold of either of them to ask them just that."

Nick stood up, "well I'm going to go back to digging myself deeper into the wrong side of the web."

Chris got up as well, "well I've got the last few of Frederik's properties to check out so I'll get on with that."

Sean tried Frederik first. There was no answer from the mobile number he'd given them and his office just said that he wasn't in and they weren't sure when they were expecting him. He would frequently move about all his companies not basing himself at any one of them. Sean called Joseph and his nurse answered telling Sean that Joseph wasn't well and that he was currently sleeping. She said that she'd leave a message for him but explained that in the last few days he'd been feeling very weak and in her opinion he wasn't doing well at all. Sean thanked her and made a few notes in the file on the bulletin board.

Sean checked in with James and gave him a quick update on how the three of them were progressing although in truth he didn't really have anything positive to provide. As was often the case in their assignments there could be days and days of what seemed like no progression and then suddenly things would start to slot into place and everything would speed up. This was still very much the information gathering stage so Sean wasn't fazed by the fact that he didn't have anything good to say. Once he'd finished updating James he decided to hit the gym for an hour or so in order to release some of his frustrations.

Chapter 14 (Europe)

Katie and Alek changed their plans on the flight to Lyon. They decided to go straight to Interpol HQ in order to make a start on securing the resources they'd need to begin their investigation. Their first step was to simply go through the archives and open cases to see if there were any cases of unknown women that had turned up either dead or injured within the last six months. No easy task considering the political hoops that needed to be jumped through to gain the cooperation of the various countries. Even Interpol had procedures to follow although things worked well between themselves and local organisations. The requests still needed to be handled carefully to ensure they weren't stepping on anybody's toes. At the airport they grabbed a cab to take them to the offices. Alek had never been to Interpol HQ and was wondering how he'd be received. He needn't have worried because James had already placed a call to Katie's superior to advise them of what the team were investigating and to ask for as much cooperation as they could give.

Katie and Alek got out of the cab and walked through the main doors, a security guard smiled at them, "Katie, it's so good to see you back."

"Hello Pierre, good to see you again. How's the family?"

"They are all good and enjoying life," the smile disappeared as he looked at Alek. His right hand dropped to the butt of his pistol and his left to the handcuffs on his belt, "should I take the suspect to a holding cell?"

Alek raised an eyebrow and for a split second Katie looked worried.

Suddenly Pierre smiled and extended his right hand, "it's good to meet you Alek. Any friend of Katie is more than welcome here, even the Russian ones." He winked at Katie and laughed, "we've been expecting you. Upstairs called down first thing to arrange for an ID pass for Alek."

Alek shook his hand, "the pleasure is all mine Pierre."

"They've arranged for a desk for you both on the third floor but your boss wants to see you first as soon as you've signed in."

Katie gave Pierre a smile, "thank you, I'll catch up with you shortly."

"I will be expecting lunch, I'm sure it's your turn to pay."

Katie grinned, "I'm sure it is."

They made their way to the main reception desk and signed in. The receptionist handed Alek his ID pass. Following the advice given he clipped it on his jacket so that it could be clearly seen and the pair of them made their way to the lift. Katie pushed the call button and the doors opened, they both stepped in and she pushed the button for the fourth floor.

"Do you know all the guards that well?"

"No, Pierre and I go way back. Our grandparents came to France from Algeria together after the war. Our grandfathers fought in the same French unit and after they left the army they both decided that France had more to offer so they simply left everything behind to make a new life in France."

The lift stopped and the doors opened. Katie and Alek stepped out into an open plan office space with a group of offices down one side. Katie walked to the right and made her way to the third office and Alek followed. Although the door was open Katie knocked and waited to be invited in. Alek heard a feminine 'come in' and following Katie he walked through the door.

The office was smart and tidy. Two empty chairs were one side of the desk while on the other was a smartly dressed woman who invited them to sit. Alek looked around the office as he moved towards the chair. It was incredibly neat, everything in its place. The books in the bookcase neatly organised, no paperwork in sight other than the folder in front of the woman sat at the desk. Alek sat down, he'd normally introduce himself but this wasn't his territory and he was taking Katie's lead and sitting down seemed to be the right thing to do.

"Katie, it's good to see you back. It's been too long."

Katie nodded, "it's been a while. Claudine may I introduce Alek one of the team that I work with."

Alek stood up and held out his hand, "pleasure to meet you."

Claudine stayed in her seat but shook the outstretched hand, "likewise."

"Pierre said you wanted to see us before we made a start."

Claudine sat back in her seat pausing for a moment, "Katie, as you know the powers that be were rather sceptical when it came to releasing someone to the task force that you're with. Looking at the results you've achieved proves the scepticism was unfounded however they are still guarded. Some attitudes are still outdated and behind the times. Things are moving forward and improving all the time and the world itself is changing. Some things however are much slower than others. Interpol is of course more than happy to assist wherever we can and our resources are at your teams' disposal however there are some things that take time to change. Alek I have read your file and it's impressive. Having said that, some people at the top have expressed a little concern at allowing a member of the FSB access to roam about the building let alone the ability to use our systems. Now that's not a view I share but I must make you both aware that you will be being watched very closely." Claudine looked at Alek and then across at Katie.

"That's fine, we'd expected that and had discussed it. Alek will hand his Mac over to IT for them to check it and then he will log in remotely to our systems back in the UK. It'll only be me that logs into the system here."

Alek put his Mac on the desk, "I fully understand and if we were in my headquarters right now the hoops we'd be jumping through would be considerably bigger. There'd be a hell of a lot more of them. Our administration wouldn't be rolling over so nicely and there'd be a lot of strict do's and don'ts that we'd have to adhere to."

Katie stood up, "we're on the floor below could you get the IT tech to drop the Mac back down to us once they've finished with it?"

Claudine smiled, "you'll be glad to know that I've overruled that decision. I can't have one of my top stars stuck at a desk on an admin floor. The office at the end is clear you can both use that. I've had the fridge stocked with water and there's a coffee machine in there as well."

Alek smiled, "you're certainly not one of the sceptics then."

Claudine looked him in the eye, "as long as your performance matches the facts in your file then I'm happy to cut you some slack. Especially as I know that Katie wouldn't have allowed you in the building unless she trusted you and that's more than enough for me. I've never doubted her judgement and I'm not going to start now."

"Wow, now that's a big vote of confidence," Alek kept a straight face as he turned to Katie, "your coffee making must have been much better when you worked here."

Claudine laughed and Katie just pointed to the door and said "out."

They made their way to the office at the end, the door was open and they both went in. There were two desks back to back. Both had a pile of stationary on them as well as a phone, screen, keyboard and mouse. In the corner was a larger table with four chairs. To one side was a unit that ran the full width of the office and on it was a coffee machine and all the accoutrements that came with it.

Alek put his bag down next to one of the desks, "well this is a bit more than a step up from a desk in an open plan office. You're rated quite highly aren't you?"

Katie had an almost embarrassed look on her face, "maybe a little, I might have sort of saved Claudine during an operation that went wrong."

Alek was intrigued, "sort of saved her how?"

Katie went over to the coffee machine and turned it on, "we were on an operation that was going in the wrong direction. We were dealing with a gang and we'd been tipped off that three of the gang members were at a property in Paris. A small team of us had followed their movements and were already in Paris so we went to the property to apprehend them. Turns out it was a trap. They were expecting us and there were eight of them and only four of us. We'd stopped round the corner from the house in order to put our vests and prepare on when they ambushed us. I'd managed to get my vest on but Claudine hadn't, I stepped in front of her to cover her while she got it on and promptly took two bullets to the chest. The body armour did its job but it knocked me off my feet. One of the team was killed instantly but Claudine and the other team member returned fire. Luckily for us Claudine had made the Police aware of our presence and they happened to have two units in very close proximity. Almost as soon as the first call phone call was made reporting gunfire they dispatched both units. Within minutes there were four uniformed officers supporting us and the gang backed off. In the end three of the gang were killed and two seriously wounded."

Alek looked impressed, "so you really were a rising star."

"I didn't do anything that another agent wouldn't have done," she turned two mugs over, "coffee?" she asked trying to change the subject.

"Please."

Before either of them could say anything else there was a knock at the door, "come in."

The door opened and a man stepped in holding the Mac that Alek had placed on Claudine's desk.

"This belongs to one of you I believe?"

Alek stepped forward, "yes, thank you."

"We haven't really done anything to it other than check it for bugs. I've been told you're going to connect to an external network so there didn't seem much point in doing anything other than that."

Alek put the Mac down on the desk, "thanks."

"You're welcome," with that he turned and left the room closing the door behind him.

Alek sat down, "I'll check in with Nick. Did you want to sort us out a vehicle to use?"

Katie nodded, "yes, I'll go and check with Claudine to see which rental company we've got the best deal with." She opened the office door and walked back towards the office they'd been in a few minutes ago. Like everybody else in the team his Mac and phone were linked so that they created a Wi-Fi hotspot. Alek opened the lid of the Mac and typed in his password. A few keystrokes later and he was connected to the server in Hove checking the progress folder for the mission.

Each mission had its own folder and when the team were split as they were now they could all login and update the status of their part of the investigation allowing everyone to track the progress of the overall operation. It worked well and Alek updated the section assigned to him and Katie. They would of course call each other to check in etc but this added an extra level of information. It also allowed James to get a quick overview of how things were going. Alek noticed that Charlie had booked herself off duty but available. No doubt pulling a shift at the hospital he thought to himself.

Katie came back into the office with a set of keys, "there's a pool car we can use so that makes things so much easier. James has already sent across all your details so you're covered to drive if needed."

"Well that saves us a bit of messing about."

Katie sat down and logged herself into the system, the first thing she did was to check the bulletin board to find out what was going on. She did log in remotely every now and then but as she was here she felt she could give herself an hour or so to catch up on what was happening. During the first hour they had a few visitors popping in to say hello to Katie. Word had spread that she as in the building and a number of people wanted to take the opportunity to catch up with her. As all she was currently doing was effectively catching up on the gossip as she went through the bulletin board it didn't matter to her that people kept interrupting. Once she started to focus on their current objectives however it would become a little bit irritating.

Word had also spread that the FSB were in the building and for some that was a huge leap forward and a definite step in the right direction. For others it was rather difficult to accept. Thankfully those people were in the minority and were predominantly the older staff that remember the old times at the height of the cold war. Something that some people just couldn't let go of and despite all the political advanced that had been made in recent years.

After about an hour and a half Katie got bored with what she was doing and refocused herself on the task at hand. First she reached out to a few contacts she had across Europe and asked told them she was looking into any cases of unidentified men or women aged seventeen to thirty. She had discussed this with Alek and they both knew that it was going to be quicker if they involved as many people as they could with the initial search although they weren't sure if they'd actually find anything. From what they already knew so far this wasn't a bunch of part time criminals organising this.

Alek in the meantime had reached out to an FSB contact that dealt with cold cases. Not the run of the mill stuff but cases that didn't add up with strange anomalies that would be of interest to the FSB. He then checked back in with Nick to see how he was doing. That didn't take too long as Nick was gradually working through the layers of the dark web getting ever deeper as he went.

"So I've asked a friend to run a search on any strange or odd cases that involve young single men or women that can't be identified. I've checked in with Nick and he's happily burying himself in the dark web. He hasn't found anything yet but its early days and as we know from the past never easy or quick."

"If there's anything to find I don't know anyone better that we could have searching. I've reached out and have a few people digging through recent cases and if we're lucky we might find something although I'm a little worried that the people we're after are a bit too smart to simply dump a body in a field." Katie looked up from her screen, "that's the bit that concerns me the most. Frederik and Joseph both said that they sent a message to say they'd finished with the girl and on both occasions someone arrived, collected the girl and cleaned up leaving absolutely no trace of them ever having been there. That takes some organisation and definitely takes money."

"Well we know that they're paying a large amount of money for the service so it's no surprise that it's thorough. I wish Frederik had been as meticulous as Joseph." Alek paused for a second, "I guess it's like he said and he wants to put the experience behind him. At the end of the day he did come forward."

Katie didn't reply straight away, she seemed to be staring into space, "but he didn't come forward, Joseph gave us his name."

"Well yes but he still agreed to meet us. Although maybe he didn't have a choice as Joseph had put his name forward."

Katie looked at Alek, "but what if what he told us was a pack of lies and he just gave us what he felt we'd want to hear. He must have spoken to Joseph to find out what he'd told us."

"If that is the case then Sean and Chris will find out. They're looking into his business and personal life so if there's anything that isn't right they'll find it."

"I guess you're right, let's go and get something to eat. I could do with stretching my legs and we can stick our bags in the car on the way out." They made their way to the underground car park and located the vehicle they'd been assigned. After putting their bags in they made their way to a small sandwich bar and ordered some lunch. They sat on a bench and discussed what they should do next.

Katie got the number for Josef from the file on the bulletin board and called it. A nurse answered and Katie explained that they wanted to visit just to ask a few simple questions. The nurse was a little unsure at first but Katie won her round and they agreed to meet as soon as they could get there. While she was talking Alek was already booking their flights and a local hotel in Berlin close to the airport as there was no guarantee they'd make it back to the airport for the last flight. He also booked a rental car to save a little time when they landed.

Chapter 15

Phoebe opened her eyes, it wasn't a dream. She held her eyes shut for a few seconds and opened them once again. Sadly it definitely wasn't a dream, the now familiar clinically clean sight she had been looking before she went to sleep still greeted her. She took a deep breath and slowly sat up. Looking around the room nothing had changed and she knew that no matter how hard she prayed this was real. She pushed back the duvet and swivelled her body round planting her feet on the floor. The room seemed to be at the perfect temperature, even the floor appeared to be heated. She sighed and stood up walking to the bathroom door. She put her hand on the handle and opened it slowly. The room was as she'd left it, she moved over to the toilet and paused before sitting down. She looked around the room desperately looking for the cameras that she now knew were in the room. They must be, she'd been thinking about it long and hard and didn't think for one second she'd be allowed the common courtesy of being able to sit on the toilet with any privacy.

She slowly lowered her shorts and sat down as quickly as she could. Her body told her that she needed to go but her brain wouldn't let her. She sat there for five minutes before nature took over and she was finally able to overcome her brains constant reminder that she was being watched. She hadn't ever sat on the toilet with someone in the room and even though she was alone she knew that the cameras were watching. She tore off a couple of pieces of toilet paper. She stood up and pulled her shorts back on. As she turned round to flush the toilet she suddenly became conscious of the fact that she had pulled her shorts up as if she were at home, almost with all the time in the world. She shocked herself, had she done that knowingly or had she momentarily forgotten about the cameras. She washed her hands and moved back into the bedroom.

She sat back down on the bed, one foot on the floor and one up on the edge of the bed. She thought about what to do next, not that she had many options to be fair. She stood up again and moving over to the screen she selected a fairly updated playlist. She turned the volume up slightly and started to do a few basic exercises. Nothing too strenuous she decided but just enough to wake herself up. After twenty minutes she paused. Without realising it she had already completed three sets of her normal warm up routine. She hadn't done that for a while, not even when she was attending the gym five times a week. She stopped and stood up, deciding that no matter how she felt the time had come to take a shower. The first one ever in front of a camera. She'd been in a shower with someone before but that was decidedly different. This time she was alone but being filmed or watched and that just didn't seem right. She knew that she had to get over herself and that she somehow needed to block out the fact that she wasn't alone.

She looked at the screen expecting to see something, it was blank. Was she being watched all the time she wondered, she brushed her hair back and decided that she had to put it to the test. She stood up and headed back into the bathroom, one step at a time she thought. She faced the shower, it didn't have a traditional door as it was a wet room but she still kept her back to the mirror as she undressed herself. Now naked she stepped into the shower and turned the dial to warm and set both the shower head and the side jets to come on. Her logic being that if she stood slightly in front of the jets whoever was watching wouldn't necessarily see her clearly. This gave her a little comfort but she still felt awkward. She took a deep breath and stepped into the water standing slightly in front of the side jets so that they were spaying across her back.

The warm water was nice and she tilted her head back a little so that it was directly below the main shower. She ran her hands through her hair to make sure it was thoroughly wet. She suddenly realised that no matter what or who was watching she still needed to keep clean and with that in mind she decided to spend the first five minutes showering herself as she would normally do. While she was rubbing the shower gel in she realised that when she was at home and relaxed she did in fact sometimes play with herself whilst in the shower and had even taken herself to the point of orgasm. But that was on her own without someone watching her. She bent down to wash her legs and feet and realised that without thinking as she'd bent down she had moved back slightly and as a result was now presenting her naked butt for anyone to see. She quickly stood up and just let the water run over her body removing all of the shower gel till she was just stood in the water contemplating her next move.

She took a deep breath and decided to take the next step but a sudden thought came into her mind. She'd never faked an orgasm before and didn't know if she could. Whoever was watching would know straight away, or would they? She was worried now, could she actually do this? She stood still once again the water cascading off her. She decided that she had to do something to satisfy her captor, even if it was only putting on a small show. She took a deep breath and turned round. She took a slight step forward so that she was directly in line with the jets and directly underneath the shower head. One step at a time she reminded herself, she grabbed the bottle of shower gel and squeezed a fair sized amount into her palm. She put the bottle back on the shelf and took a small step forward so that the majority of the water was now flowing down her back. Rubbing her hands together she started to gently rub her left shoulder. Making slow small circles she worked her way across her neck swapping hands so that she could do the same on her right shoulder. She moved both hands down to the top of her breasts still making small slow circles. Closing her eyes trying to think of nothing else but the feeling of her hands moving over her breasts. She felt her thumbs brush across her nipples and she felt them respond. She cupped her breasts in her hands and moved her thumbs in small circles around her nipples.

She smiled, she was genuinely enjoying this and was beginning to feel a little excited. She left her right hand where it was and slowly moved her left down towards her stomach making more of an oval shape. Feeling more relaxed she arched her back slightly and moved her hand lower. She had her right nipple between her thumb and forefinger and was ever so slowly rotating her nipple, which by now was fully erect. Her left hand had reached the top of her thigh and she slowly parted her legs, she was moving her hand from one thigh to the other.

She extended her thumb and rubbed it gently over her clit, she shuddered slightly as her thumb moved back and forth. She slowed suddenly doubting what she was doing. Her hand dropped by her side and she dropped her head. She sudden realisation of what she was doing and where she was hit her hard. Her right hand fell from her breast and she simply stood there under the running water. She barely moved for five minutes not knowing quite what to do. She'd been kidnapped and she was god knows where in a shower playing with herself. Just what was happening to her, she shook her head and decided to get out of the shower. She dried herself off quickly and walked back into the bedroom with the towel wrapped around her.

She stopped in front of the mirror staring at the girl looking back at her. Could she do this? Should she do this? She sat down on the bed, her legs straddling the corner. She took a deep breath and tried to make sense of what she was doing, no matter how hard she tried to she couldn't. One step at a time she decided, standing up she removed the towel. She went over to the dressing table and picked up the bottle of moisturiser. Taking another deep breath she told herself if he wants a show I'll give him one and see just what I get in return.

She sat back down again squeezing a nice amount of cream into her left hand, she put the bottle down on the bed next to her and slowly rubbed her hands together allowing the cream to cover her hands. She slowly and gently rubbed her hands over her breasts taking care to cover every little bit, both nipples responded instantly and as she moved her hands back and forth she occasionally flicked her thumb out so that it caught the edge of her nipple making her jump. She felt the excitement rising in her and she closed her eyes her back arching slightly and she began to lose herself in the moment. She moved both of her hands to the top of her breasts and moved them down in unison.

As her hands got to the middle of her stomach she stopped, with her left hand she picked up the bottle of moisturiser again squirting a nice amount directly onto her stomach. She put the bottle back down again and slowly lay back on the bed. Her hands reaching down she gently rubbed the cream into her stomach and the very top of her thighs. As her legs were straddling the bed she was able to move her hands to the inside of her thighs with ease. She moved her right hand back up to her breasts as her left teased her inner thighs. She was still silky smooth as she had recently had a full wax which definitely added to the excitement she could feel beginning to pulse through her body.

She ran her middle finger straight down her lips adding a little pressure so that parted ever so slightly, she felt the tingle as she moved her finger back up and it brushed over her clit. She could feel the heat between her legs and suddenly knew that she could do this, in fact she now wanted to do this. Her middle finger slid inside as she dropped her wrist neatly parting her lips with the fingers either side. She moved her middle finger round in a slow circular motion so that she could feel her knuckle inside herself. She orgasmed surprisingly quick her eyes opening with shock as the waves of enjoyment hit her. She stopped moving both hands and lay still, her breathing still shallow and fast.

She finally sat up, the shock of what she'd just done hit her and she felt a little ashamed. She slowly sat up and picked the towel walking back into the bathroom she put the towel on the rail and went back into the bedroom. She opened a drawer and selected a t shirt and pair of shorts. She moved to the side of the bed and pulled the duvet back. Climbing into bed she pulled the duvet over herself and lay there with her eyes closed wondering if she should be enjoying the feeling between her legs or ashamed of performing in front of a camera. She moved her left hand and turned the light off plunging the room into darkness.

She tried to clear her mind but it simply wasn't happening, she was not able to focus on any one thing, her mind was in turmoil. The normal feelings she felt after an orgasm had already left her even though she could still feel the wetness between her thighs. The problem was that the minute she had turned the light off she immediately care back to earth and realised exactly where she was. Or more to the point realised that she really didn't know where she was at all and that frightened her. She knew that nothing had happened to her so far and that despite the circumstances she was in what seemed like a good place. The room was comfortable, she had everything she needed, except her freedom. She definitely didn't have that.

She tried to switch her brain off, she even tried to sing some of her favourite songs but nothing worked, she couldn't stop worrying about what was happening. She'd been fine last night so what had happened, what had changed? She didn't have the answer and was just beginning to get annoyed with herself. Sighing she sat up, turning the light back on she swung her legs over the edge of the bed. Taking a deep breath she stood up. She decided that maybe a few minutes of exercise might force her mind to ease up a little. She started with a couple of sets of sit ups, taking deep breaths and getting into a rhythm. She then moved to a couple of sets of push ups and suddenly she could feel her whole body starting to relax again.

She carried on and after twenty minutes of various exercises she felt much better. She went into the bathroom and turned the shower on. Quickly stripping off she stepped under the jets of water and let her body soak. She just stood there letting the water cover her body. She slowly turned herself around even though it wasn't really necessary as the spray of water from the shower head above her covered her entire body without her moving at all. Once she'd completed a full rotation she stopped and putting a small amount of shower gel in the palm of her hand started to gently wash herself. She put some more shower gel in the other hand and took a step back from the jets of water. She quickly washed herself all over and now covered almost head to foot in a coating of bubbles she stepped back under the water.

She stayed under the jets for about five minutes before turning the shower off. Picking up the towel shed used earlier she dried herself off thoroughly putting the wet towel back on the rail once again. She slowly made her way back to the bed and got under the covers. Feeling far more relaxed now and closing her eyes she took herself back to the feelings of elation she felt as her body had given in to the earlier orgasm.

Chapter 16 (North America)

Cass and Kelly were waiting at the airport for the others to arrive. They'd been working out of a small office at the local Police station and had managed to convince the Police Chief to assign them a larger room now that the team was getting bigger. They'd spent their time so far going through CCTV footage from the coffee shop to try and find as much footage of Phoebe and the mystery woman as they possibly could. So far there'd been mixed success, they'd found four instances when the two had met but none of the meetings had given them a clear view of the mystery woman's face. Cass was beginning to think that it wasn't anything they were going to be lucky enough to get.

Every single time she was careful enough to avoid the cameras and they'd happily taken a break to come to the airport to collect the others. Cass was disappointed with what they'd found so far as none of it really helped except for the fact that whoever it was that was meeting Phoebe was linked with her disappearance. It wasn't a coincidence that she was avoiding the cameras, she was a professional and clearly very good at what she did.

They hadn't been waiting more than ten minutes when Drew, Jake and Boyd came out of the main terminal building. Jake noticed Cass and made his way over with the other two in tow, "hi Cass, been waiting long?"

Cass opened the trunk for the guys so that the guys could stick their bags in, "no, we've only been here about ten minutes. We figured if we were late you'd grab a coffee."

Jake smiled, "we were going to but we thought we could grab one on the way or wait till we get to the office."

"Okay, well now that we've got a bigger office we can grab some food and drink on the way back and then we'll bring you up to speed with where we are currently."

"Sounds good to me," with that they all got in and Cass pulled out into the flow of traffic leaving the airport. The journey was uneventful and Cass had said rather than go over anything as they were driving she wanted to wait till they were all able to focus and concentrate. They stopped on the way and grabbed some sandwiches and various snacks. They all knew they were in for a fairly challenging task as scanning through endless CCTV footage wasn't exactly an exciting thing to do. Especially under the circumstance, every little bit of footage they can find may help to build a picture and they were very aware that at the moment they didn't have a great deal at all to go on.

They arrived at the Police station and Cass parked in the same spot that she'd used earlier. They all got out and followed Cass into the station. It was a hive of activity and she stopped at the front counter to get some ID badges for the guys that had just arrived. Once that had been sorted she led them all to the office that they were now using. They all sat down, Cass had closed the door to try and keep some of the noise out. It was a busy area and the noise level always seemed to be quite loud. Luckily the stuff they'd been watching didn't have any audio so they didn't need absolute silence.

"Okay guys so here's what we have so far, we've found four meetings between Phoebe and her friend. We haven't managed to find any more than that and in every single meeting the friend makes sure she's not caught on camera. We're hoping to find some footage of her initial visit to the coffee shop but to be honest I don't think it's going to help. She really knows what she's doing and I think we'll find that even when she was checking the place out she won't make the mistake of letting us see her face. As soon as the CSI team finished at the apartment we went in to have a look. We were careful not to touch anything at all, we simply observed and took photos. We have got permission to go back again and we'll do that together in the hope that between us we can find something that helps or at least gives us a clue as to what happened." Cass paused to take a drink

Kelly took over, "so we have managed to find two CCTV cameras that have a view of the apartment. The angle isn't that great and we should get footage from both cameras tomorrow morning hopefully. I've got to be honest and say that we're a little bit disappointed so far.

142

We had hoped to be able to have found something that would have at least given us a starting point but as it stands at the moment we haven't really got anything at all."

Jake put his drink down, "so how do you want to tackle this?"

Cass paused for a second, "well the best way forward I think is that we take a day's footage each from the coffee shop and work though them. Now that you're all here we'll be going through five days at a time. Sadly even at high speed it still takes about three hours to go through the whole day and even if we do find something early on we still have to go to the end of the day in case they appear twice in the same day. It hasn't happened so far but we can't risk missing anything and we're beginning to think that we won't actually find anything useful from the coffee shop at all."

Cass passed three flash drives across the table, "there's one each, the tech team here have set it up so that it's stored in chronological order and here's a list of the days that we've covered so far. Let's pick a day each and make a start. We should be able to get another five days done before we go and get something to eat."

The next three and a half hours passed quite quickly, the net result was one more meeting between the two women but again nothing that was going to be of any use in identifying the mystery woman. They catalogued the date and the time and copied the relevant section of footage into the folder they'd been building.

Cass closed the lid of her Mac, "okay guys let's go and get something to eat, anyone got any preferences?"

No one had any particular wishes so they decided to go to the burger joint just down from the station. They left the car in the car park and walked the short distance. It was fairly busy when they go there but were seated at a table straight away. They didn't need much time to order and the waitress got the drinks back to the table quite quickly.

Jake put the menus down on the table, "so how do you want to approach the apartment Cass?"

"I'm not sure and that was something I wanted to discuss. We've been allowed to thoroughly search it if we want to but I'm not sure if we'll actually get anything useful. I think first of all I'd like to build up the best picture of Phoebe that we can from what we find there."

"Have we got any results yet from the search the CSI team conducted?"

Kelly shook his head, "not as yet, they did find some fibres and a couple of fingerprints that didn't belong to Phoebe but I'm guessing they haven't identified them yet otherwise they would have got back to us. They know that this is time sensitive and they have been more than willing to share information so they aren't holding anything back. I think the fact that they haven't said anything yet is simply because like us they haven't found anything useful at all."

Jake grimaced, "there was me thinking this was going to be the easier of the two investigations."

Cass put her glass down on the table, "no, I think from what we've seen so far that this is going to be far from easy. She hasn't given away anything on CCTV and I don't think we're really going to find anything here that'll help. So far this looks like a very professional job and I have a gut feeling that this is going to be a long hard slog in order to find something that'll help."

Their food arrived a few seconds later, Cass had gone for a straightforward cheeseburger and fries. Two of the others had gone for half pound BBQ burgers with onion rings and fries. The other two had gone for what amounted to a breakfast burger which was a half-pound burger with bacon and a fried egg, they'd also gone for onion rings and fries. The food was really good and while they were eating they stopped taking about the case and simply caught up with what was going on in their own worlds. They all came from very different backgrounds and the conversation eventually wound up with Cass explaining how the team got involved in the first place which then led to being asked what else they'd done in the past.

An hour later they'd all finished and Cass paid the bill, "okay so let's call it a night and we'll go straight to the apartment tomorrow." They all agreed and made their way to the car. Cass drove the short distance to their hotel and they all made their way to their rooms. They were all a little disappointed with the lack of progress so far but as was the case with a number of previous assignments. As always tomorrow was another day and could well be the day they get a breakthrough.

Chapter 17 (North America)

A few hours later they were all back in the office. Joss had got there really early with Scott and they'd both finished their reports and had found a couple of whiteboards that they'd added the key parts of each report to. The others arrived and they worked through the debrief. As well as the numerous files a number of boxes of donuts and pastries had appeared and they were coming to the end of the session when Levi was escorted through to them.

"Morning gang," he added a couple more boxes of donuts to the table, "thought you might like these."

Joss smiled, "thanks Levi, better late than never I guess and I hope you bring good news and not bad."

Levi sat down next to Joss, "well it's good and bad I'm afraid. The DEA have been working this case for some time and it's taken them six months to get an agent inside. They don't want any agencies coming in and destroying what they worked on so far. In fact they've politely asked me to tell you all it's a no-go area as far as you're concerned."

"Well Levi," Scott said with some humour in his voice, "I suggest they grow a pair and tell that to the General because I can't see him just casually backing away for them."

"No he won't which is why I've managed to get them to agree to get the undercover agent to meet us and got through what information they have so far in the hope that it'll give us what's needed to avoid having to go back." Levi looked round the table and saw some doubt on the faces looking at him, "look I know it's not what we want to hear but the agent will be here in about ten minutes. So let's reserve any judgement until we've heard what they've got to say."

Joss picked up her coffee mug, "we can do that I guess, now as you've managed to have ducked out of this assignment so far you can get me a coffee."

"That's not strictly true but to shut you up I'll do it."

Joss smiled, "so what does the agent know about us?"

"Well not a lot, I've told them that we're a multi-agency task force and that we're dealing with a sensitive case that has the backing of some senior people. I've tried not to indicate that we could get their operation shut down and that ours would take priority as we may need their intel and more importantly their help with boots on the ground especially as they have a live operation in place already."

Levi put the now full mug of coffee down in front of Joss and was promptly given two more mugs to fill. "Come on guys I was on assignment not off enjoying myself."

Danny laughed, "well that's what you get for going off on your own and leaving the team behind."

Levi shrugged his shoulders, "I guess I don't have a choice." His phone chimed. "Ah saved by the text, that'll be the DEA agent letting me know they're downstairs."

Clay got up, "It's okay Levi, I'd hate for something to interrupt your team bonding I'll go down and get them. Hopefully by the time I get down there they will have cleared security."

Levi sighed and made his way over to the coffee machine, "unbelievable way to treat a colleague, if only the General was here to see this."

Joss spoke without even looking up, "Levi if he was you'd be filling up his mug as well and you know it. He'd say its character building now stop moaning and hurry up."

Ed was smiling, "you guys really do work well together don't you?"

Joss looked up and paused for a second, "to be honest the type of assignments we get sent on we'd fail most of the time if we didn't get on the way we do. There's no rivalry, we may be from a variety of organisations but the only way this works is if we work as one and so that's exactly what we do. We may joke and wind each other up every now and then but that's just the way we let off steam."

Joss saw Clay walking towards the conference room with the DEA agent in tow, he came into the room and closed the door. "Everyone this is Stevie Wells, the undercover DEA agent. Stevie I'll leave you

146

with them as I just need to sort out a few things but I'll be back shortly." Clay turned to the team, "start without me and I'll catch up in a bit." With that Clay did an about turn and left the room closing the door behind him.

Levi stood up and made his way around to Stevie. "I'll start the introductions, I'm Levi on assignment to the team from the DEA. I'll take you round the table and introduce you to the team."

As he said that Stevie started to look around the table and suddenly stopped, her eyes widened and before she could stop herself she exclaimed "Jarhead."

The room went silent and Scott smiled, "hello Stevie it's actually Scott, and before anyone says anything Stevie is the barmaid from the club last night." Scott looked straight at Danny, "so no need to start putting two and two together."

Danny feigned a shocked look, "I don't know why you're looking at me."

"I do," Joss said, "now can we please get back on track as this is kind of important and discussing Scott's conquests isn't on the agenda."

Scott sighed, "it's started already, Stevie please ignore them. I'm one of a number of military specialists within the team and I'll finish off what Levi tried to start before this lot took over." Five minutes later Stevie was sat down having been introduced to the whole team and given a brief insight as to what the team do and how.

Levi took over once more, "so Stevie you've seen the rough brief of what we're working on and we really don't want to blow your investigation out of the water. I'd never live it down and would probably be reassigned if we did and I certainly don't want that to happen as surprisingly I really like working with this bunch of misfits."

Stevie had a serious look on her face, "I get that but I'm not sure if the two investigations can work side by side. The second one of us makes a move it'll blow the cover of the other," She looked round the table, "I've been working on this for over six months now and we're fairly close to getting enough evidence to close the business down and make a bit of a dent in the cartels operation."

Joss now had a concerned look on her face, "we don't even know if what we're investigating is linked to either of these premises and all we've got is a tenuous link to some gang members that have been known to frequent either one or both."

147

"Well I can fill in some of the pieces for you, which is what I guess I'm here for." Stevie paused to get herself a coffee, she sat back down and carried on, "the gang you're looking into uses both premises. They move and distribute the drugs for the cartel. The strip club is used for the sale and distribution of large quantities and the smaller bar is for the smaller clients. From the little I know about what you're looking into the gang could easily be involved. In the past smuggling people across the border was one of their specialities and that's what got them linked in with the cartel so they are more than well enough connected to make someone disappear. The real concern I have is that we've been made aware of a new designer drug coming onto the market and from the intel we've gathered so far they're using this operation to launch it so we really don't want to blow this."

Ed now had the concerned look, "so what can you tell us about the gang? Do you think we could isolate them and deal with what we're looking into without wrecking what you're working on?"

Stevie shook her head, "I don't know, and to be honest that sort of question is way above my pay grade. I can tell you this much, the gang use two warehouses downtown. One is solely for the drugs and the other smaller one is for everything else the gang is involved in. Now from what I understand the cartel does know about the drug warehouse obviously but I think the gang have tried to keep the smaller one off the radar. I don't think they want the cartel knowing that they still dabble in all of the other activities as the cartel wouldn't be overly impressed. This is a large operation they have going on here and it's exceptionally profitable so they'd be less than impressed if they knew what the gang were up to."

At this point Clay came back into the room, "okay Stevie so I've just been brought up to speed by your Boss and I can understand with the DEA wants to protect what you're working on. Having said that we can't just ignore the fact that there is a possible link with the gang and what we're looking into. I've agreed that for the moment that we'll still let the DEA lead the investigation but if we confirm a definitive link then we'll have to reassess that and the powers that be will have to decide what direction to go in."

Joss took over, "Stevie, how far apart are the two warehouses? Could we move on the smaller warehouse without it affecting what's going on at the larger one?"

Stevie though for a few seconds and then nodded, "yes you could, they're about six blocks apart. If I'm honest I would think the cartel already know what the gang are doing but turn a blind eye as it doesn't interfere with their business. That may change if you do move in on the gang because logically you'd then connect them to the second warehouse which would then impact on the cartel."

Joss smiled, "well not necessarily, we could ignore the second warehouse and just focus solely on our investigation and ignore everything else. In the eyes of the cartel it would make us look incompetent but would leave everything in place still for your operation unless they got spooked and decided to play safe."

"I think they'd stay put as they've invested heavily into this and it works really well. With the new drug coming in they stand to make millions on top of what they already bring in and they've been working on this for some time so as they have so much in place already here I think they'd keep things going. From the exposure I've had to cartel members they are very sophisticated and clever and would not walk away from this unless they really had to. If you could keep it to just busting the smaller warehouse and ignore any evidence you find linking the two I think we'd possibly be okay. They might slow things down for a bit to play safe but that wouldn't be for long."

Clay jumped back in again, "right, so we keep it small and target the smaller warehouse only. Stevie can you give us everything you've got on the layout of the building etc."

"Sure, it's on the corner of the block with a small car park at the front with a small reception area. There's a larger car park and loading dock at the rear. On the side is a fire escape coming down from the second floor. This floor only extends halfway across so half of the warehouse is full height. They've got several rooms on the first and second floor some for storage but some set up as rooms they hold people in. Now we don't have an exact floor plan because there's absolutely no reason for me to go over there and so I've just pieced together bits of information from things I hear in the break room or things I overhear when I go into some of the meeting rooms at the back of the club."

The phone next to Joss started ringing and she picked it up, putting her hand over the mouthpiece she told everyone to carryon and she walked out of the office closing the door behind her. Stevie carried on walking through the layout of the warehouse giving as much detail as she could.

Within five minutes Joss was back in the room "That was Barney and I've just given him an update. Based on what we've found so far he's made a snap decision to swap things around a little. Ed, you and I are swapping teams and Cass, Jake and Drew will be joining this team. An FBI operation is going to be set up to hit the warehouse in order to see what can be found. It'll be restricted to the smaller warehouse only and anything that links the two buildings will be ignored. That should hopefully leave the DEA operation intact and able to continue. Stevie, Ed and I are leaving for the airport straight away. Can you continue to go through whatever you can with the guys but then I would suggest maybe staying away from here and we'll make sure your handler gives you an update on what's happened." Joss and Ed grabbed the few bits they had on the table and said their goodbyes and left the room.

Clay arranged for a driver to take them back to the airport and suggested that they took an hour or so to get some food and to chill out for a bit as they needed to wait for the others before deciding on the next move. There were still a few bits that Stevie felt she could add so it was agreed that she'd hang around until the other team members had been briefed in case they had any questions.

Just over five hours later they were all back in the room along with the new arrivals, with the introductions completed Clay continued with the meeting "So Cass I think you're pretty much up to speed and as you'll be taking the lead on this I'll now step back. I'll be with you and will work as the liaison between yourselves and the local PD as I know most of them."

"Thanks Clay, okay guys we'll split into three teams, Jake and I will take the front entrance, Scott you and Marcus will take the rear entrance, Drew and Danny you'll hang back. Danny you're unarmed but we'll need some help searching and I want to keep the Marshall Service and the local PD out of the way so that it really does appear to be purely and FBI operation." Drew and Danny nodded in unison. "Right, we'll clear the bottom floor first and then work as two teams to clear each room, as soon as we've cleared the first floor Drew you and Danny can enter and start searching the ground floor for intel. Scott we've got extra jackets and body armour for you and Danny, everyone else has already got their own. Any questions so far?"

Scott spoke first, "so when are we looking to go in?"

Cass shrugged her shoulders, "I'm not sure if there is a good time but we need a few hours to go over everything a few more times so at the earliest it'll be tomorrow morning at around ten. I want to use the daylight and the warehouse has a number of skylights so that should make things easier when we're searching. From what I can see they shouldn't be expecting anything and at that time of day we shouldn't encounter many people in the warehouse. I would think that most of the activity is out of hours apart from a few deliveries so mid-morning should be a pretty quiet time. That in mind we also need to be ready for any surprises which is why the local PD will be on standby just in case."

Clay spoke next, "the local guys are all good at what they do and would really like to push the gang out of the area. They realise that isn't likely to happen but they'll be happy that at least something is being done to upset them a little. The gang seem well connected and I guess that's as a result of the cartels influence in the area. To play it safe we're not releasing any information until the briefing in the hope that we can keep a lid on it."

Cass looked round the table, "we'll use two vehicles and approach the front and rear at the same time, standard rules apply on this one guys so do not fire unless fired upon. Remember we really don't want to engage with anyone. Ideally we'll be in an out before anyone knows about it. The issue is that I can't believe for a second that they won't have CCTV and as soon as we enter someone somewhere will know we are there. Local PD will create a hard perimeter which should give us the time we need but we are going to have to be quick, grab what you can. I can't emphasise enough that this needs to be quick and clean."

Clay leant forward in his chair, "I'll make sure that the perimeter is secure and we'll do everything we can to ensure that everyone is kept out. Looking at the street view it'll be easy to keep a cordon in place and no vehicles will be able to approach so you should hopefully have all the time you need. I am however aware as to how quickly things can change so I'll make sure that in the briefing tomorrow morning everyone knows exactly what's expected of them."

Cass looked round the table, "Okay everyone we're done for now, back here for seven in the morning, get some rest. The briefing will be at eight and we move out at nine to a holding position. Questions anyone?"

The room was silent, "right then, let's get out of here, Scott there's a present for you and you need to go and find Clay as he'll be looking after you for a few hours. Danny you might as well go with him. Right let's call it a day people and get some rest."

The door to Clay's office was open but Scott still knocked on the door anyway. "Come in guys," Clay pointed to a hard case that was leaning against the wall of his office, "that's for you Scott and we'll leave in five."

Scott picked up the case and laid it flat on one of the chairs. He opened the three clasps almost certain he knew what he'd find inside. Opening the lid sure enough he was greeted with a well warn but very well looked after M4, there were six magazines slotted into pre-cut sections of the foam padding along with six boxes of ammo. "It's assigned to me but as I'm going to be at the outer cordon all I'll need is my pistol. We've got a range we use ten minutes away and I just need to make a quick call and I'll be ready. I'll meet you both downstairs shortly."

Scott closed the lid and picked up the case, "roger that." he pushed Danny out of the door and they made their way to the lift, the rest of the team were coming out of the conference room with Cass leading them, she smiled, "Scott, word of advice, whatever you do don't underestimate that child when you're at the range."

Scott kept a straight face as he replied, "don't worry, I'm a good enough shot not to have to worry about that sort of thing" and before Cass could reply he stepped into the lift with Danny and the doors closed.

Scott turned to Danny, "you know she's never going to live that down."

Danny laughed, "I know, especially as I'll be reminding her every chance I get."

"You did well to beat her, I've shot against her a few times and she's not bad at all."

"Yeh I know and I didn't expect to beat her to be honest," Danny paused for a seconds, "but I'm really glad I did."

"Well Clay has got enough ammo in here for me to zero this in with enough rounds to enable me to see how well you do with this compared to a Glock, assuming Clay doesn't mind you using it at the range. We'll leave asking him until I'm finished and if he says no then when we're done I'll get Mitch or Jess to drop us at a marine Base for a couple of days and we'll use and abuse the facilities there."

152

Before Danny could answer the door opened and they stepped out into the foyer. Through the glass front doors they could see Clay sitting in his car waiting for them. They made their way out of the building and got into the car. The journey was short and they pulled up at a large brick building. The front had a few windows and a big sign declaring that it this was the place to come for all of your firearm needs and wants.

The three of them got out of the car and Clay opened the door for them. Danny and Scott went in and as soon as their eyes adjusted to the lights they could see that they were indeed in a huge shop filled with just about everything you could want for hunting or casual shooting. Rows and rows of clothing lined one side and then there were several rows of targets and ancillaries. A huge counter stretched down one wall with four sales staff behind it assisting customers. A member of floor staff came up to them and Clay showed his badge and stated they wanted to use the range for a short time. They were all ushered to a large door to one side and once through entered an area with a few benches to one side with a variety of cleaning kits on them. Two people had weapons stripped down and were in the process of giving them a thorough clean. Clay ushered them through another door and they entered the range. It wasn't too dissimilar to the range Danny had used when he was shooting against Cass.

The main difference was that it was considerably longer which allowed for the use of assault rifles and shotguns. Clay went to speak to a member of staff and returned with three pairs of ear defenders and some ballistic glasses. He also had a couple of extra boxes of ammo. "Danny, if there's any ammo left after Scott has zeroed it in your more than welcome to fire a few shots but it'll have to be under the guidance of one of us in order to meet the range rules."

Danny grinned, "that's absolutely fine and I've got no issues with that at all assuming Scott is okay with it."

Scott nodded, "that's fine by me Clay."

Scott put the case down in the first booth and removed the M4, he took out four mags and a box of ammo. He passed a mag to Danny, "fill those two for me, I should only need two and then you can fire two."

Clay handed Danny a box of ammo, "you can use that booth there to load the mags," nodding to the booth next to Scott. Danny put the mags down and opened the box. As he finished loading the second one he heard Scott fire the first sighting round having already sent a target down the range. Five minutes later Scot had reloaded after bringing the first target back. He had decided not to move the sights at all as the weapon was almost perfectly set up for him. He sent the second target down range and as soon as it was far enough away he worked his way through the second mag. It was set to single shot but even so Scott was ejecting the empty mag within seconds. He hit the switch to bring the target back to the booth and was happy with the results.

He'd split the mag and gone half and half with head shots and centre mass, the two groups were rather impressive and clearly showed that he knew what he was doing with this sort of weapon. He turned to Clay, "I'm more than happy with that so if you're happy Danny can fire two mags down range."

Clay didn't hesitate at all, "fine with me."

Scot stepped to one side and allowed Danny to move into the booth. He put the two mags he'd filled down and placed a fresh target on the pegs and sent it down to exactly the same spot that Scott had put his. He picked up the first mag and inserted it. He loaded the first round in and took the safety off with his thumb. Taking his time he emptied the mag into the target, following Scots example and putting half the mag into the centre mass and half into the head area. He'd taken longer than Scott but had counted the rounds. Flicking the safety on he dropped the empty mag out with a round still in the chamber and slotted the fresh mag in. He removed the safety once more and repeated the process. He hadn't worried about changing the target as it wasn't quite so important for him as he was just shooting for fun. He counted the rounds again and put the safety on once more when he'd fired the last round. He ejected the empty mag and placed the M4 down in front of him. Stepping back he allowed Scott to move in and hit the switch to bring the target back up.

Scott nodded, "that's pretty good, well done."

He took the target down and laid it next to his own. Danny had done well, his grouping was tight although not quite as tight as Scott's but still pretty good none the less. Scott put the M4 back in its case along with what was left of the ammo and closed the case.

Clay had been looking at the targets and was smiling, "well now I see why Cass was so shocked that you'd beaten her. That's probably a better grouping than I'd get. That's damn good shooting Danny."

154

"Thanks Clay," Danny seemed a little embarrassed, "I don't get a lot of chance to practice to be honest but when I do I listen to what I'm told and remember my training."

"Well it certainly pays off, that's impressive." Clay led them back out of the range and they headed back to the office so that Scott could put the M4 into the armoury for the night. Once done they all headed to the hotel bar for a drink and something to eat. They didn't hang around for long in the restaurant as they all wanted a good night's sleep before the early start.

Chapter 18

She opened her eyes, she'd slept quite well despite the initial problems getting off to sleep. The exercise and shower must have helped. She suddenly realised she'd gone to sleep naked, something he only usually did when she was in bed with someone else. Her body told her she needed to go to the loo so she got out of bed and went into the bathroom. When she came out there was a message on the screen, it simply said 'Amazing.' without realising it she said, "thank you," out loud. The screen responded with 'No, thank you.' She heard a soft click and knew the door had been unlocked again. She quickly grabbed some shorts and a t-shirt from a drawer and put them on.

She opened the door and breakfast was on the table but so was a box, quite large but plain. Moving over to the table she sat down and pulled the box towards her. Taking a deep breath she opened it and looked inside. The first thing she saw was two books. She'd read both before but it was still nice to have them. She found a couple of new t-shirts that would be really comfortable to sleep in. Although she enjoyed sleeping naked last night so she wasn't sure if she'd even use them. There was a large bottle of baby oil which she guessed was going to be a new part of her routine when she performing for the camera. She found a few magazines towards the bottom of the box. The usual sort of women's monthly glossy mags you'd find at every newsstand. Not really the sort of thing that she would normally read but to be honest but under the current circumstances she was grateful for anything to read. Especially if it allowed her a bit of an insight as to what was actually happening outside. Her mind briefly drifted to the outside world. She shuddered when she considered that she was feeling grateful for a monthly magazine to update her.

She shook her head slowly and looked into the box. All that remained was a small rectangular box, rather pretty and inviting. She took the box out and opened it up. Nestling neatly inside amongst some soft pink tissue was a bullet vibrator. With a bit of a blank look she took it out of the box. She knew exactly what it was as she'd owned quite a few over the years. She had found them a rather nice way to enhance and improve her masturbation technique. Under the circumstances though she didn't seem to have quite the same feelings of elation holding it in her hand.

She put it back in its box and took everything though to the bedroom and paced in on the bed. She went back in and sat back down at the table deciding to focus on breakfast. She started off with some fruit and yoghurt, her normal go to option for first thing in the morning. She had made a conscious decision to eat what she could when the opportunity arouse. Not that she'd been given any indication that food would be scarce, in fact so far her host, if she could bring herself to call them that, had been more than accommodating. She moved the cereal bowl to one side and picking up a side plate with a few pancakes on it and poured a decent helping of maple syrup over them.

Before she started to eat them she got up and went into the bedroom and grabbed one of the magazines. She thought that she might as well catch up on some gossip while she ate, even if it was the type of hype and rubbish she wouldn't normally concern herself with. If only it was a photography or nature magazine which is the type of thing she'd normally read. While sitting there eating she decided that she'd ask for some specific magazines and she started to make a mental list of the things to ask for. When she finished eating she sat there for a few minutes looking round the room. She had lost interest in the magazine as each page seemed to be filled with the same sort of thing and to her it wasn't that interesting at all. She sighed and stood up, pushing the chair back with her legs as she did so. She left the magazine on the table and went back into the bedroom. She sat on the bed for a few minutes wondering what to do next, her mind drifted back to the fact that whoever it was had seemed pleased with her performance and a thought entered her mind. What if she tried to use that to get things that she wanted. With that in mind she got up and went into the bathroom, she turned the shower. Removing her t-shirt and shorts she went back into the bedroom to get the new vibrator that she'd been given. Time to test her new idea and put on a show. She placed the

vibrator on the shelf in the shower and slowly covered herself in
bubbles. Taking care to make sure that she took her time she slowly
washed herself. Deliberately taking her time when it came to washing
her breasts. For her plan to work she needed to make sure that she
really did create a show that would please. Her hope was that if she did
a good enough job the reward would be greater. She slowly turned
around in the shower as she washed as she wasn't really sure where the
cameras were so she'd decided to ever so slowly rotate as she was
cleaning so that no matter what position they were in they'd capture
her.

She let the warm water cascade over her body to wash he soap off and
she was feeling nicely relaxed as she took the vibrator off the shelf. She
was in a good place and as a result the orgasm was natural and
occurred rather quickly. The familiar shudders flowing through her
body as she climaxed. She stayed in the shower for a further five
minutes enjoying the warm water flowing over her body. She finally
reached out and turned the shower off. The bathroom falling silent as
the soft noise of the droplets of water hitting the floor tiles came to a
stop. She stepped out of the shower cubicle and picked up the towel
that shed put on the towel rail to warm up, after drying herself off she
went through and sat on the bed. She let her mind wander for a few
minutes just daydreaming. She removed the towel and lay back on the
bed naked. Closing her eyes she took herself back to a few weeks
earlier when she was at college. She thought about how some days
she'd been struggling with the workload and had wondered if it was
worth the effort.

She sat up suddenly, how had it come to this? Effectively a prisoner
god knows where forced into performing for god knows who? The
anger started to rise, she could feel herself getting more and more
agitated. Up until now she'd managed to convince herself to remain
calm and to go with the flow after all no one was getting hurt and as
yet she hadn't been asked to do anything that she didn't already do.
Doing those things in her apartment was one thing, performing in
front of a camera was something completely different. She wanted
answers, she looked around the room "Why am I here?" She waited for
the now familiar response to appear on the screen, there was nothing,
"come on talk to me, why have you got me locked up?" She waited
again but still nothing, she'd never been ignored before, the screen had
always almost instantly come alive with a response. With her anger

rising she quickly got dressed, it was as much of a protest as she could manage. After all she knew that every room had multiple cameras so she could go and hide anywhere so it suddenly dawned on her that her only way to protest was to cover up.

Now fully clothed she sat down on the bed, her mind racing, she'd lost all of her composure in just a few minutes. The realisation that she was being held captive dominating her thoughts. It wasn't really news to her considering her surroundings, she'd worked it out straight away. She'd tried to remain positive and as she hadn't actually been in any danger, she'd allowed herself to go with the flow. Now her state of mind had suddenly shifted, she didn't deserve this and whoever was doing this to her had no right to take away her freedom. She paced round the bedroom a few times before stopping at the screen, "why are you doing this to me?" She could hear the anger in her own voice.

Suddenly the screen came into life, 'I would have thought that was obvious.'

She stared at it for a few seconds, "no, it's far from obvious and I want to know what's going on, why are you doing this to me."

'Well, that's a very easy question to answer, simply because I can.'

She looked away from the screen and stared at the camera in the corner, "what do you mean? I'm not an object or possession. I'm a person and you've got no right to keep me here against my will," she could feel herself losing control as the anger inside her became more intense, she sat on the bed to try to calm herself down.

'As you've asked what I mean I'll explain it to you. It's quite simple really, I can do whatever I want with you as I own you.'

Phoebe stared blankly at the screen, her mind racing, she understood the words but couldn't put them into context, "nobody owns me and I'm a free person."

The response on the screen was almost instant 'Really? Look around you, how free do you feel?'

Instinctively she looked around. "I don't understand."

'What don't you understand, I would have thought by now things would have been obvious.'

"I want answers not riddles," her voice had a much harder edge to it now and the anger was really beginning to show.

'Then answers you shall have, but first how much do you want to know?'

159

Phoebe didn't hesitate, "everything, I want to know what the hell is going on." The screen went blank, she waited but nothing happened, the voice made her jump.

"I'll tell you everything but first I need to know that you really do want to hear it?"

Phoebe could tell it wasn't a young voice, it seemed to be coming from all around her. She instinctively looked around even though she knew that she was alone in the room. She hesitated before speaking, hearing a human voice for the first time for several days had unnerved her a little, "I do want to hear it. You have to tell me what's going on."

"This wasn't how I intended to introduce myself to you however we don't always get what we want in life as I'm sure you're aware. In a nutshell you're mine to do with as I please, I own you."

Phoebe looked stunned, "what the hell do you mean you own me?"

"Exactly that, I own you. I paid a significant amount of money to have a particular person delivered to me. Somebody that met the specifications that I'd given and that someone is you."

Phoebe sat still for a moment trying to take in what she'd just heard, "you .... you can't buy people," her voice was faltering, and she suddenly felt unsure about everything. Her mind was trying to comprehend what she'd just heard.

"Oh I can and I have, I paid a pricey sum for you and you're mine to do with as I please. Up till now I've been nice and I've respected you but that can change."

Phoebe noticed a sudden harshness in the voice, a definite change in tone that suddenly made her feel very vulnerable. She looked around and for the first time didn't see the room as a bedroom she saw it for what it really was, a prison cell. She stared at the screen, it was blank, and she suddenly had trouble thinking as her mind was racing. She couldn't take in what she'd just heard, she heard a noise and turned around in a panic, there was nothing there. She realised the noise was her heartbeat and it was racing.

"I suggest you calm down, have a drink of water and try to relax, we'll talk again as soon as I think you're ready."

"No," Phoebe hadn't realised she shouted, she took a couple of deep breaths, "no, I want to know what's happening here." Her voice much calmer this time although she was still struggling to comprehend what she'd just heard.

"You're my guest Phoebe, I have certain needs and desires and as soon as they are fulfilled you'll be free to go. As long as you meet those needs then everything will be fine."

Phoebe hesitated before she spoke, "and if I don't meet those needs?"

There was a pause before he replied, "if that was the case I'd have no use for you and I'd get rid of you." The cold edge was back in his voice

Her eyes open in shock, "what do you mean get rid of me?" She could hear the concern in her own voice.

"When you have no use for something you discard it, you throw it away. I would hate to have to discard you Phoebe so let's hope it doesn't come to that."

Phoebe stared at the screen, even though there were no words on it she didn't know where else to look. Her mouth was open and her eyes wide, "when you say discard me, you mean let me go?"

"No," the voice now had a menacing tone about it, "I would simply kill you Phoebe, if I have no use for you then there's no need to keep you alive."

Phoebe tried to speak but she couldn't find the words, the world suddenly came crashing down around her "But...... I ......" No matter how hard she tried there were so many thoughts flashing through her mind that she couldn't put a meaningful sentence together. She looked around the room, the sudden realisation that she was a prisoner hit her. Even though ever since she'd come to in the room she'd known she wasn't free at no time did she look at it from the perspective of actual being held against her will. Perhaps it was something that she'd subconsciously avoided thinking about. Now that had changed, her whole world had changed and she was suddenly angry.

"It's a lot for you to take in so I'll leave you for a while." The steely edge had gone from the voice and been replaced with a tone that was a lot more caring "have something to eat and we'll talk again shortly, I'm sure you'll have some questions."

"I've got questions now," Phoebe snapped in reply.

"No, eat and then we'll talk," as if to enforce the order the door to the dining area clicked, a noise that Phoebe now knew that indicated the door was open.

The click made Phoebe jump and she turned to look at the door, she didn't move. She'd known that she wasn't free to go anywhere. That had been obvious from the moment she awoke but to have someone tell her that she was their property to do with as they please was something that she hadn't really been prepared for. She sat on the bed for five minutes before standing up, she knew she was hungry and despite the fact that she was trying to come to terms with what she'd just heard she needed to eat.

She opened the door and walked into the dining area, the food had been laid out for her along with several drinks. She looked at the table, realising that one of the things that had made her feel less of a prisoner had been the food. It was restaurant quality, everything was perfectly cooked, even the sandwiches looked above average. Maybe that was one of the things that had fooled her mind into not seeing things as they really were. She looked around, still unable to even begin to contemplate the reality of the words she'd listened to she sat down.

She picked up a sandwich from the plate and then put it back down again. She could feel her heart racing again, she took a sip of water and tried to calm her breathing down. After a minute or two she felt a little calmer and forced herself to focus on the here and now. She was desperately searching for the rational part of her brain to take over and to make some sense of this. No matter how hard she tried all she could hear in her head was 'I would simply kill you Phoebe' She was annoyed with herself for having not realised sooner the predicament that she was in. How could she have just gone along with everything over the last few days without questioning it. She felt disgusted with herself, she'd openly played with herself in front of a camera several times for the entertainment of some sick pervert. Her body brought her back into reality, the smell of the food in front of her making her aware once again just how hungry she was. She selected a few sandwiches, some salad, a few tomatoes and filled her glass up with water.

As she ate she tried to replay the conversation once again in her head but she kept coming back to the same short sentence every time. The way he'd said it with such a matter of fact tone, almost as if it didn't bother him at all. Phoebe put the tomato she was eating down, the realisation suddenly hitting her. It didn't matter to him if she lived or died, she was a prisoner and she either did what he wanted or he'd kill her. She felt sick, she took a drink of water and closed her eyes trying to force herself to remain calm. She wasn't doing a very good job, she could feel her heart beating faster again. She opened her eyes and tried to relax, taking deep breaths in through her nose and pausing before exhaling through her mouth. She did this until the nauseous feeling left her. She looked at the food on her plate, realising that she couldn't eat anything she pushed the plate away from her.

Standing up she grabbed two bottles of water and a couple of pieces of fruit for later, she knew that when she went back though the door she'd hear a click as the door locked and she knew that she'd need something to eat later. At least part of her brain was thinking clearly she thought. Sure enough as the door closed behind her she heard the click as it locked. She put the water and fruit down on the side and laid down on the bed. Why did I have to ask she thought to herself, if only I'd kept quiet things would be so much better. She stared at the ceiling and accepted the fact that her brain was telling her that the reality was that even if she hadn't said anything the situation she was in would have been no different. She was a prisoner and had little or no control over what was happening. What had she done wrong in life she wondered, there was no answer.

For an hour or so she laid on the bed desperately trying to make sense of what was happening. She wasn't a stupid girl and always considered herself to be quite sensible but no matter how hard she tried she couldn't come to terms with what she'd heard. She tried to be rational and to lay out the facts in simple terms but the only facts she kept coming back to were two points, she was a prisoner and he'd threatened to kill her if he had no use for her. What did he mean by that? If he was going to kill her why hadn't he done that already? Gradually she started to put a few pieces of the puzzle together. He hadn't killed her because she was giving him something. The shows that she'd put on in front of the camera was what he wanted, he was simply some do sort of freak that got off on watching women perform.

She looked round the room, her mind was racing, struggling to take in what she'd just heard. She replayed the conversation once again in her head, she looked around the room again beginning to understand what this meant. She stood up slowly and made her way back to the bed, before she laid down she looked at the camera, "please don't lock the door, I will go back to eat some more but I just need a few minutes to try to get my head round what you've just said."

"That's okay Phoebe, I'll leave the door unlocked until you tell me otherwise," with that door unlocked itself once more.

"Thank you."

She lay down on the bed and fought to control her breathing. Closing her eyes she focused, slowing breathing in through her nose and pausing before exhaling through her mouth. After a couple of minutes she felt better and was able to open her eyes. Her mind now no longer racing she felt that she was back in control once more. She sat up, realising that she was still hungry, getting off the bed she made her way back into the dining room. She sat down once again and started to eat while she considered her next move. Which in light of what she'd just been told was limited to either complying with what was expected or die.

The rational part of her brain was working overtime as she tried to process what this meant to her. In reality so far, despite being imprisoned, she hadn't really had to do anything that she hadn't already done hundreds of times on her own. Okay so now it was in front of a camera and she was restricted to a couple of rooms but that wouldn't last forever, would it? She decided to take one step at a time and the first thing she needed to do was make sure that she finished eating. With a renewed focus she carried on eating allowing her mind to simply wander as she forced herself to look around the room taking in every detail as if it was the first time she'd seen it. This she decided was her coping strategy, when things got on top of her she'd do some deep breathing and then just concentrate on describing everything in the room to herself.

It worked to a degree, she managed to finish eating what she wanted and picked up an unopened bottle of water taking it back into the bedroom. A shower next she decided, not because she felt the need to perform but because she felt she needed to refresh herself. She undressed in the bedroom and walked through to the shower. She washed herself thoroughly, not in a pleasurable way, she did play to the camera in as much as she rotated herself as she washed so that he could get a good look at her body. By the end of the shower she had regained some of her confidence, drying herself she made her way back into the bedroom and put on a pair of knickers and a loose-fitting t-shirt. She lay on the bed and allowed herself to drift off to sleep.

Chapter 19 (North America)

Bright and early next morning having had a fairly decent breakfast at the hotel Cass and her team were all stood on the sidewalk outside Phoebes apartment block. On the way they'd decided that the first thing they needed to do was to see what they could spot from the outside. They were hoping to find at least one camera that had a view of the entrance. They had however already managed their own expectations knowing that whoever the mystery woman was would have probably have taken this into account already and they didn't hold out much hope. The apartment block was one of four in a row and on the street opposite were a number of smaller brownstone buildings. It would have been helpful if there'd been a few shops nearby as they often have cameras but sadly it wasn't to be.

They made their way into the building and up to the apartment. They had already discussed what they were going to do and in the first instance they were simply going to walk round the apartment without touching anything. They needed to catch a break with this and felt that firstly they'd all make independent notes regarding what they saw in the hope that one of them may see something that helps.

They split up and took a room each, every room was clean and tidy, everything had its place and Phoebe was clearly a very organised person. She obviously took pride in what she did, that was clear from simply walking around the rooms. They made notes as they went so that they could compare their observations a little later. Once they'd completed the walk round they split into two groups and started on the first two rooms. They went for the kitchen and main bedroom first as they hoped that these two rooms might give them something to go on as they were probably the two most used rooms in the apartment.

Cass and Kelly took the kitchen between them, again they made notes and took pictures as they checked the cupboards and drawers. Kelly opened the fridge door and looked over the shelves for a few seconds, "I think we can definitely count out the fact that she may have gone away for a few days."

Cass stopped what she was doing, "what makes you so sure?"

"Well there are just too many items of food that are out of date, look around the apartment. Phoebe took pride in this place and I don't think for one second she'd allow herself to have a fridge full of out of date food and drink. It just doesn't fit with how she keeps the place."

Cass made her way over to the fridge, sure enough the bread, fruit juice, pastrami and milk were clearly well past their sell by date. She imaged several items and took a step back. "Although not quite enough on its own I think this is a fairly definitive indicator that she hadn't intended to go away. You're right she wouldn't have gone to the trouble of buying half of this stuff if she had plans to go away."

They carried on for the next few hours making sure that they documented everything as they went. Boyd had left the others to it and had made his way back outside the apartment again. He was determined to try and find something outside that would assist them in finding out what happened to her. Having spent the last few hours going through her apartment with a fine tooth comb Boyd felt a personal attachment to Phoebe and was determined to do everything he could to help find out what happened. He took a few steps back and started to scan the apartment block window by window, once he'd done that he made his way round the back. He followed the same process again taking several pictures for later use although he hadn't seen anything with the naked eye.

The others were still searching so he crossed the street to look at the block from further away, he still didn't see anything of use but still took a few more pictures, this time from a slightly different perspective. As he took the last one a resident came out of the front door of the brownstone behind him. The man was in his fifties and stopped to look at Boyd for a moment before speaking, "can I help you?"

Boyd flashed his badge, "sorry, we're investigating the possible disappearance of one of the residents of the apartment block opposite and I was just taking a couple of reference photos from this side of the street."

The man shook his head, "nasty business, the Police were going door to door and asking questions two days ago. I couldn't help at all, I know the girl by sight, seen her several times but never to speak to." He paused for a second and sighed, "nasty business," he said again. "She looked like such a nice girl too, damn shame."

Boyd smiled, "well we'll do everything we can to find her."

The man's face softened, "good, I'm glad someone is looking out for her." With that he sighed again and started walking down the street. Boyd turned to face the apartment block once again. He had one last look and then started to cross back over to make his way up to the others feeling a little disappointed that he hadn't found anything at all that was helpful. He'd got halfway across when he heard someone call out. He turned round to see the same man he'd just been talking to coming back down the street. He had his hand up as if he was trying to make Boyd aware that it was him that had called out.

"Excuse me," the man was a little out of breath now, "just then you said that you were doing everything you could to find her, well that made me think of what I could do to help."

Boyd took a breath before saying anything, in his experience with this type of investigation he had always found that a number of supposed helpful people had come forward with information that was of no use whatsoever. He was always a little apprehensive when people came forward to volunteer information, even so he smiled, "yes I did and we will do everything we can."

"Well, have you looked to see if our camera caught anything?"

Boyd looked blank for a second, "what camera?" He was sure he hadn't seen one when he'd looked at the front of the brownstone, it was one of the first things he'd looked for.

"It's behind the glass above the front door, we had it installed a few months ago as one of the residents was having trouble with an ex-partner who was on a bit of a vendetta and was damaging their car. The camera was put in to catch them in the act so that the Police could prosecute."

Boyd spun round and looked above the door, he still couldn't see anything. He took a couple of steps closer to the door and suddenly the unmistakable outline of a camera could be seen behind the glass. Boyd cursed himself for not having seen it but was now rather grateful that the man had come back down the street to speak to him.

"If you like I can let you in to speak to the Super, she lives in one of the ground floor apartments."

Boyd nodded, "yes please that would be great, do you know if it's on all the time?"

"I think it is, well that's what we all agreed when we discussed everything before installing it. We were concerned that if it wasn't recording all the time we'd miss something."

They made their way inside the building and the man knocked on the door to the first apartment on the left, a few seconds later a well-dressed woman opened the door.

"Hello Cynthia, this young man is investigating the disappearance of the girl from the building opposite and I mentioned to him that we have a camera that, if they're lucky may have something stored on it."

"Oh," she suddenly looked a little sheepish, "I didn't think to mention that to the Police when they were here the other day, do you think it'll help?"

Boyd thought for a split second, "we're grateful for any assistance anyone can offer, can I send someone round to copy any footage that you have for the past few weeks?"

"Of course, but if you want I can give you a copy right now. I have a backup copy in a safe that you can take with you as long as you can return it to me."

"That would be great, before I take it can I have a look at what the camera is capturing right now?"

"Yes, sorry how rude of me please come in." She took a step back and Boyd went in, "you might as well come in as well Stan and I'll make you a coffee," she turned to face Boyd again, "would you like one."

"Oh, that's really nice of you but my colleagues are still searching the apartment across the road and I need to get back to help them."

"That's okay, Stan you'll have to wait a second while we go and get the backup."

Boyd followed Cynthia along the hallway and into a room. It was setup as a home office, a computer with two screens and a half decent looking printer next to them. She opened the safe and withdrew a hard drive. "This has got the last two months on it, unfortunately we only keep two months at a time so hopefully they'll be something of use on there." She turned the screen on and sat down. After a few seconds the live feed from the camera was being displayed on the screen in front of Boyd. "As you can see it's really setup to catch what's going on in front of our building but you can see the block across the road although I don't know how useful it'll be."

The quality wasn't too bad and Boyd could make out a fair bit of detail of the block Phoebe lived in, he smiled, "that's great and I'll get a copy done as soon as I can and will get this back to you."

Cynthia passed the hard drive to Boyd, "no rush, as long as we get it back."

"You will do I can assure you, I'll leave you both to your coffee and thank you for your help."

Boyd made his way back across to the apartment and made his way upstairs to the others. They were just finishing off and wee about ready to leave. Cass tuned as Boyd entered the room, "find anything?"

Boyd held up the hard drive, "the last two months footage from a camera mounted above the door in the brownstone opposite. The view isn't great but it may give us something to work with. We'll never pick out a usable image of any facial features but it may give us some sort of timeline."

"Okay let's get back to the office with everything we've got and make a start on going through it all."

Kelly looked at Cass, "why don't we grab a coffee and something to eat while we discuss who does what next."

"Great idea, we'll go to the diner near the Police station as we have to pass it on the way back."

Less than thirty minutes later they were sat down in the diner, food ordered and drinks in front of them. Jake took a sip of his coffee, "Cass how do you want to do this?"

"Well I think Boyd should run with the new footage that we've got and make a start at going through that. We'll all compare notes and start to catalogue the images we've got and see if we can possibly piece something together. I've got to be brutally honest though and say that at first glance I don't think that we have anything that's going to help."

Kelly spoke up, "the only thing I've taken from this morning is that I don't think she planned to leave to go anywhere. The feeling I get from what I've seen is that she was well organised and structured, she wouldn't have all that food in the fridge if she was intending to go somewhere."

"I agree," Cass thought for a second, "it seems as though we're no further ahead other than more or less confirming that she seems to have been taken."

That statement seemed to dampen the mood a little although they hadn't really expected to find much. Their food arrived and while they were eating they all used the time to catch up with messages and emails on their phones. An hour later they were all back in the office feeling a little better after having eaten something. Boyd had managed to find a large monitor that he'd now attached to his laptop and was starting to review the footage from the brownstones CCTV. The others began the somewhat laborious task of going through the images making sure they were stored in the correct folders. They had to check each one first to make sure they hadn't missed anything first time round.

It was slow going and the minutes turned into hours. Three hours later and none of them had found anything new. They'd had several breaks and a few coffees and were beginning to feel a bit frustrated Cass closed the lid of her Mac, "guys I'm going to stretch my legs and call Barney to give him an update, won't take me long at all really," the others could hear the frustration in her voice.

Jake stood up, "while you're doing that Cass I'll call Joss and get an update on how her team is doing."

"Okay everyone let's take five and all stretch our legs, we'll come back and do another couple of hours before calling it a day."

Everyone stood up glad for the opportunity to take a break, this was the hardest part of any investigation and the hours they'd put in so far hadn't yielded anything at all and it was already beginning to feel like a waste of time and in real terms they'd only just started. A short break was what they all needed and they left the office to stretch their legs. Cass walked round the block while giving Barney and update and Jake did the same but went in the opposite direction. The hustle and bustle on the street was quite nice and Jake enjoyed the distraction as he paused for a few minutes before walking back into the Police station.

It was clearly a busy time of day as there seemed to be a near constant stream of officers going in and out. Jake guessed it must be a shift change because it was way too busy for it to be the norm. He made his way back up to the office they were using. He was the first back so he went and got himself another coffee. That was one of the good things about being in a Police station, a near constant supply of half decent coffee. He stopped for a few minutes to catch up with a detective that he'd briefly spoken with earlier in the day. As he got back to the office the others arrived and seeing him with a fresh coffee they all went to get themselves one.

When they were all back in the office Cass updated them with the information Barney had passed on. Jake then gave them an update on how Joss and her team were doing. All in all so far neither team seemed to be doing very well at all. With fresh coffee and with a new sense of optimism after their short break they agreed to continue for another couple of hours. After about thirty minutes they all regretted that decision as the tedious nature of what they were doing crept back in.

Suddenly Boyd let out a triumphant, "yes" everyone stopped what they were doing and looked at him, "sorry guys, I've just found what I believe to be the first sighting of Phoebe and the mystery woman. Annoyingly the resolution isn't anywhere near good enough to ID her but it's definitely Phoebe and I'm fairly sure it looks like the woman from the coffee shop."

"Okay make a copy of that section and let's see if we can build a picture of what happened and a timeline of sorts."

"Will do," Boyd had a more positive tone in his voice now and continued to watch with renewed interest. Within the hour he had three instances of them coming and going. They had now all agreed to carry on in the hope that they found something that would lead to a breakthrough. Forty minutes later he had another section of footage showing them both arriving at the apartment and an instance of the mystery woman leaving on her own. He carried on looking for another forty minutes and then stopped.

"Cass, I think I've found something that doesn't seem to make much sense."

Cass stopped what she was doing and came round the table to sit next to Boyd "Okay what have you got?"

Boyd played her every clip that he'd found so far, "now this is the last clip I have of them arriving together and then about two hours later the mystery woman leaves by herself. The thing is there's nothing after that and I've gone through the next day and a half."

"Right so what have we got so far?"

Boyd looked at the files he'd created. "Three instances of them coming and going together, four instances of Phoebe leaving and coming back on her own then this instance of them arriving together and the woman leaving alone."

The others now stopped what they were doing and crowded round the screen Boyd was using.

"Play the last clip of them arriving and the woman leaving," Boyd opened the first clip and clicked on the play button, everyone watching could see the pair of them walking into shot laughing as they walked, Phoebe opened the door and they both walked in. A minute or so later the light comes on in an upper window. The camera angle doesn't get the whole window just the bottom part but enough to show that someone had just turned a light on. Boyd leant forward, "by my reckoning that the front room window of Phoebes apartment, now here's the clip showing the woman leaving." He clicked play and they saw the front door open and the mystery woman steps out and walks down the street and out of the frame.

Jake leant forward, "Boyd can you play that last clip again but go back a minute or so before she walks out of the door."

It took Boyd a few seconds to get to the right point and he then once again he clicked on the play button. There wasn't any audio to listen to but the room was silent as they all intently watched the screen. They didn't see anything else that helped and Cass turned to Jake, "why did you want to see that bit?"

"The light isn't on anymore in the front room and I wanted to see when it went off."

Boyd took the footage back another couple of minutes and clicked play once again, this time the light was on in the window and almost instantly it went out. "It's almost as if she turned the light off before leaving."

Drew joined in, "it could have been Phoebe turning it off though."

Jake shook his head, "yes possibly but if Phoebe was in the apartment when the woman left I'd expect the light to stay on till she went to bed and turned it off."

Kelly spoke up, "let's not get ahead of ourselves here and make something out of nothing. I know that we're desperate to get a step ahead but before we start trying to fill in the blanks we need to make sure they're the right bits we're adding."

Cass nodded, "I agree, let's get a coffee. Boyd I'll get yours can you set it up to play from the minute they arrive and we'll watch the whole thing real time until the woman leaves."

Five minutes later they were all back, this time they'd moved their seats round, closed the door to the office and turned the lights off so that they could see more detail on the screen. Cass put her coffee down, "okay Boyd let's see what we've got." Once again Boyd clicked on the play icon and the clip started.

They watched intently as the two women came into the shot from the left and made their way to the door of the apartment block, Phoebe pauses for a second, presumably to get her keys out and open the door. The resolution wasn't good enough to be able to zoom in far enough to see any clearer so they carry on watching. The light comes on in the top right of the screen and then nothing else happens other than a few vehicles driving past. After that a couple walking their dog and a delivery driver dropping off a pizza to a resident in the next block along. Just over an hour later after a couple of pauses and a coffee refill they see what looks like two college students arriving carrying a heavy sports bag between them. They press a buzzer and a few second later open the door and go in, they watch the screen for another five minutes and Jake asks Boyd to pause it.

"So did anyone notice anything after they went in." Jake looked round the group, nobody said anything, "if you watch the clip again you'll see that no other lights come on in the windows after they've gone in. Now assuming all the apartments are laid out the same they've either gone straight into someone's bedroom or they've gone to Phoebes apartment. The kitchen isn't really big enough for those two and the owner of the apartment to be in. Now I could be wrong but to me it looks like they've gone to the one apartment with a light on in the living room."

Boyd set the clip running again and just over forty minutes later the same two men come out still carrying the sports bag, they walk off back in the direction they came from. Twenty minutes after that the light goes off, a few minutes later the mystery woman comes out of the front door of the apartment block. She walks off in the same direction as the two men that had just left.

Jake sat back in his chair "I have no idea what we've just seen but it seems a little too coincidental that they leave and a short while later the woman leaves."

Kelly looked at Jake, "I agree but there's not enough to really link the two together. They could have gone to another apartment, though unlikely bearing in mind what we've just seen, it's still possible."

Cass stood up, "let's leave it there and get something to eat, we'll review the footage again tomorrow and hopefully get a fresh perspective on it." They all agreed and went about putting the office back as it was and closing their laptops and Macs down. Once done they made their way down to the car and made their way to the diner again. They'd decided to go back there as the food wasn't at all bad and it was conveniently placed and meant they didn't need to go too far out of their way. They didn't talk as much as they did during their previous visit. They were more interested in eating and the toll of scanning photos and watching CCTV footage had dampened their enthusiasm a little. It didn't help that despite having got some half decent footage they weren't really any closer at all to piecing together what had happened to Phoebe.

Over drinks in the hotel bar they agreed to start again early in the morning and to review everything they had so far and feeling a little despondent they all agreed on an early night.

Chapter 20 (Europe)

The flight to Berlin was nice and straightforward with absolutely no delays at all. They collected the keys from the rental desk and Katie drove them to the address they had for Josef, it was a forty five minute drive from the airport and they made good time. They had one slight issue when the Satnav took them down a country lane that became a dead end but a short while later they pulled into the driveway that led up to Josef's property. It was a large country house with immaculate gardens running the whole length of the driveway, they pulled up outside the house and got out.

Alek looked around, "well this is where I'd want to retire, just look at it." No matter where he looked everything was just perfect, the lawn, the flowers and the house itself.

Katie made her way to the front door, "it is rather impressive."

Before she could ring the bell the door was opened by a young girl in a nurse's uniform, "good morning, my name is Trude and I'm one of the nursing team tending to Josef. He's asleep right now but should wake shortly. Won't you please come in." Alek and Katie followed Trude into a large hallway with an elegant sweeping staircase off to the left. Trude closed the front door behind them and then led them into a large drawing room that was, not surprisingly, elegantly decorated.

"I apologise for the fact that he isn't awake but we let him sleep whenever he wants and I'd rather not wake him. He's fairly weak and needs all the sleep he can get to keep his strength up."

Katie smiled, "please don't apologise, we should be the ones to do that and I can assure you we wouldn't bother him unless it was absolutely necessary."

"That's Okay, can I get you a drink while you wait?"

Alek nodded, "yes please."

"I'll bring a selection through and then you can both choose." With that the nurse turned round and left the room. Alek moved over to the window and looked out. The garden to the rear of the property seemed to be endless and similar to the grounds at the front was picture perfect. Katie was looking at the artwork on the walls. "These look like the originals." she exclaimed looking at them admiringly "They are." came a deep guttural voice from the doorway.

Both Katie and Alek turned to see a smartly dressed thirty something man standing in the doorway "Good morning, I'm Karl Josef's nephew."

Katie stepped forward, "hello Karl, I'm Katie and this is Alek."

"Alek, my uncle has spoken about you, I think you met him previously."

Alek tried to hide his surprise, "yes, I met him with one of my colleagues."

"He has told me everything, I would like to thank you for the time you have invested in him. After he'd spoken to you he seemed to be a changed man and it was as if a huge weight had been lifted off his shoulders. As you can imagine the events he described to you is something the family would dearly love to put behind us."

Katie decided not to beat around the bush and to take a direct approach, "I take it from your tone that you're not happy we're here and I can understand that but before you ask us to leave we really could do with speaking to Josef once more."

"Ideally I would like you to leave however my Uncle would never forgive me if he knew that I'd turned you away and I will respect his wishes. I would ask though that you keep everything to an absolute minimum. He isn't well and I fear that he doesn't really have very long left with us and I most certainly don't want him to be interrogated and put under any stress."

"Karl we aren't here to put him under any stress at all," Katie's voice had softened, "we value the information he has provided and simply have a couple of questions relating to the friend that he put us in contact with."

"I appreciate that but I'm sure you understand that I do not wish for my uncle to be in any more discomfort than he already is. I worry that reliving his experience may well be distressing for him." There was a distinct edge to Karl's voice.

Katie jumped in again, "Karl it is not our intention to talk through the events. The questions we have don't relate to the event in anyway," she kept her voice as soft as possible to try to remove some of the obvious anger that Karl was experiencing.

The mood was further softened by the arrival of the nurse pushing a drinks trolley. Karl turned to the nurse, "Trude please extend every courtesy to our guests and ensure that they leave having every question they have answered." The nurse didn't reply she simply nodded her head to show that she'd understood. With that Karl left without saying another word.

Trude pushed the drinks trolley into the centre of the seating area "Karl is very protective of his uncle and the family are understandably in shock and ashamed of Josef's actions."

Katie's face softened, "we can understand that and I assure you we are here with the best intentions and have absolutely no desire to make Josef relive the events."

"I know, I spoke to him before he went to sleep and he was keen to see you. He sees any little bit of assistance he can offer as a positive and a step nearer to absolution," she stepped back from the trolley, "please help yourselves and as soon as Josef is awake I will come and get you. Feel free to walk in the gardens should you choose to. I have no idea how long it'll be before he does wake up. If you do go outside please take the phone on the trolley with you and I will call it should he wake up while you're outside."

"Thank you Trude."

"My pleasure and enjoy." With that the nurse turned around and walked out of the door closing it behind her.

Alek spoke first, "I can see where Karl is coming from and I guess the old school German upbringing is what makes his attitude seem a little hostile and direct."

Katie walked over to the drinks trolley, "I get it too, and in a way I sympathise with him." She poured two coffees and passed one to Alek. As they enjoyed their coffee they wandered the room looking at the various bits of artwork, the books in the rather extensive bookcase and the various ornaments, "there's no shortage on money in this room."

Alek had to agree, "I'd say it runs into the millions in this room alone."

They finished their coffees and put the empty cups on the trolley, Alek picked up the phone, "let's go and enjoy the garden rather than sit in here." Alek opened the double doors that led out to the garden area and was greeted with a wonderful burst of floral scents as he did so. For forty minutes they admired the structured gardens finding a secret path that led to a wonderful hidden water feature. The phone rang in Alek's pocket, he answered it and listened for a second, "thank you Trude," he put the phone back in his pocket, "Josef is awake and eager to see us."

Katie turned away from the statue she'd been admiring, "shame I could spend hours out here."

"Me too but I don't want to outstay our welcome."

They walked back up to the house to find Trude waiting for them. The drinks trolley had vanished, so Alek gave her the phone, "thank you, please follow me," she turned and went through the doors and up the staircase. Following her they both admired the art on the walls as they ascended, they followed Trude to the second room on the first floor. She opened the door and stood to one side so that they could enter. As soon as they were both through the door she closed it behind them.

The bedroom was incredibly spacious. Two large bay windows sat either side of a very large comfortable looking bed. Josef was propped up on pillows and looked a little lost in the centre of the bed, "Alek, so nice to see you," the look on Josef's face was one of genuine happiness. Alek moved towards the bed, two chairs had been placed beside the bed. "Please do sit down, how are you? How is Cass?"

Alek smiled, "I'm fine Josef and Cass is doing well. She's currently in America at the moment following up on a lead over there."

"That's wonderful, and who is this?" Josef was looking directly at Katie.

"Hello Josef my name is Katie."

"French if I'm not mistaken, from your looks and accent I'd say at some point your family was from a French Colony."

Katie was more than a little surprised, "well..... yes they were."

"An old trick, I used to study accents and would take great delight during meetings to demonstrating my talent. Well enough about my now useless abilities how can I help you both?"

"Well we have a few questions but I can assure you we don't need to go over anything you've told us. This is more about any extra information you may have regarding your friend Frederik and maybe any other friends you spoke to or referred," Alek had tried to be as direct as he could.

"Frederik spoke with you? Oh that is good, he can be a bit of a challenge at times and I wasn't sure if he would meet with you. I do hope he was as forthcoming as I was," Josef had a bit of excited tone in his voice.

Katie lent forward slightly in her chair, "yes he did but we were wondering if there was anyone else that you may have spoken to about this."

"No, the only one I ever trusted was Frederik. I believe that he may have spoken to a couple of his close friends. He moved in far bigger financial circles than I did."

Alek looked around and thought about what he'd seen of the house so far. "He didn't mention anything when we spoke to him but I have to admit I didn't ask him the question when we saw him."

"Ahh then there's your mistake Alek, Frederik isn't inclined to give you any more information than you ask for. He would never volunteer any details unless you asked or were paying for them."

Alek smiled, "in that case Josef when I next see him I'll have a list of questions for him."

"That would be a wise idea," Josef paused for a second and then looked into space as if he was thinking of something to say. Katie looked at Alek who shrugged his shoulders. Neither of them spoke they simply waited for Josef not wanting to disturb his train of thought.

With no warning Josef snapped back to reality and stared at Katie first and then Alek, a sudden look or recognition filled his face again, "Alek how wonderful to see you, Trude said you'd been in contact."

Alek reacted quickly and composed himself, "hello Josef, so good to see you."

Josef looked at Katie, "who's this then Alek, it's not the young lady you had with you last time."

Katie was quick to answer, "hello Josef, my name's Katie."

"Well Alek you're lucky to have found someone so pretty, now what brings you here?"

"Nothing important really Josef, I just had a question regarding your friend Frederik."

The look on Josef's face changed instantly, "damn steiner, that man's not my friend, far from it he's nothing but a villain, built his whole life on lies. Don't listen to a word he says as its all lies and half-truths." He closed his eyes for a few seconds and then opened them again, "so Katie are you and Alek going to have a second crack at Fredrick then?" His voice and facial expressions seemed to have returned to the same state they were in when they'd first spoken.

"Yes we are but now thanks to you we'll make sure that we have the right set of questions to ask him."

"Good idea," there was a definite softness in Josef's tone again, "he's a slippery one that Frederik and you need to be direct with him otherwise he won't tell you anything." Josef looked at Alek, "it's been wonderful to see you again and please have a drink and something to eat before you leave. I need to get some rest otherwise I'd join you."

"Thank you Josef, you get some sleep and we'll see you soon," Josef had already closed him eyes and didn't reply. Alek and Katie got up and quietly left the room taking care to open and close the door making as little noise as possible. They made their way down the stairs to find Trude waiting for them.

"Did you get everything you needed?"

"We did thank you," Alek paused not sure if he should say anything, "part of the way through he seemed to drift off and then returned almost as a different version of himself."

Trude sighed, "yes that happens a lot, it's the medication he's on and there's no telling when it'll happen. Sometimes it days between episode other times it happens three or four times in the same conversation."

"It only happened once during the conversation for a couple of sentences and then he was back to normal."

"I'm glad you saw him as his normal self, sometimes he wakes up in the wrong mood. Is there anything else you need?"

Katie held out a card for Trude, "there's nothing else and you've been a great help thank you. If you have any problems or if he asks after us please give us a call and can you thank Karl for his understanding."

Trude nodded, "I will and thank you for coming to see him."

Trude saw them both to the door and said goodbye before closing it behind them. Alek and Katie walked towards the car, before getting in Katie looked up at the two bay windows of Josef's bedroom. "Well I do hope that he's going to be okay."

"I'm sure he will be, although the medication is obviously having a bit of a serious side effect." Alek and Katie got in the car, "let's find somewhere to make some notes and then we'll head back to the airport." As they were making good time Alek checked to see if he could change the flight, there wasn't any point in staying at the hotel overnight if they didn't need to. A couple of phone calls later and the flight had been changed and the hotel cancelled. They made good time back to the airport and after handing the car back they found themselves a quiet corner and sat down with some food and drink.

They had only started recording when they'd been sat with Frederik so they both recalled the initial conversation with Trude and Karl as best they could. They listened to the conversation with Frederik a couple of time before writing it down. Once done they made their way to the gate and waited to board. Luckily for them they didn't have to wait long and benefited from a nice smooth flight back to Lyon. As soon as they landed they went straight to Katie's parents as they felt that there wouldn't be a great deal to achieve by going into the office for an hour or two and they could do everything they'd do there at home.

Chapter 21 (Europe)

They had a relaxing evening and as a result were in the office the next morning by 07:00. They'd grabbed breakfast on the way in not wanting to wake the rest of the house. Armed with coffee and pastries they set about dissecting what they'd learnt. It was becoming far clearer now that perhaps Frederik hadn't been as truthful as he could be and they had no reason to doubt Josef's words of caution regarding his friend. They knew that Sean and Chris had been looking into Frederik and had already sent Sean a text to let him know they'd updated the file and that he should have a look.

All four of them were now focusing on Frederik and after a conference call they'd split up the remaining properties and financial searches between them. Annoyingly so far Sean and Chris hadn't found anything at all that would suggest anything was out of place. Maybe despite everything he was actually above board and telling the truth. The Interpol searches had turned up three bodies that matched the criteria they'd set and Katie and Alek were now reviewing the cases. The investigations to all three had found nothing and were simply listed as unsolved. A young girl had been strangled and dumped, the other two had been shot, both found in shallow graves and both found by accident. In all three cases all that was confirmed was cause of death, a rough timeline and basic details relating to the bodies.

Alek was currently looking into the girl that had been strangled. She'd been found dumped just outside Moscow and despite their best efforts the local police hadn't been able to identify her. Alek knew straight away that she wasn't a local girl. Her skin was tanned all over and it was clearly natural and not sudden. This was someone that had lived in a significantly sunny climate and that definitely didn't describe Moscow or the surrounding are for quite a few hundred miles. She had no defining features but Alek decided to send it across to the team in the states because he felt there was a slim possibility she could be one of the missing people that they had identified.

Katie wasn't faring so well, every single search she conducted on Frederik came back as being genuine. Every financial check very property check and every business check. She'd looked on the bulletin board and could see that Sean and Chris were experiencing the very same thing and she was getting frustrated. The hours flew by and it was mid-afternoon when Katie gave up. She'd just conducted the last business search on her list and once again everything checked out. She sat back in her chair and closed her eyes. She opened them and stood up, "Alek I'm going for a quick walk and I'll take a fresh look at it all when I get back, I just need to stretch my legs."

"Okay, can you grab something to eat if you're going out as I have a feeling this is going to be a long day." Alek was half way through the file on the second body that had been found. The investigation had been through but once again absolutely no way of identifying the body and all they'd managed to ascertain was that it was a 9mm bullet that had been used. The ballistics didn't match anything on record and so had just been labelled as an unsolved murder and put to one side.

Katie came back with a bag of sandwiches and cakes, Alek got them both a fresh coffee and they spent half an hour throwing suggestions backwards and forwards with regards to the next move. Sometimes openly discussing things had its benefits but after an hour they were no further forward and had agreed that as yet they hadn't missed anything. They called Sean and Chris once more for an update and it quickly became apparent that all four of them hadn't found anything untoward. Sean made it worse by letting them know that Nick hadn't managed to find out anything as yet either. They each had a few last things to check before they had to accept that they needed a new line of enquiry.

Alek decided to go back to basics and almost start again with a view to looking at the cases from a different angle. The first thing he did was to email images across to Cass for her to check them against any missing persons lists they had been able to access. He then started to create a timeline for each of the victims, he took his time reviewing every detail of each case in order to build the best possible picture of what happened. He was aware that what he was doing was a long shot but then at this stage of the research that was often the case.

Happy he now had a more in depth profile for each of them he circulated to a number of contacts in the hope that it might shed a little more light or in the worst case highlight some other victims that presented similar circumstance. He was really hoping that wouldn't be the case, but with the information that they had already managed to find, there was a better than average chance that sadly there'd be a lot more cases.

Katie needed a break from what she was doing as she was simply going round and round in circles, it was often the case but that didn't stop her from getting more and more frustrated. She made a coffee and then asked Alek to update her on what he'd managed to find out so far. The team often did this during an investigation that involved so many unknown facts. It sometimes gave them a fresh perspective, more importantly though it allowed them to sense check what they were doing.

Having gone through everything Alek had been working on they turned the tables and Katie worked her way through the small, and somewhat almost unimportant facts, that she'd managed to put together relating to Frederick.

She paused for a second, "so if you had the money would you buy someone?"

Alek looked at her with a bit of a shocked expression, "no I wouldn't."

"What even if money wasn't an issue?"

Alek took a deep breath and thought for a second or two, "I suppose the real answer is that unless I was actually in that situation I don't know what I'd do. Right now the thought of it just simply doesn't register with me. If I had multiple millions of dollars in my bank account I'd like to think I still wouldn't even contemplate it."

Katie nodded, "so why do they do it? Is it a statement of their wealth?

Alek shrugged his shoulders, "some people are just born that way and have a sadistic streak within them. For others the money probably distorts their judgement. Having said that I honestly don't think it's something I'd do. I have killed people in the past but that was either in combat or in self-defence," he laughed, "I expect a good lawyer would be able to argue that in essence my actions are no different to that of someone taking a life intentionally."

"You're probably right but there is a difference. These people are paying for the privilege of doing whatever they want to another person. There just isn't any justification for that at all."

"No there isn't but the world in which we live in is far from perfect and sadly whether we like it or not the facility is thee for someone to offer that service. It seems as though whoever is running this operation has found a very niche and profitable market, effectively it's tailor-made slavery for the rich and powerful."

"How someone comes up with this sort of idea beats me."

Alek smiled at her, "it's always been the same Katie, supply and demand. No matter where you are in the world they'll always be someone exploiting others. It's unfortunately one of the darker sides of human nature and something that we'll always be struggling to control."

The next few hours went by in exactly the same way the rest of the day had gone. They had turned up absolutely nothing. Katie decided that enough was enough and they'd call it a day. They made their way down to the car and Katie drove to her parents picking up from fresh veg on the way. She'd decided she was going to cook and wasn't sure if her mum had everything she need so it was just easier to grab it all on the way. They enjoyed a nice relaxing family meal and afterwards just sat and talked in the garden enjoying the mild evening.

Chapter 22

He was watching her on the larger central screen, a bank of smaller screens surrounded the large central one. Each screen showed a different camera angle allowing him to see her no matter where she was. The audio was fed through a cinema style surround sound system. At the moment he had the sound tweaked up to one of a number of presets controlled from his keyboard. The room was filled with the sound of her deep rhythmic breathing, he would often sit and watch her sleep, he found it somewhat calming and stimulated his mind. From where he was sat he could control every aspect of her environment. The lower left screen showed a series of readings for each of the rooms, temperature, lighting, humidity. Within a few seconds he could dramatically change virtually everything. At times like this he liked to raise the temperature of the bedroom slightly so that she subconsciously pushed the covers of her whilst sleeping. He liked to see the shape of her body. Twice he'd slowly raised the temperature to just the right level to cause her to wake during the night and take her t-shirt off, falling back to sleep with just her knickers on.

His fingers tapped a few commands on the keyboard and looking over at the screen on the left he saw visual confirmation that the changes that he'd entered had been confirmed. Sitting back in the chair he stared at the large central screen, there was eagerness in his eyes now as he thought about the hours ahead. He stood up and with one last longing look at Phoebe he left the room. It was a short walk down to the master bathroom and once inside he closed the door. The walk in shower was huge and could comfortably fit at least four people in it.

The whole bathroom was state of the art and absolutely no expense had been spared.

He stripped off to reveal a completely hairless body. He regularly visited an exclusive beauty parlour that catered for his exact needs. He touched a single button on the showers command panel and instantly the large shower cubicle was filled with several jets of water from above and the sides. He stepped in, closing his eyes he slowly rotated himself so that his entire body was wet. From a shelf he picked up a bottle of shower gel and poured some onto a soft sponge. The shower gel was odourless and created a soft foam that soon covered almost his entire body. Lifting the shower gel off the shelf had sent a command to the control panel and the water pressure had dropped off to create almost a fine warm mist. This prevented the layer of foam from being washed off too quickly.

Touching a tile at the back of the shower instantly returned the water pressure back to the jets of water. Once again he closed his eyes and slowly turned himself round in the shower allowing the jets to clear away all of the foam. Touching another tile the water stopped and after waiting for a few seconds he stepped out of the shower cubicle. To the right of the shower was a much smaller cubicle, slightly larger than the standard sort of thing you'd find in a normal bathroom. He walked across the heated tile floor and stepped in. Placing himself in the centre he stood with his legs parted and his arms out to his sides at about forty five degrees. A series of sensors picked up on the fact that he was in the right position and suddenly warm jets of air flowed out of barely visible slits in the walls.

In essence he was now stood in a full-size air dryer. The jets of air designed to gently dry the water on his skin. Similar to when he was in the shower he rotated his body round but moving far slower now so that the warm air could dry him. It was strangely satisfying and the pressure was set so that he could feel the air gently massaging his skin. Ten minutes later he stepped out and the dryer shut down instantly. Walking across the warm tiles once again he looked at himself in the floor to ceiling mirrored wall. A special glass and clever temperature control stopped the wall from misting up when the shower and dryer were on. The cost of the bathroom alone was greater than most people spent on their first home. He didn't really care, money meant very little to him.

Stepping over to the basin he brushed his teeth and took a bottle of moisturiser from a shelf. Like the shower gel it was odourless, he took his time to make sure that after applying it he'd rubbed it all in thoroughly. He stepped over to the mirrored wall again and looked at himself. Happy that he couldn't see any evidence of the moisturiser he made his way back to the screens. The rhythmic breathing was still coming from the speakers, seemingly deeper now, but that is exactly how it should be. While he'd been in the shower a powerful odourless anaesthetic had been pumped into the room that Phoebe was sleeping in. Developed by one of his companies it had no lasting effect other than the render the person unconscious. Less than one in a thousand had any after effects. It had been designed so that when the subject came to they weren't even aware that they had been unconscious.

Knowing her weight and height he had been able to ensure that the exact amount of anaesthetic necessary to knock her out for two hours had been administered into the air she was breathing. He looked at the bottom left screen once again to check all of the readings. They confirmed that everything had gone perfectly. It showed the exact dose and the time it had been administered. She was completely unconscious and would be for at least the next two hours. He only needed an hour so he knew that he'd given himself enough of a margin for any error. Not that there had ever been any errors.

He walked over to the wall at the left of the screens, touching a small panel a door suddenly opened and he stepped through it. Phoebe's breathing was still rhythmic and he could hear that nothing had changed. He was naked apart from a smart watch he was wearing on his left wrist. He touched the screen on the watch and the door closed behind him. In his left hand he was carrying a condom, odourless and lubricant free which was important. He couldn't leave any hint behind that he'd been in the room and the last thing he wanted during this was that his excitement would get the better of him. In his right hand was a pair of pants that he would need once he'd finished.

He stood looking at her for a full five minutes before pulling back the cover to reveal her body. She was lying on her back, one arm to her side and the other resting on her stomach. It was gently moving up and down as she was breathing. Her t-shirt had ridden up a little revealing her knickers, her legs were slightly apart. Looking back up he could see the outline of her breasts under her top. His excitement already showing he put the condom on. Taking a step closer he looked at her once again, so clean and perfect. He touched her foot and ran his hand up the length of her leg stopping at the top of her thigh. His heart beating faster he could feel the excitement and thrill coursing through his body. He ran his fingers down the inside of her thigh and traced a line down to her knee and back up again stopping just short of her knickers.

He removed his hand and placed the palm on her exposed stomach. He paused for a second savouring the feel of her smooth warm flesh. He moved his hand up under her t-shirt and stopped just short of her breast. His heart racing now. He knew that he was exactly where he wanted to be. He moved his hand slightly higher and felt the softness of her breast, his thumb moved across her nipple, despite the drugs the sensual receptors around her nipple responded and he felt her nipple become erect. He took a deep breath savouring the moment. Enjoying the power he had over her, he exhaled and paused to feel his body respond to the excitement he was feeling. He moved his hand back down and taking it out from under her t-shirt he used both hands to move her top up to reveal her breasts.

Although he'd seen them on the screen already the fact that he was now inches away from them only served to heighten his level of desire. He paused for a second allowing his breathing to calm a little and then slowly bent over her. His lips stopping just short of her nipple, he extended his tongue and allowed it to flick back and forth over her nipple. Opening his mouth as far as he could he lowered his head taking as much of her breast in his mouth as he could. Taking care now to mark her skin he slowly released the smooth skin from his mouth. Standing back up he allowed himself a minute or two to gently play with her breasts taking care not to squeeze too hard. Part of his sexual gratification came from the fact that she would be totally unaware that he had molested her.

He stepped further back in order to allow himself to calm down. He could feel himself losing control and he didn't want it to be over yet. He ran his hand over his own body as he looked her up and down. His breathing once again under control he stepped forward once more. He pulled her legs up slightly so that her knees were bent and gently prised her legs apart. Moving back up to her breasts he cupped one in each hand and gently moved his thumbs across her nipples. From previous experience he had found that despite the drugs doing this to other women in the past had caused their body to function as if they were awake and caused them to become wet with excitement.

He got off on having this kind of power over someone that was helpless. More than that they were unaware that they were being abused and that just fuelled his desire. Moving his hands from her breasts he turned around and knelt down beside her. He rested the palm of his hand on the inside of her knee and slowing moved his hand down. Enjoying the feeling of her soft warm flesh against his hand, he paused for a second allowing his hand to rest on her knickers. Closing his eyes he savoured the feeling of her warmth through the thin material. A full two minutes went by before he opened his eyes once more and allowed his hand to move up the inner thigh of her other leg.

Pausing for a second he moved back down again his hand returning between her legs, he slowly pulled his hand back until the tip of his middle finger dropped off the edge of her knickers and onto her soft tantalising flesh. He was almost at the height of his mental excitement. Knowing what was coming next, he moved his other hand between his own legs so that he could savour his bodies mental and physical stimulation simultaneously. Moments like this were impossible to recreate in the outside world. To have complete control in this way was something he'd only been able to replicate under these conditions and the feeling was just exquisite and worth every penny.

He slowly moved his hand forward pushing down with the tips of his fingers so that this time they went underneath her knickers. He curved his palm slightly so that it followed the natural curve of her body between her legs. Keeping his fingers together he slowly moved his hand back and forth keeping the rhythm of both hands at the same speed. In less than a minute he stopped moving both hands as he knew he wasn't far off from losing control and he wanted this moment to last longer. He let go of himself and let his left hand rest on her leg. Before moving again he listened intently to the sound of her breathing and matched her speed with his own. He found that being in synch with his victim gave him an extra buzz.

He could feel his excitement and desire getting the better of him and he slowly increased the pressure of his middle finger and his heart started to race as his finger slowly slid inside her. Holding his finger still for a second he took a deep breath and slowly drew his hand backwards so that his finger followed the line of her body gliding over her clit. Withdrawing his hand he moved it up to his mouth and extending his tongue he tasted her juices. Moving his head forward he closed his lips over his finger and ran his tongue round it. She tasted every bit as delightful as he'd imagined and he allowed himself to imagine going down on her, his tongue darting in and out. He stopped himself and removed his finger, for now a simple fingering was all he was allowing himself but next time he would feast on her juices.

He moved his hand back inside her knickers once more, this time he allowed two of his fingers to slip inside her he performed a sort of slow stroking motion with his fingers. Pushing down with the palm of his hand so that he could feel her clit at the base of his fingers as the tips stroked back and forth, taking himself back in had once more he again matched the pace of both hands. As he felt his body respond he picked up the pace slowly, closing his eyes he savoured the noise his fingers were making inside her as he allowed himself to lose control. He held his fingers steady inside her as he felt his orgasm pulse through his left hand. Just before the shudders of his orgasm had finished he withdrew his right hand and placed his fingers once again inside his mouth. He ran his tongue over his fingers marvelling at the exquisite taste.

He stood up, making sure the condom was still in place he walked over to where he'd placed his pants and pulled them on. He moved back over to Phoebe he looked at her for a few seconds before slowly moving her legs back down so that they were flat once again. He carefully lowered her t-shirt back down to cover her breasts and took one last look to make sure she was in the same position that he'd found her. Happy that everything was just right he made his way back out of the room leaving absolutely no visible trace that he had been there. The only real sign was a barely noticeable damp patch on Phoebe's knickers where his fingers had come into contact with them as he withdrew his hand.

He made his way back to the control room to check on her, he watched the monitor for a minute or so and then made his way back to the bathroom. Removing his pants he removed the condom and threw it in the bin. Turning the shower on he stepped under the jets and washed himself once more, he then stood there allowing the jest of water to wash over his body. His mind racing and feeding off the power running through his body after having violated someone without their knowledge. She'd wake up shortly and be completely unaware that he'd been touching her breasts and had been fingering

191

her. Even tasting her juices without her being aware. God he loved the power and tomorrow would be even better as for the next step he'd allow himself to go down on her. He smiled as he felt himself start to harden again as he imagined the feeling of her soft thighs against his head as he used his tongue to explore.

Fully erect once more he closed his eyes and taking hold of himself started to replay the whole scene over once more in his mind, slowly increasing the speed of his hand as he went. He'd done this many times before and had perfected the art of timing his orgasm to the scene in his head. As he thought about his fingers moving in a gentle stroking motion inside her he felt himself losing control and once again he felt his own orgasm pulse through him. He let go of himself and tilted his head back, a huge smile on his face marvelling at the power he had. This is what life is all about, these moments of pure pleasure. He stayed in the shower for another five minutes washing himself once more before stepping out and moving over to the drier. Once dry he walked out of the shower room and into his bedroom, selecting a pair of pyjamas he put them on and got into bed.

Chapter 23 (North America)

Bright and early they were back in the office once again. They'd decided to skip breakfast and to get something to eat after they'd finished going back over what they had already. They were all sat watching as the two men walked off screen and there was silence for a second.

"Well I didn't see anything new," Kelly said as he finished his coffee.

"I don't think any of us did," Cass looked round at each of them and was greeted with blank looks, "damn I was hoping to see something we'd missed." Boyd had left the footage running and she watched as the mystery woman closed the front door and disappeared. She looked away from the screen again, "I guess we start to write up what we've got and begin cataloguing the photos so that we can ..." before she could finish the sentence Drew interrupted her.

"Stop the recording and go back a minute or so," his voice sounded a little excited.

Cass looked at him, "what have you seen?"

"I want us all to see it in case I'm mistaken."

It took Boyd just a few seconds to go back, "okay here we go."

The recording started again and they all looked at the screen expectantly, suddenly a people carrier appears from the right and drives off down the street. "Boyd take it back so that the vehicle is in line with the camera and pause it," within seconds Boyd had the frozen image on the screen.

"That's the two men, look at their tops."

Everyone looked at the image and realised that they were indeed looking at a slightly blurry shot of the two men that had been carrying the sports bag in and then out of the apartment block.

Drew smiled, "so all we need to do now is find another camera somewhere down the street that gives us the vehicle details."

Thirty minutes later they'd not only found the vehicle on a traffic camera two blocks away but had the registration. Sadly it didn't help them as it belonged to a vehicle that had been stolen two days before and very quickly became a dead end. To make matters worse forty minutes after that they lost the vehicle and couldn't find it on any cameras. It had been heading out of town but they couldn't be sure which route it had finally taken.

They'd been relaying the information back to Grace as they went and she'd sent them a map of the area showing the locations that the van had pinged and they found them. She'd reached out to a few other organisations and was waiting to hear back to see if any of them had managed to get a hit on the van but as yet they had nothing.

The atmosphere in the room had gone from one of excitement to one of almost despair and they were almost back to square one. Cass decided to split the team up, "okay everyone here's what we're going to do." She looked round the table before speaking, "we know the van was stolen so I want two of you to follow up on that and see what you can find out, see if there are any clues that may help. Drew and Boyd see what you can find out. The rest of us are going to work with Grace to see if we can predict where they may be heading."

Drew and Boyd left the office to find an officer that could help them to liaise with the local force that dealt with the initial theft of the van. The van had been stolen from a business in Kansas City, Missouri and they caught a lucky break when they found one of the detectives worked the area for five years before transferring. He was able to reach out to a colleague and within twenty minutes they had all the case notes on the screen in front of them. Two people had broken into a yard and stolen two vans. The CCTV footage hadn't given the investigating officers much help and although they had managed to get some possible fingerprints they didn't return anything when they were put through the system. An hour later they returned to the office where the others were in a video conference call with Grace.

Cass looked over to Drew as he sat down, "no luck, we struck out. They didn't find anything that'll help at the scene when the van was taken and the CCTV footage doesn't give us any more than we already have."

Cass looked back at the screen to find that Barney had joined Grace, "did you hear that Grace, we don't have anything extra on the van."

"Yes, I heard Drew and he's sent me a quick update. I'll add it to the file but there isn't much that's going to be of use."

Barney joined in the conversation, "Cass I've just had an update from the other team and I need to swap the teams around a bit. We're going to run and FBI led search on a warehouse and I want you, Jake and Drew to swap with Joss and Ed, we need to increase the FBI presence and to add to the realism I want you three to join them so that if anyone does any digging it won't look out of place."

Cass wasn't surprised at all by this decision, the teams would often have to swap around to ensure the right balance for various tasks, "no problems when do we go?"

"Jess will be leaving shortly and she'll pick up Joss and Ed and then come straight to you so I guess you've got a couple of hours before you need to be at the airport."

Cass nodded, "okay we'll do a bit more here and then we'll leave."

"Good, I'll make some arrangement with the airport and get someone to meet you there to speed things up," with that Barney got up and moved out of view.

"Grace is there any way we can even remotely predict anything at all with regards to where they were heading?"

Grace shook her head, "not with any certainty at all. It looks as though they're heading up state rather than towards the border but that could be a rouse and they could just be taking a scenic route before heading south."

"I had a feeling that was going to be the case. Well we'll keep looking and see what we can turn up although now I'm beginning to think we may have lost the trail." Cass turned her head as Drew got up from his seat.

"Give me few minutes, I'm just going to try something," with that Drew left the office.

Cass looked back at the screen, "Grace, let Barney know I'll get everyone together and we'll leave for the airport shortly. I'd rather be there with a bit of time to spare than arrive late."

Grace nodded, "will do and I'll keep trying to see if I can come up with something that'll help," with that call ended and the screen went blank.

Drew came back into the office with a smile on his face, "so the detective that we spoke to a while ago was chatting with a couple of the others over a coffee and they want to help. They've reached out to some colleagues in neighbouring areas and have given out some details of the vehicle that we're looking for so we've now got a lot more eyes on the problem."

Jake looked up from his laptop, "that was a great idea, what made you think of it?"

"When Boyd and I were initially talking to him he seemed visibly upset at the prospect of people being kidnapped for money. Sorry Cass but we had to give him a bit of an idea as to what this was really all about in the hope that he'd be more engaged. It paid off as there's now four detectives calling round for favours. It may lead to nothing at all but with us, them and the people Grace is working with I'm hoping that we'll at least get one more sighting of the van. That'll give us a bit more of an idea as to the direction they're heading."

"Excellent idea, sadly we're not likely to see the results first hand as Cass wants us to get our stuff together as we're leaving shortly."

"Okay all I need to do is grab my laptop and stick it in my bag and I'll be ready."

Within the hour Cass, Jake and Drew had left leaving Kelly and Boyd to continue the somewhat challenging task of looking for the proverbial needle in a haystack as they searched different traffic camera networks in the surrounding towns. After two coffees and a quick break to get some sandwiches they were no closer. The first break came twenty minutes later, one of the detectives came in with a big smile on his face, "we've got a sighting on a traffic camera in a town thirty-five miles north east of here."

Kelly felt an instant wave of relief, "that's excellent, can you send me the clip and the location so I can forward it to the rest of our team."

"Already have," before Kelly could say anything else the detective had left the office. Boyd got up and walked out into the main office. There was an audible buzz now and he noticed that several groups of people were clustered around monitors. Word had got out regarding the hunt for the vehicle and more and more people wanted to be part of it.

196

Boyd was amazed at the interest the search had generated and went over to the original detective that he'd been dealing with.

He'd been joined by a colleague and they were now jumping a couple of towns down from the latest sighting in the hope of finding it again. Much to Boyd's astonishment the screen let out an audible tone as an image of the van appeared. They'd found another hit, ten minutes led to twenty minutes and then thirty without any more success. Suddenly the excitement had reduced and it looked as though they'd lost the vehicle.

Kelly had already sent Grace the second set of details and was busy trying to plot a possible destination. The assumption was that the van had turned off somewhere after the last sighting as it didn't appear to have reached the next town. Another two hours went by without any further sightings. Strings had been pulled and a local car with two uniformed officers in it was patrolling the road that the vehicle had last been caught driving down on CCTV. Nobody really held out any hope but it was worth trying especially as they had no other leads and were now relying on pure guess work. Most people had lost interest now and gone back to doing what they should have been doing in the first place leaving Kelly, Boyd and the original detective still scouring though CCTV clips.

An hour later the call came in stating that by sheer fluke they'd found the vehicle. The uniformed officers out looking for it had responded to a call and on arrival it transpired that the call had been a bit of a false alarm but the caller was amazed at how quickly they'd responded. They then explained why and the caller advised them that there was a vehicle similar to the one they were looking for down a track that they walked their dogs. The officers asked them to show them the track on a map and they set off, fifteen minutes later they were parked behind the vehicle calling it in.

Ten minutes later the detective came into the office, Boyd and Kelly were both busy desperately trying to work out what to next and they didn't notice the detective standing there. "Guys," they both looked up suddenly aware that he was in the room with them, "the uniforms found it."

Boyd had a blank look on his face, "found what?"

"The vehicle, they're parked right behind it now and they've requested a tow truck."

"You're kidding," the doubt clear in Kelly's voice.

"No, straight up they're sat behind it right now. They're waiting for a call to advise as to where you want the vehicle to go."

"Can they get it towed to here so we can get a forensic team on it?"

"Yep, we can use our CSI team if you want. I'm sure I can clear it with the boss."

"Yes, definitely, that's great how on earth did they find it."

The detective spent a couple of minutes explaining what had happened before leaving the office to call the uniformed officers back and to get the vehicle towed in. Kelly sat still for a few seconds unable to work out what to say. "Well that's a surprise and a huge step forward."

Boyd didn't seem quite as excited, "well it is and it isn't."

Kelly looked at him blankly, "what do you mean."

"Well we have the vehicle but they're either on foot in the countryside or they're in another vehicle and I'm happy to bet that they certainly didn't go out on foot. So that means we've got the original vehicle but have no idea as to what they're driving now."

"Right we need to get out there to see if there's anything at all we can learn."

Kelly and Boyd both got up and went to find the detective once again. They found him at the coffee machine and a quick five minute conversation was all that was needed to get permission to use a car to go out to the scene. The Chief was pleased that his team had helped and went even further by authorising the detective to drive them both out to the scene to assist and liaise with the locals if needed. It was almost 85 miles away and they pulled up behind the marked Police car and hour and fifteen minutes later.

On the way Kelly had called Grace to update her and to advise that they were heading out to the scene to see what they could find. They'd borrowed a camera from the CSI team and started taking as many images as they could. The tow truck was there waiting to take the vehicle away and as soon as Kelly had got the photos he wanted he told the tow truck driver to load the vehicle and take it back so that the CSI team could make a start on it.

They thanked the uniforms one last time and got in the car and drove back to the station. The drive back took considerably longer as they stuck to the speed limit and once back at the station they found Joss and Ed waiting for them. Kelly quickly brought them up to speed. Joss decided that as things stood they'd definitely taken a step forward even though this could now be a bit of a dead end as they had no way of knowing what vehicle they'd changed into.

By way of a thank you the first notable thing that Joss did was to order a whole load of Pizzas for everyone. Without the help and cooperation of the detectives at the station they certainly wouldn't have been in possession of the vehicle this quickly if at all. The Pizzas were a great hit and without doubt secured the help of the whole floor for the next two days as more often than not when the detectives had helped outside organisations in the past they had been lucky to get a thank you so the appearance of numerous pizza boxes cans of soda were gratefully received.

An hour later the tow truck arrived and the vehicle was unloaded into the corner of the garage that the CSI team used for vehicle examinations. They got straight to it and started work. Joss knew that they'd probably be a while before they were done so suggested calling it a day and starting again first thing in the morning. They invited anyone that was interested on the floor to the local bar to join them for a drink. Without realising it that second act of thanks towards the Police Department was going to make all the difference to the investigation.

For a few hours the conversation drifted from story to story about the good cases, the unsolved cases and the ones that got away. One by one the detectives left until it was only the team still in the bar. Joss knew that the CSI team would need some time so she suggested meeting up at 09:00 to review everything they had by which time she felt that they should have at least the preliminary report from the forensics on the vehicle so they all made their way back to the hotel and called it a night.

Chapter 24 (North America)

They were all back in the office for half six the following morning. Rather than paperwork the desk was now covered in body armour and weapons. Both Scott and Cass had M4's as well as sidearms, Jake, Marcus and Drew had sidearms and their back up pistols. Everyone had extra mags although they didn't really expect any trouble Cass had agreed with Clay that they wouldn't take any chances and would go in prepared. Although Danny didn't have a weapon Scott had added a few magazines to the slots in the assault vest that Danny had in front of him.

Cass put the folder down that she was holding, "listen in everyone this is how it's going to work. As mentioned yesterday we'll approach in two vehicles, Jake and I in one and we'll park at the front. The four of you will approach from the rear and Drew and Danny will stay in the vehicle until we give the all clear once we've cleared the first floor. Drew you and Danny will then enter the building and gather whatever you can. Once the building is secure, we'll get the local PD in and we'll then collect everything possible. Anyone got any questions?" Nobody said anything so she stood up, "okay let's go and see what we can find."

They all headed out of the building and got into their respective vehicles, Drew was driving as he and Danny were staying in the vehicles. Clay had already met up with the local PD and called them a few minutes after they'd started driving to inform them that the outer cordon was in place and they were ready for them. Five minutes later both vehicles were waved through and approached the warehouse. Cass stopped out front and Drew drove straight past her and circled round the back pulling up just short of the rear door.

Cass got out with Jake almost at the same time as Scott and Marcus got out, Drew and Danny stayed where they were. They all had earpieces in and heard Cass say, "heads up teams, let's go," Jake and Marcus got to their respective doors first. As Cass and Scott had an M4 each they were covering them. Jake and Marcus both picked the locks on the doors almost simultaneously and both said "I'm in" almost at the same time. Each of the two teams kept up a running commentary so that they knew exactly where each other were. It also allowed Drew and Clay to keep a mental picture of the team's location.

The two teams worked their way through the bottom of the warehouse without any incidents at all. It was made easier as there didn't seem to be much stored here at all. Two separate areas of crates and boxes towards the rear entrance but other than that it was clear. They made their way up the stairs and started to clear each room, calling out as they cleared and moved to the next one. Within twenty minutes they were making their way up to the second floor. Cass called for Drew and Danny to make their way into the building to start checking for intel.

Danny made his way through the door behind Drew, the warehouse opened up in front of him. It was about a hundred metres wide and two hundred meters deep. To the right of the door was a huge open space. Walkways painted a light grey with bright yellow edges broke the open space into large areas that goods would be placed in. To the left were the same walkways but all of the areas between them were full of crates. Danny noticed that most of the crates were about a meter high and three metres long. The bulk of them were stacked three high but there were a few stacks of two and a couple of single crates as well. The offices were in an L shape with the majority of them above the empty section of the warehouse. Danny followed Drew through the crates to a workbench that ran along the length of the wall, and there were several sections that contained drawers so they started searching each of them. Danny could hear the teams in his earpiece and as a result of their movements echoing around the warehouse. They'd got halfway along the bench when Danny heard a noise behind him. Drew heard it at the same time and they both turned in unison. A door that wasn't on the plans they'd been studying before entering had now opened in the wall next to the base of the stairs and two people had emerged carrying pistols.

Danny dropped the pile of papers that he had just retrieved from the drawer he was searching and started moving towards the crates that were about ten feet to his right. Drew moved almost as quickly but Danny had reacted just that little bit faster and was behind cover before the shots rang out. Two rounds hit the crate that Danny was behind and the noise was deafening in the almost empty warehouse. Two more rounds had been fired and Drew had been hit in the leg. He had fallen to the ground before reaching the crates and returned fire hitting the person that had shot at him.

"I'm hit," Drew was breathing hard, "I've been hit in the leg but I've managed to get one of them. I can't see the other one but I think there's only two of them," he took a deep breath, "FBI, put your weapons down and your hands up." Drew had his weapon pointing towards the open door in the hope of spotting the other shooter.

A shot rang out and just missed Drew. He was on the ground about two feet from the crate that Danny was using as cover and due to the way he'd fallen his feet were the closest part of his body to Danny. Danny stayed in cover, "Scott, there's two of them and I think Drew hit one and he's down. I'm behind cover but Drew is out in the open," just then another shot rang out and again hit the crate that Danny was behind.

Scott's voice sounded in Danny's earpiece, "stay in cover we're moving back down but we can't see anyone."

Danny made a quick decision, he reached out and grabbed Drew's leg pulling him into cover. Two more shots rang out one hitting Drew's body armour the other hitting him in the hip and Danny could see instantly that Drew was in a bad way. "Drew's been hit again but is now in cover." Danny could hear the others cautiously making their way down the stairs.

Danny heard Scott's voice in his ear, "talk to me Danny."

"Scott, he's been hit twice, once in the leg and once in the hip. The leg shot is a through and through but the hip shot isn't and he's passed out and there's a lot of blood." Without realising it Danny was now breathing rapidly.

"Okay take it easy, we're almost there. Take a couple of deep breaths and stay in cover. Can you reach Drew's pistol?"

Danny took it from Drew's hand and taking a fresh magazine from the front of his vest he ejected the one in the pistol and put the fresh one in. "I've got it Scott and we need to be quick, Drew needs help."

Danny suddenly heard Clays voice in his ear, "don't worry Danny help is already on its way."

"Danny we're back on the first floor do you know where they are?"

"Scott be careful, they came out of a door at the bottom of the stairs and I'm not sure where they are now. I think the guy that Drew hit has moved."

The next voice Danny heard belonged to Cass, "Danny we've split, two of us are coming down the stairs the other two are covering from the first floor landing, call out if you see any movement."

Danny had seen where the shot had come from and wanted to be able to give Cass and Scott some sort of idea as to where they needed to be looking. With the pistol extended in front of him he carefully looked out from behind the crate. Luckily they were behind a single crate so Danny was able to stay on one knee and had a good stable firing position. Next to him were two crates on top of each other so he had something to move behind if he needed to. He scanned the area in front of him and suddenly stopped as he saw movement. He aimed the pistol on the movement and found himself in the same position as the person that Drew had shot. Danny's brain registered the bloodstain on the other persons shoulder. He knew what he needed to do but hesitated for a split second. This wasn't a paper target and it could fire back. Which is exactly what happened, luckily for Danny the shot went wide and hit the crate next to him. Danny didn't hesitate any longer and fired two shots in quick succession. He saw the first hit the target in the shoulder again and the second was a headshot which would have possibly missed but for the fact that the first shot made the target move to the left putting their head in front of the oncoming second round that Danny had fired.

Scott's voice sounded in Danny's ear, "talk to me."

"Scott one of them is down and definitely not getting up again."

"Well done now stay in cover while we find the second one."

"Roger that," as Danny went to move back into cover he froze. Out of the corner of his eye he could see movement. His head naturally turned to track what he'd seen. It was in that second that his lack of combat training showed as the weapon he was holding didn't move with the same speed his head did. He'd only turned the weapon half the distance his head had turned and was now in trouble. The second person Drew had seen had made his way through the crates and now had a nasty looking grin on his face as he had Danny bang to rights in the sights of his gun. Danny's eyes widened in horror as he realised to late that his pistol wasn't where he desperately needed it to be. He started to move it faster towards the target but he knew he was going to be too late. He was almost there when he saw the other guy's trigger finger tighten. Everything seemed to slow down in Danny's world, he started to move his body but he knew he was not going to make it in time and the gunshot rang out.

After leaving Danny and Drew they'd split into pairs as they searched the rooms. Taking a room each they were leapfrogging each other as they cleared each one. Standing either side of the door one of them would open the door with enough force to give each of them a clear view of the room. They entered each room in textbook fashion talking as they went so that everyone listening was aware of their progress. Most of the rooms were empty offices with absolutely nothing in them at all. A few had some office desks and chairs in and a few had boxes and smaller crates in them. They'd worked their way up to the second floor quite quickly although they weren't taking any risks even though every room had been clear so far. Things changed when they heard the first shot and Scott now took the lead. Up to that point he'd been quite happy to allow the other three to lead as this was more of a law enforcement search than a combat situation but that had now changed.

All four of them were out of the offices on the second-floor landing. Scott held a finger to his lips and they followed him moving quietly as they went not wanting to make any noise. They reached the first-floor landing quite quickly and Scott motioned for Cass and Jake to move further along the landing while he and Marcus made their way back down to the ground floor. Scott took the lead and made his way down the stairs. Instinct had already forced him to move the selector from single shot to burst. He was almost whispering when he spoke so that he didn't give away his location. He was scanning the crates desperately looking for the second gunman. He spotted a movement and the gunman came into view. Scott didn't have a lot to aim at as most of the targets body was behind a crate but his head was exposed and that's all he needed.

Cass had made her way along the landing with Jake following. She too had changed from single shot although not in the instinctive way that Scott had she'd realised it was the better option as she made her way along looking down amongst the crates. She saw the gunman at about the same time as Scott and they both fired within a millisecond of each other. Neither of them had taken a chance and they had pulled their triggers twice.

The bullet never came towards Danny as he watched the gunman's head explode followed almost instantaneously by his chest. The noise of the shots reverberated around the warehouse and Danny finally blinked as the body hit the ground. Scott suddenly appeared from a crate behind the now very dead gunman.

Danny pointed towards the door that the two men had come out of and then noticed that Cass and Jake had now made it back to the ground floor. From the position she was in Cass had seen the door and was already stood by it as Scott approached. Scott took the lead again and entered through the door with Cass and Jake close behind. Marcus had made his was over to Danny who was now tending to Drew's wounds as best he could. Suddenly Danny was aware of more noise as a dozen or so people entered the warehouse through both doors. Marcus called out and two medics appeared next to Danny and took over.

Danny was clearly in shock as Clay approached him but before Clay could say or do anything Scott appeared by his side. Danny was looking at Drew and jumped when he heard his own name.

"Danny look at me." Danny raised his head and found himself looking at Scott, "way to go Little Fella. I'm proud of the way you handled that now I want you to listen to me. You need to make the pistol safe and hand it to Clay." On hearing that Danny seemed to spring into action and instinctively ejected the magazine and pulled the slide back to eject the chambered round. Instinct kicked in again and he caught the round and without thinking fed it into the magazine putting the magazine back in place. Now that it was safe he handed the pistol to Clay and Scott took him by the shoulder and led him outside. Cass was now with Scott and as soon as they were outside got a bottle of water from the car and got Danny to take a drink.

Scott looked at Danny, some of the colour had now returned to his cheeks, "right mate I want you to talk me through what happened step by step."

Danny looked at him for a second and then started walking through the steps that he and Drew had taken. Scott listened carefully and when Danny had finished Scott slapped him on the shoulder, "now let's go back in and check on how everyone is doing," Danny nodded and followed Scott back inside.

The warehouse was now a hive of activity. Clay had already split everyone into two teams, and they were gathering up everything they could find. A second team of medics were dealing with the two dead gunman and Marcus had already removed their wallets and anything else that they'd had in their pockets. A pile of evidence bags was beginning to build up on one of the crates and more were being carried out from behind the door that the two gunmen had appeared out of.

Drew was still conscious but now had an oxygen mask on as he was lifted on the gurney, which made Danny feel a whole lot better. Scott seemed to pause for a second, "Clay can you finish up here with Marcus and bring all the evidence back to the office with you both?"

Clay nodded, "yes, we'll be a while but we can manage that."

"Great, Cass and I will take Danny back. Jake can drive Drew's car back and meet you all at the office." Scott turned to Cass, "grab Danny and meet me at the car, I need to make a call," Cass nodded and moved off to get Danny.

Scott took his phone out of his pocket and dialled a number, "Barney its Scott, I need a favour. Can you call James, I need him to get hold of someone as quickly as possible and get them here," Scott listened for a few seconds, "no, the immediate team are fine but Drew took two bullets and is in a bad way. The medics have just left with him and hopefully he'll be fine. The thing is that it was Danny that took the guy out that shot Drew, a few seconds later he was in the sights of the other guy who had him bang to rights. Luckily Cass and I took him down before he could fire. I want Cole Deakin here as quickly as possible. He's an ex-Seal turned shrink who I've worked with in the past. I trust him so I want him here doing an after-action report with Cass and I first and then with Danny," Scott listened again, "no I know that the FBI, CIA and the Marshal Service can supply someone but that's not good enough. Barney, the kid was staring down the barrel of a gun. It's not what he signed up for and add that to the fact that he's just killed someone I want to make sure that he's given the right help and that starts instantly with Deaks spending some time with him," Scott listened again, "thank you."

He put the phone in his pocket and made his way to the car. Cass was talking to Danny who was leaning against the passenger door with a bottle of water to his mouth, "right then Cass let's get back and get something to eat before we clean these weapons, you up for that Little Fella?"

Danny gave Scott his usual smile, "yep, sounds good to me."

Once they'd cleared the Police cordon the journey back to the Marshalls office was fairly quick. Danny spent the journey looking out of the window letting his mind wander. He didn't know what to feel, in fact he didn't know how to feel. He was toying with asking Scott how it felt when he'd first killed someone and then stopped himself, and he closed his eyes for a second telling himself that he could deal with this and that it was no big deal. After all a number of the team had killed people in their line of work and they were functioning on a daily basis without any problems whatsoever. He opened his eyes to see that they were about to pull into the car park and he took a deep breath as Cass parked up.

They all got out and made their way to the conference room they'd been using, Cass had called ahead and arranged some food, the table had several bags and cans of drink on it. Scott was the first into the office and grabbed a bag of food and a can, "alright you two grab some food and we'll take it down to the range and clean the weapons down there. We can eat and clean at the same time and hopefully by the time we're done some of the others should be back."

Cass and Danny grabbed a bag each along with a drink and turned round to walk back out. Cass paused and turned back to grab a second bag of food, Danny looked a bit puzzled and Cass smiled, "I'm hungry, I haven't eaten for a while and we're going to be at least an hour cleaning the weapons so I'm making sure I've got plenty to eat and if I were you I'd grab another one as well," Danny laughed and picked up two more bags knowing that Scott would probably eat half of his if he didn't. They made their way down to the range and put everything down on the table in the outer section. The range was empty so they had the whole place to themselves.

Scott and Cass made the M4's safe followed by their pistols, "okay Little Fella," Scott said, "we'll start on the M4's if you start on the pistols. Neither pistol was used so it'll be a fairly straight forward job cleaning them."

Danny nodded, "sounds like a plan as long as I can eat as I go."

Scott laughed, "that's the plan," he slid a cleaning kit across to Danny and then opened up the food bag. Cass and Danny did the same and were pleasantly surprised to find a fairly decent choice inside. Cass had requested that the food bags contained a variety and were substantial and whoever had gone out and got them had certainly made sure of that. Scott wanted to keep Danny busy to take his mind off what had happened and by eating as they were cleaning Scott knew that Danny would be far too busy to worry or to talk. An hour flew by in which time Danny had finished the first Glock and was well on his way with the second. They'd both opened their second bag of food and were making short work of the second lot of sandwiches.

Unbeknown to Scott Cole Deakin was on loan to a team of Rangers that were on a joint exercise working out of Luke Air Force Base. It had taken James less than thirty minutes to locate him and arrange for him to put on a temporary assignment with the team. Less than 45 minutes later he was buckled up and taking off on his way down to meet up with Scott. James had briefed him and had spoken to Mitch and suggested that they leave the plane at the airport and travel to the Marshalls office with Deaks. Mitch had agreed that the more friendly faces Danny saw the less he'll focus on what's just happened. They hadn't briefed Jess other than to let her know that they were flying down to meet up with the team and to grab some evidence that had been found. All of which was true but Mitch knew that Jess would be worried and he made the decision to tell her as soon as they were wheels down. For now he just wanted her to focus on flying rather than worrying.

The flight was straight forward and apart from a little delay in landing they made good time. Jess shut the plane down while Mitch and Cole talked in the back. Once she'd finished she left the cockpit and went into the main cabin. She knew something wasn't right as soon as she looked at Mitch, "what's wrong?"

The look on Mitch's face softened, "take a seat for a second Jess," as soon as she was sitting down Mitch continued, "I didn't fully introduce you to Cole. He's an ex-seal who's now working with the Military as a Psychiatrist and trauma counsellor. He's going to be carrying out the after action briefing with the team. You've already been briefed and you know that the team were involved in a shooting and two suspects were killed. The bit you don't know is that one of them was killed by Scott and Cass."

208

Before Mitch could continue jess interrupted, "yes Barney told me that but what I didn't understand is why Cole was being flown down. The after-action report would be handled by whoever is leading the investigation. In this case the FBI and they've got loads of people to hand and if they didn't the Marshall service certainly do."

Mitch paused for a second before continuing. "That's perfectly true but Scott requested Cole for a specific reason, and I guess there's no easy way to say this but you have to give me a chance to explain before you say anything."

Jess suddenly looked nervous "I'll listen but hurry up you've worried me now."

"No need to be worried Baby Girl. Scott has worked with Cole in the past and he trusts him and I mean really trusts him and wanted him down here no matter what to deal with the situation as he knows that Cole will make sure that everything that can be done will be done. You already know that two suspects were killed during the operation. Well, what you don't yet know is that it was Danny that shot and killed the second suspect."

Jess now had a horrified look on her face and took a deep breath before she spoke, Mitch held his hand up, "wait a second, I haven't finished. Danny is absolutely fine, if he wasn't then we would have told you straight away. There's nothing physically wrong with him at all. It's the mental side Scott is worried about and that's why he wants Cole to deal with Danny. The after-action report is a bit of a red herring as such. Yes, we have to do them but they are usually very quick and dealt with locally. Scott has spent enough time around incidents like this to know if it's handled correctly at the outset then the end results further down the line are far more positive. Hence why he insisted on having the best person he knows to deal with Danny. We spoke about this at length and felt that as he wasn't injured we could wait to tell you. If we'd told you before we'd taken off, I wouldn't have let you in the cockpit and that would have been worse for you and I'm sure in time you'll see that, so sorry for doing it this way but it's for the best."

Jess looked less worried now, "can I go and see him?"

Mitch nodded, "yes, arrangements have been made and we're leaving the plane here, someone should be here to collect us and take us to the Marshalls office. Scott has got Danny cleaning the weapons with him and Cass to take his mind off it until Cole gets there. We're going to get Cole to do a quick meeting with Scott and Cass to make it seem more normal and then Cole will spend some time with Danny."

"Okay in that case considering what Scott has done so far don't let Danny know I'm here until after he's spoken to Cole. I won't be able to control myself when I see him and that could make things worse."

Mitch stood up, "we'll drop Cole off and then we'll go for a coffee and something to eat and wait for them to call us."

Jess nodded and stood up, they all left the plane and made their way into the terminal building to find Jake waiting for them, before Jake could say anything Jess blurted out, "how is he?"

"Well Jess he's absolutely fine and busy stuffing his face while cleaning the weapons with Scott and Cass," he held out his hand, "I'm Jake and I promise you that Scott has made it perfectly clear that we're to treat him as normal and to let Cole do his thing."

Jess shook his hand and then smiled weakly, "sorry, I promised myself I wouldn't do that."

Mitch put an arm round Jess and laughed, "that's Okay Baby Girl we know you're usually fairly cranky so it's no surprise."

Jess punched him on the arm, "you're such a bell end."

Introductions done they made their way out to the car, and all got in. Mitch had already asked Jake to drop Cole off and then drop them off to get something to eat and Jake had suggested that he stay with them to run through what happened and how things are going. The drive to the Marshalls office was straight forward and before they knew it the three of them were in a diner ordering some much needed food and drink. While they were eating Jake updated them on what had happened so far.

Clay met Cole and took him up to the conference room they were using, Cole didn't waste any time and asked if someone could get Cass and bring her up. Clay said he'd do it himself and within minutes she was sat down going through the events from her perspective as they happened. Twenty minutes later she was back down in the range telling Scott to go up to see Cole. It took Scott and Cole less than ten minutes to go through it all and Scott spent the next ten minutes describing what Danny had experienced. By the time Scott had returned to the range Danny had finished cleaning the second pistol and they were both neatly laid out. As Scott had already finished cleaning the M4 that

Clay had loaned him he asked Cass to deal with the weapons while he took Danny up to see Cole.

Scott dealt with the introductions and then excused himself leaving Cole to debrief Danny first and then to spend some time digging deeper. Scott grabbed an elevator and went to the diner to meet the others as he knew that Jess would be concerned about her brother and he wanted to try and put her mind to rest a little. He entered the diner and saw the three of them sat at a corner table, the diner wasn't particularly busy and even though he'd eaten while cleaning the M4 he felt hungry. He ignored the feeling and made his way over to the others. As soon as Jess saw him she was up out of her seat and rushed over to hug him. As she let go and moved back Scott could see tears in her eyes. Choking back the tears she looked Scott straight in the eyes "I can't even begin to thank you for looking out for Danny. Not just the day-to-day stuff Scott but arranging for Cole to sit down with him. I don't have the words to thank you," at that point she burst into tears and fell into his arms again sobbing.

The waitress looked over and Mitch quickly asked for another round of drinks and some pie. With that the waitress lost interest in Jess and Scott and busied herself getting the order together. Jess finally let go of Scott and they both sat down. Before anyone could say anything the drinks arrived and Scott asked for a black coffee. Seconds later the waitress was back with Scott's coffee and the pies.

In between mouthfuls Scott updated them all and gave them a bit more background relating to why he'd asked for Cole to be involved, many years ago Scott's Seal team had been in a fire fight. The Seal team were fired upon first and they instantly returned fire and although only a four-man team they sent back a barrage of rounds that was not only quite substantial but also highly accurate. The team had taken cover and the team leader called a cease fire. Scott described the silence as total until they heard someone call for a medic, at that point the four of them instantly knew they'd been involved in a friendly fire incident. They identified themselves and moved forward. The incident had involved a local army unit with several embedded advisers. The sentry who had fallen asleep had been woken as Scott and his colleagues approached and without thinking had opened fire without first challenging who was approaching. One of the advisors knew instantly from the sound of the weapons that this wasn't an enemy patrol and he ordered the sentry to stop firing. Which was pointless as the sentry had been killed almost instantly by the Seal Team.

No one knew who had fired the fatal shot as the sentry had been hit by numerous rounds. It was Cole that dealt with the after-action reports as at the time he was in Country attached to a unit that was close by. Scott and Cole developed a close friendship from that point on and Scott was very aware of the effect that Cole had on him and the help that he had given him further down the line which is why he had insisted that Cole was involved from the outset with Danny.

"Jess, Cole is the best person I know when it comes to dealing with this sort of thing and there isn't anyone else at all I'd rather have looking after Danny right now."

Jess had tears in her eyes again, "thank you Scott."

Scott reached out and took her hand, "listen, he's a tough kid and with the right help he'll be fine and right now he's got the right help. What he needs is to be kept busy and to have friendly faces around him which is why I'm going to call Barney and suggest we grab our gear and head back. I'll ask Clay to scan everything they find and send it to us."

Jess nodded, "can we go to him now."

Jake got the attention of the waitress and she came over, he asked for the bill and when she returned he left a decent tip. They drove back to the Marshalls office and went straight up to the conference room. Cole and Danny had been joined by Cass and Clay and they were reviewing some of the evidence that had now made its way back from the warehouse.

Jess went straight to Danny and gave him a big hug, "you can let me go now Sis," everyone laughed.

They all sat down and Scott introduced Mitch and Jess to Clay. With that out of the way he outlined his plan for the team to head back and asked Clay if he could arrange for all the evidence found to be scanned and sent to them at Luke. Clay agreed and then gave them all a quick update on Drew. He was still in theatre but everything was looking promising even though he'd lost a lot of blood. The initial prognosis was that he'd make a full recovery although he'd need a good deal of rehab but the important thing that everybody agreed on was that it was great news to know that he was going to be okay.

Clay looked round the table, "I just want to say a big thank you to you all before you go. Despite the incident at the warehouse it's been great having you around. The Marshall Service don't always come off very well when working with other agencies, but this has been an eye opener. We've got the FBI and DEA asking us if we'd share the intel. Normally we'd be told to hand everything over but somehow you guys have elevated us and we seem to be taking lead on this, which I've got to say is a good feeling."

Cass smiled, "Clay it's been our pleasure, you've made this far easier than it could have been and well while we may not look like much the guy that pulls our strings has a lot of weight. I made some suggestions that as a thank you for what you've done for us that you and your team should be given credit and although we dressed it up as an FBI operation the overall lead was always documented as being yours, so it was quite easy to make that official."

Clay looked a bit sheepish, "I've got to be honest Cass when I was first approached I tried to push back. I didn't fancy opening up our services to a bunch of civilians but I'm glad I did. You're a great team and it really has been a pleasure to work with you all. What are your next steps?"

"Well we're temporarily based at Luke Air Force base and that's where we're going to head back to. We'll spend an hour or two imaging the evidence you already have here so that we've got something to start with when we get back and then we'll be on our way."

"I'll sort out two cars to take you to the airport just give me a shout when you're ready to go as I'd like to say goodbye," with that Clay got up to leave the room.

Scott stood up, "Clay your M4 is back in your office. Thank you for the loan. I thought it was a bit of overkill at first but I'm real glad I had it."

"Not as glad as I am," Danny said with a big smile on his face.

"I'm glad I could help, it would have been nice if things had been straightforward but as Drew is going to be fine it worked out well in the end."

"We're very used to things not being straightforward Clay, it seems to be the nature of the assignments we're given. All we need to do now is hope that we get something useful from the stuff that we found."

Cass stood up and looked at the rest of them, "listen up you lot let's go and get some boxes and bring them up and start imaging what we can."

They all stood up and made their way to the outer office where the boxes were beginning to pile up. They knew that most of what they found would be worthless, but everyone hoped they'd find something that would be of use.

The boxes kept coming in and before they knew it the team were overwhelmed with paperwork. It seemed that the gang had documented just about everything they'd ever done, there were receipts for everything and anything and they were beginning to wonder if they'd actually find anything of use at all. Three hours later they gave up and decided that it was time to head back to Luke. They'd just got a call to let them know that Drew was out of surgery and in the recovery room but wouldn't be able to receive any visitors for a while as the surgery hadn't been as straightforward as they'd have liked and they wanted to keep him under close observation for a while longer.

They all grabbed their kit and said their goodbyes. Just as Clay had promised two cars ran them to the airport and while Jess and Mitch got the aircraft ready for take-off the others grabbed a coffee. Before long they were in the air and heading back to Luke for what they hoped was a bit of rest but in truth they knew that the hard part was just beginning as they had to sift through the mountain of images they had obtained already.

Chapter 25 (Europe)

The following morning, they entered the offices in a slightly subdued mood. Even though they both knew that the investigations sometimes had dry spells and significant amounts of wasted hours searching dead ends and false leads it didn't help their mood. They'd agreed to start from scratch again and look for any anomalies they may have missed. They toyed with asking Claudine to borrow a fresh pair of eyes but discounted that idea for the moment. They decided to spend the morning reworking what they had and if by lunchtime they hadn't found anything then they'd ask. They didn't get past eleven o'clock before things suddenly changed. Katie took a call from Cass asking her to check out an airport in Spain. She'd explained that they had traced a medical repatriation plane that had left the states carrying one of the missing people they'd been investigating.

Katie had put the call on speaker so that Alek could here to save having to relay the information, with the called finished she looked over at Alek, "well that's changed things for us. Sean and Chris can finish the last few bits while we investigate this. I'll make some calls."

Before Katie could do anything else Alek's phone rang, he took it out of his pocket and saw it was Barney. He answered and spent the next couple of minutes listening and every so often asked a question. He ended the call and looked at Katie. He could tell from the look on her face that she'd understood part of the conversation and knew that someone had been shot, "before you ask let me relay what Barney said. They raided a warehouse, something went wrong and one of the team was shot. It wasn't any of our team it was an FBI agent that had been assigned to help. He's in surgery now but by the looks of things he'll be fine. Cass and Scott were involved and shot someone and unfortunately Danny was involved and he shot someone as well. The two dead guys were gang members so it's a justified shooting but they wanted to let us know in case we saw something on the bulletin board later."

Katie looked a little less worried now, "how on earth was Danny involved in a raid?"

"I don't know, we can read the report later to see what happened but at least everyone is okay."

"Okay, so back to our situation. If the plane did land there then we're going to need a lot more information than we can get over the phone. Can we get one of your Spanish colleagues to meet us there so that we can deal with it first hand?"

"Absolutely, I'll go and talk to Claudine and ask her who the best contact is in the area."

Ten minutes later Katie was back. The airfield wasn't big enough for the standard commercial aircraft so Alek had found a smaller company that regularly flew there and had booked them tickets for a flight that left in just over an hour. It was going to be tight but as it was a smaller concern they wouldn't need to go through quite the same process as a commercial flight. They actually went through a smaller separate terminal building off to one side of the airport. They quickly drove to the airport and checked in. The flight was a very no-nonsense affair and was over really quickly, on arriving they cleared security and walked into the arrivals lounge.

A smartly dressed woman approached them as they landed, "Katie, Alek my name is Adriana, my colleague and I have been assigned to assist you. Claudine called our boss and described you and told us which flight you'd be on in case you're wondering how I knew who to look for."

Katie laughed, "that doesn't surprise me."

"Carlos is parking the car and he shouldn't be too long. We've been given a brief idea of what we're doing here. Can we grab a coffee while we're waiting so that you can update me?"

"Absolutely, we'll probably be here a while so we might as well bring you both up to speed."

Alek nodded to the main door as a smartly dressed man walked though, "that'll be Carlos then."

Adriana looked at Alek, "how did you know that, is it that obvious?"

Alek laughed, "no not at all, I saw him looking through the window as he walked to the door. As soon as he saw you he stopped looking and walked in so it was a bit obvious."

Carlos made his way over and they introduced themselves, once that was done they grabbed a coffee and Katie gave them both a shortened version of the operation so far. She only included the bits that led them to the airfield as they didn't really need to know the rest. Once they'd finished they made their way over to the main information desk and introduced themselves. They were quickly taken to the main offices and the airport manager introduced himself immediately offering full cooperation. They followed him into a meeting room and Katie gave him the flight number and asked for as much information on the flight as possible but also access to any previous flights. She explained that she'd also need to see any CCTV footage and logs they may have relating to any deliveries or passengers that may be associated with the flight.

The manager left the office for about ten minutes and then came in with two other people, he introduced the first as the head of security who would take them to the CCTV monitors and go through whatever they needed. The other was the manager in charge of the logistics at the airfield and she was responsible for all the freight linked to incoming and outgoing flights. As this was a medical flight any patients would be classed as freight.

The team split up and Katie went with Carlos to check the CCTV while Alek went with Adriana to go through the freight manifests. The manager offered to go back though the records to dig out the previous visits made by the aircraft so that they could then check those flights as well. Although he did apologise and say that they may not have any CCTV footage but they would have the freight manifests on record as these needed to be kept for a number of years for audit purposes.

The CCTV footage wasn't great, certainly not to the same quality as the footage from the airfield in the states. Luckily the aircraft was at a stand close enough for them to make out what was happening. They saw an ambulance pull up and a short while later a gurney with a patient was moved from the plane to the ambulance, after a few minutes the ambulance left. The plane didn't hang around for long before it was taxiing back out to the runway to take off. They made a copy of what they'd seen then changed to the main gate cameras in order to get the details from the ambulance. Twenty minutes later they had clear enough images to be able to get the registration and name of the ambulance company. They checked the gate logs, which thankfully were all electronic, and confirmed the name on the ID of the driver.

Alek and Adriana were having some similar luck. They'd already copied the manifest for the flight in question and noted that only one passenger had been declared coming in on the plane and it showed zero passengers for the onward journey so there was a really good chance that the passenger on board was the one they were after. The computer system was quite thorough, and it was an easy job to locate other flights and manifest that the plane had made. A total of six trips in the last four months, it took a little longer to find all of the manifests but an hour and a half later they had everything they needed.

They'd been given the use of a large meeting room and Alek and Adriana were busy imaging the paperwork when Katie and Carlos re-joined them. Alek could see that Katie was happy with what they'd found and she was even happier when she saw what Alek had managed to get hold of. When they'd been shown the room they could use Alek had asked for some drinks to be organised and these arrived shortly after Katie and Carlos joined them, "I didn't know what everyone wanted so I just asked for some hot and cold drinks," Alek picked up a bottle of sparkling water and sat back down.

Katie sat opposite him after poring herself a coffee, "so what have we got?"

Adriana took a quick mouthful of water from the bottle she'd picked up, "well we've got the manifests for six trips that the plane has made. We already know that on the last trip they arrived with one passenger and left with none. We'd just started to look at the other five trips when you came in."

"That's a great start, we've got some clear footage of an ambulance arriving at the front gate before it went airside. We've got some not so great footage showing a passenger being taken off the plane and loaded onto the ambulance before it leaves."

Alek stopped what he was doing, "so how do you want to handle this Katie?"

"I guess the quickest thing to do would be to stay as we are and if you and Adriana go through the manifests Carlos and I will follow the trail of the ambulance."

"Carlos, Adriana anything you'd like to do differently or are you okay with that?"

Carlos looked at Adriana, it was clear that the question had thrown him. "Well we've just been assigned to assist so we'll do whatever it is that you need."

Alek smiled, "that's good to know but that's not how we do things. We're a team and anyone joining us is part of that team and we always discuss our next moves so if you can think of anything that would need to be done differently, please don't hesitate to say something."

Carlos shook his head, "no, if I was calling the shots it's exactly what I would do so yes let's split."

"Good," Alek picked up a bottle of water, "we'll image everything as we go and upload it so that the rest of the team can see it straight away."

"Good idea," Katie looked at Carlos, "we'll go and make some phone calls they've got a second office we can use, and it'll save disturbing you while you're doing that. It'll mean that you can spread all the paperwork out which will make things easier," she didn't wait for a response and left the room with Carlos close on her heals.

As Adriana was laying out one of the piles of paper for imaging she paused, "do you always work this well with everyone?"

Alek took a few minutes to explain what it was that the team did and how they did it, "we've always found that it's far easier to bring everyone in and work as we always do than to try and adapt to the different ways agencies work. As an example Katie is on loan to us from Interpol which is why it's been so easy for us to get you two assigned to us."

"So are you with Interpol as well?"

"No I'm not, I'm what you might call a bit of a wildcard and one of the reasons as a team we're pretty much able to go anywhere in the world," Alek could see that Adriana was intrigued.

"So go on then Mr Wildcard who's loaned you to the team?"

"Well not wanting to miss the party I've been loaned out by the FSB."

Adriana looked at Alek with a huge grin on her face, "oh of course you have."

Alek put the piece of paper down that he was holding and removed his wallet from his pocket, he opened it up and slid it across in front of

Adriana. Pure luck saw it stop in front of her the right way up and Alek's official FSB ID was there for her to see.

The look on her face instantly changed, "oh my god, you are."

"Please don't sound so shocked, we are human you know."

"I didn't mean it like that I'm so sorry. I'm just surprised that Russia and America have people on the same team."

"That's okay most people have that reaction. The powers that be realised that in order for us to do what we do we really did need to be able to go anywhere in the world. The only really issue we have is China and we're working on that although I'm not sure if we'll ever get to jump over that hurdle."

Adriana pushed Alek's wallet back over to him and he put it back in his pocket, "it must be nice to be able to work across borders without the political interference."

"Oh, believe me that doesn't change. It's still there but because we've usually been given the assignment because none of the internal agencies want or can't get involved so it gives us an edge and we can, more often than not, skirt round the political challenges."

"That's got to make it easier."

Alek paused for a second, "yes and no, take this case for example. We're now investigating across several countries dealing with numerous agencies simultaneously which makes things a bit challenging."

"That must generate an enormous amount of paperwork."

Alek nodded, "yes it does and like any investigation we always end up with huge amounts of information that we either don't or can't use as it takes us down a dead end or is false and we lose countless hours of investigation as a result but it has to be done. The recent visit to Josef is a prime example."

Adriana looked intrigued, "how so?"

Alek stopped what he was doing, "well we had hoped that a further meeting with him would give us some further details about his friend Fredrick as we've found nothing at all on him to help us. Katie and I went to see him but he didn't give us anything that we didn't already know. It may be that the medication he's on is having an effect on his memory as whilst we were talking, he had a funny turn and for a while it was as if we were talking to someone else, there was a real personality change."

"That must have been difficult to deal with."

"It was," Alek picked up his bottle of water and took a drink, "luckily it only lasted a few sentences and then suddenly he was back to normal. It was odd to hear such bitterness in his voice as he swore about his friend and told us to watch out for him as he wasn't to be trusted. He has such a gentle personality it was a real shock."

Adriana was now very intrigued, "what did he say?"

"Well, everything was okay and then he looked into space for a second and it was if he hadn't been talking to us, he said hello to me and when I said that we had a few questions relating to his friend Fredrick he said "Damn steiner, that man's not my friend," then preceded to berate his friend for a few sentences before pausing once again and returning to normal. He hadn't realised that his personality had changed. Apparently, it's one of the side effects of his medication."

"That couldn't have been easy to deal with."

Alek shook his head, "no it wasn't, I know he's done some bad things in the past but it wasn't nice to see him affected in that way."

"Must have been strange to hear someone with a placid personality suddenly change and start swearing, what did he say?"

Alek looked a little confused at the question, "well he said damn steiner."

It was Adrianna turn to look confused now, "but damn isn't that bad I thought you were going to say something far worse than that."

"He called him a damn steiner and although we can't find reference to that from the tone of Josef's voice it can't be good."

"Steiner isn't a swear word."

Alek looked stunned, "what?"

Adriana smiled, "my grandfather is German and fought in the war, when I was growing up he taught me all the swearwords much to my parents despair and trust me steiner isn't one of them, it's actually a surname."

Alek had a blank look on his face, "are you sure?"

Adrianna nodded, "fairly sure, if it was a swear word believe me my grandfather would have known it."

"God how can we have missed that?"

"To be fair unless you spoke fluent German you wouldn't necessarily know."

Alek grinned, "Adrianna you're an absolute star and this could explain a few things," Alek got his phone out and hit the speed dial for Nick, "it's me, can you set up a new search for Frederik Steiner, run the search for his parents using that surname as well," Alek stopped talking for a second, "I know but someone has just pointed out that the assumption we made was probably wrong and if this is Frederik's surname it could explain the lack of earlier family history," he paused again, "thanks Nick." He put the phone back in his pocket, "well let's see what that turns up, you could have just turned a dead end back into an active lead."

Adrianna smiled, "glad to have helped now I guess while we wait we have to return to the super exciting task of imaging this lot." By now they have multiple piles of paperwork that had been sorted into some sort of order.

There wasn't any enthusiasm in Alek's voice as he replied, "yes we do indeed."

The next couple of hours flew by as they imaged the various pile of paperwork, to try and relive the monotony they discussed places they'd visited challenging cases they'd dealt with and even discussed what they'd order to eat. Once they'd completed the last page Alek sent Katie a text suggesting lunch. While waiting for the reply they stacked the various piles neatly. As they'd been imaging each page they created a target address for each group of paperwork so that it would be easy to find when they were searching later.

Over lunch Alek filled Katie in on the news regarding the discovery that Adrianna had highlighted. Nick hadn't come back to Alek yet but that wasn't necessarily a bad thing as Alek knew that Nick would have multiple searches running for various team members and would always get back to everyone as quickly as he could. Katie took the opportunity to update Alek on what they'd found out about the ambulance. The company that owned it ran nearly twenty similar vehicles throughout Europe mostly carrying out patient transfers from one hospital or country to another. About fifteen percent of their work related to international repatriations and five ambulances and crews were assigned to that. This made things a little easier for the team as it narrowed down the number of people they'd have to investigate. As yet Katie was waiting for the details of the various crews to be given to her but the Company had been cooperating so far so if all went well they should have the details by the end of the day. In order to speed things up she told Alek that she'd arranged for two colleagues to visit the company to meet in person so that when she'd got in contact they were expecting the call. It worked perfectly because they almost fell over themselves to cooperate with Katie's requests.

Katie had been clear when talking to them regarding keeping the investigation low key at this stage. She'd explained to the Human Resources director that the last thing she really wanted to do was to open a formal investigation into the Company in order to get the information she needed. The director instantly confirmed that they would comply without hesitation as their reputation didn't need to be tarnished with the fact that there was an active investigation. No matter how hard companies tried once a formal investigation was started the media always seemed to find out and that was something that a high profile company like this didn't want to experience. Especially as almost two thirds of their contracts were with large blue-chip organisations or government departments throughout Europe and the negative publicity a formal investigation brings was certainly something they wished to avoid.

Katie had been incredibly clear regarding the fact that none of the employees were to be informed and if it transpired that they had been alerted by anyone at all then not only would a formal investigation regarding the staff be started but a second larger investigation regarding the leak would be implemented and that sort of thing could be the end for any high profile business. Corruption relating to any government contracts always attracted the wrong sort of attention and any hint of a formal investigation would be very bad news indeed. Katie had hoped that the fear of that alone would ensure the complete and immediate assistance of all involved.

"Okay so next steps?" Katie looked round the table at the other three.

Alek leant forward, "I suggest we go back to the local office and do some digging and work through the manifest information we have so far to see if we can find any other obvious patient drop offs."

"Sounds like a plan," Katie looked at Carlos, "do you think we can utilise a few extra resources for when we get the details regarding the ambulance crews?"

Carlos nodded, "yes that shouldn't be a problem at all as long as it's basic financial and background checks."

"It would be at this stage, and we'll need some really quick answers as I'm a little worried now that more and more people are being made aware of the investigation."

"That's okay, I know a couple of analysts that will gladly help and they're both very good at what they do. If there's anything to find they should be able to find it fairly quickly."

Katie smiled, "that's good, okay let's go," she looked over at Alek, "on the way to the office we can make some calls to update everyone on where we are and hopefully get a bit of an update on their side of things as well."

The drive to the office wasn't too long, they'd thanked the airport staff and as they were walking to the car Alek and Katie had both started to make the calls to the UK and the States to make contact with the others. It's probably why the journey didn't seem to take as long as they'd expected. They hadn't been paying much attention to the drive itself as they were focusing on the information they were passing on. Followed by the fact they were then processing the updates they were getting regarding how the investigation was going elsewhere. They were both surprised when the car engine was suddenly shut down, they finished their respective calls quickly and got out of the car.

They were in an open air car park in front of a modern two story building, the car park contained about fifty vehicles. Carlos led the way as they walked towards the main entrance, "you'll both need to have your ID showing at all times, the boss is a little strict on that," Alek noticed that both Carlos and Adrianna now had their ID's on display. Katie took hers out of her pocket and clipped it to the pocket on her jacket.

Before Alek could say anything Adrianna spoke up, "I'll get you a temporary ID Alek."

Alek smiled at her, "thank you, that's probably for the best."

Carlos stopped and turned round, "how can you not have your ID on you? Its basic protocol to have it with you at all times unless you're undercover."

Alek shrugged his shoulders, "well I can use my ID if you like but I'm not sure if your boss would be overly impressed at the commotion I'd be causing everywhere I went."

Carlos had a look on his face that clearly showed he didn't understand what Alek was talking about which caused Adrianna to laugh at her partners expense.

"It's okay Carlos he's not with us so doesn't have a formal Interpol ID, he's with the FSB."

Carlos laughed, "of course he is."

"Yep that's what I said," she looked at Alek, "nobody takes you seriously do they?"

Alek shook his head, "no they don't," he took out his wallet and opening it passed it to Carlos.

Carlos looked at the ID and his face changed, "oh my god, you are."

Alek nodded, "Adrianna said that too."

Katie stepped forward putting her arm round Alek's shoulder, "it's okay Carlos he's house trained, and I'll keep an eye on him."

The expression on Carlos's face changed to one of embarrassment, "I'm so sorry Alek I didn't mean that to sound as bad as it did. I just assumed that you were from the same office as Katie," he passed the wallet back to Alek.

Putting it back in his pocket he looked at Carlos, "it's fine and please don't worry it happens all the time."

They made their way to the door and walked into the reception area, Adrianna spoke to one of the reception team who very quickly produced a visitors pass and passed it to Alek, "we have two types of visitors pass, one allows unsupervised access to the building and the other one is obviously a must be supervised at all times pass, the one you've got is the former."

Alek raised an eyebrow, "really, I'm surprised you have gone for the always supervised option."

"Oh don't worry I did think about doing that," she had a mischievous look on her face, "but then Carlos would have to escort you everywhere and explain why and I didn't think he'd enjoy that."

Carlos looked embarrassed again, "okay let's move on and pretend I didn't say anything."

Adrianna laughed, "we'll use conference room two to start with and I'll go and get the boss so that we can update her with what's going on." The conference room was big enough to seat ten around the main table in the centre of the room. It was basic and yet functional. Katie led the update and kept it simple. She'd added at the end that it would be helpful if they could use a couple of additional resources to enable them to speed up the background and financial checks and that request had been signed off without hesitation. After the briefing Carlos had left to go and find the two people he wanted to help them.

Katie had received two emails from the medical company that owned the ambulances. The first basically stated that the company would assist in any way possible and that they would not withhold any information. There was a whole paragraph dedicated to what amounted to a plea for some sort of confidentiality regarding the investigation. In essence they were asking that in return for their complete cooperation that the investigation be kept under the table. The second email contained several attachments relating to staff, routes, patients etc. Katie forwarded both emails to the others as they all began setting up their various devices that they'd need in the next few hours. Carlos came back and a few minutes later they were all joined by two analysts, Carlos introduced everyone to Jacques and Pierre, introductions done they sat down and opened their laptops.

Katie gave them a quick insight as to where they were so far and the help they needed. When she'd finished she looked at the two newcomers, "so what do you need us to do to help you?"

Pierre had a blank look on his face, "sorry, what do you mean?"

"Well, I've just explained what we hope to achieve in regards to background and financial checks," she paused for a second, "I now need to know what you need from us to help you."

"Oh," the blank look was still there, "well normally we're just given a whole load of data and expected to make sense of it and deliver the desired results."

"Yes, that doesn't surprise me but we don't work like that so what I need to know is what information you need from us to make things easier and faster for you."

Pierre looked a little less blank now, "well, all we really need is the employee details in order to make a start."

"Okay that's easy I'll send that to you both now," Katie looked down at her Mac, "what are your email addresses?"

Pierre rattled off the addresses and Katie sent the email, "so that's done. Alek can you work through the manifest details and find any other anomalies. Adrianna could you look into the routes etc for the five crews for the past few months. There's a lot to go through and I'll help you with that. Carlos, could you set up a localised folder so that we can start to drop all of the information into it. It'll need to be outside the normal structure so that Alek can view it."

Jacque spoke for the first time, "I've already done that," he didn't look up from his screen or stop typing while he was talking, "it's on the secondary drive and I've simply called it Operation Outsider," he suddenly stopped typing and looked up, "wait, you said it needs to be outside the normal structure for Alek?"

"Yes I did," Katie paused for effect, "Alek doesn't have an Interpol login so he can't access the secure system."

Jacque looked across at Alek, his eyes resting on the visitor's badge. "Oh." he looked up at Alek's face to find Alek smiling at him, "erm okay I can move the folder easy enough it'll only take a second," he looked back down at his screen again, a few seconds later he looked back up, "there it's all done, so you're not with Interpol then?"

Before Alek could answer Carlos said, "oh god here we go again."

Katie jumped in, "no he isn't, both Alek and I are on loan to a multinational team and every so often we fall back to enlist the help and assistance of the actual agency that we're with hence why we're here right now."

The next couple of hours flew by as each of them focused on the area they'd been given. Every so often Alek or Katie would receive a text or call from other members of the team, they were all making notes and adding to the folder which was gradually growing in size. Pierre and Jacque were very good at what they did, very good indeed. Before long they had completed all of the background checks on the five ambulance crews. The financial checks had already been started and the first few bits of information were now dropping in. Katie made everyone aware that she was going to pause for a short while so that everyone could get together what they had so far and have a mini update so that they all had an idea as to where things were heading. She explained that this would allow her to re task everyone if she needed to add more resource to a particular area of the investigation.

They all broke to grab a drink and spent five minutes or so pulling all the useful bits of information together so that they could each give a concise update. Alek went first, "so I've managed to find four further examples of the plane dropping off a passenger at the same airport in the last six weeks. Each time they fly in from the states with one passenger and leave with none. I can't tell yet if it's the same medical Company that take the passenger away but I'm working through the gate logs now in the hope of linking that all up."

Katie nodded, "okay that's good in one sense but not great in the bigger scheme of things as this seems to look as though it's becoming a bigger problem than we first thought, Adrianna how are you doing?"

Adrianna quickly looked down at her notes, "each ambulance is GPS tracked and we have the password to view the data. The challenge is that the first thing I need to do is go through the daily workload for each vehicle in order to work out how many stops it should have and where they are so it's far from an easy task. All I've managed to complete so far is the route for the day we're interested in and a day either side. The system is just plotting the route maps for me now to compare. I hadn't realised how challenging this was going to be, sorry."

Katie nodded, "that's okay and it's why we do exactly this. Alek and I will both stop what we're doing and help with that as soon as we're done. Carlos what have you got so far?"

"Well as soon as the folder was set up I started to add some of the stuff that we'd already imaged. I've also created an action log detailing what we've done so far just in case we need to refer to it at a later date. I have a feeling that this isn't going to be a quick case."

Katie shook her head, "no it isn't, we may get a quick initial result but I think the evidence will be appearing for some time to come and as we unearth each new lead we'll find a whole load of new things to deal with."

Without waiting Pierre spoke, "we've had the background checks come back for all ten employees and to be fair as you'd expect they are all clean. It's not a surprise as anyone wanting to work for this company is put through a very stringent vetting process before they start so if there were any concerns they wouldn't have been employed. We've started the financial checks but that takes considerably longer, it may be a while before we get anything that we can actually work with."

"Okay so I think it's fair to say that we need to focus on the routes the vehicles actually take compared to what their work logs show," Katie looked round the table, "let's pair up and take a crew each. One of each pair plots the route as per the job list supplied by the company the other checks the GPS tracking log to see if they divert off route. We'll break in a couple of hours for something to eat."

Alek leant forward in his seat, "why don't we send someone out for some sandwiches and coffee now and then we run straight through till we've had enough."

Katie nodded, "not a bad idea to be fair, is everyone happy with that?" Everyone agreed and Jacque made a list of what they all wanted. There was a local sandwich bar that operated a delivery service which made things really simple and within forty-five minutes the table they were sat at was covered with sandwiches, cakes and coffees.

It was hard going, each day an ambulance had a pre-planned patient list with various drop off and pick up points. Although they appeared to only move five or six patients a day on average it still took a quite a bit of time to plot out the route taken. They all gradually got into a bit of a rhythm, and they were ever so slowly working their way through the days. Alek had selected the crew that they already knew had carried out an unscheduled collection and delivery. he was scanning through their worksheets and plotting the routes as Adrianna overlaid them onto the GPS tracking routes. On the day in question they had already confirmed that the collection they'd seen on CCTV was indeed unscheduled.

The hours moved on, they were making some headway and had found another potentially unauthorised pick up from the airfield. Rather worryingly it wasn't the same crew which meant they now had to assume that at least two crews were involved and they had rather hoped that it would have been the same crew as that would have made things easier. Katie had already updated Barney and had promised to get back to him with a further update as soon as she could. Half an hour later Alek confirmed a third possible pick up carried out by the original crew they were investigating. Katie immediately asked Jacque and Pierre to focus on the financial records of the first crew. She needn't have worried as they had already set the original ambulance crew up as the first searches they started.

The hours ticked by and Katie became conscious of the time. She knew that her and Alek would carry on for a few hours yet, but she gave the others the chance to call it a day and go home. Without hesitation they all said they'd continue so she ordered several pizzas. With all the financial searches set up and running all six of them were now focusing on matching the crews' worksheets with the tracking reports. By ten in the evening they had four probable cases spread over a five week period, three of which were involving the original crew. Katie called a halt to everything at that point suggesting they all left for the evening and started again first thing in the morning. Everyone agreed and the lights in the room were finally turned off at half ten after a very productive but somewhat exhausting day.

Chapter 26 (Europe)

The following morning in Hove Sean was up early, as he had to collect Charlie from the airport. When they got back neither Nick nor Chris were up yet so he took Bruce out for a walk. Something was niggling at him and he couldn't put his finger on it. He took his phone out of his pocket, flicking through his recent calls he tapped the name as it appeared, "Alek it's Sean, can you talk?" the response was instant, "good, you've met both Joseph and Frederik did you get a feeling at all that they were hiding something?" Sean listened for a second, "I'll be back in the office in about twenty minutes. Give me a call in an hour," with the call finished he put the phone back in his pocket and walked Bruce back to the office. He fed him some breakfast and then started to prepare his own.

He went for a fry up and knowing that the other two would magically appear when they smelt food so he did enough for all of them. Sure enough just as he was frying the eggs Chris and Nick appeared, "make the coffee Nick, breakfast will be ready in a couple of minutes."

"So Nick, have you had any luck finding anything out?"

"Not yet, I have now got a more detailed list of properties and holdings which are far more extensive than I expected. The bank records are still running and as yet I've got nothing on the girl. No records of anyone being found matching her description but I think that Katie will have more luck with that so I'll focus on looking into Frederik."

"I'm not sure if we'll find anything to be fair."

He nodded, "you may be right, everything that I've found so far seems to be legit and I haven't been able to find anything negative at all on any wider search. He may be a bit of a dead end although there's hardly any mention of him before the age of eighteen."

Charlie didn't look surprised, "not unusual, life in Germany back then wasn't as straight forward as it is now and they had a whole load of restrictions in place."

"I'll keep looking, so what's you plan now?"

"Just waiting for James or Barney to decide if they need me. If they don't then I can pull a few shifts at the County while I wait for them to assign me to something." Charlie was still an active member of the British Army and would frequently help out at any local hospital whenever she wasn't on assignment. It allowed her to keep up to date with the ever changing world of surgery. It was also part of a wider initiative the armed forces were backing whereby they lent out some key members of staff to assist with civilian organisations every so often. Part of a domestic hearts and minds campaign that had been dreamt up. Charlie was lucky enough not only to be part of the Generals team but also to have built a good enough relationship with the local hospital which allowed her to get some valuable hours in the operating theatre.

Nick made his way over to the kettle and got four mugs ready. Chris grabbed some cutlery and took it through to the table. Alek was due to call in fifteen minutes so Sean knew he just about had time although they could take the call while eating if need be. He served the food up onto the four plates he'd already got out and took it through. Nick had already taken the mugs of coffee through and Chris had poured them each a glass of orange juice.

Sean told the others about the call to Alek explaining that there was something that he couldn't explain but it was bothering him, "I suppose it's this, why stop at one? If you've got that much disposable income would you stop or would you go again?"

"Well, I haven't picked up on anything in the recordings or notes that would lead me to believe that they would. I mean they're both trying to confess in their own ways to make things right," Nick cut into his second sausage as soon as he stopped talking.

"But if you've got that much power and have had a taste of full control over someone, would you give it up or want more?"

232

Chris put his glass down, "I can see where you're coming from and yes I can imagine that someone that was a sadistic power hungry billionaire might want more."

"That's what I'm worried about, are we missing something? Alek has spoken to both men and I want to get his opinion. I couldn't get hold of either of them last night and if I'm honest I'm not sure if they'll even be truthful with us which is why I want to run it past Alek."

Charlie got a text from James stating that for the next couple of days unless something big came in she'd be free. She thought that would be the case as Sean, Levi and Chris were at the office so they had enough people around to be able to spare her. She let the others know and picking up her plate left them to it. For the next couple of minutes they ate in silence, all finishing at around the same time. Chris picked the plates up and took them out to the kitchen, placing them in the dishwasher he then added the frying pan and saucepans as well. He walked back into the dining area just as the phone beside Sean rang, "hi Alek you're on speaker phone and Chris and Nick are with me."

"Nice of them to get up, Katie will be joining me is a second she's just getting some breakfast."

Sean laughed, "that'll be a healthy croissant or a pastry or two then, we thoroughly enjoyed our fry up."

"Yeh thanks for that, she's back now so stop talking about her like that."

"Morning Katie ignore him we weren't talking about you at all."

"I know you weren't, but I don't doubt for one second that you were teasing him about breakfast."

Sean laughed, "we might have been, how are the croissants today?"

"They're lovely and fresh thank you and I suppose you fat gits had a delightfully healthy fried breakfast."

"There is a distinct possibility that we may have done."

"So predictable, now why are you bothering us at this ridiculous time of the morning?"

"Katie I've got a question for you both. Do you think that Frederik was being completely truthful? I've listened to the recording and I've read the reports for both Frederik and Josef and I can't help but feel something isn't right but for the life of me I can't put my finger on it."

"I only met Frederik but he seemed to be genuine but that doesn't mean he was withholding something."

Alek spoke next, "so I met both and I would honestly say that the emotion that Josef showed would lead me to believe that he was being totally honest and I don't think he was withholding anything at all. Frederik on the other hand in comparison seemed almost blasé about the whole thing. He did express remorse and the fact that he'd found god etc but it was all said with virtually zero emotion or shame whereas Josef struggled to talk to us at times."

"I agree, I listed to both recordings several times last night and that's what has made me ask the question. There's no doubt that both men were or are sadistic power hungry control freaks. It's why they've been as successful as they have. I tried to get hold of both of them last night and failed. Josef isn't well and Frederik wasn't answering."

"Sean I'm not saying that I think Frederik hasn't been truthful with us but if you compare the two then yes there's a possibility he withheld something."

"Okay that's cool, I'm going to try to get hold of them again and if I can't I might catch a flight across to meet Josef face to face as I know where he is as I spoke to his nurse yesterday and he's at home and in a bad way."

"Who have you got to go with you, is Charlie around?"

"No Alek she's just left to go to County for a couple of theatre shifts, I'd go across with Chris."

"If you're going to go Sean I suggest that Katie meets you and you go together, Josef is old school and when we met him he was far more receptive towards Cass than he was to me, I think this is a case where a female is more likely to get more of a positive response from him."

"Are you up for that Katie?"

"Yes definitely, what about if Alek and I go from here, we've got the initial people searches underway and are now just waiting for any results that come back so we're effectively playing a waiting game for now."

"I'm good with that and it makes sense. In that case do you want to make contact with Josef or his nurse and let them know you're going to see them?"

"Yes, we'll do that right now."

They all said their goodbyes and the call ended.

In order to free Nick up Sean and Chris started digging into the information they'd found on Frederik. It wasn't absolutely necessary as

234

he hadn't been able to give them as much information or details as Joseph but rather than sit around they decided between them to do something at least marginally useful rather than do nothing. Levi had received a call and had been summoned back to the states, something to do with a DEA case that he'd been working on. This often happened with some of the team members, during quieter periods they'd return to their various agencies to carry out refresher training or to help out with ongoing investigations. Levi had been gone for a six-week period before recently coming back to the team and as luck would have it with a fair few members of the team stateside if he was released quickly he would be able to join them.

As always, any investigation involving the dark web was far from easy. Nick had followed the emails and was three or four levels down. Each level had more complex security and Nick had quickly realised that this wasn't a group of amateur's emails that he was tracking. The encryption was far from simple and just as he thought he was getting somewhere he'd hit another level of protection and would have to work his way though it before progressing. The hours rolled on and he suddenly realised that he needed a break. He took a shower and then went to find the other two, they were set up in one of the meeting rooms and Bruce was keeping them company.

"Right guys I need to get something to eat, do you want to join me or are you okay?"

Sean looked up, "no, I'll happily take a break this is getting boring now. I know it's better than doing nothing but I'm losing interest."

"Me too," to prove his point Chris shut the lid on his Mac and stood up, "right where are we going?"

"Well, I need a bit of exercise so we can either walk down to KFC in Boundary road or walk along to Burger King."

"Ok so let's do Burger King but we'll drive there. Order at the drive through and then park up and walk across to Hove park and that way Bruce can have a run while we walk round the park and eat." Bruce had heard Sean mention his name but hadn't moved anything other than his left ear. That changed when Sean got to the bottom of the stairs and opened the back of the Audi, "come on then boy," Bruce was instantly up and on his way, expertly bounding down the stairs and jumping into the back of the car. They arrived at the drive through and once they'd got their order they parked up and went for a leisurely stroll around the park. After an hour they made their way back to the car and went back to the office to continue with the laborious task that they'd left behind. This they all agreed was the worst side of the job that they did. Unfortunately, it took up quite a high percentage of the investigation but it was something they accepted and they knew that without the research and background checks they'd never dig up the clues they needed.

Nick, Chris and Sean hadn't stopped, the volume of information they'd gone through was incredible. They had managed to make some headway though and although things weren't moving anywhere near as quickly as they'd like they were happy with what they'd found so far. Nick had been focusing on the emails and had managed to get to the point of identifying five shell companies that the emails had been routed through. Now he had the additional emails that had been found on the laptop in the warehouse in the states he'd managed to confirm that they all used the same encryption. More importantly it gave them definitive proof that they were now on the right track and that they were all investigating the same thing. As each hour went by, he got a step closer although he knew that the likelihood of actually tracking everything back to the original sender was unlikely he would hopefully be able to find out enough to give them a starting point.

Chris and Sean had been running countless searches for the Steiner family, not easy considering the sheer volume of families that shared that name. They'd split the search, Chris was focusing on Frederik and Sean was searching for broader family connections. It was time consuming and they'd been met with numerous dead ends forcing them to start again. Sean got up to stretch his legs and to make them all a coffee, deciding they could all do with something to eat he quickly knocked up a couple of fried egg sandwiches each. Taking the coffee and egg sandwiches the other two he returned to the kitchen to grab his. Once back at his desk he started yet another search widening the parameters once more. A few seconds later the first results came in and he started the somewhat laborious task of sifting through each of the hits. Fifteen minutes in he was looking at a black and white photo taken in February 1945, it showed an SS officer being awarded a medal for his services on the Eastern Front. The translated caption under the photo read 'Major Karl Steiner of the 11th SS Panzer Division receiving his medal with his family'

Underneath that was a short paragraph explaining how his five year old son Frederik had stood to attention as his beloved father was awarded his medal. Sean did a bit more digging and found the full names of all three family members, a little exited he started to dig deeper. Two hours later he found that the trail ended in 1957 and he couldn't find anything at all after that, having learnt a few things from Nick over the years he sat and thought for a few minutes to work out how he could change the search parameters to achieve a different result. An hour and a half later he uncovered a record showing that Frederik Steiner had formally changed his surname. Sean had to assume it was to detract from any association from his Fathers service in the SS, although his Father had fought in a combat unit and wasn't linked at all with any atrocities that the SS had been accused of Sean guessed that Frederik wanted to distance himself all the same hence the name change.

With his newly found piece of information Sean went to see Chris to see if he'd managed to find anything. Chris hadn't been as lucky but now Sean had found a possible link he could do a few different types of search. They worked together for a bit, bouncing ideas off each other and after a short while had a second bit of luck. Chris had managed to find three properties that were linked to Karl Steiner. Two in Berlin and one just over 50 miles away in a small town. They took a property in Berlin each and started to see what they could find and a short while later found that both properties had been sold a short time after Karl Steiner had passed away. His wife had died the year before him and the properties were left to Frederik who it seems sold them almost immediately. They couldn't find any references at all to the third property. From what they could tell it had remained in the family name but appeared to have been left alone. They'd already gathered information of Frederik and there hadn't been any mention of the property at all.

They added it to the list of things to be checked, a list that was growing longer by the hour it seemed. As was often the case during an assignment they'd end up with numerous leads to chase down. A large number of which could be done electronically. There were always a few things that needed to be checked out physically and that's where things often slowed down as they only had so many bodies available to them and there were often significant distances separating the things that needed to be checked. Sean made a call to a contact he had in Berlin asking if they could do a bit of digging locally, once he'd done that, he called Katie to give her an update on what they'd found.

Chapter 27 (North America)

Less than twelve hours after the shooting at the warehouse Angie and Damien were sat in the outer office on the 18th floor of Stephen Goodbanks main office. It wasn't advertised as that, he had another office block that was listed as his main headquarters. For someone that desired privacy it was no surprise that he had an alternative office to use in a daily basis. The outer office was just as stylish and immaculate as the main office itself. Even though hardly anyone ever managed to make it up to this floor there was a receptionist sat at a desk, a desk that was clutter free, no phone just and Mac, mouse and keyboard. None of the usual paraphernalia you'd expect to see on a receptionist's desk, maybe because this was no ordinary receptionist. She was a mercenary, one of a number on Stephen Goodbanks payroll. Her job was to ensure that the only people that made it through his office door were the ones that he had invited.

The office door opened and despite the late hour Stephen Goodbanks was dressed immaculately, he stood at the door for a second before speaking, "come in, sorry for the delay," Angie and Damian stood up and made their way into the office. As usual it was immaculate however unlike their last visit the chairs at the table had been pulled out and it was obvious that this is where they were going to sit. Made even more evident by a smartly dressed man already sat at the table.

Goodbanks closed the door and turned round, "sit down both of you please," he made his way round the table and sat down. Angie and Damian sat next to each other both now very aware that this meeting was very different from the one they'd had not so long ago. "I'm glad you both got here as quickly as you did," he paused for a second before continuing, "this is Miguel, and he's here to assist me with a small issue that has presented itself."

Angie knew straight away that something was wrong, sitting at the table rather than the comfortable chairs at his desk was the first indication but the real give away was the business like edge to Goodbanks voice. She knew that this wasn't good and for the first time ever she was concerned.

"I'm guessing that neither of you know why you're here at this hour," he looked from one to the other, Damian shook his head and Angie managed to say, "no," her voice lacked its normal clarity and confidence.

"Then allow me to shed some light on this for you both. It has been brought to my attention that an element of one of our current operations has possibly been compromised, and that simply isn't good enough." There was now a real hard edge to the tone of his voice "Miguel is here as it has an indirect effect on one of his revenue streams and he will be taking care of things for me to ensure that the issue goes away immediately."

Angie was desperately trying to work out where she'd made a mistake or what she could have done to have created this problem, Damian was doing the same but Goodbanks didn't give them long enough to think before he continued.

"So I'm sure you're wondering what the problem is, before we get to that I want to make something perfectly clear. I value the job that the pair of you do. You each have your strengths and weaknesses and up till now I've never needed to question my decision with regard to the projects I get you to oversee. Now though I do have some concerns and believe me when I tell you that is not a position in which I wish to find myself."

Not that he needed any confirmation but the look on both of their faces told him that he had their undivided attention. He left it a few seconds before continuing, he wanted the gravity of the current situation to really settle in so that there could be no illusion as to how serious he considered things to be, "you are probably unaware of an FBI raid earlier today in which two gang members were killed, an FBI agent shot and in intensive care and a large amount of paperwork and drugs seized. Now the drugs on the surface aren't my initial concern. The paperwork seized is, as is the fact that the FBI felt the need to raid the premises in the first place. It transpires that they were following a lead on a missing person that led them to a couple of establishments that are run by a particular gang. It seems that the FBI managed to link the warehouse to the gang. Thankfully they missed a larger warehouse contacting significantly more drugs and a variety of weapons. Imagine my surprise, no make that my astonishment to find out that the missing person they are looking for is none other than one of our client's purchases."

Goodbanks looked at Angie and then at Damian, Angie had a slightly confused look on her face whereas Damian had the tell-tale signs of concern on his face.

"Angie, I can imagine that you are trying to quickly work out where you may have gone wrong and what you may have done. You needn't worry as in this instance the issue doesn't sit with you. Damian you on the other hand do need to worry as the missing person is one of the people that you arranged for delivery."

Damian now looked uncomfortable and found himself in a position that he'd never been in before. Angie was visibly relieved and her whole body seemed to have relaxed. Damian went to speak but before he could get a word out Goodbanks raised his hand indicating that Damian should keep quiet, "you'll have a chance to speak when I'm ready but for now you need to listen. The gang that you chose to use have an existing relationship with a Mexican Cartel. A rather large and somewhat unpleasant Cartel that does not take kindly to anyone interfering with their distribution network. The gang are a little low level to be honest but do move a significant quantity of merchandise and up to this point have been rather useful. The Cartel now feel however that the gang have served their purpose and that a message needs to be sent. The Cartel is going to remove the gang and are willing to concede that they'll need to look for an alternative in the area. The reason for such a drastic approach is twofold. Firstly they really do want to send a message to everyone that they are not to be messed with and failure has its price. Secondly, they are hoping to make it look as though the gangs dealings were completely linked to the drugs and weapons in the hope that the FBI drop the investigation into the missing person."

Goodbanks looked directly at Damian and could see more than just a little concern on his face, "do you have anything to add Damian?"

Unsure if the current mood warranted any familiarity Damian decided to choose his words carefully, "I've used this gang before a number of times and they have always been discreet and have delivered without any problems. They have always been aware that anything they do for me is of a sensitive nature and that they need to make sure they don't make any mistakes. I've always kept a close eye on what they do and they haven't ever made a mistake. Do the Cartel really need to send a message?"

"Now Damian that is a good question and one that I think we should ask them," Goodbanks turned to the man sitting next to him, "Miguel, do you really need to send a message?"

"Yes I do believe we do Stephen," Miguel turned and looked at Damian, "it's an understandable question Damian, may I call you Damian?" Miguel's voice was soft with only a very slight hint of an accent but the words were spoken with a dangerous authority. Damian knew instantly that this wasn't someone to mess with.

"Yes please do and I didn't mean to question your judgement."

"That is perfectly okay and I do understand why you would have asked. However I think after I've finished speaking you'll understand why I cannot allow this unfortunate incident to go unchecked. I was born into the world of drugs and guns, my father ran the Cartel somewhat successfully and realised from an early point that if we were going to stand above the other Cartels we needed to be smarter and stronger. Stronger is easy as you simply hire tougher men than your opposition, smarter however is not so simple. He sent me to live with a distant cousin in Texas and I was schooled in the US. I was educated to the highest level with private tutors and I excelled. I focused on business studies, economics and law, it wasn't easy and when I'd finished my education I was approached by several global companies but I politely declined all the job offers and returned to Mexico. My father handed over control of the Cartel to me and I set about changing our structure and business model. We may not be the biggest but I do know that we are the most profitable and that's not due to over inflated prices but due to the way we conduct our business. There are no second chances, if you do business with us you are made aware of that from the outset. It is for this reason that an example will be set. The gang in question have risked a highly profitable revenue stream and I will not allow that to go unchecked. It is only a matter of time before the FBI involves the DEA and they will discover a second property that the gang use. That property has a significant amount of drugs and weapons stored in it. That is going to be moved and all evidence of the gangs involvement with my Cartel will be removed. I think you will understand and agree that in order to maintain a strong working relationship with all of my suppliers and distributors I am not in a position to let this sort of thing go unpunished."

The room was silent and stayed that way for several seconds. Damian didn't know what to say first. He realised he'd made a big mistake. He'd used the gang for several things before but knew now that involving them in abducting people was a monumental mistake and he was worried about what the cost of that mistake was going to be to him.

Goodbanks broke the silence, "Damian, up until now I've never had reason to question or doubt anything you've done. This however is an error of judgement that is going to cost me considerably. I have to be honest and say that I'm surprised by your lack of judgement and I'd like to think that moving forward you'll reconsider the methods you use to fulfil any requests that our customers have."

"It's not a mistake I'm going to make again, I can assure you."

"Good, I really do hope that we don't have to have this type of conversation again. Can you please wait outside while I discuss with Miguel how we tidy things up. I want to speak to you both afterwards about other matters and I don't want to hold Miguel up for any longer than necessary."

Angie and Damian got straight up without saying a word. They knew from the tone of Goodbanks voice that he wasn't looking for any acknowledgement. Less than thirty minutes later the door opened and Miguel walked out, he stopped in front of Damian, "this error has cost your boss a significant amount of time and money, you're lucky that he holds you in such high regard. Let me be clear, if you had been working for me and displayed this error in judgement I would have had you permanently removed from the organisation," the menace in Miguel's voice was evident and Damian didn't doubt for a second that he was telling the truth. "I have assured Stephen that this mess will be cleared up straight away and that nothing will come back in his direction. I have also told him that he needs to be aware that no matter how high his regard for you is that you and I will never work together on any project no matter how small your involvement."

Damian could think of nothing else to say other than, "I understand."

"Good," Miguel didn't even acknowledge Angie, he simply turned away and made his way towards the lift.

Goodbanks appeared at his office door, "you'd both better come back in," his voice hadn't quite returned to its normal pitch and they'd worked for him long enough to know that this incident wouldn't be forgotten for some time to come. They made their way back into the office. As if to reiterate the current mood he sat back at the table again rather than his desk, keeping the meeting more formal than it would normally be.

"I'm sure I don't need to tell ether of you that this is a setback I could have done without. Miguel is going to deal with it and he assures me the problem will go away. It won't surprise you to know that he has dedicated teams that deal with this sort of thing and that they are particularly thorough."

Damian paused before speaking, "Mr ..." before he could say anything else Goodbanks held up his hand.

"Stop there Damian, its Stephen now that we're on our own. Having said that please don't think that this means that I'm okay with what has happened because I'm not. The next mistake like this will not be treated so casually."

"Sorry Stephen, the people I use are vetted and they've never made a mistake like this in the past."

"I don't think they made a mistake this time, I think they've just been very unlucky and somehow came to the attention of the FBI. That being said we cannot afford to have anything derail what we're doing and it does need to be dealt with. I have no idea what Miguel has in store for them and I don't want to know. I trust his judgement and he'll do what is necessary to protect our business arrangement."

Miguel knew what he was going to do even before he'd left the meeting the night before. He'd set things in motion as he'd left the office and was now simply awaiting confirmation that everything had been dealt with.

The team had split into two teams of four and while one team positioned itself at the front of the warehouse the other was at the back. Each of the team leaders had a screen strapped to their left forearm and they were both looking at a live feed from the CCTV system inside the warehouse. Every member of the eight man team looked almost identical. They were all in black. A pistol in a thigh holster and another in a holster on their chest plate with a suppressed M4 as their main weapon. A variety of concussion grenades and flashbangs were attached to their kit as well as a number of magazine pouches.

They looked and behaved as you'd expect any Special Forces team to do. However this team wasn't attached to any part of the American armed forces. In fact they weren't part of any recognised armed forces at all. This eight man team was one of three that Miguel De La Cruz had at his disposal. The Cartel had long ago realised that normal armed members of the Cartel were okay for most of the day to day stuff but some situations required a higher level of expertise. Miguel had arranged for a select number of men to be put through a yearlong training program run by four mercenaries. The end result was that he now had three eight man teams of elite fighters with skills and weaponry that matched or bettered a large number of Special Forces teams worldwide.

As each sub team leader was focusing on the screen on their forearm the number two of the team was busy picking the lock on the door in front of them. Almost simultaneously they both stepped back indicating that the doors were now unlocked. Alpha one spoke "Alpha and Bravo teams we have eleven targets inside all on the lower floor, no targets currently on any other floor or in any office." There weren't any individual replies, instead the last member of the team tapped the team member in front on the shoulder, as soon as Bravo team leader felt a tap on his shoulder he replied, "Bravo team ready."

Almost at the same time Alpha team leader felt a tap on his shoulder "Alpha team ready." Somewhere close by someone tapped a command into a laptop and the CCTV system in the warehouse shut down. "Alpha and Bravo teams go," without hesitating the two teams entered the warehouse via their respective doors. They'd already studied plans of the warehouse and had seen CCTV footage showing them were various pallets and boxes were stacked.

The teams entered the warehouse and spread out in pairs, each person had a pre designated arc of fire to ensure that none of the team were in danger of getting caught in any crossfire. A strange buzzing sound filled the air for about thirty seconds and then there was complete silence. "Alpha team clear." "Bravo team clear." Less than sixty seconds after entering the warehouse all eleven gang members were dead. Three trucks moved into the warehouse loading bay and started to reverse up to the loading doors. Two men jumped out of each truck and moved into the warehouse to open the doors and as soon as the trucks were inside the doors were closed.

Alpha and Bravo team left the warehouse and made their way back to the two vehicles they'd arrived in. Once in they made their way to the rear of the strip club. The displays on the team leaders forearms now showed a different set of CCTV images. They had eight targets left to eliminate and they could see five of them at the strip club which meant the remaining three were at the restaurant or elsewhere. Once again from somewhere close by Alpha team leader was given the go ahead as the CCTV images went blank. For the second time things went like clockwork and in less than a minute there were three dead in a large storeroom and two dead in an outer office.

The two teams moved location to the restaurant. This time there was a complication as only two gang members could be seen on the CCTV. Photos of the remaining three targets were now displayed on the team leader's screens. Ten seconds later they had the home address of the missing gang member. Bravo team headed over to that location while Alpha team moved a block away. They had allowed for this but were hoping that all of the gang members would be together at the three locations. They knew they didn't need to worry about the smaller warehouse as that was still under the control of the FBI and they knew the gang wouldn't go anywhere near it.

"Alpha team, we've just passed the target heading towards you but don't know if he's heading to the strip club or the restaurant. We've just turned round and are following him, wait out."

"He's heading to you eta thirty seconds."

The vehicle pulled into the parking lot and the second the engine was turned off the driver was dead. Alpha team split into pairs again and entered the rear door of the restaurant. The remaining two targets were in the first office on the left and were dead before they'd even realised the office door had been opened. Alpha team retreated back into the parking lot and got into their vehicles. Their job was done and so they drove off into the night. Less than an hour from arriving at the location their task had been completed.

The first two lorries had been loaded and the third lorry was over half full when the lead driver received a call to let him know that the main team had completed their task, "listen in people let's get this last truck loaded, I want to be out of here within ten minutes," there was a flurry of activity and nine minutes later the doors were being opened again and the trucks pulled out. They stopped once outside and one person from each truck jumped in after having closed the loading doors. The trucks pulled out and went their separate ways into the night loaded with all of the drugs and weapons that the gang had been handling for the Cartel.

Miguel received a text. 'All dead, no collateral' he'd been clear that he didn't want any innocent people killed. This was one of the times that he wanted the Cartel to carry out a precise targeted execution. Another example of what happens if you make a mistake whilst working with the Cartel. He sent a one-word text to Goodbanks, it just said 'Done'

Miguel sat back content with how things had gone. He'd been fairly confident that it was going to go well when he selected the team he was sending. They had an almost perfect record and he'd been exceptionally clear when explaining what he wanted. The success was more than just about cementing his reputation. He'd been working for some time now in conjunction with Goodbanks on a new high end drug and that alliance was going to make him countless millions and so it was vital that nothing came in between the two of them to cause any rifts or issues.

Chapter 28 (North America)

They all met for breakfast at eight and after a quick update from Cass they made their way back to the precinct. As soon as they arrived they knew something wasn't right. The floor the office they'd been using was on seemed to be overflowing with people. The noise level was certainly higher than it had been and there seemed to be a serious amount of frenzied activity. They made their way to the office and sat down. Getting their Macs and laptops out they got themselves ready for the day. Kelly was the first to get himself set up and volunteered to go and find someone from CSI to see what they'd found out so far. He hadn't been gone for more than two minutes before he was back.

Joss looked up from her Mac, "that was quick."

Kelly had an odd look on his face, "well yes, but that's because I didn't get any further than the second desk outside the office. It seems as though we've made an impression and after leaving us pretty much everyone agreed to lend a hand and well you've got to come and take a look," with that he left the office again and everyone followed. The Captain was talking to one of the detectives and when he saw them all standing there he came over.

"Morning, so I've got to say I'm grateful for whatever it is you've done to bring this team together like this."

Joss looked a bit shocked, "well we haven't done anything really."

"You're wrong there, the night shift got the initial results from the CSI team and ran with what they had. A few favours here and there and they'd run the prints and fibres through the databases. Sadly no hits but they're still trying a few other options. Most of the day team came in early and most of the night team are still here."

247

Joss was almost lost for words, "I don't know what to say."

A detective that had been one of the first to leave the bar the night before overheard Joss and came over, "it's simple, we get allsorts coming in every now and then asking for help or favours and we get the odd thank you or update every now and then but you've all made us feel part of the team."

"That's just how we work, we've always found that involving the people we're working with rather than just using them nearly always gets better results."

"Well it got me thinking and when I left you last night I came back here to talk with the guys on nights and asked them if they'd mind doing a bit of digging if they got the results from the forensic team and that's exactly what they did. One thing led to another and before we all knew it we'd all agreed to come in early or stay late to see what we could find out."

Kelly spoke up "This is great news, have you managed to find anything new?"

"Well yes and no, so we've found a few new bits of CCTV and we've now put everything together so that we've got a timeline and route up to the point that they ditched the vehicle. Two of the guys have worked through the possible routes they may have taken and selected the two most likely based on probable destinations. It's all guesswork and based on a hunch they've concluded that they were most likely heading to either one of three major cities or one of two airfields."

"Do they want to come into the office and brief us on what they've concluded?"

"Yes I think they'd definitely want to do that."

With the help of several of the detectives in just under an hour they'd reviewed everything that had been gathered so far. Sadly it hadn't given them any definitive results but the traffic cameras in the three most likely cities were being looked at and what limited CCTV was available from the two airfields was being sent over.

Joss sat back in her seat, "thank you everyone, what we've achieved here is quite remarkable considering what little we had to go on. I know that we haven't managed to identify anyone but at least we have a good starting point now."

Kelly stood up, "let's get a quick coffee and take five, after that we'll hopefully have the airfield footage to go through."

The office emptied, Boyd had volunteered to go and get some doughnuts and the others made their way to the break room. Just as Joss stood up her phone rang, she looked down at the display to see that it was Cass, "hey Cass how's it going?"

Within seconds Joss had a look of concern on her face. Kelly had seen Joss answer the phone before he'd left the office so he'd grabbed Joss a coffee and had just come back into the office when he saw the worried look that Joss had now adopted, "thanks for letting me know Cass and I'll update the others, if you need anything let me know," Joss ended the call and put the phone back on the desk.

Kelly passed over the mug of coffee that he'd got her, "what's wrong."

Joss took a deep breath, "Drew has been shot during the search. He's is surgery now and they don't have an update as yet on his condition. Cass wanted us to know just in case the news came in from somewhere else."

"Is anyone else hurt."

"No, well none of the team anyway. They killed two suspects but Cass didn't give me the full details all she wanted to do was give us the heads up really. We'll get an update shortly I would imagine."

"Hell that's not the sort of news we want if I'm honest."

Joss looked at Kelly, "no, it most certainly isn't."

The team came back in but the detectives had gone back to their desks. Some getting back onto the cases they were dealing with and some making calls to friends who were running the CCTV searches in the cities they were interested in. Joss briefed the team as soon as they were all sat back down. Boyd had returned with the doughnuts and the room now had a rather subdued feeling about it. Just then one of the detectives popped his head round the door, "we've tracked the van through the first city and clean out the other side so we're just trying to pick it up again."

"Okay everyone here's what we're going to do," they all looked at Joss, "Kelly you and Boyd go out and join the detectives trawling through the CCTV. It'll show some appreciation if we get amongst them. Ed and I will go and get some lunch for everyone and then we'll split the remaining CCTV footage up amongst all of us."

After they spent another three hours going through various bits of CCTV footage they'd lost the van. Joss had stood all of the detectives down and had spoken to their Captain. As far as she could work out for the moment they'd done everything they could and after a lengthy conversation with Barney it had been decided that the team should head back to Luke. They said their goodbyes to the detectives and after thanking them all once again headed off to the airport to meet Jess or Mitch for the flight back.

As the team took to the air on their way back to Luke some distance away the light on a server started blinking as it uploaded the latest routine back up file from a CCTV system. Just four miles outside of the zone the team had been searching the server finished the upload and the files were stored. One of the files previously uploaded contained the clear images of a vehicle arriving and pulling up to a plane belonging to a reputable medical company. The footage clearly showed a female patient being loaded onto the plane.

Barney now had both teams back under one roof and a huge challenge ahead of them all as the evidence they now had was mounting up at an alarming rate. Although neither team had registered a solid breakthrough they had both gathered some good intelligence that may or may not get them to the next step. He'd stood both teams down for twelve hours to allow him to work with James to come up with a suitable strategy to hopefully get them to the next big break.

Grace had been working flat out trying to keep up with the vast amount of data both teams had been sending back. She'd enlisted the help of a couple of the on base techies to help her catalogue everything. Between them they'd just about managed to keep on top of it and she was now adding some finishing touches to a software program that would enable them to search through it all and group relevant bits of data together. It hadn't been easy as they had to tag each file with keywords in order for the software to collate it all. She'd been working with Barney and James to create a number of keywords that they'd put together to enable them to run several searches to give various results. She was pleased with what she'd done so far and typed the commands in to allow the software loose on the thousands of files they'd uploaded.

Barney had told Grace to call it a day and to be back for 08:00 when he'd brief the teams. He made several calls and took a few. One of them being an update on Drew, who was out of the woods and recovering as well as can be expected. After that call Barney sat for a while mulling over in his head what had happened and what he could have done differently. Eventually he accepted that as far as he could see he'd made every allowance possible and that the team on the ground had acted in accordance with the plan. It was just one of those unfortunate incidents that you can't always allow for no matter how well you plan. His mind drifted back to him and Sean approaching the house before it blew up in front of him and he shook his head. All things considered taking into account what the teams did they'd been lucky not to have succumbed to more knock backs than they had.

His phone rang again and he answered it, he spoke for a few seconds then listened for several minutes. He ended the call and then rang James to update him. He put his phone on the desk and leant forward resting his head in his hands. After a few minutes he got up and went to get himself a coffee and something to eat before crashing out for the night. He'd grabbed some food and noticed that Cole was sitting at one of the tables. They'd already spoken before Cole flew out to meet the team and so Barney made his way over, "mind if I join you?"

Cole looked up, "no please do, as it happens it'll be nice to give you a quick rundown before you see my initial report in the morning."

Barney nodded in appreciation, "so how is he?"

"Well he's a tough kid and like most people his age is quite happy to bottle his feelings up. Luckily for me you've got a couple of people in your team he really looks up to. Scott has worked wonders with him and helped him to open up but it was after a lengthy phone call to one of your team in the UK that he really let his guard down and spoke freely and honestly."

"That'll be Sean he spoke to, we've got a number of people in the team that have seen combat but Scott and Sean are the two that Danny really looks up to. I know that Sean has been doing some weapons training with Danny and I'm sure during that whether Danny knew it or not Sean will have been discussing the effects of the various situations and the coping strategies that he uses."

"Yes it was Sean, I spoke to Scott afterwards and he said the same as you. I gave Sean a call and had a long talk with him and he gave me a good idea as to how he feels Danny will be coping and the best way to get him to open up. I've got to say it saved me some serious time as almost straight away he became more open. He feels guilty, he knows that he had to pull the trigger and he's very aware of the consequences if he hadn't but none the less he feels guilty. He's questioning himself and wondering what he could have done differently to have avoided taking those shots."

"Do you think he could have done anything else?"

Cole lifted his coffee cup pausing for a second, "no, I don't think he could," he took a mouthful of Coffee, "I've spoken with Cass and Scott and from the information I have there isn't anything else he could have done. In fact his actions made all the difference and if he hadn't acted the way that he did then the outcome would have been very different indeed," he put the cup down, "you've got a great team and I'm sure you don't need me to tell you that. They look out for each other both physically and mentally. I think he'll be absolutely fine but it might be an idea to keep him back a little bit for a while if you can."

"Well for the next 24 to 48 hours we're going to be firmly based here while we go through everything we have and to then come up with a plan for our next steps so there's going to be plenty for him to do on base."

"Good, it would be a good idea to get him to spend some dedicated one on one time with Scott. I know what that guy's been through and he'll definitely have some sound advice that Danny will listen to and take on board."

"I will do, we need to return a few favours to various people on base so I'll get Scott and Danny to head that up."

"That'll be perfect, as far as I can tell there's no reason why he can't handle a weapon again and that's in my report. In fact a little bit of range time with Scott would be a good thing. Whatever training you've put him through has created a solid kid who's got great instincts and a good head on his shoulders. I really do think this'll be something he'll bounce back from. It'll never go away and the doubt will always be there at times but with the right support he'll be okay and from what I've experienced of your team so far you've definitely got the right environment for him to be in right now."

Barney smiled, "thanks Cole that means a lot."

"Hey don't thank me. It's you and your team that have created that environment and it's really good to see."

"Shouldn't you old folks be in bed by now catching up on your beauty sleep, which by the way you really do need?"

Barney didn't even need to turn around to see who it was as the voice gave it away, "sit down flyboy and if you can't say anything sensible then I suggest you keep quite."

Mitch sat down next to Barney, "whatever you say Granddad."

Barney sighed, "What have I done to deserve this," he turned to face Mitch, "Listen poster boy, the only reason we tolerate you is due to the fact that Jess says you've still got a way to go before she's happy with your flying skills."

Mitch laughed, "I wouldn't mind but that's probably true. I've flown with some incredible combat pilots in my time but that girl is one of the most naturally gifted chopper pilots I've ever seen."

"Well in that case behave or I'll tell her how disrespectful you've been."

"Okay old man I'll dial it down."

Barney smiled and took the conversation back to where they'd been, "I just wish we'd had a better start to the investigation."

Cole spoke up, "Barney, at the risk of using a cliché you can't make an omelette without breaking some eggs. You've got a challenging operation on the go and whether you like it or not on the way you're going to make a number of people unhappy and some people more than annoyed. That's just the nature of what you're doing."

Barney pushed his now empty plate to the side, "I know, the frustrating this is I know that we've done well to get as far as we have but from the initial briefing from the two teams we seem to have hit a dead end. The evidence and stuff we have so far indicates they've been taken and we're on the right track but the trail has gone cold. Unless we're extremely lucky and turn up something in the documents we've found we're going to be treading water."

Cole stood up, "well then I guess we need to crash out so that we're ready to start working through it all in the morning. I'm on a few rest days now as the unit I'm working with are out on a three day exercise so if you like I'm happy to jump in with you all and help out. It'll give me a chance to speed a bit more time with Danny."

"That would be great Cole and I'd really appreciate it."

"Think nothing of it, I owe Scott a few favours and from what I've seen of your team so far I'd be more than glad to pitch in and do my bit."

The three of them got up and made their way over to the array of trolleys that were sat there waiting for the numerous trays of cutlery and crockery that would be used throughout the day. They were billeted in different parts of the camp so they said their goodnights and made their way back to their respective rooms.

Chapter 29 (Europe)

The following morning they made an early start. They wanted to expand on each of the four examples they'd found from the day before. Alek contacted the airport security to request the CCTV footage. While he was giving them the dates and times he needed footage for Katie was going through street level maps to check out each of the drop off points. The challenge was that although they knew the ambulance had stopped they had no way of knowing where the crew had gone. The assumption was that they would park fairly close to wherever it was they were delivering to but there was no guarantee that it would actually be the building they stopped at. Alek had finished his call and was now helping Katie, they were hoping to find an obvious CCTV camera but one of the challenges was that the maps weren't necessarily up to date. After just over an hour they both agreed that this would need to be done in person. Katie started making a number of calls to local offices to see if they could spare anyone to go and do a physical check of each location. While she was doing that Alek gave Nick a call to see him and the others were doing.

Katie had been staring at yet another street view map trying to see if she could spot any obvious CCTV cameras. She put the phone down and was about to update Alek when it rang again, this time it was Danny. She listened for a couple of minutes occasionally acknowledging what Danny was saying. She put the phone down once again and turned to Alek "So the first call was Sean, they managed to find a link to Frederik's family relating to an old property just outside of Berlin. On paper it appears empty and he's contacted someone local to do a bit more digging. The second call was Danny and a little bit more important and worrying. Nick has managed to decrypt a series of emails and it appears that there were in fact two kidnapped girls on the plane so there's a fifty percent chance that the girl we saw being dropped off on the CCTV footage isn't actually Phoebe."

Alek looked surprised, "that's something I didn't expect, I thought we had the passenger manifest?"

"We did but it seems they loaded one official patient and one unofficial patient on the plane before they flew down and picked up Phoebe."

"Right so we need to go over the plane's flight plan again then. We based our assumptions on the fact that it was Phoebe they'd dropped off but if it wasn't then we need to try to work out where the second girl was dropped."

Katie was working her way through the folder tree on the server, "here's the official route the plane took. After dropping the first girl off it went to Paris, Berlin then Amsterdam before eventually leaving there to fly back to the states."

"So now we need to get hold of any footage we can get from those three airports."

"That's easy, I'll get the local offices straight onto it. We may not be able to get the footage particularly quickly but we should at least be able to find out what drop off or pickups there were as that'll have to be documented." Katie made a few calls while Alek carried on the now laborious task of looking for CCTV cameras. They had a bit of luck and had managed to find a few but the issue now was the lack of boots on the ground. They'd already used a few favours to get some extra people looking locally but with a number of cameras to now try to retrieve footage from they really didn't have enough bodies.

Alek sat back in his seat, "what if we split up and both of us go to two of the locations and we get Sean and Chris to fly over and cover two more?"

Katie sighed, "we may need to, there's no way I can ask for any more help from Interpol. I've pushed my luck as it is."

"So what about not worrying about it at all and calling Barney or James and ask them to contact the General and let him pull a few strings. That's got to be a much quicker way of getting things moving."

"I think Barney has probably got enough on his plate, I'll call James."

"Cool, I'll get some coffees," with that he got up and left the office.

Katie called James and explained the problem and rather than just ask him to call the General she asked what he thought would be the best move. James didn't need more than a second to confirm that the quickest and easiest way to get extra people assigned to them was bring the General up to speed with what they'd found knowing that the first thing he'd ask is what do they need. Sure enough less than twenty minutes later Katie got a call back from James letting her know that local Police were now going to secure any CCTV footage at the list of locations that James had provided. This gave them a little breathing space and meant that they'd possibly achieve a result much quicker.

They still had a long way to go and things were becoming much harder as new information was being found by numerous teams and as they knew from past experience if they weren't careful they could easily miss a vital clue. Katie called Sean and asked him if he and Chris could take a step back and start to coordinate all of the details that were being fed back. Sean confirmed that wouldn't be a problem at all and in fact it would be made a little easier as Charlie had finished her stint at the County as was back in the picture. Katie thought about asking one of them to come over and join them to make up the numbers but decided against it for the moment. She updated some notes on the server to reflect what was now happening and turned her attention back to helping Alek.

Less than five minutes later Alek took a call from the head of security at Schiphol airport in Amsterdam to advise that one patient had been taken from the plane by a private ambulance belonging to one of the larger local hospitals, Alek put his phone down "Well that's the first one and it seems to be a legitimate drop off so that just leaves Paris or Berlin."

Katie nodded, "let's hope they get back to us just as quickly. As soon as we know which one it was we'll head straight there as we've got enough local bodies here to continue to follow the trail we already have." It was Katie that received the next call a few minutes later but it wasn't one of the airports it was one of the local police stations just wanting to confirm exactly what it was they were looking for. While Katie was on the phone Alek had started to check out flight times to Paris and Berlin in order to attempt to give them the opportunity to plan ahead. They knew they'd be flying somewhere but had no idea as to how quickly they'd find out.

Alek closed his Mac, "why don't we just go to the airport now, we've got our bags and we can sit in the airport lounge and more or less do exactly what we're doing now. At least that way we can react a little quicker. There are regular flights available and we'll save ourselves a bit of time if we're already at the departure lounge. I know we can't go airside but the second we know we can get tickets and if it takes too long then we could always split up and take one airport each."

Katie agreed and they both quickly made a few calls whilst packing their stuff into their bags. They took a cab to the airport and found themselves a nice quite corner that allowed them some privacy so that they could talk openly without having to worry about anyone hearing what they were discussing. They'd just finished their first coffee when Alek took a call from someone at Berlin airport. They could confirm that two people had been dropped off. Similar to the patient at Schiphol airport one of the patients was taken away by a liveried ambulance belonging to a large local private hospital. The other was collected by an unmarked private ambulance and they had no onward details. Although they hadn't heard back from the last airport in France they took an educated guess that the unmarked ambulance had collected the kidnapped girl. They quickly got a couple of tickets for the next flight to Berlin which luckily for them was due to leave in just over ninety minutes.

It was going to be tight on time as they head to clear security and then get to the gate but luckily the airport was fairly quiet and they'd made their way through security in just over twenty minutes. Once airside Alek called James to let him know what they were doing and Katie called Sean to update him. She asked Sean to find out the details of the head of security and to book a car and accommodation for them as it was mid-afternoon already and by the time they'd landed and got all the information they needed it would be quite late and they would need to stay locally. They boarded without any fuss and although it was a short flight they were both asleep just after take-off. They knew that they would need to be focused as soon as they landed and although it wasn't for long a short sleep would be of benefit. It was something that over the years had become second nature.

After landing they both made their way to the main information desk in the arrivals lounge. They asked to see the Security Manager and after a few minutes were informed that he was currently busy and would be with them as soon as he could. Katie explained the importance and pointed out that they had in fact already spoken with him and they were expected. She waited while another phone call was made only to be told the same thing again. Alek decided to take an alternative approach and walked over to two armed Police officers that were patrolling the arrivals lounge. Over the years his knowledge of the German language had become fairly extensive and he spoke to them in German showing them his ID asking for their assistance. He obviously chose his words well because after a short radio conversation he was asked to follow them.

Katie and Alek followed the two officers who took them through the arrivals lounge to a secure set of doors that were off limits to passengers and led to the administrative side of the airport. After following them down a couple of corridors they came to a lift. It shot up two floors and the doors opened revealing an open plan office area filled with desks and screens. It was laid out in an organised and logical manner and from what they could see already was clearly the central hub of the Airport security system. All four of them stepped out of the lift and almost instantly a smartly dressed man strode over to them in a purposeful manner. He acknowledged the Police officers who, having completed their task, simply made their way back to the lift.

He held out his hand to Alek, "sorry for the confusion, Mateus Stroell, please call me Matt."

"Matt, I'm Alek and this is Katie," they both held up their respective IDs for him to see.

"Please come this way, I think I understand what it is that you need but I just want to check in order that we don't waste your time with the wrong information."

"Thank you," both Alek and Katie had expected a certain amount of efficiency as in the past all of their dealings with the German authorities had been very formal and by the book. They both followed Matt across the open plan floor space and down a corridor to an office. One of the walls consisted of floor to ceiling glass and overlooked the arrivals lounge.

Alek walked over to the window and looked down on the people below him, "wow, now that's a nice way to keep an eye on things."

Matt and Katie joined him, "I had it put in to remind me as to just who it is that I'm charged with keeping safe." He turned around and walked over to his desk, "please take a seat," he indicated the two seats on the opposite side of his desk, Katie and Alek both sat down.

"Can I get either of you a drink at all?"

Katie spoke first, "actually could we have a couple of coffees please."

Matt nodded, "of course," he picked up his phone and asked whoever picked it up to arrange for three coffees to be brought through to him. "So from what I understand form our phone call you're after any CCTV footage or information we can provide relating to the recent arrival of an air ambulance."

Katie and Alek had already discussed who should lead any discussions and they'd agreed that it should be Katie. Not because she was a woman but because an Interpol agent was far more likely to get a positive response than an FSB agent. People were far less likely to be guarded or suspicious when dealing with Interpol.

"Yes, the tail number we gave you when we spoke belongs to a plane that we have a particular interest in. Before I explain anything further I will point out that we are very aware that you will have followed strict protocols with regards to patient transfers and we are of the opinion that as far as you're concerned all of the paperwork is genuine. Unfortunately from what we've found so far we're dealing with a very well organised and highly financed operation."

"As a precaution I have already had the paperwork checked." Matt removed a folder from a drawer in his desk, opening it he removed two pieces and passed them over to Katie. "Everything checks out, the patient information the transfers etc, nothing was out of place and we had no reason to suspect otherwise."

Katie handed Alek to two sheets of paper, "Matt there's nothing at all on here to make you think otherwise. In fact you could have done all the due diligence you wanted and you'd find absolutely nothing wrong. The patient that was transferred to the local hospital ambulance is completely above board. It's the patient that was collected by the private ambulance that we're interested in."

Matt handed the folder over to Katie, "you'll find everything we have on the plane and the two ambulances. You'll also find two flash drives in there containing every bit of CCTV footage we have. The paperwork and footage actually cover the last three visits that the plane has made to this airport. From the conversation we had on the phone I felt it made sense to give you as much assistance as possible."

Katie had a surprised look on her face, "that's great Matt thank you."

There was a knock at the door and a member of staff entered carrying a tray with three coffees, a bowl of sugar and a milk jug. Matt took the tray and placed it on his desk, "thank you Astrid," without saying a word she left closing the door behind her.

"Please help yourselves," he picked up the cup nearest to him and placed it on the desk.

Katie leant forward and put some milk in both cups, giving them a quick stir she passed on to Alek.

Matt picked up his cup and taking a mouthful of coffee paused before speaking, "do you mind if I ask the extent of what you're looking into?"

"We're limited as to how much we can share at this stage," Alek looked at Katie, "the problem we have is we're still gathering information and to be honest we don't know how big or how deep this goes."

Matt nodded as if he understood, "in other words you have no idea as to whether I or any members of staff may be involved or at least aware of what is happening."

"Speaking openly Matt, that's exactly where we are right now. We have absolutely no reason to suspect anyone here currently. Whoever is running this is incredibly knowledgeable when it comes to airport protocol and procedure and from what we've seen all of their paperwork is absolutely faultless. Which sort of leads us to believe they don't need anyone on the inside as they're doing everything by the book so there's no need for any internal help at all." Alek drank some of his coffee.

"Then you really do have quite a task ahead of you then."

Katie jumped back in, "yes we do, and the information you've given us will help no end. We're staying locally this evening as we want to check everything out. All things being good we won't have any further questions but if we do could we come back in tomorrow morning first thing?"

Matt nodded, "of course, if there's anything at all you need please don't hesitate to ask."

"Thank you," Katie drank the last bit of her coffee and put the cup back down on the tray. Alek did the same and they both stood up. Alek picked up the folder that Matt had given them and put it into his bag.

Matt stood up, "I'll see you out to the lift and get one of my team to get you back into the main arrivals area."

At the lift Alek held out his hand, "thank you Matt, you've been more than helpful and hopefully we won't need to bother you again."

He shook both Alek and Katie's hand, "please if there is anything just call."

Five minutes later Alek and Katie found themselves back in the arrivals lounge and made their way to the exit to grab a cab to take them to the hotel. They'd purposely chosen one close to the airport as they knew all they needed were a couple of rooms for the night before hopefully flying back. If things changed they knew they could simply book somewhere more suitable if needed. There were plenty of taxis at the rank and they were at the hotel within twenty minutes. Fifteen minutes later they'd checked in, they had adjoining rooms and Alek had unlocked the door that linked the two. He heard the lock disengage on Katie's side and the door opened. They called down and ordered some food and drink. While they waited the set the Macs up and started to read through the paperwork that Matt had provided in the file. As expected it was incredibly thorough and contained absolutely everything.

There was a knock at the door. Alek opened it and invited the porter pushing the food trolley into the room. The food and drink was placed swiftly on the table and giving the porter a tip Alek closed the door behind him. They'd ordered various sandwiches, snacks and soft drinks. At this stage they didn't know what lay ahead of them so soft drinks were the obvious choice. They settled in for what was probably going to be a late night. They took a flash drive each and started to watch the footage making notes as they went. Just over two hours later they had both managed to work their way through all of it. They'd both made lots of notes and now they had to work out what to do next. As they'd been working each bit of the paperwork and footage had been added to the relevant folders on the server so that the rest of the team could see what they had.

Alek suggested they stretch their legs before starting the next stage which would involve them going through the key bits together and to go through the notes that each other had made. They walked down to the reception area and made their way out onto the street. A brisk thirty minute walk was enough for both of them to feel refreshed enough to start again. Once back in the hotel room Katie ordered some fresh coffee and they sat down began going through the first flash drive again. Katie jumped to the bits that were important and they discussed what they were seeing. An hour and a half later and they had gone through both drives and had managed to isolate the clips they needed and put them together.

They had clear images of the ambulance driver and copies of his ID, they'd already started a search on him and the vehicle. They couldn't get a clear image of the patient although they were fairly certain it was a woman. After making contact with the local Police station they managed to put a request in for a review any CCTV footage that may be available from street cameras. Taking into account the information they had and what they'd managed to find out themselves they'd both agreed that the ambulance from the local hospital was in fact genuine. They'd put a call into the hospital and had spoken to the administration team who had confirmed that a patient had arrived for a surgical procedure and was now on a ward recovering. They updated the files once more and after making a couple of calls decided to call it a night. They didn't have a firm plan for the morning and elected to make a final decision on what to do next over breakfast.

Chapter 30 (North America)

Damian was in pain. It wasn't a physical pain, not even close. This was mental pain and at a level he'd never experienced before in his life. Right now he was wishing it was physical pain because he knew how to deal with that. He'd made a colossal mistake, well actually he'd admitted to himself he'd made numerous mistakes that had led to him being in the position that he found himself. He put the half empty bottle of Jack Daniels down on the counter. He was sat at the breakfast bar in the kitchen of his apartment looking out of the window at the lights of the city below. He tried to clear his head but he kept coming back to the same thought. God this was a complete fuck up.

He'd become greedy over the last four or five months and had allowed the desire for money to come before the logic and common sense that he'd shown at the beginning. For a while he had chosen to mirror the approach that Angie was using to select targets. She used the personal approach, finding an individual target. Making sure that they met the exact requirements and carefully removing them from society so that no one noticed. As the demand grew he began to get frustrated working on one at a time and wanted more. His desire turned him towards an old friend who had risen through the ranks of a street gang and was now one of three key Lieutenants within the gang. He'd described what he wanted and after some negotiation around the finder's fee the gang leader agreed to help.

Damian had made it clear that the people they found couldn't come from the area and they needed to make sure that they only sourced one person from any one area. To be fair they'd stuck to that and had enable Damian to deliver five or six people every month. The rewards had been great. Not only had he seen a substantial financial benefit from the arrangement but the gang had supplied him with cheap drugs and women. Not that finding women had ever been a problem but the women the gang supplied were nobodies and weren't looking for anything other than some easy cash and that suited Damian perfectly.

He picked up the bottle and swigged another mouthful. He knew drinking himself into a stupor wasn't the answer but right now it seemed like the best thing to do. The conversation that he'd had with Miguel had really messed with his head and now the gang had been removed from society in brutal fashion. He'd been trying to get hold of his friend for a few hours and had then called someone else that he knew in the area. The conversation that followed had resulted in him picking up the bottle of JD. The whole gang had been systematically slaughtered and not a single member was left alive. The information he'd been given left him in absolutely no doubt as to who was responsible. The reputation that followed and preceded Miguel wasn't based on rumour or belief. It was based on fact. Quite often facts that couldn't even remotely be distorted or questioned and lead to Miguel being feared wherever he went.

After hearing that Damian had called a contact in the local police force and was given a far clearer insight as to what had happened. As far as the police were concerned it looked like the whole gang had been targeted by a very thorough military style group. Reports and CCTV had shown a small highly trained group had entered various establishments and systematically killed every gang member. Nobody else had been hurt at all. It had been a very well carried out mass assassination. The police were investigating but they weren't classing it as a priority as the gang had been somewhat of a thorn in their side for years. The simple fact that they were now not a problem was actually seen as a positive thing. Though his contact did say some officers were shocked at the way it was carried out. A few veterans within the force instantly likened it to a Special Forces operation. The footage they'd seen showed a very small very well equipped team making the whole thing look like a training exercise.

Damian wasn't at all surprised as Miguel had significant influence and could easily afford several groups of highly trained mercenaries prepared to do anything he wanted. The rewards for a job well done would be significant and from what Damian had already heard this was definitely a job well done. Damian wasn't overly worried about his connection to the gang as it had only been via a couple of burner phones. The face to face meetings with his friend had been well away from any of the properties that the gang owned or frequented. All payments had gone through several shell companies before arriving in the gangs account and he hadn't ever done anything in writing.

It wasn't so much any of that which was causing the mental anguish it was the sudden loss of a very lucrative revenue stream. One that whilst rewarding him financially had enabled him to shine within the organisation. That shine had very abruptly disappeared and now he was, for the first time ever, a part of something that Stephen Goodbanks would rather forget. It wasn't a position that Damian ever thought he'd be in and the very one sided conversation with Miguel had rattled him so much he simply couldn't focus his mind on finding a solution. That's where the drink came in. He'd decided to drink himself to sleep in the hope that when he finally woke up he'd find himself in a better mental state.

He picked up the bottle again, putting it to his lips he paused for a second. The logical part of his brain was fighting back and he put the bottle down once again. Taking a long hard look out of the window he tried to focus his mind on the here and now. He put the top back on the bottle. Drink wasn't the answer, he toyed with emptying the half full bottle down the sink but as he had four or five other bottles there didn't seem much point in wasting it. He stood up and walked out of the kitchen into the next room and placed the bottle back in the drinks cabinet. He walked over to the window and looked out at the sprawling city below him once again. This time with a more focused mind.

He walked back into the kitchen and got a bottle of chilled water out of the fridge door pausing before he closed the door he realised he was hungry. He quickly made a couple of pastrami sandwiches and took them and the water back into the other room. He opened the door that lead onto his balcony and sat down in the fresh air. Taking a bite of the first sandwich he sat back in the chair and stared out into the distance. He needed to work out his next step. It had to be a significant one as he was very conscious that the spotlight was on him and for all the wrong reasons. As he ate the sandwich and drank the water he tried to clarify in his mind as to where he actually was in this rather abysmal situation.

He shook his head, this was a bloody mess and there wasn't an easy way out of this monumental screw up and he knew it. He thought about calling Angie to ask for some advice but decided against it. The last thing he needed right now was Goodbanks finding out that he couldn't find his own solution to the problem. He didn't think Angie would say anything but he couldn't take the risk and actually if he was honest with himself he was better than that. Yes he'd made a mistake but it wasn't anything that he couldn't bounce back from. His image might be tarnished for a while but he can remedy that with a bit of hard work.

Time to get back to doing things himself, he had two people that still needed to be found. He opened his laptop and signed into his secure email account. He read through the two descriptions and decided that although he could probably find both locally that he should distance himself from the area for a while. He opened his web browser and checked on flights to several cities. He had three options available to him with flights that left in three hours. Not having made a final decision yet he packed a bag and called a cab electing to make the final choice once he was at the airport. He'd packed two fresh phones and plenty of cash so that he didn't leave too much of a trail behind. Under the current circumstances he felt that it was best to be a little cautious. Despite the drink he was thinking clearly and not taking any risks.

Unbeknown to him his name and address were stored in the phone of the gang lieutenant that he'd known. The gang leader had insisted on knowing who he'd been dealing with and the lieutenant had supplied the information required which unfortunately for Damian included details of their friendship from years before. If someone looked close enough there was a breadcrumb that could lead straight to his door. In the big scheme of things it wasn't so much a breadcrumb as a whole loaf and had he known this his course of action may well have been different. As it was he was sitting comfortably in the back of a taxi on his way to the airport.

Less than an hour and a half later he was boarding a plane heading for Chicago on the hunt for a 26 year old brunette that was at least five foot six with fair skin and no tattoos. During the flight he made a few notes and created a to do list. Normally he'd be a little more flexible and work from more of a blank page but he wanted to get back on the right side of his boss as quickly as possible so a new approach was needed. The more structure he gave to the approach the better he felt. He could now see why Angie took such a methodical approach to the job.

By the time he landed he actually had a pretty solid structure to work from and booked himself into a downtown motel that gave him access to several gyms and swimming baths. Gyms were a good place to start looking as a high percentage of woman of that age were interested in keeping up appearances and the gym was a good place to do that. The swimming pool was always an easy way to check for tattoos. The type of women that he had sourced in the past had all been the bikini wearing types so little chance of him missing a tattoo.

Arriving at the motel he booked a room for three days with a view to either extending the stay there or moving to another motel in a different part of town. He dropped his bag on the bed and grabbing his tablet made his way to one of the local bars. He was tired but didn't want to waste any time at all so had elected to spend a couple of hours trawling a few bars to see what he could find. All he needed to get started was a few names, which would lead to a Facebook search to ascertain relationship status age etc. He'd found that was always a good starting point as it often allowed access to friends etc so if the original target wasn't suitable for some reason then there was a chance that a friend might be. It usually gave him good access to photos as well to enable him to match the target against the client's criteria.

The first bar he stopped at was far too noisy and dark to be of any use so he had one quick drink then moved on. Whilst there though he made a list of all the local gyms and pools so that he could plan a few trips the following morning. Going from gym to gym didn't worry him as he was fit enough to be able to do a couple of workouts back to back. Especially as all they needed to be was good enough to look plausible which meant he didn't need to push himself too hard. The second bar was much better, more of a wine bar than an actual bar to be fair and a good number of younger people present which was what he needed. Sitting at the bar gave him a good opportunity to listen to conversations and more importantly would every so often enable him to glance at someone's ID. The bar staff would almost certainly request it for anyone that didn't look remotely old enough.

An hour later he had two names to be getting on with, they both loosely met what he was looking for and it was enough for him to make a start. He left the bar and made his way back to the motel feeling slightly happier about the situation that he was in. Back at the motel he opened a bottle of water and started his searching. He quickly found the first Facebook profile but was disappointed to find that looking back through her photos that she was a natural blonde. He flicked through her friends but didn't find anyone that jumped out at him. He'd go back to them if he needed to later. The second was in between relationships which was good but had far too many friends and recent posts. He needed to find someone that wouldn't necessarily be missed. He trawled through her friends and once again couldn't find anyone that was suitable. However he did find a link to a book club and that from his past experiences was a good place to look for loners that wouldn't be missed. After making a note of the detail he closed the laptop and had a shower before getting into bed to get some much needed sleep.

Sleep didn't come easily and after only an hour he was awake again, the guilt had suddenly hit him and he couldn't shake the feeling that he'd let Rick down. His carelessness and greed for money had got Rick killed. He sat up unable to stop his mind from getting back to a suitable state for sleep. He'd gone through high school and college with Rick, they found themselves together on day one and the friendship grew from there. After college Rick lost his way a little and ended up getting involved on the side-lines with a local gang and as he got deeper and deeper he found it impossible to get out. Damian had kept in contact with him even lending him money when Rick hit rock bottom. Damian knew it wasn't a loan and that the likelihood of Rick getting back on his feet was slim but he didn't care. His friend needed help and he was in a position to do so.

As Damian seemed to advance and go up in the world Rick seemed to be doing the opposite. Although Damian kept in touch and offered what help he could it simply wasn't enough and Damian had watched as Rick slipped further and further into the gang lifestyle. Damian had tried to boost Ricks position within the gang by making them aware that it was in fact Rick that had suggested that Damian approach the gang for help. Now it seems that all that Damian had actually done without knowing it was rather than help Rick he'd been instrumental in his death. He looked around his room in despair. Shaking his head he could only think one thing and that was that he'd created an awful mess and the death of a number of people firmly rested on his shoulders. Taking a couple of pain killers he went back to bed and focused his mind on the details of the girls that he was going to follow up on.

Chapter 31 (Europe)

They were both up early and used breakfast to catch up with emails and phone calls. The Police had tracked the van to the city limits but then lost it. The analyst that had been tracking it stated in their report that they were fairly certain that the van hadn't stopped. The timeline on all of the recordings had been consistent and didn't show any gaps that would indicate that the van had stopped. They did have a general direction but that was all. While they'd been sleeping the initial reports on the driver and passenger had come back. Neither of them had any previous criminal record and they both lived locally. Alek put a request in for a financial record check on both. The van had come back as being registered to the driver and had been purchased just over two years ago from a dealer that specialised in used emergency services vehicles.

They now had a bit of an issue. The next step they really wanted to take was to arrest the two men and search the two addresses but they knew that could create an issue if they showed their hand too early. Katie decided to call James to discuss what options they had. After a lengthy discussion they both agreed an arrest would be too risky and that setting up some sort of surveillance would be a better option. After finishing the call with James Katie rang Claudine to ask if she wanted the surveillance to be handled by the local Police or if she wanted Interpol to deal with it. Claudine didn't need much time to decide. As the investigation already spanned numerous countries she didn't want to being handled by the Police and she authorised the use of an additional team of four to work under Katie's guidance.

Katie finished the call and looked at Alek, "well it's beginning to become a bit of a handful. Claudine has assigned four more agents to us and after reviewing everything we've reported back to her she's added two more to deal with background checks etc."

"We may have to consider you heading back to coordinate it all rather than being on the ground. We could either go back together and get Sean and Chris over here or we split up and I stay here and we get the boys to split and join us."

"Well I guess it makes sense for me to be back at HQ so that I can oversee everything as this is just going to get more complicated and I can't very easily see what's happening elsewhere from here."

"You call Claudine and let her know what we're doing. I'll stay here and work with the surveillance team when they get here. I'll give Sean a call and get him to meet up with you and Chris can come to me, or now Charlie is back she could join one of us leaving one of the boys to stay back with Nick. I'll call Sean and let them decide. It may be that Nick needs one of them more than the others and right now we don't need any of their specific skills."

They ordered coffee to be delivered to Katie's room. Although they'd been using the room Alek was in Katie needed to leave so she could pack what little she had while she was on the phone. Once in the room Alek called Sean and explained what was happening and Sean told him to give him a few minutes and he'd call him back. While waiting Alek called the front desk to ask them to organise a taxi to take Katie straight to the airport. They advised him that they actually had a shuttle bus leaving for the airport in half an hour and Alek asked them to reserve a seat.

Sean called back after five minutes. They'd discussed it between them and decided that Sean would join Katie and Charlie would fly across to meet up with Alek. As Chris had the stronger IT skill set he'd stay back and help Nick as much as he could. Alek agreed and told Sean to get Charlie to send him her flight number and he'd meet her at the airport. Katie had called Claudine to update her on what was happening and suggested that as she was now leaving Berlin it may be an idea to assign a senior agent to the surveillance team so that they could act as the local liaison. Although in reality it would only take a couple of phone calls for any member of the team to be given overall command on the ground. In the past the team had found it far better to keep the command assigned to local agents as it avoided the majority of the political red tape.

Katie left for the airport and Alek busied himself getting a set of briefing notes ready for the incoming Interpol team. He sent Charlie all the relevant links to the files by email so that she could catch up on the flight over. She was already on her way to the airport with Sean and was due to be with Alek in just under three hours all things being equal. Alek took a call from the lead Interpol agent explaining that they would be with him an just over two hours. They needed to collect some extra kit and would base themselves at the same hotel as him to start with. Alek called down to reception to book some extra rooms for a night. It didn't need to be for any longer as he knew they'd base themselves closer to the targets addresses once they had a plan.

At the same time he booked the rooms he booked one of the many business rooms that the hotel had available. He got some stationary arranged and asked reception to organise a couple of street maps. The room had a projector and screen in it and Alek set up his Mac to check it out. Happy that everything was working he ordered some coffee and caught up with his messages while he waited. In theory the Interpol Team should arrive about an hour before he'd need to leave to meet Charlie which would be enough time to brief them all and bring them up to speed.

The phone in front of Alek started ringing, it was the Interpol Team leader letting him know that they were in reception. Alek put his phone down and made his way out to the reception area. Four smartly dressed people were stood off to one side. Alek knew they were the people he was after. Not just because they were dressed smartly. It was the fact that as a group they had positioned themselves in the perfect way to be able to survey everything around them. Between them they could see every entrance and exit and they were stood exactly were Alek would have positioned himself. As he approached one of the team said something to the person with their back to him, the agent turned round to face Alek.

Alek held out his hand, "I'm Alek, if you follow me I've got a room organised and we can do the introductions once we're there."

The agent shook Alek's hand, "Karl, and that's a good idea."

They made their way across reception and down a corridor to the room, the team were only carrying laptop bags and once in the room they placed them on the table and all took a seat. Alek introduced himself and Karl introduced his team, which comprised of Ralf, Karla and Erica. Karl explained to Alek that the team had worked surveillance before and had purposely created two male and female pairs as they found it looked less suspicious when they were on foot. Alek ordered some drinks and gave them an outline of what he and Katie were looking into. He made it clear to Karl that this was an Interpol led surveillance operation and that Karl had the lead and Alek would only step in if they needed to get something done quickly. He gave each of the team a folder containing the briefing notes he'd put together. He left them reading thought the notes while he went to the airport to meet Charlie.

He walked into the arrivals lounge and made his way over to get a coffee. He was a little early as Charlie wasn't due to land for another ten minutes and then she had to make her way off the plane and through security so realistically he probably had about an hour before she was with him. He took his coffee and sat down, getting out his phone he stared to flick though his messages and emails. He was reading though an update email from Nick when out of the corner of his eye he saw two Police offers heading towards him. He put the phone down and they stopped at the table he was occupying, "hello sir, Mr Stroell sends his regards and wondered if there was anything he could help you with."

Before responding Alek instinctively looked up towards the office that he'd been stood in the day before. Matt was stood at the window and raised a hand in acknowledgement. Alek smiled and raised a hand back, "I'm fine but more than happy to discuss why I'm here with Mr Stroell if he desires."

The Policeman nodded, "he'd like that and we've been asked to take you too him."

Alek stood up, putting his phone in his pocket and picking up his coffee he turned to face the officer, "lead the way gentleman."

They led him to the same door he'd walked through less than twenty four hours ago, the officers escorted him to the lift. Alek knew better than to tell them he knew where he was going. They will have been tasked with delivering him to the door so he just let them do what they'd been asked. The lift stopped and as the doors opened Matt was waiting for him, Alek stepped out of the lift pausing to thank the officers for their assistance. "Morning Matt."

"Hello Alek, sorry for the intrusion but after our chat yesterday I'm a little wary and was wondering if we were under surveillance in any way. I had you and Katie added to the security watch list to give me the heads up in case you came back, just being cautious and I hope you understand." Whilst Matt had been talking they had made their way to his office, closing the door behind then Matt indicated that Alek should take a seat.

Alek sat down, "not a problem at all but please understand if we did want to place you or any member of your team under surveillance it certainly wouldn't be Katie or me that would be here doing it. You can rest easy, I'm here to meet a colleague. Katie flew out this morning and I've got someone flying in to meet me, but after what you've just said I guess you already know she left this morning."

Matt held his hands up in mock surrender, "yes, and just so that you know her flight landed safely twenty minutes ago."

"No need to worry Matt, we definitely know enough already to be able to eliminate the involvement of anyone at the airport."

Matt smiled, "I'm glad to hear it although I must be honest I was a little worried."

"No need to be, the people doing this are way too organised and don't seem to need any help. The paperwork they have appears legitimate enough and they're good enough to make everything look above board."

"So you have a colleague flying in?"

"Yes she's on the next flight in from London Gatwick and due to land any minute now. All I need to do is wait for her to clear security and we'll be out of your hair."

"Then allow me to extend some professional courtesy and get her cleared as quickly as possible. Come with me and we'll meet her as she comes off the plane."

Not waiting for an answer Matt turned and made his way to the door, Alek followed and they turned left out of the office walking along the corridor to two sets of lifts. Between the two lifts was an information board similar to those in the arrivals lounge displaying the flights times. Matt quickly looked at the screen and nodded to himself, pressing the button for the left hand lift he turned to Alek. "She'll be at the stand in five minutes I'll call ahead and get her met there and taken to the office. It'll save you about twenty minutes as there are four flights coming in at the same time so passport control will be busy."

Alek smiled, "thank you."

274

Matt took his phone out of his pocket and made a call. "Stefan it's Matt, I need someone collected from the flight that has just landed from LGW, can you get someone to get," Matt put his hand over the speaker, "Charlotte Green." Alek said knowing exactly what Matt wanted. "Charlotte Green, it's not a security issue but I want her off the plane and at the side office as quickly as possible." Matt put the phone back in his pocket, "they'll get her to us fairly quickly which should save you about half an hour."

All Alek could think to say was, "thank you."

Charlie had been a bit fortunate when booking her ticket and she'd ended up with an aisle seat five rows in. As they approached the stand she got ready to get up out of her seat. She had travelled with her grab bag so she didn't need to wait for any cabin baggage to be unloaded. The plane came to a halt at the stand, unlike the majority of the other passengers in the aisle seats she didn't stand up until the seatbelt sign went off. She knew it would only take a second or two to get her bag out of the overhead locker so there was no point in standing yet. After a minute or two the front door of the plane opened and a member of the ground crew entered the plane and spoke to the Cabin Manager, who after a short conversation looked at the passenger manifest and then looked straight at Charlie. He made his way forward asking the passengers that were now standing in the aisle to take their seats for a second, he stopped at Charlie, "my apologies Miss Green but could you follow me please."

Charlie stood up and grabbed her bag, she followed the cabin manager to the front of the plane. The member of the ground crew smiled, "if you could follow me please," without waiting for Charlie to acknowledge him he turned around and walked out of the plane. Charlie followed as he set off at a brisk pace. At the top of the ramp they were met by a customs officer, once again she was asked to follow him with no explanation. "Any reason for the VIP treatment?" she asked.

"I'm sorry I don't know. I have been asked to make sure that you aren't delayed in any way and that you are given priority and to be taken straight through passport control to the security office. They haven't explained any more than that."

"I'm sure I'll find out what's going on before long," she knew that there was no point trying to get any further information. She followed him and as they approached the main customs hall the noise grew.

They'd passed a few passengers as they walked but it was clear to Charlie that a number of planes had clearly landed at roughly the same time as there were a few hundred people attempting to form orderly lines as they made their way through passport control. They bypassed all of the people as they made their way over to the far side and paused for the security number to be entered into the door, she followed her guide through the door and they turned right down a corridor. They passed a number of rooms and took a door on the left. This led through to a smarter more appealing area and the customs officer stopped at a closed door and knocked. Charlie heard someone say enter and the he opened the door, motioning for her to enter she stepped past him and entered a well-furnished office which contained two people. One was dressed smartly with what was clearly an airport ID hanging from a lanyard round his neck the other had a big grin on his face, "nice flight?"

"You idiot, why didn't you message me to let me know what was happening?"

"No fun in that is there."

"I now know why Cass and Joss hate being with you."

Alek laughed, "now we both know they'd be envious and would want to be here instead of you."

Charlie looked straight at him. "I very much doubt that and you know it."

"Miss Green may I introduce myself, I'm Mateus Stroell the Security Manager for the airport."

Charlie smiled, "please call me Charlie and thank you for your assistance in getting through security Mateus."

"You're welcome, it's my pleasure."

"Don't get too excited Charlie, Matt just wants us out of his airport as quickly as possible."

"Ignore him please, that's not strictly true," Matt quickly brought Charlie up to speed with the current situation, "so you see I'm merely offering a little professional courtesy."

"Thank you Matt it is appreciated," the jovial tone now gone Alek sounded genuinely appreciative.

"You're welcome Alek and please if there's anything we can do the help any further please let us know, now if you both follow me we'll get you out of here." They followed Matt through the door and within a minute Alek found himself at the door that led to the arrivals lounge. Alek and Charlie walked through the door into the arrivals lounge and made their way out to the taxi rank. They kept the conversation in the taxi to small talk. Alek asking how the others were and Charlie dishing the gossip on the team in the UK.

As soon as they arrived at the hotel they went straight to the meeting room. Alek quickly ran through the introductions, and they all sat down, "guys you've had time to read the briefing notes we've put together and I'd like to hear your thoughts."

Erica put down the piece of paper she had in her hand, "I guess the first thing we are curious about is why you are looking to conduct surveillance? If as you suspect they've already dropped the girl off we aren't going to learn about her location from following them."

"No we aren't but there's a concern that if we lift them we may compromise everything so we're trying to balance the investigation in Europe with what's going on in the States."

"In the notes you mention somewhere that you've already established that they seem to mix genuine jobs in with those linked to the kidnapping." Karl flicked through the pages in front of him selecting the one he was looking for, "with regards to the ambulance team in the states eighty percent of their work seems to be genuine and if these guys follow the same pattern we could spend a great deal of time learning nothing."

Ralf leant forward in his chair, "in fact what we'd be doing us giving ourselves a huge amount of work to follow up on to be able to ascertain of they're on a legitimate patient run or one we're interested in."

Karl looked round the table at his team and then looked at Alek, "while you were getting Charlie we discussed this and worked on the premise that if this was our operation what would we do and we came to the consensus of opinion that we'd conduct a dual surveillance operation. One team would follow them and as soon as they were far enough away from their homes we'd install cameras in order to hopefully see or hear something that speeds things up."

Alek nodded, "I've got no problems with that. Do we need to organise any kit or do you have it with you?"

Karla spoke for the first time, "we have everything we need already. We can do a full installation at both properties all we need is two to

277

three hours at each to do it in one go or we can do it in bite sized chunks if they come back. Luckily as they travel together we can use two teams to follow them and the third team can do the installation."

Alek thought for a second, "okay I've got no problems with that."

"Good, in that case Ralf and I will carry out the installation while you four follow them, can we access any of their schedule at all?"

"Not as yet, the problem is as far as we can see they appear to be self-employed and don't have any direct ties with any particular companies. We've got some results back from the financial checks and can see who they've been paid by but at this stage we'd be taking a huge gamble in approaching any of the companies so as it stands we have to just follow them."

Erica shook her head, "the quickest way to get ahead of the game is to get hold of some of their electrical devices so that we can download any emails etc."

"I know, the issue is that the only real way to do that is to arrest them," Alek paused, "it may come to that as to be honest we can't really wait but we if you look at the bigger picture we don't want to move too early otherwise we'll give everyone higher up the chain the opportunity to disappear or hide everything."

Karl nodded in agreement, "so let's spend the next few hours trying to locate their current whereabouts and follow up on some of the financial records that we already have."

They spent the next couple of hours trying to track the vehicle via various cameras throughout the city and surrounding area. The financial records showed similar payments that the team had already found elsewhere and they were quickly able to link them to having come from the same place. A familiar set of shell companies appearing in the trail. After finding three of the same ones as had been found previously they stopped looking as they knew that another team was following that line of enquiry. They had no luck locating the van and now had a dilemma as the only logical step forward was to stake out the two different residential addressed they had for the two men.

Alek made the decision to do just that and they all got their gear together. Charlie arranged for the rental of a non-descript car from a company that Interpol used every so often. It wasn't brand new and lacked any stickers or identifying marks that the usual hire cars had. Alek sent the Interpol team off first as he and Charlie had to wait for their car to be delivered to them at the hotel. They could have got one of the others to take them to collect it but it was in the opposite direction of where they needed to go so Alek opted for getting the two teams on the ground as quickly as possible and then as soon as the car was delivered he'd head over and join the others.

As they had three teams of two Alek opted for a relay system. Having one team waiting close by while the other two teams took a house each. Every so often the plan was to swap around so that they moved about and weren't in the same place for too long. Luckily the two houses weren't that far apart and they were in busy areas which was a bonus. Quiet residential streets tended to be harder to work in as people sitting in a vehicle stood out a little more and the quieter areas tended to have a far more proactive neighbourhood watch type of scheme going on so it was far harder to carry out any lengthy surveillance.

The next eight hours went by without incident with no sign at all of either men. The team moved about, walked on foot and watched from a distance. They decided to drop the surveillance on the passenger and focus on the driver overnight, they couldn't afford to stop altogether and they didn't really have enough members in the team to keep a twenty four hour watch so they all agreed to drop down to just watching one with the teams changing every two hours through the night. At half twelve they got lucky, very lucky in fact as the driver was using a car that they weren't aware of and they almost missed him.

He parked the car and went inside the house, although none of the lights at the front of the house came on they could see a feint glow in one of the windows indicating that he had switched on the lights in one of the rooms at the back of the house. Twenty minutes later the window went dark and suddenly the lights came on in the upper front left window. A figure appeared at the window and closed the blinds and a short time after that the room went dark. Nothing happened through the night, the teams changed over every two hours and had agreed that all three teams would be back in the area for six o'clock.

Chapter 32 (North America)

Barney was up at six and went out for a run. Two miles in he was joined by Scott and half a mile alter they crossed paths with Cass and Jess. By the time they got back to the dorms they were staying in there were eight in the group. They all had a quick shower and made their way to the mess hall for breakfast. Once they'd all finished they made their way to the conference room they'd been using. Grace was already there tapping away on her Mac.

"Morning Grace, how's it going?"

"Well not quite as quickly as I'd like but its working and we're beginning to see the results come through."

"Good, okay everyone take a seat. I want to give you a quick update and then we'll discuss what we think is the best way forward."

There was a fair bit of noise as everyone sat down and then it went silent. Barney paused for a few seconds before he started, "I got an update last night from Clay. Drew is doing fine, he's out of surgery and doing as well as can be expected. They think he'll recover completely and they'll be no real physical side effects, which I'm sure you'll all agree is a good result. The possibility of some mental side effects however is as always ever present and that really will be a time will tell thing."

There was a chorus of people agreeing and when it died down Barney continued, "the second update is a little more disturbing and unfortunate. I got a lengthy call from the chief of Police that some of you had been working with. The warehouse, strip club and restaurant that you'd been checking out were all hit. He described it as a surgical strike almost military. The precision with which it was carried out can only lead him to believe that it was a group of mercenaries. The footage he's seen and what he described smacks of a Special Forces mission. The only people killed at all three places were gang members not a single civilian was injured or put in harm's way. To show how precise it was the whole gang down to the last member was assassinated within an hour."

Cass spoke up, "do they know who or why?"

"No they don't all they can assume at this stage is that someone was very unhappy that the gang had done something that had alerted the FBI and caused them to raid the smaller warehouse," Barney looked briefly at Danny and then carried on looking round the table, "whoever it was left nothing behind other than empty shell casings. The good thing is I guess is that another gang is off the streets. The two bad things however are that all of the weapons and drugs in the larger warehouse are now missing and the DEA operation has come to an abrupt and definitive halt."

"Wow they must be pissed."

"I expect they are, and that's probably a bit of an understatement. Levi can you make some calls and see what the state of play is and offer our apologies for what they're worth as we seem to have completely screwed up months of undercover work."

Levi got up, "I'll go and make some calls now."

"Good, Scott can you call your lady friend and find out if she knows anything, Stevie isn't it?"

"What, how did you.....?" he stopped mid-sentence and looked at Danny who now had a sheepish grin on his face.

"Why are you looking at me?" Danny now had a look of total surprise on his face.

"Because, you little shit there's no one else sat at this table that would have described her as my lady friend."

"Well let me tell you, I'm certainly not responsible for describing her like that. I said you were probably shagging her."

Barney laughed, "Scott I don't mind if you are shagging her but can you give her a call to see what she knows?"

"Don't you bloody start, I didn't and have no intention of shagging her."

Jess smiled, "me thinks the boy doth protest too much."

Scott stood up and walked out of the conference room and said, "screw the lot of you," as he did.

"Please send her my best wishes," said Danny as Scott walked down the corridor.

"Right back to business." There was an edge to Barneys tone as he said it and everyone knew it was time to focus again, "we'll have to make amends with the DEA because they really aren't happy especially as whoever it was cleared out the larger warehouse. They suspect it's the cartel sending a message to everyone else they deal with and it's a very clear 'Don't mess with us message' and delivered in a very precise way."

Cass sat forward in her seat, "so we now need to make our investigation count otherwise we're going to have wasted theirs for absolutely no reason."

Barney nodded, "that's it in a nutshell, so we need to pull out all of the stops and somehow find the next clue that'll allow us to move forward. As it stands at the moment all we seem to have managed is to have found two people that have probably been taken against their will as well as a whole mountain of documents and images. Not the sort of start I was hoping for."

Cass thought for a second, "that's true but having said that we've had worse starts to some of our operations and they've eventually worked out. Don't forget that we have at least got two people that we can focus on so we've got a reasonable footing."

"Right then people, taking into account of what's happened so far we need to make sure we check every little detail. We can't afford to miss anything so please be as thorough as you can and I know it's going to be boring as hell to start with. As you know from the past these things have to be done and there's no easy or quick way to do it."

"So we've now got three rooms available to us and I've set up some kit in each of them. If we split into groups and focus on getting everything scanned in and catalogued as fast as we can." Grace looked round the table "If we split into four teams, a team each in the other two rooms that we have and two teams in here. One of those team scanning etc and the other can begin to make sense of what we've got and start looking for some extra clues."

Barney nodded, "that makes sense. Okay guys from my perspective it doesn't matter who does what so let's set a time limit and regroup here just before lunch to see how we're doing. Remember take regular breaks, we can't afford to miss anything and I'd rather it take a few hours longer and everything to be uploaded than rush it and miss a vital image or document."

Cole stood up, "I've been on base quite a while and can pull some strings to get a regular fresh coffee and snack deliveries to the three rooms if that'll help."

"That'll be a great help Cole, thank you," Barney turned to Joss, "I'm going to update James so can you get things moving for me. I'm not ducking out and I'll do my fair share, but I need to keep him appraised of what we're doing and to get an update on how the others are doing."

"Sure, that's not a problem," Joss stood up, "right let's go we know what we need to do so let's do it."

There was a flurry of activity as the team split up and set about the somewhat laborious task ahead of them. It was something they'd done many times before and it was probably the most unexciting part of any of the tasks they undertake. The high speed scanner made things a little easier and once they got into the swing of it they started to make some good progress. Cass and Joss had decided that as they'd been at the head of the two teams that they'd be the ones to start looking through everything, it made sense as they'd written up the reports and been calling in the updates. Although they'd swapped teams part way through they agreed that they'd each follow the investigation that they'd finished on so Cass was going through everything relating to Connor and Joss was searching for the clues regarding Phoebe.

Levi came back and found Barney to give him an update on the DEAs position regarding the operation that was now very dead in the water. The powers that be weren't at all happy and to be fair Barney had expected that. They did however understand and take into account that the fact that their operation had suddenly come to an abrupt end wasn't really directly due to anything Barney and the team had done. Nobody could have foreseen the outcome and the DEA accepted that they gave Barney the go ahead to carry out his investigation so if anything the DEA had shot themselves in the foot.

The fact that they'd lost countless hours of undercover work hadn't gone entirely to waste. They had managed to get some good solid leads further down the chain but it was leads going up the chain that they really wanted and that definitely wasn't an option anymore. The fact that someone had cleared the larger warehouse out pretty much declared that the cartel or whoever was pulling the strings had moved on and wasn't going to be doing any business at the strip club or the restaurant. In fact, with the gang gone there wasn't anyone at the helm so the two had been closed.

Although they were making good progress it was slow going and mentally draining, Scott decided to mix the teams up after and hour in order to relieve a little bit of the monotony and the constant flow of coffee and food helped as well. The challenge was that the boxes of paperwork and images to be dealt with just didn't seem to end. To make things worse they were still receiving emails and files from the people they'd been working with as they still had active people working the case from the scene.

The next few hours flew by and the team could now visibly see that they were making progress. The pile of boxes was growing smaller and the number of digital files in the pending folder was considerably less. The team were still in an upbeat mood even though they'd spent the last three hours or so scanning, renaming and saving files into numerous folders. Cass and Joss were now overwhelmed with things to look at and piece together. The going had become a little easier for them when an hour earlier Barney had seen what was happening and assigned himself and Scott to assist them both so there were now four of them desperately trying to piece together an almost impossible jigsaw puzzle in order to gain the bigger picture.

They'd found nothing new but had at least confirmed that they felt they had enough proof to confirm that both Connor and Phoebe were part of the trafficking ring that they were investigating. Scott suggested that half the team take a break and go for some lunch and Barney agreed. He sent both Joss and Cass off as they had been dealing with the most demanding part of what they were all doing and their levels on concentration had been far higher for longer. They'd found out the hard way in the past how easy it could be to miss a vital piece of information and had lost several valuable hours on an assignment some years back when one of them was over tired and missed a significant clue. At the time no blame was assigned but they agreed to put some measures in place to stop it from happening again. Not always easy when you've got people breathing down your neck demanding instant results. Luckily the significant success that the team had delivered in the past now gave them a little more latitude and people weren't quite so demanding.

Over the years the team had developed the ability to switch off from the current task almost instantly and so during lunch in the mess the table was awash with laughter and noise as they enjoyed a well-earned rest. Not surprisingly Danny was the most vocal especially when he got to tease Cass yet again about the rather embarrassing fact that he beat her at the range. After about fifty minutes they made their way back and swapped with their colleagues. Within minutes they were back to work with their serious faces on once again hoping to find something new.

The first lucky break came mid-afternoon, although it had nothing to do with anything the team were doing. Barney received a call from Clay saying that one of the boxes of documents that his team were going through contained some hand written notes that had been found in the hidden section of the warehouse they had searched. They were difficult to read but it was clear that whoever had written them had been describing a conversation they'd had with a collection driver. During the conversation the driver had briefly mentioned that whoever he was transporting was probably a delivery for the money men to hunt and torture. The notes were rather rambling and seemed to be a collection of key points that could possibly be used as some sort of evidence in order to blackmail someone. Quite possibly one of the gang members looking to try to make some money from someone higher up the food chain.

Barney had asked Clay if he could get someone to do some digging to see if they could come up with a time or date that linked to the note so that they could possibly then review the CCTV tapes they'd managed to get from the warehouse. With a vehicle ID they might be able to take a big step forward. Clay had already done that and as yet they hadn't found anything but at least it was something a little more concrete regarding people trafficking. Barney thanked clay and took a few minutes to call the team together to update them on the new development.

The team hadn't been going slow, far from it but the news gave them a bit of a sense of urgency and they returned to their screens with a renewed vigour. At half six Barney decided to call it a night. His initial intention of splitting the team into groups so that they could cover a 24 hour period had been binned as they were working so well together as a whole he didn't feel they'd achieve anymore by dividing the team up. They all went to the mess hall to find it almost empty which surprised them all. Cole explained that every so often exercises would overlap which left significantly fewer personnel on base and today was one of those days. Without the need to rush to clear the table they took their time and enjoyed a relaxing meal and used the time to wind down from a mentally challenging day. On the bright side they were well over halfway through everything they had and were making great progress.

Grace had managed to access some clever new software and while they were eating all of the images they had were being subjected to a number of algorithms and to tag the images to certain groups that she'd assigned. The hope was that it would simply clump relevant images into the same file in order to make the overall search that much easier. The majority of the team hit the gym followed by a spell in the pool. By the time Barney had finished updating James and the General the gym was empty when he got to it so he went straight to the pool to find that they'd got a water polo match under way. He joined the team that was at the time losing and they spent the next hour generally taking the mickey out of everyone and everything. It was one of the many occasions that Barney realised just how lucky he was to have a team like this.

Barney made an executive decision and stood the team down till the morning. He told everyone to be back in the office for 10:00 ready to go. This wasn't unusual and the team didn't need any encouragement.

A few of them simply used the base facilities and used the time to relax and truly take their minds off the assignment. Cass, Joss, Jess and Grace decided to go into Phoenix for some much needed retail therapy, a few drinks and a relaxing meal. Scott, Cole, Barney and Danny went to the range to blow off some steam. Danny once again impressed everyone. When they called it a day he'd only scored seventeen points less than the others and was rather pleased with himself.

Chapter 33 (North America)

The following morning Damian felt far worse. He'd had a bad night and hadn't slept well at all and despite the steps he'd taken in the last 24 hours he felt like crap. It wasn't the alcohol either. This was a deep psychological panic that he was experiencing and he didn't know how to deal with it. It was something he hadn't experienced in his life and he wasn't in anyway able to cope with it. The dreams in between short burst of sleep had all focused around what had happened to the gang and his mind was working overtime and was filled with images of what happened. At one point he woke up in a sweat after dreaming about being the wrong end of the barrel of an M4.

He got straight in the shower and got himself ready. Still unable to completely forget the images in his head he made his way to a local coffee shop. In the past they had been as good source of leads as quite a few people would have their ID on display and if he was lucky and positioned himself just in the right place the line of people waiting would be close enough to his seat for him to be able to read the names giving him a nice list of targets to research. He was going to hit a gym first thing but he decided that the coffee shop would occupy his mind better and right now that was definitely what he needed. His logic was that if he could give himself enough things to think about and focus on he was less likely to start drifting back to the images in his dreams.

Luck was on his side, it was a very busy morning and he'd managed to get a seat at a table. The one he chose allowed him to not only be close enough to the people waiting to order but also close enough to see some of the people waiting for their drinks. Sometimes a first name and a town was enough to bring up a profile and he had a good memory for faces so even if they'd left the coffee shop he could remember enough detail to scan the profile pictures as they came up. He stayed just over an hour and came away with five possible targets to research a bit more thoroughly later. He thought about it and decided to go to a gym next. It was located near four large office blocks so he was hopeful that he'd get a reasonable flow of people coming in. As luck would have it there was a pool as well so he also had that as an option.

He used the first half an hour to work off some of his worry. Pushing himself so that the pain in his muscles took his minds focus away from the dreams. He slowly eased off and forty five minutes in was taking it easy and making it look good without exerting much effort at all. Two potential candidates were training together and he'd overheard them mention using the pool after so he finished up and went down to the pool. He swam for about five minutes them made his way to one of the hot tubs. They were located close enough to the pool itself for him to be able to clearly see anyone coming in. Both of the women looked about the right age and now they were in the pool he could clearly see they didn't have any tattoos although one did have pierced nipples, although that wasn't too much of a problem.

He'd seen enough to know that he needed a name to enable him to dig a bit deeper into both of them. Although they knew each other and ideally he was looking for loners. He would still do the research in case they were just casual acquaintances rather than work colleagues or close friends. He showered and got dressed. Luckily the gym had a decent sized reception area with a couple of tables and some comfortable chairs. He grabbed a soda from the machine and made himself comfortable, he knew he wouldn't have to wait too long and sure enough within twenty minutes they walked through the reception area. Damian had been lucky enough to find a seat that gave him a close enough view of anyone leaving. He couldn't see anyone coming in till they walked past him but at the moment that didn't matter. It was more important to try to get a name for at least one of the women he'd been watching.

His luck held, as they both came out they walked close enough to enable him to read the full name from one of the ID tags and a partial name from the other, he also got the company name. He quickly made a note of that and sat back for a few minutes. He now had seven women to look into and decided to keep looking. He could research each of the women later at the motel but for now he wanted to keep himself occupied and see who else he could find. He thought about going back to the same coffee shop but changed his mind and decided to find somewhere different. He already had the details of the next one he was going to try and on the way he stopped off at a bookstore to grab something to read. Reading a book whilst sitting in a coffee shop didn't look out of place and it would allow him to extend his stay without it looking too odd. His mind still wasn't really in the right place to read so he picked up one of the current bestselling books knowing that it wouldn't be heavy going.

He made his way to the coffee shop and was glad to see that it was busy. Even better was the fact that the majority of the traffic was for take away which suited him perfectly. Annoyingly the ideal table he wanted was occupied but he knew that it would only be a matter of time before he could swap seats. His first coffee yielded nothing at all. Although there were a couple of women that matched the requirements he was too far away to be able to make out any names on coffee cups or ID's. Finally the couple at the table he wanted got up and left. The second they showed signs of moving he'd stood up in line and made his way up to order a fresh drink, he got himself a sandwich as well as he suddenly realised he was hungry. He made his way over top the now vacated table and settled himself down for a while. Now in the perfect position to casually glance at people as they waited, he was also now close enough to hear the names called out as the drinks were placed on the counter.

Two hours later having just finished his third coffee he got up and made his way out of the coffee shop. He'd got four more possible names and felt that he now had enough to be getting on with. On the way back to the motel he stopped at a convenience store to grab a few things to eat and some bottles of water. He was going to be in for a prolonged session of searching and didn't want to have to leave the motel for basic things like food and drink. He'd go to a bar later in the evening for a proper meal but for the moment some nice and easy quick snacks would do the trick. He got back to the motel and started making more extensive notes on each of them before beginning the harder task of searching for them on the web.

Within two hours he'd whittled the list of eleven names down to a possible two with two new names added. They'd come from the numerous friends that he'd found on the various Facebook profiles he'd searched. He also had the Instagram accounts for the four he was now interested in. They all met the requirements so it was now a case of beginning to put together a picture of their social lives. It was no good finding someone that was so actively social that they'd be missed within hours. He needed someone that posted occasionally, that had a non-essential job. Someone that blended in so well they wouldn't be missed for some time. Three of them posted far too frequently and he'd be surprised if it went more than a day before concerns were raised. The fourth however was a bit more promising. She appeared to be a bit of a loner, rarely updating her status on Facebook and only posting once or twice a month on Instagram. She had a part time waitressing job that from what he could piece together didn't offer particularly regular hours. He'd managed to find her address with a bit more digging and set out to have a look to see what sort of neighbourhood it was.

The apartment she lived in wasn't in a great area for any sort of lengthy surveillance. It was a quiet residential street and a parked car with someone sat in it for any length of time would definitely look out of place. This wasn't going to be anywhere as easy had he had hoped. He really was looking for a quick result to get him back on his feet. With that in mind he decided to head to a local bar to begin his searching all over again. He'd still attempt to carry out some sort of surveillance on her but he needed to find a few more possible targets. The bar was busy, he ordered a drink and after taking a quick look at the bar menu ordered a burger and fries. Not really what he wanted but for the moment it would have to do. He chose to sit at the bar so that he could once again hopefully get a glimpse of the odd ID or two. After an hour he began to wonder if he'd already used up all his luck. Not a single woman in the bar even remotely matched what he was looking for.

He decided to give up for the evening with a view to starting again tomorrow following the same pattern. On the way back to the motel he changed his mind and as soon as he was in the room he packed a bag for the gym and went to let off some steam hoping that some prolonged exercise would tire him out and would offer him a better night's sleep. The gym wasn't busy and he set himself a punishing routine, pushing himself much further than he had earlier in the day. Once he'd finished he spent half an hour in the pool cooling down and enjoying a few relaxing lengths. He showered and got dressed. He must have been the last to leave because he couldn't see or hear anyone else. As he walked through the door into the reception area the receptionist smiled at him. "That was a long workout."

He smiled back, "just felt the need to work off some stress, hadn't intended to be that long sorry."

"Oh that's Okay, hope it helped."

"Yes it did, I may even come back tomorrow."

"Oh I do hope so."

"Really?" He found his voice had a questioning tone about it.

"Well compared to most people we get in here you seem to be quite normal."

He laughed, "oh I'm far from normal but thanks."

He walked towards the door pausing before opening it, with one hand on the door handle he turned around, "do you fancy getting a drink?" He wasn't going to say anything but on impulse he decided that some company might not be a bad thing and she was pretty attractive.

She didn't hesitate, "I'd love to. Give me five and I'll meet you at the bar across the street."

Damian didn't say anything and crossed the street to the bar, he ordered a beer and rather than sit at the bar grabbed the first available booth that had a clear line of sight to the door. Ten minutes later the receptionist walked through the door. She paused and looked around as soon as she spotted him she walked over, "wasn't sure if you'd be in here."

"I wouldn't want to miss the chance to buy you a drink, what'll you have?"

"I'll join you in a beer."

He stood up and made his way over to the bar and ordered two beers. Returning to the table he sat back down passing over one of the open bottles, "hope you don't mind but I didn't think you'd be a glass kinda girl."

She laughed, "no, you got that spot on, out of the bottle is just fine by me. I'm Stella."

"Damian."

"So Damian, what brings you to this area? Pretty sure I haven't seen you in the gym before."

"No today was the first time, I'm in the area following up a few business leads and just wanted to unwind."

"Cool, well I'm glad you chose our gym," Damian noticed she seemed genuinely pleased.

"Pure luck but right now it seems like a very good choice."

They talked for an hour or so only stopping to allow Damian to get another two bottles of beer. They weren't talking about anything specific and Damian actually found himself beginning to relax. They finished their drinks and made their way out onto the street, he turned to face her, "can I walk you home?"

She laughed, "you almost have, I live above the gym."

"Oh well that's handy for work."

"It sure is, listen do you fancy a coffee? It's instant so nothing special."

Damian didn't hesitate, "I'd love one," he was actually glad for the distraction, the last hour or so had been nice and for a short time his world returned to some sort of normality. They crossed the street and made their way up the stairs to her apartment. It was a fairly decent sized two bed apartment, very neat and clean. She'd already told him that she was studying and working in the gym evenings and weekends. She clearly had money because there wasn't any way that she could afford to pay for an apartment like this on the salary she'd be making at the gym. Damian sat down on a rather comfortable two seater sofa. He could hear Stella making the coffee and taking a deep breath he closed his eyes for a second letting his head rest on the back of the sofa.

Stella called out from the kitchen, "milk and sugar?"

Damian opened his eyes, "just milk please," he heard the fridge door open, he looked around the room and suddenly questioned himself. What on earth am I doing he thought. Before he could think anything else Stella came out of the kitchen with two coffee mugs in one hand and a pack of cookies in the other. For some bizarre reason he'd expected her to sit in the single seater opposite but she put both mugs down and sat next to him. She turned her body so that she was facing him. In doing so her leg was almost touching his. Her body language was completely open and left him in no doubt as to where things could lead. They talked for what seemed like ages and Damian felt himself relax as the minutes went by, he finally put his empty coffee mug down on the table.

"Can I use your bathroom?"

"Yes of course it's the second door on the right."

As he stood up he made a conscious decision to act and lent down sliding his hand behind her neck he pulled her face towards his and kissed her. Gently at first but within seconds the passion and lust took over and the kiss became far more intense. He slowly pulled away and looking into her eyes said, "stay right there I'll be back."

With a cheeky smile she said, "oh don't worry I'm not going anywhere."

Within minutes he was back and as he approached her she stood up. They kissed again this time raw passion took over and five minutes later there was a trail of clothes from the sofa to the bedroom, the pace kept changing from slow and passionate to frantic and hard. Damian controlled the speed where possible, not wanting it to finish. When he felt he was close he slowed things down and spent time exploring her body before entering her once more. He finally lost control and they laid together their bodies still entwined without saying a word. Stella kissed him and rested her head on his chest, before he knew they'd fallen asleep still in each other's arms.

Chapter 34 (North America)

The following morning they were all back in the conference room just after 09:00. They'd all enjoyed a few hours longer in bed and had made the most of a relaxed breakfast. Through the night Barney had taken a call from the Captain at the precinct that the team had been using while they were investigating Phoebes abduction. One of his detectives that had been working with Joss and the team had carried on investigating. Normally on a quite night shift he'd pick up a cold case and review it but ever since the team had left they'd made such an impression on him that he carried on searching for another clue into the abduction. He'd reviewed everything they had to start with and then. When he couldn't find anything new, he widened the search area by ten miles.

There were two new airfields in the search radius and he struck out at the first one. They didn't have an active CCTV system and only members were allowed to use the airfield and it could only accommodate small planes. Although disheartened the detective surmised that it wouldn't be the sort of airport used anyway. The second one however was different, it did accommodate international flights for private aircraft and had extensive CCTV coverage of the whole airfield. Mainly as a deterrent but they also benefited from a reasonable reduction in insurance as a result. The detective asked if they would be able to send him the footage for a particular period and they said they'd get a copy straight across to him.

Two hours after he'd spoken to the security team at the airport he was watching the first bit of footage. An hour into it he saw a van enter the main gates at the airfield and the driver matched the image of one of the two suspects carrying the sports bag out the apartment block. He called his Captain straight away, who, in turn called Barney who asked for the footage to be sent straight across. He needn't have asked as the captain had already done that along with the details of the security team at the airfield.

Barney had called Grace early and asked her to meet him just after eight, between them they'd cued up the footage ready to show the team. Grace had isolated all of the cameras and separated the footage so that the team could split down into pairs to review each camera in order that they could get a complete view of the van arriving and where it went and what it did.

As soon as everyone was sat down Barney started. "We've had a breakthrough but before I start I want to say a big well done to all of you. So far in this investigation with the understandable exception of the DEA we've had nothing but positive feedback from everyone we've worked with and what I'm about to tell you demonstrates that emphatically." He then spent the next five minutes taking the team thought what had happened. As soon as he finished Grace started the first bit of CCTV footage and within seconds they were staring at the face of one of the two suspects they'd seen leave Phoebes apartment. Grace paused the image and for a few seconds the room was silent.

Joss spoke first, "how on earth did he find that?"

"Well the detectives Captain said that his whole team had enjoyed having you there and wished that they'd been able to help you all to a better outcome. It seems that they've done just that hence my comment about the impression you guys make when you're out there. The detective in question felt that he personally owed it to the team to find something no matter how trivial." Barney looked at the image that was still on the screen. "This footage is far from trivial, even though we haven't viewed it all yet the fact that we have this is a massive step forward."

Joss had a big smile on her face, "I'll say."

"Right so the normal routine applies, split into pairs and Grace will send each of you some footage to review. There are 36 cameras at the airfield so we've got a fair bit to trawl through but let's make a start and see what we find." Within seconds the team had paired up and Grace was able to send the first lot of files across. They still had use of the two extra rooms so they made the most of them and spread out. As soon as they'd all started Barney went off to sort out some coffee once more for the three rooms.

Despite having spent the last couple of days glued to the screens sifting through thousands of documents and images the team took to the task with renewed vigour. Within an hour and a quarter they'd managed to piece together the vans journey at the airfield. The final piece of footage showed a patient being moved from the van on a gurney and being lifted up into the side cargo door of a plane. The tail number clearly in view and to help even more the logo of the medical repatriation company emblazed down the whole length of the fuselage. At that point the team knew that this really wasn't just some trivial little clue that the detective had found.

"Okay guys listen in, here's what happens next. Jess, I want you to go and prep the plane for immediate take off. Joss you'll take Scott, Kelly and Danny with you. Jess will fly you down to the airfield stopping off on the way to collect the detective and one of his colleagues. I want everything you can get from there including physical copies of the footage and statements from every member of airfield staff that appear in the footage or that may have been in the control tower when the plane took off."

Jess was already out of the door before Barney had finished speaking. She didn't need to hear anything after being told to prep the plane as she knew that one of the team would brief her as soon as they were on board. Any aircraft they were using were always ready for immediate use no matter where they were in the world. Another one of the benefits of the Generals ever growing circle of influence. Nobody else had moved as they all needed to wait until Barney had finished so that they were aware of the whole plan.

"Cass I'd like you and Grace to trace the flight plan of that plane and also every flight for the three months before and any other flights up till now. Jake and Ed I need you to use your respective contacts etc and trace that van. Find out whatever you can about it no matter how insignificant it seems. I also need to identify both of the men and as we now have better quality images of them I'm hoping it'll be a little easier."

"Mitch, Cole," Barney looked across to both of them, "it's up to you what you want to do but if you're still up for helping then I can assign you to a task."

Mitch stood up, "let me go and check but I think I'm clear for the day so I can double up with Jess if you like?"

Barney nodded, "that would be great, although it's a straightforward flight it wouldn't hurt if she flew solo."

Cole didn't hesitate, "Barney I'm still available so I'm more than happy to jump in with the team flying down and can assist with gathering any intel."

Barney didn't hesitate; he'd already decided to ask Cole if he'd fly down with the team as it would give him some more time to work with Danny and to keep an eye on him. Danny hadn't shown any adverse conditions since the shooting and all of the feedback that Cole had given him so far had been positive. Even so, the fact that Cole was available and able to help gave him the opportunity to continue monitoring things. "That would be great Cole, to be honest the more the merrier."

The team left the room. Those flying down with Jess went and collected a go bag. They always went prepared and as always there was no certainty that they'd be flying back later in the day. Kelly had been with the team long enough now for some of the habits to have sunk in and he had already instinctively packed ready to move at a moment's notice. They made their way out to the hanger where Jess was just finalising everything with the Crew Chief that had been looking after their plane.

Scott was the first to get to Jess, "are we ready to go Baby Girl?"

"We will be as soon as you're all on board. We're cleared for an almost immediate take off although we may have to hold for a few minutes as there's a flight of F16's due in. They're running a little late so we may get in the air before they arrive."

The rest of the team had already boarded and Scott and Jess made their way up the steps to join them. Scott moved into the cabin and after sticking his bag in a storage area sat down next to Kelly. Danny closed the door and confirmed it was locked and armed. He made his way to the cockpit, "all in and ready to go," Jess was settling herself into the seat and glancing over the controls as Danny was talking.

She didn't look round as she spoke, "we're ready let everyone know we're about to move."

"Roger that," Danny left the cockpit and went back into the cabin, "we're about to move everyone."

Before anyone could say anything the intercom buzzed. "The F16's are running late enough for us to be in the air and out of their way before they get here so we've got immediate clearance to take off." She left it there as nothing else needed to be said. They'd all flown enough times to know what was expected of them. Mitch had been cleared to join them and he'd already completed all of the pre-flight checks so Jess was able to taxi straight out to the runway and get the plane off the ground. They settled in for the flight ahead of them. Each of them taking the time to once again review everything they had so far so that when they go on the ground, they'd be able to get to work straight away.

Cass and Grace were on the phone to different departments of the FAA trying to gain access to the flight plans they needed. As yet no calls had been made to the company that owned the plane. They wanted to gather as much information as possible before letting the company know about the investigation and the part their plane seemed to have played in it.

Jake and Ed were also on the phone. Jake was looking into the van to find out who owned it and Ed was contacting local Police forces to see if there had been any incidents involving the van. They'd already made the assumption that the vehicle was going to be dumped at the earliest opportunity in the same way as the first vehicle they'd used. If it had been dumped they weren't expecting to find any more clues but it would give then an indication of where to look for any traffic camera footage etc in the remote hope of finding what vehicle they'd swapped into.

The flight down was relatively uneventful, the only excitement was when they stopped off to collect the detectives. They'd grabbed a few boxes of donuts just before they'd go to the airport which made Danny and Scott rather happy. The short flight to their final destination was almost over before it had begun. It seemed that they'd only just taken off before Mitch announced that they were beginning the decent to land.

The owner of the airfield had assured Barney that the team would get his full cooperation and he wasn't wrong. As soon as they had landed two vehicles met them and took them over to the main administration building. Once inside introductions were made and if the owner had any previous doubts about the importance of things. Being shown the detectives ID followed swiftly by Joss flashing her CIA credentials and Mitch in his Air Force flight suit, they very quickly went away. Joss quickly explained what was needed and was pleased when she was informed that all staff that had been on duty that night had been called in and were waiting to be interviewed.

The team split up, Jess and Mitch went back out to the plane to ensure it had been refuelled and to make sure it was ready for a quick departure if needed. Cole and Danny went off to speak to the Head of Security to obtain the hard copies of all of the CCTV footage. Joss and Kelly split up and took a detective each to the two rooms that had been set aside for them to use as interview rooms. The logic being that they wanted to keep an element of calmness to the whole process so their theory was a local police officer paired up with an FBI agent should make everyone aware of the importance and need to be open and honest. They'd agreed that the detectives would lead the interview with Joss and Kelly only asking questions if needed.

In the meantime Scott had gone to the Control Tower to obtain copies of their logs and to talk to the Air Traffic Controllers. Once he'd finished there he went down to the main gate to check the logs there. He was able to get the gate logs for the night as well and as an added bonus anyone going airside had to submit photo ID so he'd been able to secure copies of that as well. Although he'd already decided that the ID was probably a fake. So far everything he'd seen about this operation was quite professional and he didn't think for one second that someone would be using their own ID.

The interviews were going well but it was obvious this wasn't going to be concluded in one day. Joss decided to send Scott, Danny and Cole back with the CCTV footage and log details as there wasn't any point in them hanging around. There were plenty of things that could be done so Jess flew them back up to Luke while Joss, Kelly and the detectives carried on with the interviewing.

Once back at Luke they updated Grace with everything they had and as soon as they'd finished with her they went to the mess to grab something to eat while they waited for Barney to update James and work out the next step. Things were beginning to speed up now as between them Cass and Grace had managed to get their hands on the flight plan for the plane covering its movements in the 24 hour period before and after they'd seen it on CCTV at the airfield. The tower and gate logs added to the positive step forward as the plane had been at the airfield three times in the previous 60 days.

Jake and Ed had drawn a blank after what seemed to be a promising start. The van had been reported stolen but after following up on that the trail had dried up and the van hadn't been reported found as yet. Jake and Ed joined the team in the mess and they updated everyone on what they'd found. Barney joined them all shortly after and said that he'd give it an hour and then get everyone back together in order to plan the next move. He was waiting for a call back from James once he'd updated the General.

They all enjoyed a relaxing hour filling up on food and drink. The variety on offer was once again outstanding and it was a chance for them to make the most of it. While they were talking Barney told Cole and Mitch they could stand down for the rest of the day especially as they were on their own time. They both took the opportunity to do a few bits for themselves and left the team deciding on what else they could eat. While Danny and Scott were going up once again to fill their plates Barney took a call from Joss. She thought they'd be done by about half ten in the morning. Once he'd finished the call he turned to Jess, "you'll need to fly down first thing tomorrow to pick the others up so once you're done here go and check on the plane and call it a night."

"I don't mind helping out for a few hours."

"No that's okay, we've got more than enough bodies here and I'd like you down there first thing in case they finish earlier than expected. I want to get everyone back here as fast as possible."

"I'll see of Mitch is free if not it's a short flight so it's more than doable on my own."

"I'm sure that Poster Boy will have nothing better to do and it'll be good for him to get a few more hours supervised flying in."

Jess laughed, "oh he'll be thrilled to hear that," with that she left to go back to the hanger to sort the plane out for an early morning take off.

"Right, everyone grab what you haven't eaten yet and let's get back to it, we've got a lot of new intel to go through and make sense of."

There was a flurry of activity as they all sorted themselves out and made their way back to the conference room. Danny and Scott hadn't quite finished and as soon as they had they cleared the table of all the trays and made their way to join the others. They didn't need to let Barney know they were doing that as it was the right thing to do and he'd expect them to do it as they were after all guests at the airbase.

Once back in the conference room there was a real noticeable sense of urgency, even more so than earlier. The team were working faster than they had been. The new information had been a real boost to the investigation and although it didn't reveal any definitive answers it was a huge leap forward. In turn added a new and somewhat expected dimension in that the operation they were looking into was global and clearly financed by someone with considerable money and connections. Cass had pieced together details of the flight after it had left the airfield and it had flown to Spain. She was getting detailed information regarding the planes movements from the FAA. As soon as they'd realised what had been happening they had been sending updates through as they got them. Very quickly Cass and Grace were able to ascertain that the plane had made several trips at the same Spanish airport.

As soon as they'd established that, Cass had given Katie a call to ask her if she could check with an Interpol contact to find out as to why the plane would make so many trips to that airport. Within half an hour Katie had called back, the airport was located close to a very large private hospital. It was favoured by celebrities and insurance companies as a result of the facilities and treatments on offer. Some at a premium price but delivered with total professionalism and speed. Cass had informed Barney straight away and they were now discussing what to do with regards to making the company that owned the plane aware of what was happening.

Like many investigations Barney now had a decision to make. Alerting the company too early could tip their hand and allow evidence and crucial details to be deleted or reworked to hide involvement. The challenge was that often they needed the cooperation of the company to assist with the investigation in order to get to the next step. This wasn't ever an easy decision and in the past he had got it wrong and had made enquiries too soon which had in turn led to delays in the investigation. Luckily the end result was still a positive one although it could have easily stopped the investigation dead in the water.

Although the decision was ultimately his at a crucial time like this as was often the case he started a discussion between the team to see what the consensus of opinion was, "okay everyone stop what you doing for a minute, we need to discuss the next move." The room slowly fell silent "Grace can you grab the others and get everyone back in here in ten minutes. That'll give them a chance to grab a coffee and something to eat if they want to."

Grace saved the file she was working on and left the room to get everyone, she'd proved to be a valuable asset and had saved the team countless hours of cataloguing and searching with some of the algorithms and scripts she'd created. Something they would have definitely have benefited from during past investigations. Barney made a mental note to speak to James to see if a tentative offer could be made to secure her on a more permanent basis with the team whenever they're working stateside. Barney closed his eyes and took a moment to enjoy the silence, everyone had left the office to grab a drink and he was on his own. As with many investigations things could move swiftly and he frequently found himself without time to think. This current investigation was suddenly gaining momentum and once again he knew that at this crucial point the right or wrong decision could make all the difference. This was where Fletch excelled and her absence was noticeable. He had a little time so, as in the past, he was going to use the collective minds of the team to put the pieces together to see what options they had with regard to the next steps. He'd found in the past that this had worked well and was always open to the opinions and thoughts of others.

A voice broke the silence, "getting a bit much for you is it old man?"

Barney didn't need to open his eyes to know who the voice belonged to "give me strength, do the powers that be not have something for you to do on this base other than to wander around abusing visitors?" Barney had opened his eyes to see Mitch stood in the doorway in his flight suit.

"Oh you know me, always like to make the visitors feel welcome," he grinned at Barney, "my boss has just given me a tasking that'll take me out of the picture for a couple of days. Pete Henshaw is on base and he's flown with Jess in the past so if you need a second pilot he'd be the first person I'd recommend. He can't cover the gig I've been given as he's only fixed wing qualified. Do you want me to speak to him?"

"If you could Mitch that would be helpful, I don't think we'll need him but as you know we never really know what's round the corner."

"That's not a problem, I'll go and find him know. In case you leave in the next day or so good luck and give Jess my regards and I'll see you soon."

"Thanks for your help Mitch, it's always good to have you around. I'll drop your boss a line and thank him for lending you out. Lord knows with your record a bit of positive feedback might make things look better for you." Barney smiled at Mitch who started shaking his head.

"Absolutely no respect these days from the older generation, have a good one old man and if I don't see you I really hope you get them."

"Thanks Mitch," with that the doorway was once again empty but Barney could hear some of the team on their way back to join him. Danny came through the door first carrying two mugs of coffee in one hand and a plate full of doughnuts and pastries. He set a mug down in front of Barney and put the plate down on the table virtually in front of him, "I'll leave it there so that you don't have to strain yourself to reach them," some of the others laughed and Barney could do no more than roll his eyes and shake his head.

Once everyone was sat down he started, "you all know roughly where we are at the moment and we need to make an important decision with regards to the Medical repatriation company. Do we contact them now or wait till we have more details regarding their possible involvement?"

Cass spoke first, "Jake and I have been going over the footage and to be honest it looks like a normal patient transfer. If you didn't know the history behind the vans earlier movements you'd think it was a private ambulance delivering a patient to the plane. They obviously removed Phoebe from the sports bag as some point during the journey and placed her onto the gurney before they got to the airfield. Watching the footage everything appears above board so there's a good chance the planes owners are unaware. It wouldn't take much to supply some forged documents to confirm the transfer to the clinic in Europe."

Barney had a concerned look on his face, "Katie said pretty much the same thing. Interpol have investigated something similar in the past and in that investigation all of the transfer papers were genuine on the surface. When they dug deeper they got nowhere as the insurance company was just a dummy with the payment coming from an untraceable offshore account."

It was Jake that spoke this time, "I'd say it's probably a similar scenario here. The company involved are quite big and do a significant amount of business in the states and if they were found to be knowingly involved it would shut them down and they'd lose several multimillion dollar contracts. I don't think it would be anywhere near worth them getting involved so my gut feeling is that they're in the dark."

"Anyone else have any input?" Barney looked round the table, he got all the way round the table to Grace, who was sitting on his left, without anyone saying anything.

"So I've checked out the flight plans for the plane and I can't see anything that looks out of place. The company run several aircraft and I've run a search on the pilots and they all come back clear. The odd parking fine but nothing else at all. We've managed to link three major medical insurance companies to their books and all of them are above board with no federal investigations even remotely linked to this sort of thing. There are a couple of malpractice lawsuits but that's nothing unusual at all. I'd say from what we've all managed to find so far that they are being used to transport people without their full knowledge. The same can't necessarily be said for the on board Doctor and nurse."

Barneys' expression changed, "what makes you say that?"

Cass took over again, "well we wouldn't expect the pilots to suspect anything, they're there to fly the patient from A to B and that part is straight forward. The medical team however would expect a patient to be displaying certain symptoms. In order to care for them in flight they'd have to have the patient's medical records and the patient isn't going to fake anything if they've been kidnapped so they've either got some pretty convincing documentation or the medical team are in on it. We've been able to get the two pilots details from the FAA however we can't get the details of the medical team without going to the owners to request them."

"At which point we possibly open everything up and create a problem for ourselves."

"Well that depends on how the company handle the information when we discuss it with them. Jake thinks if we approach them formally as with a joint CIA/FBI front they'll hopefully keep the fuss to a minimum and listen to us when we say that we're making discrete enquiries at this stage. If we go in armed with warrants etc it's more likely that word will spread quickly and we'll lose control."

"That makes sense and it's a good point, so Cass and Ed or Joss and Jake can you make an appointment to go and see them or do you think dropping in unannounced is a better approach?"

Joss was the next to speak, "well knowing how some of these big companies operate the owners are quite often rich well connected bureaucrats' so it may be wiser to adopt a bit of a show of strength and set up the initial meeting with all four of us. If we encounter anyone with an aversion to female authority Jake and Ed can lead and if we come up against someone that we can charm then Cass and I will lead. We won't know what the best approach is until we're there so I would say we hedge our bets and go prepared for anything."

Barney nodded in approval, "I like that idea, where's their head office?"

"They seem to have two but the slightly larger and the one I'd head to is in LA, close to the all-important celebrity population. Which seems to make up for a rather large part of their portfolio of key clients."

"LA it is then, Jess can you sort out a flight plan and if you need a pilot you'll need to find Pete Henshaw. Mitch is back on a live operation but Pete is available if you need him."

"That's okay I spoke to Mitch earlier and I've already spoken with Pete, he's currently on a five day rest cycle. He's got spare flying hours but the team he's working with have been stood down so he's good to go at a minutes' notice."

"Excellent, go and find him and you four had better grab your things and get to LA as quickly as you can."

The room came alive as they all made their way out of the door, "Levi can you contact Stevie and see if they've uncovered any new information. Scott and Danny can you get in touch with Katie and see if she's got anything new from her contacts at Interpol. Marcus and Boyd can you touch base with your bosses and see if there are any updates at all and confirm that they're still okay for you to be working this with us. Grace you and I have the delightful task of going through everything before we call James and the General with an update." Barney once again looked round the table although it was quicker this time as five of the team had left moments before, "if there are no questions let's make a start." Once more the room was filled with sudden movement as everyone with the exception of Grace stood up and left the room.

"Okay Grace, shall we take a few minutes and grab something decent to eat before we make a start on piecing all of this together?"

"Yes, I'll take my Mac with me and we can make a rough plan while we eat and then when we get back in here we can put it all together."

"Perfect, let's go, the others are sensible enough to know they need to eat so I'm not going to worry about telling them."

The next hour flew by, Barney and Grace mapped out the rough plan for the update as they ate what eventually turned into a group lunch as the others gradually made their way to grab some food. Within fifteen minutes of Grace and Barney having sat down the rest of the team was seated with them. Barney had received a text from Jess to let him know they were on the runway waiting for clearance to take off. She'd let him know that the flight time was just under 90 minutes and they'd already arranged for an FBI vehicle to meet them when they land. Barney let the rest of the team know just to keep them in the loop. It made no real difference to what any of them were doing but he'd found over the years that keeping everyone updated has several benefits and he'd found anything that had a positive effect on the team was a good thing.

As they were eating the various groups updated each other on what they'd found so far. They'd carry out a more formal update when they were all back round the table but a quick update as they were eating wasn't a bad thing and it had become normal practice over the years. They often found that the informal setting would sometimes allow for a bit of creative thinking and so they'd naturally adopted the habit and would bounce ideas and information off each other. Once they'd finished eating they went back and began a more formal update collating the various bits of information and getting a brief presentation together for the General.

Jess landed at LAX without any issues at all, the flight had been uneventful and they'd landed an hour and twenty minutes after taking off. Jess and Pete told the team they'd stay with the plane and to call them once they were heading back to the airport. It would give them a chance to refuel and prep the plane even though they had plenty of fuel over the years Jess had learnt that there's no guarantee that they'll be heading in the direction they thought they would be. Once they'd got the plane ready they would head over to the Pilots rest room and grab a coffee and something to eat.

The team were met on the tarmac by a people carrier driven by an agent from the local field office and he ran them straight to the Companies head Office. Cass took the lead and flashed her ID at the receptionist stating that they had an appointment. The receptionist didn't hesitate and told them to take the lift to the top floor and they would be met. Obviously someone had taken their call seriously as they'd normally be stalled and kept waiting. The lift doors opened and the four of them stepped out, they were met by a smartly dressed man.

"Good morning, please follow me they are expecting you in the board room." No request for ID or conformation as to who they were at all. They followed him noting the decor, this was a firm doing well. The carpet was soft underfoot, the pictures on the walls were clearly expensive and the colours of the walls blended in perfectly with the carpet.

Their escort stopped at an ornate and very decorative set of doors, he opened them and gestured for them to enter. The boardroom was large, a huge oval table sat in the middle with seating for twenty. The chairs were based on a vintage design and as ornate as the doors. Two large paintings were hanging on the two walls and the other two walls were simply floor to ceiling glass giving a fantastic view of the skyline. Four chairs had been pulled out. Obviously for them so they made their way over to them. Their escort closing the doors softly behind them as they entered the room. Seated opposite their chairs were four people, one of which had a notepad in front of them and was dressed slightly differently to the other three.

They all stood up, "hello, please take a seat, my name is Devlin Saunders and I'm the CEO, this is my Chief Operating Officer my Financial Director and the gentleman on the end is our attorney."

Cass introduced the team clearly emphasising that this was a joint CIA and FBI team. "Mr Saunders I'm hoping that the call we made has been relayed to you and that you're aware of why we're here."

He nodded, "please call me Devlin, from what I understand this is an informal visit."

Cass smiled, "yes it is at this stage and to be honest we were hoping to keep it that way."

The Attorney jumped in, "so you don't have a warrant then."

Cass looked directly at him, "no we don't however both agencies are currently preparing the paperwork in case we do need one."

"Simon please be quiet unless I ask you for your advice." Devlin had an annoyed look on his face but as he looked away from the attorney his face softened, "my apologies as it stands at the moment I don't feel that this discussion requires a warrant. Please understand if I feel the need arises then it would be rather remiss of me not to request one."

Cass was surprised at how quickly the attorney had been shut down but didn't let it show, "that's perfectly understandable, currently neither agency feel that the business is in question. From our investigation so far it's simply a couple of your employees that we'd like to discuss." For the next couple of minutes she explained where they were at with the investigation and that they had no issues with the pilots or the flight plans but would like to take a bit of a more in depth look at the medical team on the flight in question.

Devlin looked thoughtful as he sat listening to Cass but responded without hesitation. "The Doctor and nurse on that flight, and in fact all of the flights are supplied by an agency. We own the planes and employ the pilots, but the medical staff change depending on the patient. To be honest it's easier for us to go to an agency to request a team that meet the medical needs of the patient."

Cass smiled, "I can understand that, especially as you'll simply bill that back out with a nice bit of profit on top."

"Simple business strategy and it ensures that our base costs are kept to a minimum but that's no different to a number of industries as I'm sure you're aware."

Cass knew that she had to tread carefully as they really didn't want to have to go down a formal route to get the information they needed, "totally understandable and if I were in your position I'd be doing exactly the same."

Joss spoke up, "I can assure you that as Cass mentioned neither the FBI nor CIA feel that your company are implicated in our investigation. To be perfectly honest now that you've mentioned that the medical team are in fact hired in for each job that distances you even further. As a business you have too much to lose and from your records we've seen that this is an effective and well managed operation. Which is why we've jointly opted for the less formal approach. Your business plan works and we certainly aren't here to question your ethics in anyway."

Devlin looked at Joss, "my apologies if I came across a little defensive, it wasn't my intention. I've built this business up over the years and I am very protective. Which I think you'll agree is understandable under the circumstances. I do really appreciate the approach that you've taken and I promise you we will give you any information that you need without hesitation." With that he stood up, "if you'll all wait here I'll have some coffee served while we make the necessary arrangements to get you the details you require," all four of them left the room leaving the team on their own.

Having done this for several years they all knew to watch what they said as many businesses were known for recording meetings etc so they were already guarded and were careful about what they discussed as they sat there. The door opened and the same employee that had met them at the lift wheeled in a drinks trolley with tea, coffee and plates of pasties and biscuits. "Please do help yourselves and if there's anything else you need I'll be just outside the door." Without waiting for a response he turned on his heel and closed the door behind him.

"Well that's what I call service," Jake stood up as he spoke, knowing what everyone wanted he poured four coffees and added creamer and sugar, "if only all our meetings went like this."

Ed grinned, "let's be honest that's not likely to happen, this is clearly one of the few companies that genuinely has nothing to hide and really does want to cooperate."

Cass picked up her coffee, "either that or be seen to be distancing themselves from the issue."

"Do you think that's the case?" Ed had picked up a pastry and started to eat it as he waited for Cass to reply.

"I actually think he means it, there seemed to be some pride in his voice when he mentioned about how protective he is. Reading the company biography earlier I actually believe he may well be telling the truth. If you think about it, contracting out the fulfilment of the medical staff makes perfect sense and you can then tailor the team to the patients exact needs ensuring a dedicated professional every time. Especially as all you do is add a bit extra and you've got a rather nice profitable business and in a city like this the demand will be huge so it stands to reason you wouldn't want to do anything to tarnish that reputation."

Jake put his coffee down, "I know that some CEOs like to play on the edge and enjoy the danger of stepping over the line but I haven't seen or heard anything yet that would lead me to believe that is the case here," he looked around the office and stood up, walking over to the window he looked out at the view. "As Cass has just mentioned any involvement or knowledge of what we're looking into would destroy their reputation instantly. If they are involved they've got to know that we'd find out so I actually think for once that Devlin is being honest. If anything he's probably more than a little concerned at the moment in case this does have any backlash on the business."

With that the door opened once again and the whole team turned as one, Devlin came in and the door closed behind him. He held a folder in his hand and sat down at the same seta he'd been in before. Jake sat back down and they waited for Devlin to speak.

"I'd like to start by saying thank you for the way that you've handled this, it's most unusual for a government agency to be so thoughtful. I would have expected you to have come armed with warrants and demands however you've taken the time to approach this in a rather unusual manner and it's for that reason that I'll give you everything you need. My attorney advised against it and suggested asking for a formal request but in my eyes that would only make it look as though we have something to hide." Devlin paused for a second looking at each of them in turn. "All of our staff employed or contracted have to pass stringent checks and in the folder are the two files relating to the Doctor and Nurse on the flight in question. There's enough information in each file for you to conduct an enquiry without having to go to their employer."

Devlin got up and made his way over to the drinks trolley and poured himself a glass of water, he made his way back to his seat and sat down. After taking a few mouthfuls of water he carried on. "Part of the agreement everyone we use has to sign is that at any given time we can supply their details to any Government agency for vetting and they have to waive their rights to privacy. We currently carry out regular medical transfers for the services and have to obtain clearance to land at various military bases. It's for this reason that I'm not hesitating to supply you with their files containing all the information we have on them. A third folder contains a list of dates and times that they have been contracted to us over the last three years and the final file has a single piece of paper on it containing all of my personal contact details in order for you to avoid having to ask anyone else for further information should you need it."

He pushed the folder over towards Cass, "thank you, it would have been easy for us to have arrived with warrants and an army of investigators but that's not always how we do business. As you've been so transparent and cooperative I'll be open and honest with you. We're part a team that's made up of just about every major Government agency worldwide. Whilst we have the resources available from each agency we represent we often find that a more subtle approach at times reaps better results and the conversation we're having now just goes to prove how well our approach can work. It's been a pleasure and hopefully we won't need to contact you but let me assure you before we do anything that may impact on your business we will speak with you first."

"It's taken me years to get this business to this point and as it stands we are one of the most respected medical repatriation companies in the world. Insurance companies are constantly knocking on our door to be able to use us in order to provide premium policies for the rich and famous." Devlin paused for a second and all four team members could see a tear in his eye. "I wouldn't know what to do with myself if we were implicated in anything and it horrifies me to think that we could be."

Joss stood up and made her way round the table, she knelt down next to Devlin and he turned to face her, "I think I've seen enough already to know that you're speaking from the heart and I give you my personal guarantee that if there's anything you need to know I'll call you personally."

A tear rolled down his face as Devlin tried to gather some composure, "thank you," he managed to say.

Joss put a hand lightly on his shoulder, "you're welcome, now we'll get out of your way and allow you to get back to business as usual." She stood up and the others followed her lead. They made their way to the door and Cass looked back to see that despite trying to appear composed Devlin had the look of someone that was completely crest fallen. As the others walked out of the door and were greeted by their chaperone Cass turned round and walked back into the board room.

"Devlin, take my card, it has my number on it and if you need to call me anytime don't hesitate. We're the good guys and it's our job to stop people like you being part of the fallout as we carry out our investigations. We're good at what we do and we'll do everything possible to ensure that you come out of this unscathed."

Devlin took the card and just nodded. Cass followed the others out of the boardroom, turned round and closed the door. They were silent in the lift and didn't speak until they were outside of the building. Jake spoke first "So I know our driver is one of us but let's wait till we're on the plane before discussing anything. I like the old guy and I don't want anything to happen to him so we'll wait."

Their ride was waiting in the same spot it had dropped them at and they made their way over. On route to the airport they made small talk with the field agent and thanked him as he dropped them at the airport. Cass got her phone out and hit the speed dial. "Baby Girl we're at arrivals and on our way to the information desk." The others couldn't hear the other side of the conversation but knew that they'd be in the air fairly quick as Jess somehow seemed to know her way round every airport and procedure. Sure enough within twenty minutes of arriving at the airport they were whisked away by minibus to the far side of the runway.

The cabin door of the plane was open and Pete suddenly appeared he came down the stairs and thanked the driver who promptly drove off. Jake turned to him. "Did you know him?"

Pete shook his head, "no, not at all. Jess told me his name and told me to make sure that I thanked him. It's like she knows everyone. I'd left her in the Pilots lounge for no more than ten minutes and she was talking to three pilots referring to them by name. Being in my flight suit gets me through lots of doors but she's something else. I can see why Mitch raves about her so much. On the flight here she made everything look so simple."

Joss grinned, "she certainly knows her stuff and trust me we've given up trying to work out how she makes everything happen."

They all made their way into the plane and Pete closed the door engaging all of the safety locks before making his way into the cockpit. As they started to taxi the team heard a noise from the galley at the back of the plane, before any of them could get up to investigate they heard the intercom buzz. "Welcome back people, we'll be in the air shortly and knowing how hopeless you all are I've taken the liberty of sorting out some food and drink. It's a five minute taxi to the runway we need and we've got a short wait for clearance so please sit back and enjoy the service, by the way be nice to the staff."

With that two air force personnel appeared from the galley, one pushing a drinks trolley the other pushing a food trolley, "good afternoon everyone can I get any of you a drink?" Four coffees were quickly served and they were each given plates with a variety of sandwiches and savoury snacks. Somehow each of them had exactly what they would have ordered, before Cass could do anything else the airman bent down and took a book from the lower shelf of his trolley. He passed it over to her with the front cover facing down, "Cass apparently this is a book you've been after for a while." Cass turned it over and the other three burst out laughing. Cass was lost for words at first and then all she could say was "Bloody kids." The title of the book was clear for everyone to see and it simply said 'A military guide to improve your shooting'

Cass had her back to the cockpit and hadn't realised that Pete was taxing the plane and Jess was stood just behind her. Jess clapped her hands and had a big grin on her face like an excited teenager, "I knew you'd love it." she exclaimed.

Cass scowled at her, "get back in the cockpit and fly the damn plane."

Jess gave a cheeky salute and with a "Yes Ma'am." She turned on her heals and disappeared.

The intercom buzzed again "Thanks boys, grab yourselves a drink and something to eat. Take a seat when you're ready, you might want to steer clear of little miss grumpy for a while although she'll calm down eventually. Everyone the two boys are out of Luke and they got bumped off their transfer back to base. They saw the plane of the tarmac and recognised it as they are actually part of its maintenance crew. They made some enquiries and eventually someone found me in the Pilots lounge. I went and found them and offered them a lift so be nice to them as it's actually their plane we've stolen."

The airman sat down and one of them lent across to speak to Jake, "I'm sorry but I've got to ask, what's with the book?" He gave a quick nervous look in the direction of Cass before sitting back in his seat.

Jake had a beaming smile on his face, "well now, let me tell you a story."

Cass hunkered down in her seat and mumbled, "oh god here we go again."

Like the flight out the trip back was quick and over before they knew it, the team didn't get to discuss the case because Cass spent the whole time trying to justify the humiliation. Once on the ground at Luke the two airmen dealt with the plane which allowed Pete and Jess to join the team as they made their way to the office. Barney and the rest of the team were already there with a number of files laid out in front of them.

He looked up as they entered, "perfect timing, we're about to put the final touches to the brief how did it go?" They hadn't had time to brief Barney on the way back so Cass gave a real short version of what

313

happened and gave Barney the folder, "well that's a real positive result, well done all of you. Do you need a break or are you okay to continue?"

With a smile on his face Danny chipped in, "oh I think they had such a relaxing time Cass even managed to get some reading in."

Barney had a confused look on his face and he turned to look at Cass, "really?" he asked.

Cass couldn't contain herself and went red in the face, "you damn kids can be such twats at times."

Jess and Danny both burst out laughing as Cass threw the book in front of Barney, who desperately tried to keep a straight face but failed as he said, "may I ask if it helped at all?"

Cass rolled her eyes and then held her head in her hands, she lifted her head back up, "I'm really going to hurt Sean when I get hold of him, this is all his fault. No it didn't bloody help now stop joining in and get this circus back on track."

Barney raised his eyebrows to exaggerate a shocked look, "okay then," for the next twenty minutes Barney took everyone through what they'd prepared so far. The briefing was concise and as soon as he'd finished the last slide he asked if anyone felt that anything else needed to be added, not surprisingly nobody said anything.

"Right, Joss and Cass can you get the search started on the Doctor and Nurse. Scan the files over to James and let him run with them. Jess, now we've finished with all the files that Clay let us bring back with us can you and Jake take them back to him and then Jake I'd like you to go and check in on Drew to see how he's doing. Actually Danny are you up for a trip down there I'm sure Drew would like a bit of company."

"Yes I'll go down with them, it would be nice to see him."

"Good, the rest of you we're now at a bit of a loose end until James comes back to us so let's spend some time getting this place squared away. Work with Grace to make sure that everything is documented and filed properly in case the General wants anything sent across after the briefing."

The rest of the day went by quickly, they all helped to load up the boxes of paperwork onto the plane and in the end after a brief conversation with Barney Scott flew down to see Drew with the others. He wanted to be close to Danny just in case seeing Drew had an adverse effect on him. Barney thought that was a good idea, although Cole said that Danny was doing well he didn't want to take any chances and as they didn't have a great deal to do right now he could easily spare Scott.

They arrived back ay Luke late in the evening, Jake, Scott and Danny had spent a few hours with Drew who was pleased to see them and was recovering well. Clay was pleased to see them and Jake gave him a brief rundown on how things were going. The rest of the team had managed to get the three offices they'd been using back to normal and with a bit of effort and a lot of help from Grace they'd even managed to get all the digital files catalogued and filed exactly how they wanted them. It had been a good day, even the briefing with the General had gone well although as usual he wanted answers quicker than the team could deliver them.

Chapter 35 (Europe)

Just before six the other two teams called in to say that they were both parked in different streets a block away. They had already discussed who was going to do what and it had been agreed that Karl and Erica would stay and enter the property to place whatever surveillance cameras and microphones that they could. Having not seen the inside of the property they couldn't be sure as to what success they'd have. The other two cars would follow the driver Right now that was more to do with the fact that they wanted to make sure that Karl had enough time to do what he needed to do. They had little hope of the driver doing anything that would warrant them stepping in. They had already realised that if they were going to have any success at all it would come from something they see or hear the driver do whilst at home and not anything he does during his daily driving.

Sitting in their pairs overnight they'd had plenty of time to discuss the next steps and they had all come to the conclusion that the best chance they had of finding out anything at all was going to come from a phone or computer. They needed to get access to the driver's emails or texts. Alek was fairly sure it was going to be the emails that held the clues as everything else they'd found so far had been via encrypted emails. Taking into account what they already knew they weren't actually that hopeful that any surveillance from inside the house was going to help. Despite that they were going to do what they could and hope that maybe they'd be lucky or that the investigation would take a jump forward and they could arrest the driver.

The first sign of life from within the house came at just before six forty five, the bedroom light came on. Forty minutes later all the lights in the house went out and the front door opened. The driver stepped out closing the door behind him. Luckily he didn't engage a secondary lock so all Karl had to deal with was a standard union style door lock which he should be able to pick in a matter of seconds. Five minutes later the driver pulled away from the curb in his car with Alek and Ralf following a few seconds later. They followed him a short distance quickly noting that he was in fact on route to the second house they'd been watching yesterday so it was safe to say he was on route to pick up his colleague.

Ten minutes later the car briefly stopped allowing the drivers colleague to get in and they set off straight away. The traffic was just beginning to get a little heavier so the two vehicles following had to close in a bit to give them a better chance of being able to react in case the driver suddenly turned off. They didn't need to worry as the driver kept to the main roads and eventually turned into a small industrial estate. Alek held back at the entrance and Ralf followed the driver into the estate. The driver stopped in front of one of the small units. The passenger got out and unlocking a small side door went inside, a few seconds later the roller shutter started to go up. As soon as it was high enough the driver drove into the unit. Ralf drove past as Karla looked in just about making out the shape of what she believed to be the ambulance they'd seen on the CCTV.

Ralf drove to the far end of the estate and turned round pulling over as far away from the unit as he could. They already knew that there was only one way in and out so he could afford to hold back a little knowing that Alek would be able to pick the vehicle up as it left the estate. They didn't have long to wait before the nose of the ambulance appeared out from inside the unit. Stopping just outside for a minute or two to allow the passenger to close the roller shutter, locking the unit back up again he got into the ambulance and it drove off. Ralf followed at a suitable distance and once at the exit of the estate pulled out. Alek was already behind the ambulance and they spent the next few hours following the ambulance as it carried out what appeared to be a couple of genuine patient transfers from one place to another.

They stopped for lunch as a cafe, whilst they were busy eating Ralf and Karla took the opportunity to grab some food from a nearly shop. Although they had some provisions with them in the car they didn't want to use them if they didn't need to and as the shop was close by it made sense to hold them back for emergencies. Once Karla was back in the car they let Alek know and Charlie jumped out to do the same thing for her and Alek. Whilst they were stationary Alek called Karl to see how he was getting on.

Getting into the house had been easy, the main lock on the door was a standard union lock and once you knew the principles took little or no effort to pick. As soon as they were both inside they stayed together taking numerous photos of each room before doing anything. The images served two purposes, firstly once back at the hotel they could examine them to see if they could see anything that may be of use. Secondly and in some ways more importantly they could look at the images when they'd finished in the room to ensure that they were leaving each room as they found it.

They took their time being careful to only touch what they really needed to, in total they'd managed to place five cameras throughout the house. it wasn't as many as they'd liked to have been able to install but under the circumstances, they were just going to have to rely on what they could do. The reality of them being able to get anything useful was still quite slim although a couple of the cameras did have a good field of view and the mics were quite sensitive. They'd definitely pick up any conversations that were had in the living room, kitchen or main bedroom. Of course the clarity of what they'd hear was subject to the fact that the background noise wasn't too loud.

Once they'd finished the pair of them went through each room one last time checking each of the images against what they saw in the room. Happy that everything was being left exactly as they found it they made their way out of the house and back to the car. The cameras connected wirelessly to a unit that had been hidden in the loft which would then relay the video feed back to the team in the hotel. The wireless network wouldn't appear on any devices so unless the owner found either one of the cameras or the unit in the loft he'd never know that they were there.

As soon as they were back at the hotel they checked to see if everything was working as it should. They knew it would be because they'd checked while they were still inside the house, again when they were back in the car and they'd even stopped to check one last time when they were half way back to the hotel. The cameras were fairly high tech in as much as they were both motion and sound initiated which significantly increased the battery life. They could also be activated remotely which is exactly what Karla had done from the hotel to check them. While they were at the house they had tested the motion and sound activation on each camera after they'd been installed.

Now happy that they had eyes and ears inside the drivers house they could relax and wait for the others to return. They used their time wisely following up on some of the details they'd uncovered from the personal and financial searches that had been conducted. They ate as they worked just in case they had to drop everything to go and help the others. That wasn't going to be necessary as they'd had a rather boring and non-productive day following the ambulance on what turned out to be a whole day of legitimate patient transfers. Alek had very quickly realised that as they expected they weren't really going to learn a lot from following them around.

They followed the driver back to his house and at half eight left him walking through his front door. Despite their lack of progress they still decided to keep the surveillance in place and Alek left Rolf and Erica watching the house while he and Charlie headed back to the hotel to catch up with Karl, get something to eat and shower and change before coming back to take over for a few hours. Once back at the hotel they ordered some food from room service and had it delivered to the meeting room.

Karl had shown Alek the view from each camera and they watched the live feed a minute or two, happy with what they were getting they turned the sound down, "we now have everything in place and it's a waiting game."

Karl nodded in agreement, "yes but I still feel that the easiest and quickest step forward would be to get hold of his phone."

"I agree, I've already suggested it and I think we can probably do it in such a way that neither of them have the opportunity to let anyone know that they've been arrested. We'd obviously run the risk of them not being contactable and someone from their side investigating. As we'd have not only their phones but their computers as well we'd be in a position to see any messages coming in even if they are encrypted."

Karla spoke, "even if they were we already suspect it'll be the same encryption used for the messages we've already got so we should be able to read anything straight away. It's very unlikely that they'll suddenly change anything and if we do it right and with some authority from high up we could even keep them tucked away somewhere rather than a local police station."

"I'm pretty sure if we did decide to bring them both in we'd have to make sure they were somewhere off grid. There's too much at stake and knowing what we already do whoever is running this has plenty of money and is running a very sophisticated operation. Which means we'll have to assume that they probably have contacts in all sorts of places."

"Okay so what are our next steps?"

"As soon as Charlie and I have finished eating we'll shower and change and take over from Ralf and Erica. We'll stay there till two if you two can take over till four and then Ralf and Erica can do the four till six stint. We'll all be back there for six and in the meantime I'll see if I can get someone to make a decision about bringing them in as I have a feeling tomorrow is probably going to be a repeat of today." Almost as if he'd planed it there was a knock at the door. Charlie got up and took the tray of food, closing the door once again she put the tray down on the table.

They ate quickly and as soon as they'd finished they went up to their rooms and had a quick shower. Changing they made their way back to the meeting room to check if Karl and Karla needed anything. They'd already sorted out food and were busy adding the final touches to the backup structure for the camera feeds. Alek and Charlie left them to it and made their way back to their car and after making a quick stop at a convenience store for some drink and snacks they took over from Ralf and Erica.

Two hours into their session watching the house Alek decided to give Katie a call to see how things were progressing, "Katie you're not on speaker but it's a conference call and Charlie is on as well. Just checking in to see how things are going?"

"Hi Charlie, at the moment things aren't too bad. The only real problem is the sheer volume of information that's now coming in. We've got four sets of couriers that we can now definitely connect to transferring at least one unauthorised patient that we believe is part of the kidnapping investigation."

"So how do you see this progressing? If you haven't read the file that Charlie uploaded earlier we've tailed this courier and although we now have some information regarding what they did yesterday it hasn't given us any clues relating to Phoebe. We've installed cameras in the house but I don't have any real confidence in us being able to get anything tangible from any footage or audio we get. We've discussed this as a team and the real information we need is going to be gained when we get hold of their emails. We know they're going to be encrypted but we can already break that as it'll more than likely be the same code that's used and to be honest if it's different it won't take Nick long to crack it. The only way I can see that we can gain access is to arrest the two that we're following and I'd suggest these two as we know that they have been involved with Phoebe. I'm worried about how much longer we can afford to leave it before we act. Bottom line is worst case scenario is that she's already dead but I've got to believe that there's a chance she's alive."

"My only fear is that if we do that we may start a chain reaction that results in us losing the element of surprise with regard to arresting virtually everyone at once, having said that you're right about Phoebe."

Charlie spoke for the first time, "Katie what's your gut feeling on this?"

"If it was me Charlie I think I'd give the go ahead to arrest the two you're following as long as it can be done in a way that doesn't allow them to alert anyone. Then I'd hold them off grid for a while in the hope that we can get the information we need and then as soon as we have something either move on everyone or we just focus on Phoebe. The difficulty is that although we know Phoebe has only recently been delivered there's no knowing how many others are still out there being kept alive and although we may be in time to save Phoebe that may result in us tipping out hand and losing the opportunity to get the people that matter."

"That's pretty much where we got to in our discussions Katie. I think someone is going to have to make a decision before long because I have a feeling that when we follow these guys tomorrow all we're going to achieve is a repeat of today and that's not really going to help us at all."

"Okay Alek, leave it with me and I'll call Barney and tell him what we've discussed. I'm fairly sure he'll have already read the daily updates but I'll go through it all with him and see what he wants to do. I'll come back to one of you as soon as I can."

"Thanks Katie," Alek terminated the call and turned to Charlie, "so now we sit and wait."

"The main problem I can see is the potential to wreck everything if we move too quickly. From what I've read so far none of the teams

321

have made enough intel to be able to link this to anyone above the couriers."

"I know and that's the real sticking point. Having said that though if they can find whoever Damian is then that's a huge step forward and if we arrested all of the couriers. We should be able to gather some details from their emails etc so could possibly be able to arrest a number of people that have used the service."

"That's assuming they've not covered their tracks, remember this is a highly sophisticated operation that we're dealing with so we may find that we actually come to a number of dead ends."

Alek nodded in agreement, "yes but then we may also find that we get a number of people like Josef that haven't deleted all of their emails or haven't cleaned their email well enough."

"True, well let's wait and see what the outcome of the call with Barney is."

The next few hours were uneventful, they had the feed from the cameras displayed on an iPad so had moved a bit further away from the house. They were only a couple of streets away but close enough that they could follow on foot or by car if the driver were to leave the house. Luckily with a camera facing the door they'd have plenty of notice if he was intending to leave. Just after one o'clock Alek got a call, he looked at the display to see that it was James calling, "you're up late."

"I'm very well thank you for asking Alek, so I've just had a long call with Barney and the General. Basically if you think you can successfully arrest them without them being able to let anyone know then do it. We can arrange for somewhere for them to be taken that won't raise any suspicions or questions. The call has got to be yours as you're on the ground. The only thing Barney has said is that if you have any doubts at all leave them alone and continue to follow them and we'll just have to hope that things come together quickly."

"I'll get the team together straight away and we'll work on a plan."

"Okay, if you do come up with something then just send an updated progress report and one of us will pick up on it."

"Will do."

"Good luck Alek and off the record I hope you can come up with a workable plan because we could do with a bit of good news. We're gathering information at an alarming rate but none of it has given us a decent enough chance to really move forward, all it does is lead to more investigating and searching."

"I'm sure we'll come up with something that'll work, we'll speak to you later." Alek ended the call and looked across to Charlie, "let's head back, on the way call the others and we'll work on something straight away." As Alek drove Charlie called the other four and asked them to meet them in the meeting room as soon as they could. No more than fifteen minutes later Alek and Charlie were walking through the hotel reception after having parked the car.

The others were already in the room. On the way past reception Alek had asked for some drinks to be arranged. He updated the rest of them as quickly as he could, "as it stands it's up to us to decide the next move. Now I think we could probably arrest them at the industrial unit they use. The problem is we haven't seen inside but getting in shouldn't be an issue. It's knowing if there's somewhere inside that we could stay out of sight until they are both in, we need to get to them before they can make any calls."

Karla looked round the table, "I guess a couple of us could go and take a look now to have a look inside."

"That could be a bit risky as I doubt there's a great deal of traffic in the vicinity of the units at this time of night and we'd stand out. The last thing we'd need is for the Police to turn up after they get a call stating that someone is breaking into one of the units."

"So what if we arrest the driver as he walks to his car, we can make sure we're close enough to him before we make our move and can stop him from using his phone. One of us drives his car to pick up the passenger and as he comes out of the house the team grab him. We could either get him as he approaches the car or wait for him to get in, we could park so that he doesn't have a clear view of the driver and one of us could be in the back." Ralf paused for a second. "He's got slightly tinted rear windows on his car. I noticed that yesterday as we followed him."

Erica shook her head, "arresting them in the street is a little risky as there are too many things that we can't control."

"So what about waiting until they're both in the warehouse, and we use some sort of distraction to get their attention?"

"I don't actually think there's an easy way to do this at all." Alek paused for a second, "if we were just looking to arrest them we could

323

do it a number of ways but to actually do it without giving them an opportunity to let anyone know is very different and we don't have a great deal of time to come up with an idea."

"So let's refine the idea Ralf had," Charlie looked round the table, "we send one car straight to the passengers house, the other two go to the drivers house. We watch the camera to see when he's leaving and one team is on foot and the other mobile. Just before he gets to his car we time it so that the team on foot are almost with him and the mobile team pull up. We grab him and put him in the back of the car and drive off. We take his keys off him and one of the team drives his car over to the passenger's house where we basically repeat the process."

Karla spoke up, "I do prefer that idea rather than trying to work out a plan to do it when they pick up the ambulance."

It was Erica that spoke next, "once we've got them where do we take them?"

"Well, I can call Katie to see if Interpol have a safe house that they have the use of locally. If that's not an option then I think I have an alternative but I'd rather not use that option if I can help it." Alek waited to see if anyone had anything to add before he continued. "So I think we need to swap the teams around a little to give us the best options. Charlie you pair up with Ralf, you're the ground team that'll deal with the passenger. Erica you drive and pair with Karl, I'll pair with Karla and we'll be the ground team that take the driver. Once we've cuffed him he goes into the back of the car, Karl will already be in the back. Once he's in the car I'll get in the back as well, Karla takes his car and we repeat a similar process with the passenger. Use your Interpol ID when you make the arrest, it'll need to be forceful and quick. Karla you need take it easy on the drive over to give us a chance to get ahead of you so that I can get out and assist with the passenger. We'll use plasticuffs and soundproof hoods so that if they start screaming or shouting the volume will be kept to a minimum, any questions?"

"I'm guessing before we put them in the vehicles we're going to remove their phones from their pockets?"

"That's a good point Karl and yes we will, phones and keys to be removed straight away. With their hands cuffed behind their backs their movement will be severely restricted anyway but I don't want to take any chances. Right if there aren't any other questions then we'll meet at our cars at five thirty. You can leave all of your kit here because we'll come back for it."

They all left to get some sleep before the early start, Alek made a few calls and after almost an hour had managed to secure somewhere to take both men. Alek knew that there were several safe houses in the area but it was picking one that they could afford to compromise. With Interpol technically leading the arrests the safe house would be known and as they didn't have anything suitable of their own. Alek had to force the issue and with a bit of help from James and some pressure from the General, had managed to secure the use of a little used building on the edge of the Hohenfels Army Base. It was a bit of a drive from where they were but it did give them the ability to keep both men off the grid and once through the gates nobody would even know they were there which was exactly what they needed.

Chapter 36 (North America)

He awoke to the smell of fresh coffee and finding his boxers on the bedroom floor he put them on and made his way out to the kitchen. Stella had her back to him making the coffee. All she was wearing was a pair of knickers and he took a few seconds to take in just how good she looked. He walked up behind her and kissed the back of her neck, it made her jump. He put an arm round her waist and pulled he into him so they he could feel the warmth of her body against his. She put the spoon down as his hand moved up to her breast. She turned around and kissed him, "I think coffee can wait."

They almost made it back to the bedroom but ended up on the floor in the hall, the sex had a frantic excitement about it. Damian was surprisingly totally relaxed the recent events seemed a million miles away as he enjoyed the moment totally taken in by the smell and touch of Stella. She kissed him and stood up, walking over to the counter she finished making the coffee, he laid on the floor watching her. She put the two coffee mugs down and walked over to him. Getting down on all fours she kissed him once more and then stood up, "I need a shower and I've got a class in an hour so I need to kick you out."

"That's alright, I guess I should actually think about doing some work."

As Stella walked off towards the bathroom he stood up and collecting his clothes together got dressed. When Stella came back into the room he was sat down drinking his coffee, she sat next to him, "I know you're not in town for long but if you want to meet up tonight I finish early and we could go for dinner of you fancy it."

Damian smiled, "that would be nice. I'll probably be in town for a few more days before I have to leave."

She stood up, "good, then let's make the most of those few days."

An hour later Damian was back in the room at the motel, the walk back from Stella apartment hadn't been great as the closer he got to the motel the closer he came back to reality. The last few hours had been an amazing distraction but he was now slightly angry with himself. He was in trouble and all his effort needed to be directed at rectifying the mistakes and not enjoying himself. He had a quick shower and changed into some fresh clothes. It was time to do the coffee shop rounds once again. He took one last quick look at the notes he'd made on Megan, the one and only true possibility he had so far. He decided to swing past her apartment on the way to the coffee shop. He wanted to do that for two reasons, one in the remote chance he'd see her leaving but the more important to make himself known a little. If he walked the area every so often people might notice him and he wouldn't necessarily stand out as a stranger.

In the years he'd been doing this he found that sometimes it paid to stand out rather than try to hide. He made a point of going into local shops and making conversation, almost making it seem like he was a local. He found that he blended in this way becoming one of the crowd rather than being a stranger that people notice. True to form he stopped off at a local shop and got a paper and some milk. He'd ditch them both few blocks away, but it helped build the illusion. He left the shop and made his way past Megan's apartment block. He didn't see her, but he didn't really expect to. He took a circular route to one of the coffee shops he'd already been to dropping the paper and milk in the trash as he walked through a local park. He followed pretty much the same routine as the day before and was surprised to be able to add a couple more names to his list.

By mid-afternoon he was back in his motel room digging into the background of the two new girls. It turned out that the first one was a bit of a dark horse and although on the surface seemed to be a bit of a loner and a loser was in fact hiding a very different past to the one she portrayed. She came from money and from what Damian could work out had decided to leave all that behind and make her own way on life. She be too easily missed so he took her off the list. The other girl however did make the grade. He dug further into her social media life and after an hour was quite pleased with himself. He now had two definite matches for what he was looking for and now the real hard work started.

At this point he would normally go back to his apartment and build a thorough file on any target. He found that by doing that he was able to concentrate without any distractions. His office was set up for just that and it was a safe environment where he didn't have to worry about writing notes and using whiteboards to build timelines and profiles. He couldn't do that at the motel it just wasn't practical let alone safe. He packed everything up and took it all down to his car walking back to the reception he handed the room key back to the clerk. He turned the key in the ignition and started the car, driving out of the car park he turned left and headed for the freeway. He hadn't gone more than five miles before he turned round and started to drive back the way he'd just come from.

The logical part of his mind said get back and build the full profiles, dig deeper into each target and gather as much information as possible. The emotional part of his mind was convincing him to enjoy a relaxing night with Stella and make a start in the morning. He knew in his heart it was the wrong thing to do he should focus on the job in hand rather than let his desires take over but life wasn't always that simple. He went back to the motel and parked the car up, going back to the clerk he explained that things had changed and he paid for another night. He didn't really need the room but if he was going to go to dinner with Stella he wanted a shower and to change into something a little more presentable. The tatty t-shirt and jeans he was currently wearing just didn't really look right for a date.

Having finished in the shower he sat on the bed and checked his emails, he had several of the usual boring rubbish that he sent straight to the trash. He logged into his encrypted email account to find an email from Angie, he'd been expecting her to send something. It was short and to the point, she was worried about him and was offering to help if he needed it. They'd worked together for years now and although they didn't really socialise their success within the business had often required then to work together. He replied letting her know that he had everything in hand and was surprisingly honest telling her that he'd gone back to basics and had already found two possible targets that he was working towards. He kept the reply simple, he didn't want to admit to her that he was shaken by what had happened. He trusted her but this was business and the last thing he wanted was for Steven to find out that he was even remotely struggling with what had happened. He just wanted to bounce straight back as if nothing had happened. He sent the reply and logged out, standing up he finished drying himself off and got dressed.

He was slightly early so stopped off at a bar just round the corner from the restaurant that Stella had chosen. He'd sent her a text earlier in the day asking her to choose somewhere for dinner as he didn't feel he knew enough about the area to choose a decent place to eat. She'd selected an intimate little Italian restaurant that she'd been to in the past. She told him that she liked the food and the atmosphere and that was good enough for him. He'd called and made a reservation for two asking for a table that gave them some privacy of possible so that they could really enjoy each other's company. He sent her a message to let her know he was in the bar if she wanted to meet him there or he could meet her at the restaurant if she preferred. She replied saying that she was on time so would meet him at the bar. She also asked what he was wearing as she didn't want to be under or overdressed. He hadn't really packed much so had gone for the only shirt he had with him, which was a short sleaved light blue casual style and black trousers, she didn't reply.

He'd almost finished his drink when she walked through the door, she looked incredible. She had chosen a slightly off-white blouse, black trousers and black heels. The material the blouse was made of was thin enough for him to see that she hadn't worn a bra, it wasn't fully translucent but allowed for enough of her body shape to show through. He stood up and walked over to her, "you look stunning."

She blushed a little, "thank you, I have to be honest I don't get many opportunities to dress up, this look doesn't really fit in at college or the gym."

Damian laughed, "no it certainly wouldn't, do you fancy a quick drink, or shall we go and eat?"

"I'm sure we can fit a quick drink in as I've impressed myself and managed to get here early."

He smiled at her, "what would you like?"

"Let's see how you do under a little pressure, surprise me."

"I can handle that I think," he went to the bar and ordered two double Southern Comfort lime and lemonades in tall glasses with crushed ice. He took them back to the table and placed it in front of her. "I think that should do the trick."

She picked the glass up and took a sip, "well I'm impressed, that's a good choice."

He laughed, "I cheated a little, last night I saw you had a half empty bottle of Southern Comfort in your kitchen so it was a fairly simple choice and as it's the start of the evening I thought I'd make it a long drink rather than a short."

"Thinking on your feet, I like that, well you've certainly started the evening well."

"Well let's hope I keep it that way." Damian had a cheeky smile on his face.

Stella grinned back, "oh I somehow think that you will."

They finished their drinks and made the short walk from the bar to the restaurant, it was less than five minutes which was good because although the evening was warm Damian only had to look at the front of Stella's blouse to see that it wasn't that warm, she caught him looking, "maybe I should have thought to bring a jacket."

"No, I think I can honestly say that you look absolutely fine without one."

They were seated at a table that was located in a nicely secluded booth, a single candle on the table added to the mood and Damian ordered a bottle of white wine to get them started. He didn't go for the house white but instead selected a nice crisp French white. They talked while they looked at the menu and after a couple of minutes. They both knew what they wanted and ordered. The starter arrived quickly, and Damian was impressed. It was much nicer than he'd expected, and he suddenly realised why Stella had chosen there to eat. The talk was light hearted, much like the night before and Damian realised that he was feeling far too comfortable.

The conversation eventually came around to what they both wanted for the future. Stella wanted to finish college and to join a largish business, somewhere that gave her the ability to grow and develop into a semi senior management role. She liked the idea of making a name for herself and to maybe one day eventually sit on the board of directors. Although she did admit that in some ways that might be a bit of a tall order as women weren't really that prominent the higher up the managerial structure you went. Damian decided to go for a long-term view as the short-term ambition was to simply get out of the shit situation that he'd got himself into. He told her that he wanted to raise enough money to buy a decent sized piece of land somewhere so that he could build himself a home. Something purpose built so that it had everything he wanted.

She raised an eyebrow, "everything you want, that's a little one sided."

"Well I look to the future as I am now and that's single, if I have a partner at that point then it would be built to suit both our needs."

"Do you dream of a future with someone or do you view it as someone who's single?"

"I guess because I spend a lot of time travelling on my own I always view it as a single person," he thought for a second, "I'd never really given it much thought actually, how about you?"

She didn't hesitate with her reply, "I always see my future with someone, no person in particular but my daydreams and plans always involve a significant other. I can't really visualise a future on my own, don't get me wrong I'm more than happy with my own company currently especially when I look at the creeps and weirdos I spend my time with at college and the gym."

Damian feigned a look of shock, "well this weirdo is certainly glad to be sat here."

"Oh, that's only because you seem to be a little bit more normal than most."

"That makes me feel really special."

"It should, you're the first person from the gym I've ever had dinner with, in fact I've never made coffee for anyone from there either."

Damian felt strangely happy about that, he had no right to as he never mixed business with real pleasure and he was in this city for business and not to find someone to spend time with. Stella excused herself and went to the bathroom, Damian picked up his glass and took a mouthful of wine. Somehow in the emotional turmoil he was experiencing currently he'd let his guard down, something that didn't happen very often. Whenever he was away he would always find someone to have sex with even if he had to pay for it. Which wasn't very often but he had realised in the last hour or so that Stella was different and that frightened him because he didn't expect to be feeling that way. For the first time in a long while he understood what a normal life felt like, even if the experience had only been for the last day or so.

Stella came back from the bathroom and sat back down, the waitress came across to ask if they'd like to see the dessert menu almost simultaneously. They said no and they both knew what the other was thinking, the only thing they both wanted right now was each other. Damian asked for the bill and without waiting for Stella to say anything and a little lost in the moment he gave the waitress his card, a mistake that sometime later would cost him. Normally when he was away he paid for everything with cash to reduce the trail back to him but in that split second all he had on his mind was the thought of getting Stella back to her place.

It was a short walk back to her apartment and they walked arm in arm, as soon as they were through the front door of the apartment he took her in his arms and kissed her. Gone was the frantic lust driven desire they'd experienced the night before, that had been replaced with a level of intimacy that surprised them both. For over two hours they simply explored each other's bodies, taking their time and building such an incredible sexual tension that they finally collapsed in each other's arms completely spent.

Chapter 37 (North America)

The following day wasn't so good, overnight a political row had broken out as to who should be running the investigation. The FBI wanted to take the lead as one of their agents had been shot and the raid on the warehouse had been under their control. The DEA wanted the lead as their lengthy investigation had been wrecked by the raid on the warehouse. The CIA threw their hat into the ring on the basis that the investigation wasn't at all restricted to the borders of the USA and felt that as a result if fell under their jurisdiction. Calls had been flying backward and forward all night and when Barney woke he found numerous emails and voicemails. He had a quick shower and sent Grace a message asking her to meet him in the office as soon as she could.

On his way over to meet her he called James to update him. It wasn't a necessary call as James had also received various emails and calls demanding answers to questions as each agency tried to get one over on the other. Grace was already setup and working when he arrived, "Grace do we have any definitive answers to any of the questions that we have outstanding?"

She looked up from the screen of her Mac, "well we have a few but not enough as yet to definitively decide our next step."

"I was hoping for a miracle," he filled her in on the messages, "so we need to decide how we stop this once and for all."

"Well that's not so easy but as far as I can see it's only a two horse race, the DEA don't actually have any say in the investigation at all. Yes there operation was sunk as a direct result of the raid but we're not looking onto drugs at all so that counts them out and they just need to lick their wounds and move on. The FBI and CIA could both argue they have a claim but the good thing is that neither of them actually have the resources or contacts to combine everything in the same way that your team can. They won't ever admit it but they simply can't do it. The simplest way forward is to give them both a little bit of responsibility to make them feel better then ignore them while they run around trying to best each other while you continue moving forward. The only thing is I don't think they take any notice of you as the people making all the noise are much higher up the food chain than you are, no offence."

"None taken and you're absolutely right and I know just the person to do the talking on our behalf." Barney made a quick phone call and after five minutes put the phone back in his pocket, "Grace let's go and get some breakfast before we make a start," they both made their way to the mess where they found some of the team already sat down. Within fifteen minutes of them arriving the whole team was sat down tucking into a variety of dishes. The conversation was light-hearted and Barney decided to leave it that way. After all the serious conversation could take part shortly when they were back in the office. Forty minutes later they were all sat round the boardroom table in the main office they were using.

Barney kept the update short as he didn't need to elaborate as it was a regular issue that they often encountered when they were in the middle of an assignment. Nobody round the table was surprised that this had happened; everyone had expected it as soon as the investigation started to grow. The shooting to a certain extent was irrelevant as they'd still be in the same position with everyone fighting for control. "Okay everyone this is how we're going to move forward. I want a definitive list of what we know so far, I only want the facts. Then we create a list of what we're not sure of and finally a list of what we don't know. For the moment keep it all to what we've been dealing with and I'll contact Katie and get as much information from her as I can but I don't really want to slow her down at this stage so let's focus on what we have."

Within minutes the team had split up and had divided the workload amongst themselves. Out of courtesy Barney went and found the Base Commander. He wanted to warn him that due to the nature of what they were doing the Base might receive a bit of attention and a few enquiries from various agencies as they each built their cases to fight for control. The Base Commander completely understood and even offered his sympathies as he knew just how challenging the political bun fighting could be. Barney thanked him and let him know that he'd do everything to minimise the effect it may have on the base.

Back in the office the team were doing a good job of creating the three lists, three whiteboards had been set up and a bullet point list was developing on each of the three. An hour later and they were really getting somewhere. As they were adding each bullet point Danny was updating a set of virtual whiteboards they had set up on the central server so that all of the team could see how they were doing. James was adding notes and pointers as he added his own data to the list and Sean was going through the update notes that Katie and Alek had been sending which gave a wider picture of how they were collectively doing.

The phone in front of Jess beeped, she picked it up and read the message, "erm I think it's about to get complicated, one of the ground crew have just met a five star looking for the team."

"Oh that's great news," they could all hear the sarcasm in Barneys voice, "Scott go and find him before he creates havoc and I'll let the Base Commander know." Not surprisingly the Base Commander had already been made aware and thanked Barney for calling as soon as he knew. He told Barney it wouldn't be a problem as long as he got rid of him ASAP. Barney promised that he would although that was sometimes easier said than done.

Jess came through the door with the General in tow followed by an aide, the room went silent. The General looked around the room, "don't get up," he said sounding somewhat annoyed.

Scott smiled and threw a salute from where he was sitting and Danny said, "that's a result as we're all quite comfy thanks."

Jake stared at Danny with a look of total shock. He'd been in a couple of meetings with high ranking military officers and knew that they demanded a certain level of respect. He looked over at Joss who on seeing the expression on his face smiled, "I know, you think someone of his age would be less grumpy by now."

Jake didn't know how to respond and the General let out a scowl, "Jake isn't it?" Jake just nodded not sure what to say, "please ignore the lack of respect shown by certain people in the room, I'm not sure what I've done during my career to deserve to be in charge of such a bunch of…." before he could finish the sentence Danny cut him short, "I think it's us who usually question what we did wrong to find ourselves under your command."

335

As the General turned to look at Danny his look softened and he walked round the table to him. Resting a hand on Danny's shoulder he looked him in the eye, "how are you doing son?"

"I'm fine Sir," suddenly there was a clear tone of respect in Danny's voice.

"Make sure you continue to work with Cole and if there's anything at all you need or you just want to talk to someone you don't hesitate you call me."

Danny nodded, "I will do I promise."

"Good, now get me a coffee."

With a "Roger that," Danny got up and went to get the General a coffee.

The General sat down in the seat that Danny had been occupying, "okay people bring me up to speed." For the next fifteen minutes Barney, Joss and Cass gave a pretty concise update detailing exactly what they knew the General would need to know. To be fair they already knew that he was aware of the majority of what they were saying but to give the update some context they started from the beginning. Back in the UK James would have been sending the General regular updates from the whole team so he would have a very good idea as to where they were.

After they had finished speaking the General paused for a few seconds, "right, time for a fresh perspective. Grace what do you feel should be our next move?"

Grace was clearly taken aback at not only being spoken to but also being asked for her perspective, "well I .... I'm not really sure I'm the best one to ask," she looked round the table, "you're team are much better placed to make that sort of decision."

The General looked directly at Grace and smiled, leaning forward in his chair he said, "let me tell you something about the team of clowns you're working with. Despite the way they act and sometimes look they're exceptionally good at what they do and I trust them implicitly. Believe me when I tell you that if they didn't believe in you then you would have already been reassigned. Now I work on the principle that if you're sat at a table with them then you're a trusted and valued part of the team in which case your opinion matters, so, tell me what you think the next move should be."

Grace had a flushed look on her face, "I don't know what to say." She looked round the room and paused for a second to compose herself, "at the stage we're at I don't feel we have enough to make a move on anyone just yet. I know that we have enough on the Doctor and nurse on the plane to act and Katie's team have enough on the ambulance crew but doing that now would be far too soon as we want the people in charge not just the ones at the frontline. I say we need to dig deeper and wait until we have enough information linking to someone higher up that is calling the shots. So we focus on the financial trail and find where they are receiving the payments from that we've identified as unusual."

The General sat back in his chair, "I like that, you've considered both parts of the investigation and not just on what you're dealing with here and I like that a lot. No wonder the reports I've been getting back speak so highly of you."

Grace looked at Barney who shrugged his shoulders, "don't look at me, I feedback reports on everyone that's assigned to us. We always have and I'm nothing but honest in those reports. If my report speaks highly of you it's because you deserve it. That goes for all of you, believe me if you're assigned to us and you don't deliver then you're reassigned. It's nothing personal but we need the best at all times as more often than not our backs are against the wall and the clock's ticking."

The General put his coffee mug down on the table, "the reason for my visit is to discuss where we are at the moment. This assignment has been catapulted into the limelight. I'm not quite sure why just yet but it seems that a number of people are already fighting for control. The two obvious front runners are the FBI and CIA. The danger as I see it is that if they get control of the investigation they'll immediately run into a shit storm as they have to start running every decision through the political chain of command. If that happens the whole investigation will slow down and that isn't what we want to happen. So ladies and gentleman let's work on a solution that allows us to retain control but gives them some sort of smug feeling that they're in the driving seat."

Jake didn't hesitate, "putting my credentials to one side and looking at this from the team's perspective that's a tall order. Neither agency is going to step aside. I suggest we don't ask them to and instead we make it appear that we're leaning on them for support. We ask for help from the FBI financial forensics team and we turn to the CIA for use of their contacts in Europe, let them both think they're running things and if and when we secure a result." He turned to look at the General. "We then simply sit still and let you deal with the end result. From what I've seen so far this team doesn't work to gain recognition. It works to gain results and so if someone else claims the credit I can't see anyone sat round this table that's going to lose any sleep."

The General smiled, "sound assessment Jake and I guess you've summed up things pretty well, anyone else got any comments?" He looked round the table.

Cass spoke up, "yes, I think we should give the DEA some credit in all of this and we should ask them to work with us to analyse some of the data and evidence we have from the warehouse raid. The FBI can deal with a bit of it but some of it does relate to the gangs drug interests so we should give the DEA a bone and let them run with that. The bigger part is whoever is running the trafficking side of things and that's what we share between the FBI and CIA."

"Good point Cass and not a bad idea, the DEA are particularly annoyed with us so if we can give then anything that allows them to salvage something then that would be good," the General sat back in his chair, "suggestions for moving forward right now?"

With some new found confidence Grace spoke first, "I'd say we split ourselves into two teams. One team needs to focus on the financial trail and work with whoever the FBI supply if they play ball and the other part of the team dig into the movements of the medics on the plane and try to see if they can find anything at all on the couriers that drop the patients off or any more instances where that's happened. We can get a full patient list for that plane that covers the last twelve months from the owners especially as they want to cooperate as their reputation is on the line of this investigation goes the wrong way for them."

"I like it, right Joss can you head up one team and Cass can you head up the other. Barney I need you to bring everything together as Katie and her team seem to be gathering pace with their part of the investigation. Between you and Nick we need to link it all up so that when the time comes we can close in on both sides of the water at the same time. Barney I need some time with you to dig a little deeper into a few bits and pieces so we'll leave the rest of you to split up and get cracking." The General waited a second before speaking again, "Cass one last thing, make sure you leave yourself a bit of time in amongst all this so that you can get in a few hours at the range" he looked across to Danny and winked.

Cass went red in the face, "bloody hell is there anyone that doesn't know and I would have expected better from you than stooping to their level."

The General held up his hands in mock surrender, "I admit that was a bit low," then with a huge grin on his face he added, "but then so was your final score."

Everyone burst out laughing and Barney stood up, "best we go somewhere else before she bursts a blood vessel."

The General stood up and followed Barney to the door, turning before he left he said, "you've all done a great job so far but we've still got a hell of a way to go so keep at it and let's see just how quickly we can bring this to an end." Barney and the General left with the Generals aide following close behind.

Ed broke the silence, "that was surreal, did we really just have a meeting with a real five star General?" He looked round the table for some sort of confirmation

Cass was the first to reply, "yes we did, trust me when I say he can be the stereo typical arsehole when he wants to be."

"That wasn't anything like I expected at all."

Jake jumped in, "I've got to agree with Ed I wasn't sure what to expect but I certainly didn't expect him to be so human."

Joss laughed, "believe me the conversation doesn't always go that way. So let's split straight down the table, Barney can jump in and out with the two teams as he sees fit." With everyone agreeing they all got themselves ready for a few hours of research and digging.

Two hours later Barney came back with a couple of trays of food, he'd been to the mess hall and had managed to get a few bits and pieces so that they could work straight through lunch. A few minutes after he arrived a drinks trolley appeared. They all took a quick break to grab a drink and something to eat. Barney sat down next to Grace and asked for an update on who was doing what, Grace explained that Joss and Cass had made contact with agency and had offered their assistance and access to everything they had so far. Both the FBI and CIA jumped at this as they each wanted to get one step ahead of the other. She explained that the two teams were now liaising with newly formed teams within each agency that had been setup to deal with the investigation. The bit Grace was most thankful for was the assistance she was now getting from the forensic accountants at the FBI. It made tracking the money so much easier that she wasn't now trying to do it on her own.

Danny was still busy with Jess now helping him update the whiteboards, they'd shared the virtual ones with the FBI and CIA and they were starting to add bits of information. Despite the number of people now sifting through the information and evidence they had it was still slow going. After a further three hours although they had uncovered some extra clues they still didn't have a money trail to follow or a breakthrough on the couriers.

Once again they had to accept that no matter what they did it was simply a matter of working their way through the evidence they had and being patient. There wasn't always a way to fast track the results, having said that they now have over twice as many people working through it all and they were actually getting somewhere although it didn't seem that way. Gradually they started to see some real progress, one of the FBI team had managed to trace a link between the payments made to one of the gang members and the medical team on the plane. The payments went through a number of companies and eventually led back to one single account. Unfortunately the payment was still made via an offshore account but now they had a definitive link that tied two spate parts of the investigation together.

Less than an hour later the FBI scored their second win when they managed to identify one of the two men that had appeared in the CCTV footage at the airfield when Phoebe was transferred to the plane. He had a record, nothing too serious but the petty misdemeanours he had been arrested for had got his prints and details onto the system and an image search from the footage had recorded a match. The FBI were in the process of building a profile around what they had and trying to identify the person with him.

Almost at the same time that the FBI confirmed an image match Levi took a call from his contact at the DEA that was leading the investigation. After going through several sets of phone records they'd managed to connect the gang to a known drug cartel, although nearly all of the phones had been burners previous records from other investigations linked the numbers together. They'd also come across some encrypted emails that they were looking into but as yet they weren't having any luck as the level of encryption was quite complex.

In fact far too complex for a run of the mill street gang to be involved with. Levi had the emails sent across so that Grace could have a look and asked to be updated if they found anything else.

The odd thing that Levi found when the emails had been sent across was that they weren't too and from the gang leader. They were in fact on an email account that was owned by a member of the gang that was a couple of levels down which stood out. Levi spoke to Cass about it and told her that in light of this discovery he was going to go through some of the paperwork that had been imaged from the warehouse. Cass thought it was a solid lead and suggested that Levi took one of the others off what they were doing to give him a hand. He didn't really want to do that as he knew they were all busy trying to sift through the mountains of information they had so he asked Danny if he'd be able to help.

Danny jumped at the chance as he wanted to get more involved. Updating the boards was important as it allowed everyone to see where things stood but it wasn't interesting and Danny wanted more so between the two of them they started to read through the numerous documents that had been seized during the warehouse raid. It was heavy going as a huge amount of what had been found was simply paperwork that related to goods in and goods out linked to the legitimate part of the gangs business which was in place to keep everyone's attention from the illegitimate part of their business which was far larger. The going got a little easier as they began to recognise the companies and documents that were tied into the legitimate side of things and simply eliminated them from the search.

Danny was working through a notebook that had been found on the same gang member that the emails were too and from. It was heavy going as the writing wasn't easy to read but he found two separate entries on different pages but were almost identical. Both entries just read 'Call D ref pick up' Danny spent the next hour trying to find something that would indicate who D was, unable to find anything and a little frustrated he call Clay, who had been working with his team to identify the gang members and to dig deeper into each of them if possible. In their investigation they'd managed to find the home address of the person Danny was looking into if they had even conducted a search. They had a laptop and several boxes of paperwork and notepads that they had found at the warehouse and were now in the evidence locker but hadn't managed to get to yet. Danny asked if

Clay would object to him arranging for someone to come down and go through them and Clay was more than grateful for the extra help. Danny ran the idea through Levi who agreed that it would be a good idea at which point Danny then went to Barney to run it past him.

Within the hour Jess was flying Danny and Scott down to meet up with Clay. As Danny had made the discovery Barney had decided to let him go down and see what he could find, he sent Scott down as well not because Danny wasn't capable but because Barney was still a little worried about how well Danny was coping with the shooting. Although the feedback from Cole was encouraging he didn't want to take any chances. Clay met them at the airport and despite the fact that it was late in the day they went straight to the Marshalls office. On arriving they spent a few minutes catching up with the people they knew in the office and being introduced to those they hadn't met before. Clay took them through to one of the meeting rooms and stacked neatly to one side were almost a dozen boxes "Well that's what we have, we haven't had a chance to go through it yet so not sure if you're going to find anything useful."

"Thanks Clay," Danny picked up the first box and put it on the table, "is it okay if we make a start? We've booked a couple of rooms locally but rather than wait till morning we'd like to get started."

"Absolutely, you know where everything is and as soon as you're done one of the night team will run you to the motel."

Danny took the lid off the box he'd just put down, "thanks."

Without another word Clay left them to it, Scott picked up a second box and sat down opposite Danny. It was slow going as they weren't sure what they were even looking for, they put the laptop to one side and it needed a password and neither of them had the skills to even begin to get past it. Two boxes in they had a small pile of paperwork they were interested in but hadn't found anything ground breaking. Putting the lid on the box he'd just finished going through Scott put it to one side, "Danny, as this is your lead what do you want to do, carry on for a bit or call it a day and start again tomorrow?"

Danny stopped reading the piece of paper he had in his hand, "I'm up for carrying on, maybe order a pizza and a few drinks if that's okay with you?"

Scott smiled, "I don't have a problem with that at all." As it was gone eight in the evening the day shift had left and there were only three members of the night team on duty. Scott asked them if they fancied pizza and wasn't at all surprised when they all said yes, he ordered a delivery of half a dozen large pizzas and drinks. One of the night guys agreed to go down and wait for the delivery and within twenty minutes Danny and Scott has resumed their search but now had a large pizza each and a couple of cans of drink.

An hour later Scott found details of a bank account that as yet they hadn't been aware of. Danny then found some references to a 'D' in a journal, the entries were almost diary like but were written in such a way that Danny felt they were part of some sort of therapy regime. Various thoughts and feeling were described that related to events that had happened. A couple of entries related to the mysterious 'D', one of them read 'Spoke to D today, was good to catch up with him, reminded me of when times were simpler and far less complicated. Wish I'd stayed were I was rather than coming out here and getting caught up with the gang' Danny didn't want to deface the journal so he took images of the sections that he was interested in.

By two in the morning they'd found numerous references to 'D', an old photo that wasn't very clear but showed the gang member with someone, the back of the photo was dated seven years previously so Scott had put it to one side in case the other person in the snapshot was 'D' They'd found yet another bank account and several phone numbers that had been documented. One of them was significant as the phone number was preceded by the letter D. The night team were having a slow shift and had offered to help. During quite periods they'd fall back to investigating the evidence from the warehouse so they felt that they might as well assist Danny and Scott with what they were doing as technically they were still investigating the warehouse evidence and there wasn't currently any indication as to what to go through first.

Now that there were five of them going through the boxes the useful bits of information started to mount up, Danny and Scott didn't have the ability to investigate the bank accounts or phone records but they could request the later so each time they phone a phone number of interest they sent through the formal request. Hopefully by the time the rest of the team at Luke got back into the office some of the records would be available. At four in the morning Scott found the best bit of evidence so far. It was a small notebook with dates, times and financial entries. Further into the notebook were locations that appeared to be collection points. There were eight entries in total that he could find and after going through the notebook twice Scott believed that this was in fact the details relating to eight separate collections of people, he was able to piece together a time, date, location and first name of the person along with what appeared to be payment details.

Chapter 38 (Europe)

Alek woke up at half four and had a shower, James had managed to arrange a few other things to make it easier for them. The main one being a van they could use to make transporting the two men much easier. They'd still take the three vehicles they'd been using so that they could remain mobile. He went through everything one more time in his room before making his way to Charlie's room. Knocking on the door she opened it almost instantly. As they walked down to the car Alek updated Charlie with the arrangements that James had sorted out. By the time he'd finished they were at the car and the other four were already waiting for them. He quickly filled everyone in and asked one more time if anyone had any questions. They were all happy and so with nobody raising any issues they split into their new teams and headed towards the two houses.

There were any number of things that could have gone wrong during the arrests but luck was on their side and both men were secured and in the back of the vehicle without any problems what so ever. They hadn't really put up much of a struggle although Alek had a feeling that was simply down to the speed at which the team had acted. James had given Alek the location of the van that he'd arranged to be left for them and Alek was a little surprised to find an actual prison van parked where he'd been told to go. Complete with two individual cells that were isolated from each other it couldn't have been more perfect. With the prisoners now safely stowed away Karl drove the van with Alek giving directions, the other three cars followed behind.

James had already given the vehicle and personnel details to the security team at the base so when they arrived as soon as their ID had been checked they were waved through. An MP escorted them to a quieter area of the base that was rarely used. In fact they were using one of the buildings that made up an area that was once used for close quarter battle training. The building itself replicated a police station complete with cells, the only drawback was that the cells were open but they weren't too worried about that in all honesty as they didn't expect either of the men to actually give them any information so the fact that they could talk to each other didn't really matter that much.

Once they were inside Alek arranged for some food to be sorted out and sent Karl, Erica, Ralf and Charlie back to the hotel firstly to get everyone's kit and then to the two houses to conduct a search to bring back everything they could. When the others had left Alek and Karla conducted an interview with each of the suspects. Even though they didn't expect to get any information out of them Alek felt it was still worth going through the motions especially as they couldn't really do much while they were waiting for the others to come back. Having spent just under three hours attempting to extract some useful information out of the two prisoners Alek decided to give up. Before starting the interviews they'd connected both phones they'd managed to take from the two men up to some clever software that Karla had. By the time they'd decided to give up both phones had been unlocked.

Alek connected the phones to his Mac and called Nick to let him know that the first one was all ready for him. Within minutes Nick had copied the contents of the phone to the server in Hove and within fifteen minutes had the second phone copied as well. Alek disconnected the call and put both phones into individual evidence bags. He left it to Nick to go through the various texts and emails as they were encrypted and they'd get the results far quicker if Alek left it to Nick to deal with. While they waited Alek and Karla wrote up the interview notes and saved them to the ever growing group of documents the team had collated so far.

With time on their hands and the prisoners safely in their cells they explored the Police station. It was basically a shell, the walls and doors were in place but the bulk of the building was completely empty. The only thing they found every so often were the standard infantry targets set up so that the rooms could be used for building clearance training. Downstairs however half a dozen rooms had been set up to look and function like a real Police station complete with furniture and working showers. The team had managed to secure some sleeping quarters within one of the main barrack blocks and had already agreed to work a rota with two of them manning the Police station at all times whilst the other four rested. It wasn't a great solution but they knew it wouldn't be for long because they'd be handing the two prisoners over to the local police just as soon as they could so the current setup was hopefully a very temporary thing.

Six hours after leaving the others returned, they'd collected several boxes of evidence from the two properties as well as all the team's personal items from the hotel. The searches of the two properties had been straightforward and they'd managed to get hold of several files of paperwork as well as laptops from each of the two houses. Now they were faced with the task of cataloguing all of it. As they had a number of desks to use they'd all agreed that to spend the next few hours working together to enable them to speed the process up a little. They took a bag each and began methodically working through each piece of evidence. Some items were straightforward and just needed photographing and numbering before being placed in individual evidence bags. Other items like bank statements also needed to be followed up with a financial search so that they could start to create a bigger picture.

Karla worked on the two laptops as she was probably the most qualified and it made sense to leave them to her as she was the one most likely to be able to extract the information they needed from them. The time ticked by and despite working almost nonstop they were still only half way through everything they had after four hours. Between them they agreed that Karl and Charlie would take the first two hour stint while the other four went to get something to eat. Ralf and Erica would then take over to complete their two hours with Alek and Karla covering the next two. Ralf said that they'd bring back some food for the prisoners when they returned.

The next ten hours passed without incident, the team changed shift every two hours and had all but finished the cataloguing of all of the evidence they'd gathered from the two house searches. Alek and Karla where about two hours into their shift when Alek received a phone call. It was from Nick and it was short and direct. He had managed to work through the encrypted emails and texts to find an address for the drop of location for Phoebe. The call was short because Nick had informed Alek that he'd be getting a further call from James fairly soon with all of the details. Arrangements were already being made with regards to searching the property and the team needed to be ready to

347

move as soon as things had been finalised. While Alek jumped on the server to read the full report that Nick had filed Karla called the others to update them and let them know that they may well be heading out shortly.

Alek had just finished reading Nicks report when the door to the Police station opened. Expecting to see the rest of the team walk through the door he was mildly surprised when two MPs entered, "how can I help guys?"

"Sir, we've been ordered to take over from you, we've been advised that the prisoners aren't to be released to anyone without your authority and that no visitors are permitted."

"Thank you Lieutenant."

"A German MP team is waiting by the front gate to escort you, I've spoken to them and they are waiting for you to advise on the destination. All they know so far is that they are to escort you to wherever you need to go and to provide assistance if needed."

Just as the MP stopped speaking the rest of the team came in through the door and the phone in Alek's pocket started to ring. He answered the phone before replying to the MP "Hi James," Alek didn't say anything for a couple of minutes he simply listened, "okay we'll call you as soon as we've made contact."

The room was silent everyone was looking at Alek waiting for an update "Right guys so this is what's happening, James has managed to track down the address that Phoebe was delivered to. There's no guarantee that she's still there but it's the best lead we have so we're going to go there. We've got an MP escort to get us to a holding point half a mile from the property. We'll be met there by a hostage rescue team and they'll take the lead on the rescue. We're simply there to provide what intel we can and to act in a supporting role. As soon as they have completed their part then we take the lead again so grab whatever gear you need and meet at the front gate."

There was a flurry of activity as the team immediately left to go back to their rooms to collect the kit they'd need. Alek handed over the keys to the cells and gave the MP a quick update on why the prisoners were here. Once he'd done that, he grabbed his go bag and left the MPs to it. As he walked out of the door, he could see one of the cars already on its way back to collect him. Karl was driving and as the car pulled up next to him he opened the passenger door and got in. Karl didn't wait for the door top close before he pulled away, "we need to collect Charlie on the way to the main gate. She wanted to grab some extra kit to be on the safe side."

Alek nodded, "I've just been sent the address so we've got everything we need, as soon as we get to the front gate we can leave."

Karl drove through the base observing the speed limits despite the urgency of the situation. Knowing full well racing around the base at breakneck speed wasn't going to help one bit and would probably cause them to lose more time than they could afford. He pulled up at the main entrance to the medical wing, as he did Charlie came out of the side door with a Bergan on her back and a large holdall. Alek got out and opened the boot for her, she put the bag in first then taking the Bergan off put that in the boot next to the bag, "I've grabbed a trauma kit and a field bag to give us a bit of a chance in case we have any medical issues."

Alek smiled, "Good idea," they both got into the car and Karl started driving to the main gate, as soon as they got there they saw that Erica and the others were in their car which was parked between two German Military Police vehicles. Karl pulled up behind the rear most MP vehicle and got out. He walked towards the front of the now four vehicle convoy, an MP got out and met him. Karl introduced himself and gave the MP the destination address. The MP explained that they had already been briefed and that his team would do everything they could to assist. Walking back to his vehicle he stopped to let Erica know that he'd pull in behind her as they moved off, she passed him a radio. "So that we can keep in touch with the escort, the channel has already been set."

Karl took the radio and got back in his vehicle, he passed the radio to Alek and pulled in behind the car Erica was driving as the vehicles moved off. As they got to the main road the lead vehicle turned his lights and sirens on, the rear vehicle did the same and they moved off. The journey was going to take about an hour at the speeds they were travelling at and Alek used the team used the time to gather as much information as they could regarding the house they were heading for. The drive was fairly straightforward, they encountered some traffic, but the sirens made things significantly easier and they arrived at the RV in just under fifty five minutes.

Chapter 39

Phoebe opened her eyes, rolling over onto her back she looked up at the ceiling. She thought for a few seconds and then realised that despite what she'd been told yesterday she'd had a really good night's sleep and felt strangely refreshed. She couldn't understand why as she remembered struggling with the thought that she was being held hostage. She laid there without moving her mind going over and over what she'd read. She sat up crossing her legs and dropping her head in her hands. Her hair flowed over her shoulder, she sat like that for a few minutes regulating her breathing trying to figure out what to do. She finally lifted her head up and looked around the room thinking to herself that so far, no harm had come to her. Other than the messages yesterday she hadn't really been hurt in anyway and maybe if she played along for a while longer an opportunity would present itself.

Having made her mind up she uncrossed her legs and got out of bed. She went straight into the bathroom and sat down on the toilet. Whilst she was sat there she took her t-shirt off and threw it onto the floor. A plan forming in her mind, well not so much a plan as an idea to just do as she'd been asked and to carry on performing for the camera. After all it's just an act at the end of the day and if that makes someone happy then so be it. Standing up she flushed the toilet and made her way back into the bedroom. She made the bed with slightly more enthusiasm than normal. Exaggerating some of the movements so that her breasts moved more than they would normally.

Once the bed was made she did some warm up exercises and stretches. She then spent just over half an hour putting herself through an exercise routine finishing it off with a few yoga poses that enabled her to not only relax but to put on what she felt was a worthy show. During the exercises she'd decided to hold back her anger and frustration and not to let it show. She'd perform and put on an act whilst trying to formulate a plan to enable her to escape, if escape was at all possible. She actually felt rather good after her workout and decided to have a shower. Her mood significantly more upbeat than it had been recently.

She undressed in the bedroom making sure once again to exaggerate some of her movements, before going to the bathroom she tapped the screen next to the bed and raised the temperature on the thermostat slightly. If the room was slightly warmer, she could get away with wearing less clothes and therefore hopefully get rewarded for good behaviour. Inwardly she was furious with herself at having to stoop to such levels but she realised that as it stood at the moment she didn't have any other option. She was very aware that she needed to do whatever was necessary to ensure that she didn't put herself at risk.

Stepping into the shower she turned the water on and set the temperature to a nice warm setting. Letting the jets of water bounce off her body as she slowly rotated, she took her time making sure that she paid particular attention to her breasts as she washed herself. Once she'd rinsed herself off she towelled herself dry and made her way back into the bedroom. The room was now warm enough now to get away with just putting on a pair of knickers. Drying her hair she took the towel back into the bathroom.

Walking back into the bedroom she picked up one of the books that she had been reading and laid down on the bed. Every so often she'd change position slightly, bending one leg at the knee or resting her hand on her naked stomach only moving it when she needed to turn the page. Having read a few chapters she decided the time was right to put on a bit of a show. After she'd turned the page she let her hand drop to just above her belly button. Flexing her fingers she started to trace small circles on her bare flesh. She slowly made her way up towards her breasts, she stopped to turn the page once more and placed her hand back just below her right breast. Rather than circles she started to stroke herself just below the breast. She stopped reading the book and imagined her fingers caressing her nipple. She knew what would happen and she was pleased with herself when her nipples became erect before she'd even touched them.

Putting the book down and closing her eyes she let her fingers dance across her breasts, she didn't rush anything, there was no need to. She let out a soft moan as her fingers danced across her nipples. She let her other hand drift down to the top of her thighs, opening her legs slightly she placed the flat of her hand against her knickers and slowly moved it back and forth. She could feel the excitement building from within and pulled her hand up slightly higher pushing back down so that it slid inside her knickers. She didn't need to insert her fingers to find out if she was wet because she could already feel that she was.

She smiled to herself and with her eyes still closed she started to stroke her clit using two fingers. She let out another audible moan as the feelings of pleasure coursed through her body. She focused on the feelings of pleasure and made sure that she didn't rush. Keeping up a nice rhythmic speed moving her other hand from breast to breast every so often. Suddenly she let out a gasp as she felt the first wave of spasms as the orgasm took hold of her. Increasing the speed at which her fingers were moving she felt her whole body ripple as the final wave of spasms shot through her. Phoebe smiled to herself, partly because she had enjoyed the orgasm and partly because she knew that she had put on a good show. Removing her hand from her knickers she placed her fingers in her mouth and made a show of licking her fingers clean.

Picking her book back up she started to read again, her free hand resting on her breast she could feel a wet patch starting to develop in her knickers. With her legs slightly apart she carried on reading. After about half an hour she got up to go to the bathroom. As she went back to the bed she heard the now familiar click as the door to the dining area opened. She suddenly realised how hungry she was and quickly grabbed a t-shirt from a drawer and threw it on as she opened the door and went into the dining room.

As well as a variety of food on the table she saw two new books, a couple of magazines and a MacBook Air, the Mac had a post it note on it and she took it off to read it 'This is preloaded with several groups of coursework and study guides' She sat down suddenly full of mixed emotions. Her immediate thought was that it meant she would eventually get out of the situation she was in. Her spirits lifted as she looked through the various files on the Mac. Pleased to see that everything she'd looked at so far had been directly related to the course she had been taking. She finished eating and grabbing a bottle of water and a couple of bits to snack on later she picked everything up and went back through to the bedroom.

She put the books and magazines down and sat cross legged on the bed, opening the Mac she carried on flicking thought the multitude of files. Completely absorbed she lost track of time, occasionally changing position on the bed she'd worked her way through most of the folders. She was now laying on the bed, her legs bent at the knees and feet crossed over watching one of the study guides. The minutes flew by and before she knew it she'd been studying for three and a half hours, she felt great again and really felt like she'd achieved something. She closed the Mac and rolled over onto her back and let her mind drift as she stared at the ceiling. Smiling to herself as she thought about all the documents and videos she just read and seen.

She rolled over and stood up, making her way to the bathroom used the toilet and went back into the bedroom. Looking at one of the cameras she said thank you. It was a heartfelt gesture, and she really was grateful for the Mac. She decided to show her thanks and taking her t-shirt off she went back into the bathroom. Kicking off her knickers she laid down on the floor, knowing that it was heated she knew that she could lay down without any worry about the floor being cold. She pulled her feet in tight to her bum and let her legs naturally drop open. One hand casually caressing her breasts she used the other to tease and rub herself. As her legs were spread it gave the best possible view to the camera she was facing.

She'd decided to put on a real show as a further way of showing her thanks. Placing her index and middle finger together and putting them to her mouth she licked and sucked them before moving them back down between her legs and inserting them inside herself. She'd treated him to a standard orgasm but now she was going to let him experience what happens when she gave herself an orgasm by stimulating her g spot rather than just her clit. The results in the past had been spectacular and very messy, a friend of hers had taught her how to make herself squirt and over time she'd perfected the art to the point she was able to do it with some real power. That was part of the reason she'd come into the bathroom, she didn't want to make the bed soaking wet.

She kept her fingers together and used a slow beckoning motion so that the tips of her fingers brushed across her g spot. Keeping a gentle rhythm going, closing her eyes she focused all of her thoughts into what her two hands were doing. Her nipples were fully erect and she could feel her excitement building. Every so often she'd stop the back and forth motion of her fingers and move to a circular motion. She could feel herself responding and more importantly she could feel herself becoming more and more aroused.

She knew she was close, arching her back increasing the speed of the fingers inside her and ignoring the feeling that she was going to pee she relaxed allowing the feelings to flow through her whole body. She now started to brush across the top of her clit with her other hand and suddenly the intensity peaked and she felt the first wave of the orgasm. Clear fluid went everywhere, she didn't stop the movement of both hands knowing that there would be several waves. The spasms raced through her as she continued to squirt, the inside of her thighs were dripping wet and a sizeable puddle was growing on the floor below her.

She moved her fingers faster and faster, letting out a scream she felt and heard the juices pulsing out of her, she dropped back down to the floor with a big smile on her face. Despite the fact that she'd been playing to the camera she had genuinely enjoyed herself. Running her hands over her things and stomach she found that she was dripping wet. Laying there for a few minutes she closed her eyes and enjoyed the feeling of satisfaction. Opening her eyes she stood up and walked over to the shower, turning it on she stepped under the warm jets of water. After a couple of minutes, she washed herself and stepping out she grabbed a towel and quickly dried herself off.

Walking back into the bedroom she tapped the screen and chose what food she fancied for dinner. Still naked she picked up one of the new magazines she been given earlier in the day and laid down on the bed. She was halfway through an article about how celebrities deal with the pressure of social media when she heard the door click. Putting the magazine down she got up off the bed and grabbed a pair of knickers and a clean t-shirt out of the drawer. Once dressed she made her way into the dining room and sat down to enjoy what she knew was going to be another perfectly cooked meal.

The evening flew by and she fell asleep whilst reading a book, when she'd returned to the bedroom she'd taken the t-shirt off and lay down to finish the magazine article. Once she'd finished it she got up and picked up one of the new books. The new books and the Mac had completely changed her mood and she found that she was incredibly relaxed. The book was really easy going and had a good enough storyline to keep her engaged. Without realising it her eyes closed and her hand holding the book dropped to her side.

He'd watched her in the bathroom, completely transfixed as she'd squirted again and again. This was something he hadn't seen any of his previous subjects do and he loved every second of it. The decision to give her the gifts had paid dividends and he was hungry for more. As soon as she finished showering he'd stopped watching her and had gone straight online to research what had just happened. Like many men he hadn't realised that a woman could have different types of orgasm and after reading a few articles he understood that he had just witnessed a g spot orgasm. After reading this he decided to change the plan for the evening and he now had a desire to feel her g spot for himself, having read about it he wanted to feel the excitement as his fingers stroked it. He knew that he couldn't repeat what he'd seen earlier because he didn't want to let her know that he was violating her while she was drugged. Not yet anyway, that would come with time.

A few hours later he was back in the control room watching her sleep on the monitor. Pressing a button the pumps started to push the gas into the room, in half an hour she'd be out cold again and ready for him. He left the room and went straight to the shower, following his normal routine he thoroughly cleaned himself and got mentally prepared for the fun ahead. The anticipation of what was going to happen built inside him, the familiar feeling of the power he held over another human being making him smile.

Once he'd been dried off he walked back into the control room, checking her breathing to make sure everything was as it should be he made his way to the door leading into her dining area. Pressing the screen he stepped through the door as it opened. As before the only items with him were his watch and a condom. He walked up to the side of the bed listening to her rhythmic breathing. She was still laying on her back, he leant over and moved the book slightly away from her. Without wasting anytime he lifted both of her legs up so that they were bent at the knees, he carefully removed her knickers and gently pressing on both knees he spread her legs as far as they'd go.

His eyes drifted down the inside of her thigh and rested on her now exposed inner lips and clit, he allowed himself a smug smile. She was definitely worth every penny. Probably without doubt the most exquisite girl he'd purchased so far. He ran his fingers down her leg tracing the outline of her vagina, he sat down on the bed the excitement building in him. He massaged her inner lip between his thumb and index finger, her breathing still regular he gently massaged the other side. Fully erect now he stopped to put the condom on, once in place he moved his hand back between her legs, allowing his eyes to travel up to her face he felt complete power as she slept unaware that he was about to violate her once again. The power surged through his body, using both hands he parted her lips and leant forward.

He savoured her smell, his nose less than an inch from her body, taking a deep breath he lifted his head slightly and sticking his tongue out allowing the very tip of it to rest of her exposed clit. Moving his head further forward he allowed himself to suck on it for a few seconds flicking his tongue back and forth. He heard her breathing change and slowly pulled his head back. The power rushed to his head as he closed his eyes and ran his tongue over the rook of his mouth savouring the taste of her. He knew that he had to be careful, whilst the drug did render the subject unconscious it didn't prevent subconscious movement and there was every chance that she would move if she got too aroused.

He moved his head back already overjoyed with the fact that he'd tasted her. Fully aroused mentally and physically he had one last thing to do before he left her. With the middle finger of his right hand extended he slowly slipped it inside her, probing gently he moved it around until to his delight he felt the subtle different in skin texture. A huge smile appeared on his face, filled with a huge sense of elation he allowed himself to sigh. He'd found her g spot, he slowly stroked it keeping himself in check. In truth he wanted to make her squirt but he knew that would be a huge mistake at this stage and he had many other things to do to her before he got to the stage of violating her to the point that she was aware that it had happened.

He swapped hands so that his left middle finger and index finger were inside her. Masturbating himself with his right hand it wasn't long before he felt the first sign of his impending orgasm. Making a quick decision he removed his fingers from inside her he placed them inside his mouth tasting her juices once again as he came. As soon as the orgasm had finished he stood up. One hand holding the condom in place he used the other to put her knickers back on. It wasn't easy but he managed it, once back on he lowered her legs back down. The last thing he did was to pull the bedding slightly to remove any evidence of him having been there. Satisfied that when she woke up she wouldn't see any marks to indicate he'd been the he calmly walked out. Once outside the bedroom he let go of the condom and tapped the screen on the smart watch. The door closed and he walked to his bathroom. Removing the condom he threw it into the toilet bowl and stepped into the shower once more.

Once out of the shower he dried off and went back to the control room to check everything was okay, she was still sound asleep. Looking at the screen he spoke, "life is good Phoebe, life is very good and tomorrow you're going to experience our first proper sexual encounter together when I get to feel the joy as I slip deep inside you."

Chapter 40 (Europe)

Alek wasn't sure what to expect when they arrived but he certainly didn't anticipate them being alone when they got there. However that was the situation he found himself in. They were in a car park that was alongside a wooded area. The house they were interested in was just over a mile to the north. They didn't have line of sight on the house as the trees were in their way but that was a tactical move so that they could meet up and plan their next move without being seen by anyone in the house. Their four vehicles were still parked in the same formation they'd been travelling in. The MPs were stood by their vehicles. One of them on the radio calling in to advise that they'd arrived at the RV. The team were stood by the car Erica had been driving all except for Alek. He was still sat in the passenger seat of his car on the phone to James.

"There's nobody here yet James, do you know who we're supposed to be meeting?"

"Yes, it's an HRT from GSG9, Peter will be the team leader from what I understand."

"That's good to hear, I was hoping you'd say that." Alek looked around and seeing some movement in the trees shook his head. "It's okay James they are hear, I'll update you as soon as I can." Alek put the phone back in his pocket and watched as a four man team emerged from the woods in a tactical formation, their weapons weren't quite at the ready but they weren't far short. Alek grinned as he recognised the person at the front of the group. The team had been in Germany a few years before and had been working with a hostage rescue team lead by Peter and they had performed flawlessly. Since then Alek and Peter had kept in contact every so often trading information and tactics, it was a huge positive to have Peter assigned to the task.

The team of four stopped, the team leader stepping forward lowered his weapon even further, "can I ask what you're all doing here?"

Alek had already lowered the driver's window and before any of the team could answer called out, "yes, we've been sent here by the powers that be because there have been reports that the local circus has lost control of its clowns and they're wandering around doing what clowns do," with that Alek opened the passenger door and got out with a big smile on his face.

"Oh Christ," the team leader exclaimed, "no wonder it's such a shit show the bloody FSB are in charge."

Charlie, who up to that point had been slightly hidden behind Karla and Ralf, stepped forward, "play nicely now boys."

The team leader turned to look at her and suddenly a look of recognition washed over his face, "Charlie, it's so good to see you," with that he let go of his weapon and the harness took its weight, he walked towards her, "I'm so glad they haven't just let him run around our wonderful country unsupervised."

Charlie laughed, "you should know better than that Peter."

Alek was now stood beside Charlie, "right people gather round everyone and I'll formally introduce you to Coco and his troop," the reference to Coco the Clown hadn't gone unnoticed. Alek motioned for the MPs to join them as well, he had a slightly more serious tone to his voice when he started talking again. "So, this is Peter and as far as the entry to the property is concerned he's very much in charge. We're to act in a supporting role only. He's a team leader within GSG9 and possibly one of their best operatives so what he says goes." Alek introduced the team to Peter, introductions over he turned back to Peter, "what's the plan?"

"Well we've been here a while and the good news is that we've been able to set up three observation posts already. The bad news is they aren't detecting any movement at all on or in the property and they've got nothing on infrared either."

"That's definitely not what we wanted to hear."

"I had a feeling it wouldn't be, the thing is we've been briefed and the property is being supplied with electricity and phone lines. Bills are being paid monthly and they're consistent with a property of that size.

If I didn't know that I'd say from first inspection that it's been empty for a while. From what I can see through a scope I'd confidently say it hasn't been used for some time so either someone has got their information wrong or whoever currently occupies it is very good at making it look as though no one is at home."

"So what's your next move?"

"Well on top of the Op's that we have set up I've got three teams searching the perimeter to ensure that it's all clear. As soon as they confirm that's the case then the current plan is two teams to enter the property and clear it room by room. Under the circumstances we aren't going to go in loud, we're going to take a stealthy approach."

Alek nodded in approval, "makes sense. I'd do the same."

"We've got a staging area so I suggest we make our way there and wait for all of the teams to check in." With that Peter and his team started to make their way back towards the tree line.

Alek turned to the team, "two MPs need to stay with the vehicles and the rest of us will move forward with Peter, any questions?" When nobody spoke Alek simply turned and started to follow Peter into the trees. The going was quite easy and they followed the path that the GSG9 team had created. After about five minutes they came to a bit of a clearing where the trees thinned out, there were several vehicles parked up. A larger vehicle had the rear doors open and Alek could see from the array of antennas that it was clearly a command vehicle of some sort.

Peter had stopped short of the van to talk to one of his team that hadn't been with him when he'd come to meet them. As Alek approached, he could hear that Peter was being given an update, he turned to Alek, "two of the teams have reported nothing unusual around the property. The third however have reported a barn on the southern edge of the property boundary, there are some relatively fresh tyre tracks leading into the barn. They've sent some images across, come and have a look." He walked across to the back of the van and Alek followed.

The van itself to look at from the outside wasn't that impressive at all, it had a few LED work lights at the front and the rear and slots that currently contained a variety of aerials and antennas but other than that nothing special at all. Inside the rear of the van however was a completely different story. A desk ran the full length from the rear doors to the bulkhead behind the driver's seat. Two swivel chairs were bolted to the floor, four big monitors were mounted to from a large rectangle, at the moment the four screens each showed different images but they could be combined to show one large image across all four screens. Two slightly smaller monitors sat either side of that display on swivel brackets so that they could be moved to allow others to view them.

On the opposite side of the van a weapons rack ran from the back door to the edge of the sliding door containing a variety of assault rifles, shotguns and pistols. Shallow drawers below that contained various types of ammunition and grenades. On the bulkhead a series of shelves ran the full width of the van, some containing cameras and lenses others containing a variety of drones. Under the desk a number of lockboxes acting as footrests contained a whole host of surveillance equipment. Every available piece of space had been utilised for something and no matter where you looked you could see a variety of gadgets or bits of kit that had been very cleverly stored to allow easy access.

The operator in the back of the van pulled one of the monitors on a swivel arm. Peter picked up a track pad and called up a series of images on the screen that showed a large barn. Other images showed the vehicle tracks and a number of them showed the barn at various angles. Alek noticed that there wasn't a padlock on the doors, "electric doors to the barn, that's a little high tech."

"That's why the guys took the extra images, they haven't tried to enter it yet as they are aware that the house is the priority." Peter put the track pad down. "So as it stands the plan is still to enter the house and conduct a systematic search of each room. Two teams one from the front and one from the rear." Before Peter could say anything else a voice sprang into life from the radio in the van "Boss are you there?"

"Yes. Go ahead."

"There's something you need to see, check out the live feed from my scope."

Peter picked up the track pad once more and after a few seconds they were staring at the image seen from the rifle scope of the team in one of the observation posts, "what am I looking for?"

"Well we've been here for a while now and checked the property out from several angles and there's absolutely no sign of life at all. We've even use an 800mm lens to confirm that there aren't any footprints leading up to the front door or the back door. In fact we can't find anything at all to signify that anyone has been here for some time. Now look at the bush below the lower left corner of the window that you can see in the scope."

Both Peter and Alek looked hard at the screen in front of them, Alek saw it first, "the bush is moving."

"It is but the bushes either side aren't so it's not the wind. I think there's either an air or heating vent of some kind that is obscured by the bush and the air escaping from the vent is causing the leaves on the bush to move. It's barely noticeable which is why we haven't picked up on it before now."

"Good catch, I'll update you shortly on the next steps."

"Okay Boss."

Peter put the track pad back down again, "it's possibly not empty then?"

"Well it certainly doesn't seem so yet from what you've said and what I've seen there aren't any visual indicators that support that."

Peter looked at Alek, "how do you want to play this?"

"As far as I'm concerned it's still very much your show, this is what you guys are here for so it makes sense for you to follow through with your initial plans. The air coming out of the vent doesn't change that, if anything I guess it warrants a higher emphasis on a stealthy approach."

"Right, we'll stick with the two four man teams one entering from the front and the other from the rear. We'll pick the locks on the two doors and conduct a full search. Alek you stay here with your team, you can watch from inside the van as the entry teams will have body cams so if you can see what we see and direct us if needed to anything you want investigated." Peter picked up a radio and keyed the mike, "entry teams, the rest of you continue to observe." He put the radio back down.

While the two entry teams checked each other's kit in the staging area Alek briefed his team and told them to be ready to move out once the entry teams had finished their search. Alek climbed into the back of the van and sat in the vacant seat. The display on the four screens changed as the operative next to Alek changed the input to bring up a variety of feeds. The top two monitors were now split into quarters and showed the individual feeds from the body cams of the two four man entry teams. The lower left was displaying the images from the scope cams being used by the teams in the observation posts. The monitor to the left of the operative now had a larger view from Peters body cam and the monitor to the right of Alek had an enlarged view from the body cam from the team leader of the rear entry team. The fourth larger monitor that made up the central display came to life with a feed from a drone that Alek hadn't been aware of until now.

As if anticipating a question the operative next to Alek spoke. "We don't launch the drone until the very last minute and it's currently at a thousand feet so it won't be heard from the ground and although we can't zoom right in we get a good enough image to be able to see the bigger picture." As if to prove it Alek could now see the two teams approaching the house. They split as they moved into position at the front and rear. Picking up the radio he keyed the mike. "Boss it's all yours, everything is on track here and we're good to go."

He didn't get a verbal response just a single click to confirm that Peter had heard. Alek watched the monitors, his gaze drifting from screen to screen. He saw the two teams stop briefly at the doors and then they were through. They were taking a stealthy approach so the radio was silent and everything was being communicated by hand signals. Alek watched the search unfold on the various body cams. The drone was still up but was just showing a view of the house, suddenly the view switched to thermal and Alek could see the vague shape of the teams as they moved room to room. The going was slow as they took their time in order to retain some element of stealth.

Alek watched the cameras as the teams moved from room to room, so far they'd found nothing at all and from what Alek had seen so far it definitely appeared that the house was indeed empty. Every room showed some evidence of being unused for some time, dust on shelves and surfaces and now footprints on the floor as the team moved around the rooms. The lower rooms had all been checked and the first team made its way up the stairs with Peter taking the lead position. At the top of the stairs his team turned left and started to systematically search each room once more. Within ten minutes every room had been searched and two of the team had even checked the loft space.

The radio burst into life, "Alek this is Peter, there's absolutely no sign whatsoever that anyone has been inside this house for several years."

Alek picked the handset up, "I can see that, it doesn't make sense though. It's been confirmed that both power and water are being used and have been for some considerable time. The fresh footprints you've all created tell me that nobody has been in the house for some time before you guys entered."

"You may not see it on the monitors but there's dust in the air that we've created as we've moved about so I can safely say that we are the first people that have been in here for some considerable time."

"Okay Peter I'll get the power and water usage checked once more, can you all give the outside a once ever especially that bush that we saw moving through the scope."

"Will do, guys you heard let's move and give the outside a once over."

Alek watched the monitors as the two teams made their way to the outside of the property, they took their time and made their way round the exterior checking every window. Peter arrived at the window that they'd been looking at through the scope and Alek watched the monitor carefully as Peter approached. He used his boot to move the bush to one side and revealed a cleverly hidden vent. Alek watched and saw Peter remove the glove from his left hand, placing the back of his hand against the vent he stood back up again.

"There's warm air coming out of the vent. There's not much pressure behind it which is why the leaves on the bush are barley moving but it's definitely warm so there must be a cellar under the house because there's absolutely no heat inside the house at all. Okay back inside and check all of the floors and walls."

"It can't be inside Peter otherwise we'd have seen footprints or at least some sort of evidence of someone having been there."

"Well you've watched us go over the outside Alek and there's nothing out here either so we'll double check the inside."

Alek turned to the operator sat next to him, "this doesn't make any sense at all."

"No it doesn't, the drone footage doesn't show anything either, there must be something that we're missing."

"But what, there's no way someone could make the interior look like it does. That dust isn't something that you can fake."

"No it's not but maybe when they go back in they'll find something."

"They won't, we're missing something and I can't work out yet what it is."

Before Alek could say anything the radio came alive, "be advised we've got noise from the barn, a vehicle has just been started," Alek noted the screen on the right was now showing to image from the scope of the sniper that had called it in. The barn looked exactly as it had earlier but he didn't question what the sniper had said. He knew all too well that if he said that he heard noise from inside the barn then there was indeed something happening.

The drone operator wasted no time and Alek watched the monitor as the scenery changed rapidly as the drone suddenly darted away from the house and headed towards the barn at the edge of the property. It stopped above the barn but the feed from the camera didn't show anything. Alek made an instant decision and jumped out of his seat. "None of the vehicles here will get to the barn before the doors open. I'm going to try to get to ours and try to cut anyone off that leaves." He jumped out of the van and started running back to where they'd left their cars. He wasn't entirely sure that he'd get back to the vehicles quick enough but there was no way any of Peters vehicles would get there at all, there wasn't a direct route and it would take way too long for them to drive round.

Alek wasn't the only one who had thought about using their vehicles. Charlie was already well ahead of Alek, he could see her in the distance as she sprinted through the trees. Alek hadn't thought to pick up the radio on the desk so he had no way of communicating with Peter to let him know what was going on but knew that someone in his team would update him. He was slowly catching up with Charlie but with the head start she had she was going to be at the vehicles well before he was. As he reached the edge of the tree line he could see the two MPs vehicles were already parked side by side with the passenger doors open. He saw Charlie jump into the first one closing the door as the vehicle moved off.

As he ran across the open ground he realised that Charlie must have asked one of the MPs that had been with them in the staging area to call ahead to get their colleagues to have the vehicles ready because there was no way they would have known to have moved the vehicles and to have been ready for them as they ran out of the woods. Reaching the MPs car Alek literally jumped into the vehicle telling the driver to go before he'd even tried to close the passenger door. They raced after Charlie, the driver was doing his best to make up some ground and wasn't actually that far behind as they turned into the lane that lead down to the barn. Alek could see the doors opening and as soon as there was enough space he saw a vehicle come racing out.

Alek watched as the vehicle Charlie was in came to a controlled stop, swerving slightly to the left before turning right to partially block the lane, the boot opening as the car came to a standstill. Alek saw Charlie and the driver both get out and rush to the boot of the vehicle, suddenly in their hands they had assault rifles and they took a defensive position behind the vehicle bringing the rifles up taking aim at the vehicle approaching. Alek heard the boot open as his driver hit the button on the dash and their vehicle came to a stop blocking the rest of the lane. Alek was out of the vehicle before it had come to a full stop and making his way to the boot he looked down to see two G36c's in a rack pulling both out he handed one to the driver who had now joined him at the back of the vehicle.

Moving to similar positions as Charlie and her driver Alek put the weapon into his shoulder and removed the safety catch. The vehicle heading towards them was now slowing down almost as if the driver wasn't sure what to do now that he was faced with a roadblock. As the car came to a stop Alek spoke, "we shoot the tyres unless fired upon. I want to take whoever is driving alive if possible." As if someone knew what Alek what thinking they all heard a shot and the front nearside tyre popped and deflated, a split second later the nearside rear did the same. Alek realised that the shots had been taken by the sniper who had initially called in to advise of movement in the barn.

Alek could hear the drone overhead and knew instinctively that Peter would have sent some of his team over to assist and as if by magic two teams of two appeared on the rise to the left of Alek. In between the house was a dip and the four men had been in the dip until they crested the slight hill. They were all coming from an acute angle, and it took Alek a few seconds to realise that they were taking this approach to allow the sniper an unrestricted shot should the need arise for him to take it. The two teams of two arrived at the fence line weapons at the ready. They were about fifty yards ahead of Alek who now stepped out from behind the vehicle and started to advance slowly towards the stationary vehicle in front of him.

The two teams of two covered each other as they climbed over the fence and started to advance at the same pace as Alek. Realising that they now definitely had the superior fire power he shouted out in German. "Turn the engine off and get out slowly." Alek could see that there were two people in the vehicle and he was quite relieved when the engine died and the two doors open. As the two teams approaching from the left had the passenger covered Alek moved over to the right. "Move right to cover the driver, they've got the passenger covered." The four of them slowed their advance and moved to the right, the driver and passenger of the car in front of them now had four assault rifles trained on them but Alek was still taking a very cautious approach, "hold here and wait for them to get out."

The team leader heading up the group to the left of Alek called out to the passenger telling them to get out of the car slowly and to lay face down with their hands behind their head. Alek shouted the same command to the driver of the vehicle. Slowly both passenger and driver got out and lowered themselves to the floor putting their hands behind their head. Out of the corner of his eye Alek saw one of the four man team lower his rifle and remove a set of plasti cuffs from his assault vest. He advanced taking care not to cross the line of fire that his colleagues had. Leaning down he secured the passengers hands behind their back. Alek told one of the MP's to do the same, as soon as the driver was cuffed the team leader called out to Alek. "We're advancing on the barn to secure it." Without waiting for a response the team of four moved forward in tactical formation heading towards the barn.

The MP to the left of Alek instinctively moved over to cover the passenger now that the others were moving towards the barn. Alek advanced towards the driver, motioning for Charlie to join him they advanced, the driver was still face down, "let's see what we've got here," looking at Charlie he said, "You cover him while we get him to his feet."

Charlie moved to a position that put her about ten feet away from the prone driver. Alek and the MP took no chances and slung their weapons over their shoulders so that they wouldn't get in the way. Bending down and taking an arm each they hauled the driver back to his feet. The driver started shouting straight away, "get off me, don't touch me," he tried to fight his way out of their grip but they were too strong for him. "I want my lawyer now, you have no right to do this, get your hands off me." His face was contorted with anger, "you have no idea who you're dealing with and you're going to pay for this, I'll have your jobs for this," he'd stopped trying to break free from the hold that Alek and the MP had him in. His face was really red and full of anger and hatred.

Even though she was very close to the driver she was looking through the scope her body in the perfect firing position. She moved her head away so that the driver could actually see her for the first time and she smiled inwardly as a sudden look of confusion replaced the anger on the drivers face, "hello Frederik, so nice to see you again."

"You!" Was all he could think to say.

"Us actually."

Frederik's head snapped to the left and he found himself looking at Alek, suddenly the look of confusion was gone, "you have no right to arrest me, let me go immediately."

Alek smiled, "we haven't arrested you Frederik, you're simply helping us with our investigation," he turned to Charlie, "let's put him the back of your car and the passenger can go in the back of mine." Five minutes later Frederik and his passenger were seated separately in the back of the two MP's vehicles, turning to the MPs Alek spoke, "guys, keep an eye on them and don't answer any questions."

"I'll leave two of my team here as well."

Alek looked to his right to see that Peter had now joined them with him team.

"The house is secure and the local Police will be here shortly so it'll raise fewer questions if we're guarding them rather than the MP's, they can act as support."

Alek nodded, "that makes sense, okay let's go and join the team at the barn."

They made their way to the barn, the team leader met them at the open doors. "the barn is secure, the stairs lead down to a door that is locked. We've found a security panel that contains a palm reader and we can't see any other way in."

Alek looked around the barn, it was incredibly clean. A van was parked to one side and next to it a slope dropped down to an underground lower level and Alek could see a door and two of Peters team working on an access panel on the wall. Alek walked down the slope, "any luck?"

One of the team turned to him, "not yet, to be fair I have a feeling it'll take us a while, the quickest way would be to blow the door."

Peter had now joined Alek. "I'd rather not do that unless we have to."

Alek nodded "Okay so let's do it the easy way and bring the passenger down here and use their palm print to open the door."

Peter instructed two of his team to go and get the passenger and bring them back, less than five minutes later they returned. The passenger was struggling and the two team members were almost dragging him. Alek stepped forward as they got near him "I have no idea what you think is going on here but I'm going to offer you a onetime only deal. You cooperate right now and I'll personally make a recommendation that your assistance is taken into consideration when this goes to court, and trust me when I say this, you will be going to court."

The passenger stopped struggling and stood still, looking straight at Alek he spoke, "what assurance do I have that you'll do what you say you will if I help?"

Alek smiled as he replied, "let me put it this way, if you don't assist us right now I'll make sure that I make it my duty to assist the powers that be in charging you with every single thing they can and I'll do everything possible to help them hand out the strongest punishment possible to you for your involvement."

The look of defiance was no longer there and had been replaced by a look that portrayed severe concern, "I'll help you," he sighed and then his shoulders dropped and it was obvious to all present that he had suddenly resigned himself to the fact that he was in a difficult position and had no other way out, "if you remove the handcuffs I'll open the door."

Peter stepped forward and pulled a rather wicked looking knife out of the sheath attached to the left shoulder of his tactical vest, he spun the man around and cut the plasti cuffs free, "you get one chance at this, the minute you stop cooperating or lead us in the wrong direction your back in the cuffs and out of here," he spun the man back around to face Alek.

"I'll do whatever you need," there was an audible level of concern in his voice now.

Alek walked him over to the door and stopped just short of the access panel, "now before you open this, you're going to tell us what we can expect on the other side. I'm going to ask you some questions and you're going to give me an honest reply. If we go through that door and you've lied to us then you'll be looking at some serious consequences, do you understand?"

The man nodded vigorously, "yes, yes I do."

"Good, firstly what's your name?"

"Emile."

"Emile how many people are on the other side of this door?"

"There's only one."

"Who is it that's in there?"

"A girl, she's contained in the guest area."

"Contained?"

Emile now had a very worried look on his face, "yes, she's restricted to two rooms within the complex and cannot get out. The doors can only be operated from the control room."

"So she's a prisoner then?" Alek now had a hard edge to his voice that hadn't gone unnoticed by Emile.

"Yes," Emile suddenly lowered his head and his shoulders dropped, "she's been a prisoner from the moment she got here." He suddenly lifted his head, "she is fine though, she's been fed and looked after while she's been here." A little confidence had returned to Emile's voice almost as if the fact that he was letting them now she was okay and unharmed was going to work in his favour.

"How many entrances are there?"

"There's only one way in and out and it's through this door."

Alek paused for a second clearly thinking before he spoke, "how many rooms and describe the layout."

Emile took a deep breath, "there are twelve main rooms, the complex is more or less a big square split into four quadrants. As you walk through the door you'll find a corridor going left, right and straight ahead. If you walk straight ahead the first three rooms on the right are my quarters, the first three rooms on the left are the kitchen and utility rooms. You'll then come to an intersection, when you cross that the three rooms on the right are the two guest rooms along with the main control room and the remaining three on the left are the owners' quarters."

"So can we get into every room to check it's clear?"

"You'll be able to access every room except the two guest rooms. They are controlled via an access panel and either need a palm print or a manual override from the main control room."

"Right Emile this is how this is going to work, you'll open this door and three teams will go in and check each room. As soon as they confirm its all clear we'll then re asses our next move."

Emile simply nodded.

Alek turned to Peter, "I'm prepared to take a bit of a gamble. I'd like one team to go left and clear the first three rooms on that side, a second team to go right to clear the three rooms that side and a team to go straight up the middle to secure the control room. I want to get to her as quickly as possible."

Peter nodded his head in agreement, "I understand why you want to do that but that leaves the last set of rooms uncleared so I suggest a team of four goes straight up the middle and they split, two clearing the rooms on the left and the other two secure the control room. That way you eliminate the risk and we clear the complex quicker."

Alek smiled, "Sounds like a plan to me. I'll need you to pair me with one of your team."

"The guys don't know you and to them you're an outsider and an unknown entity, they spend hours and hours training together working as teams and have unfaltering trust with each other. They simply won't have that with you and as good as you are you can't expect them to and I wouldn't ask them to. I'll go in with you, we've worked together in the past and I trust you. We'll deal with the control room while the other three teams clear the rest of the rooms."

"While you brief your men I'll go and let Charlie know what we're doing." With that Alek left Peter to brief his team and he made his way back out of the barn. He could see Charlie talking to the two MP's by the two cars which had now been joined by what looked like a couple of local Police officers. Charlie made her way down to meet Alek. He quickly briefed her on what was going to happen next and asked her to grab a spare mag for his G36 and then to meet him in the barn as he wanted her on hand as a precautionary measure in case whoever it was left inside needed medical attention. Peter's team contained medics but Charlie was more than that and if as Alek expected the girl was Phoebe then he wanted to make sure that she got the best medical help as quickly as possible. Charlie agreed and made her way back up to the MP's to get the spare mag that Alek needed.

Alek made his way back into the barn to find that Peter and his team were ready, "I just need a second, Charlie is getting me a spare mag. I'm going to get her to wait here and as soon as we have cleared the complex, I'll get her to meet us just in case we need her inside."

"The local Police have arrived and I've left four men guarding the house along with two Police officers. The rest of the team have split between us and the surrounding area until we've declared this complex safe and then we'll probably stand down and hand it over to them."

Alek nodded in agreement and turned to Emile, "before we go in what's the girls name?"

Chapter 41 (North America)

The night guys had been supplying regular coffees and neither Danny nor Scott had any idea as to what the time was until a voice from the doorway announced, "morning, early start?"

Danny and Scott both looked up, looking at his watch Danny was shocked to find it was just before seven, "erm well a late finish actually," Danny looked around the room and noticed that they now only had three boxes that hadn't been checked as yet.

"Well in that case why don't I drop you at the motel for you to freshen up then we'll grab some breakfast and come back and finish off."

Danny nodded, "that's a great idea," both Danny and Scott stopped what they were doing. The guys that had been helping them overnight had already left as their shifts had ended so they followed Clay down to his car and he drove them the short distance to the motel. Although they weren't going to be long he left them there as he had a couple of things he could do while they were getting ready. Forty five minutes later he was back outside the motel and both Danny and Scott came out looking a little bit more refreshed. Clay drove to the local diner that they'd used last time they were here. Over breakfast Scott thanked Clay for his help and explained how useful the night guys had been. Clay was pleased but not surprised that once again his team had acted in an exemplary manner. "I think you'll find that they are more than happy to put themselves out as they feel that the respect and gratitude you have shown them so far warrants their help."

"You've got a good team there Clay and the respect we've shown is well deserved, they're a credit to you."

"Thanks Scott, I only hope that you find something that'll help."

Danny grinned, "well so far with their help not only have we already got far more information than we'd hoped to get we've got it significantly quicker than if we'd been going through it ourselves so once again you're team have made a huge difference."

"Well let's finish up here and see what else we can help you find in the last few boxes."

They made their way back to the office and both Scott and Danny picked up another box each and made a start on going thought what was inside. They hadn't been sat there for more than ten minutes when Clay walked through the door with one of the other Marshals. Clay picked up the last box and placed it on the table, "tell us what it is you're looking for and we'll help you work through the last few bits."

Danny quickly ran through the key things that they were looking for. With the four of them going through the last remaining boxes they had it all completed within two hours. They'd managed to find over a dozen more key bits of evidence and Scott was actually quite hopeful that what they had managed to find would give them a real boost. Danny called Jess and asked her to fly down to get them as soon as she could. As she'd been expecting his call she was pretty much ready to go and told him she'd call as soon as she was on the tarmac.

Danny had finished imaging everything they needed and was in the process of putting the final notebook into an evidence bag when Clay came back into the room, "let me know when you want a lift to the airport and I'll drop you off."

Danny put the evidence bag into the box in front of him, "Clay we can't thank you enough for the help you've given us."

"To be honest having you guys around is surprisingly refreshing, my whole team seems to be impressed with you all."

Scott laughed, "that's probably pizza related."

"Maybe," Clay paused, "knowing them as I do though it's more directly related to professional respect for the way you all handle yourselves. There's nothing pretentious about the way you work at all and you demonstrate a level of engagement that they very rarely see from an outside agency. I know you're going to say that you aren't an agency but it's clear to everyone that you should be."

"That's nice to hear Clay, we've all spent years working independently with various agencies and units and we've found over the years that we get far better results being the way we are."

"Well it's impressed the hell out of us and that doesn't happen easily."

"We've got a short while before Jess gets down her to fly us back so how about Danny and I take you out for some lunch?"

Clay grinned, "I thought you'd never ask."

They went back to the same diner and while they waited for their food to arrive Danny put a call though to the local Pizza shop and ordered a dozen large pizzas, sides and drinks to be delivered to the day shift. It was the least he felt they could do to repay the guys for their help and support. They had a slow lunch during which time they gave Clay a rundown on where they were with the operation. Not surprisingly Clay offered his support should they need anything going forward. Scott thanked him and promised Clay that if they ever needed anything they'd get in contact but also stressed that if Clay ever needed anything at all to give the team a call straight away.

Scott asked for the bill and once he'd paid it Clay gave them both a lift to the airport, they didn't see the point in waiting for Jess to call before going there as they could just as easily sit in the airport lounge and wait. They both said their goodbyes to Clay and asked him to pass on their thanks once again to his team. They made their way into the airport and grabbed themselves a coffee while they waited. They didn't have to wait for too long before Danny's phone started ringing. Jess advised him that she'd just landed and was in a position to take off again as soon as they got to her.

They worked their way through the crowds to the boarding area for private flights. As soon as they were at passport control they were ushered through and were told to follow a member of staff who would take them airside. Neither of them was surprised by this as Jess had been here a few times now and probably knew everyone there was to know. Sure enough when they drew up level with the aircraft Jess came down the steps and thanked the driver by name.

"Okay boys let's go," as soon as they were all aboard she raised the steps and closed the door. The second the door was closed the plane started to taxi, "bit of a long flight back I'm afraid as we have to stop off at an air force base to collect a few parts and some staff." Before either of them could reply she'd disappeared into the cockpit. They both settled in taking two seats each as they both knew they'd be sleeping for most of the flight if not all of it. They both woke up as they landed. It wasn't the plane touching down that woke them it was the sudden change in noise as half a dozen air force personnel came on board. A few cases containing the parts that were needed were also loaded into the cargo section. Within forty minutes they were in the air again and on their way back to Luke. The flight time was just under ninety minutes and within five minutes of taking off Scott and Danny were asleep again. Working through the night had caught up with both of them although Scott still worked on the principle of sleeping whenever he got the chance. It was the same with food, a bit of a throwback to his operational days with the Seals. You never knew when you're going to get to sleep and eat so make the most of it when you can.

The flight was straightforward, and they landed at Luke eighty five minutes after taking off. Scott and Danny left Jess dealing with the plane and they made their way to the now very familiar meeting room they'd been using. The rest of the team were there split into little groups still researching and digging trying to piece things together. They said their hellos and grabbed a coffee each before sitting down. Scott let Danny brief everyone on what they'd found. During one of the catch-up sessions Scott had with Cole they discussed Danny and Cole said it would be good to get Danny involved in something that kept him mentally active which was why Scott was letting Danny take the lead on this. He'd run it past Barney first who was in total agreement and thought it was a great idea.

Danny finished the briefing and looked around the table, "I believe if we can dig into his past a bit deeper and work out who 'D' is then we may well find ourselves a step closer to the top."

Scott jumped in, "I think we have three positive leads to follow now, the money trail, the phone numbers and finding out who 'D' is."

Cass leant forward in her chair, "let's focus the FBI on the money trail. The CIA on the phones and we'll dig into his past and try to put a name to the face in the photo."

Barney nodded, "Cass, Joss can you both call your contacts and give them the fresh intel that we've found, Jake, Levi can you start to piece everything together once more now that we have new information. Ed, Marcus can you carry on digging into the courier that dropped Phoebe off. Grace and I will contact Nick and James to update them and hopefully find that they've had as much luck as we have. Danny, Scott I'd like you both to go and get something to eat and get some rest and before you say anything I'm aware you worked straight through last night. I have a feeling we're going to be very busy in the next couple of days so I need you fully rested so don't even think of pushing back."

Scott and Danny both knew better than to attempt to argue and they made their way to the mess to get something to eat. The others broke off into their groups and got on with the task at hand. Barney and Grace went to one of the other offices so that they could set up a conference call with James and Nick. The call was actually easier to set up than they'd expected as James was with Nick in Hove. He was working with Chris and Sean, Nick was slowly getting somewhere with the encrypted emails but it was taking up all his time so James had decided the best thing he could do was to pitch in and help. As a result, the conference call involved all four of them which was good because it gave Barney a much broader picture of what was going on.

The call lasted for over an hour with both sides pitching ideas for the best way to move forward, time was against them and they knew it. They'd never openly discussed the fate of Phoebe but Barney raised the issue pointing out that although they had absolutely no idea where she was or if she was even alive they now needed to consider the fact that she may well be and every minute counted. That little revelation stopped the conversation dead for a few seconds. It was a sobering thought and not one they all wanted to linger on. Nick said that he knew someone that could help with the encrypted email and Barney told him to do whatever was necessary. James said that he'd liaise with Katie and follow up on some of the leads she was generating, Sean and Chris said that they'd keep digging into Frederik. Barney was happy with the direction they were going in and finished the call.

He then called Katie for an update before calling the General to brief him. As was often the case their assignments became so broad they had to rely on the assistance of others and Barney was very conscious that this particular assignment already involved a broader range of outside help than they'd ever had to use before. The General was concerned about the overall size of the trafficking operation especially as what they'd uncovered already led them to believe that with was very well financed and as a result what they'd found so far could simply be the tip of a very large iceberg. Human trafficking had always been a problem particularly across borders but this was proving to be something very different indeed. The General gave Barney another 24 hours to get as much information together as possible before joining a conference call involving all agency heads. This assignment was now beginning to get noticed and the General wanted to get his ducks in a row before anyone started asking questions.

Barney knew that twenty four hours wasn't anywhere near long enough for him to have any real results but then having said that he thought about what Scott and Danny had just uncovered in the same period. "Grace I think we need to have a quick meeting to decide on where best to direct the teams time."

Grace had been taking notes from the call and closed her Mac, "I'm not sure if there are any of the leads they're following that aren't important. Looking at everything we've gathered so far I would say that we've split the team up as best we can and our only option would be to ignore one of the leads to focus a little more on the others but I can't honestly see which one you'd drop."

Barney let out a deep sigh, "you're right," he paused for a few seconds, "so we update the team and ask for any suggestions as to how to either speed things up or ideas on how we direct the resources we have available to us."

"That makes sense, if you take my Mac back with you I'll go and organise some drinks."

"Thanks Grace," with that Grace left the room and Barney sat there for a few minutes contemplating his next move. His thought process was interrupted as his phone started ringing. He looked down at the display to see the Generals number staring back at him. He picked the phone up, "General, did I miss something?"

"No Barney you didn't, I've just had a very interesting call from the US Marshalls office singing your teams praises. It seems that you've all made a rather good impression, so much so that they formally wanted to know if we needed any assistance with our investigation. They can spare us a team of fifteen and I didn't hesitate to say yes so I guess you'll need factor that into your immediate plans. Not sure how or where you'll use them, but it seemed to good an opportunity to miss."

"That'll make a significant difference to how we go forward, who's the point of contact?"

"They've assigned Clay to lead the team and apparently he'll have the team ready to go in less than an hour so the clock's ticking."

"Thanks, I'll get things moving," Barney was up and out of his seat before the General had terminated the call. This changed things and gave them a better chance of getting somewhere. As he walked back to the main office he called Jess and told her to get the plane ready. He was tempted to split the team and to send some of them down to Clay. By the time he'd got back to the main office he'd made up his mind as to what to do next.

"Guys there's good news and bad news, we'll go with the bad news first. In just under twenty four hours the General is going to be hosting a meeting with all of the agency heads. The investigation is gathering pace and growing and before long it could easily get out of hand so his idea is to contain it a little by updating all concerned and maybe distributing roles slightly differently to ensure we still have everyone's cooperation. That doesn't give us long at all to come up with as much evidence as we can." Barney looked round the table and was pleased to see that nobody seemed at all surprised by that "The good news is that the Marshall Service has created a team to help us. Clay has been chosen to head that team, so Cass I'd like you to take Scott and Danny with you and head straight down and dig deeper into the evidence that Scott and Danny found. Jess is already getting the plane ready so I suggest you go and get your bags and go and meet her."

Without even acknowledging Barney they were on their way out of the door, at the end of the day they didn't actually need to say anything. "Those of us left will work the medical crew from the plane and the courier in the hope that we can create a strong enough case to get some surveillance in place."

Three hours later Cass, Scott and Danny were getting into a cab at the airport, in no time at all they were walking up the stairs to the first floor where Clay and his team were based. The security team at the reception had instantly recognised them all and issued visitors badges. They walked through the main doors that lead and there was a noticeable level of activity in the office, far more than they'd noticed before. Danny walked over to Clays office while Cass and Scott said hello to the team members they knew. Clay had his back to the door of his office, he was on the phone sounding a little agitated. "I know that we've been set up to help them but I need to work directly with them. Having to go through you guys to liaise with them isn't going to work." He listened for a few seconds "No I get that you want to be kept in the loop and I can assure you I'll do that but you've got to let me contact them direct, it'll speed things up." he listened again for a few more seconds and saw Clays shoulders slump down. "Have it your way, we'll go through you and let you contact Barney and his team. We'll just sit here and wait for you to get back to us." He listened again. "I told you I won't contact them. Just get on the phone to them and find out how we can help. I've no idea who's looking for glory here but by going about it this way you're just slowing things down and you damn well know it." Clay ended the call and threw his phone on the desk in obvious disgust.

Danny waited for a second before speaking, "I guess I can help speed things up if you like."

Clay span round with a look of confusion on his face which was very quickly replaced with a look of pure joy, "boy am I glad to see you."

"Sounds like you're having a few problems."

"That's an understatement. somebody is glory hunting and has decided that it should be them that gets the recognition for setting up the team to help you."

"Oh don't worry about that, the General is very aware that any recognition regarding the outcome of this will go directly to you and your team, we'll make sure of that."

"I really appreciate that Danny, you're not down here alone are you?"

"No don't worry, they've kept me under close observation since the shooting," he said grinning, "my sidekick is out there with Cass saying hello to everyone."

Clay took a step towards the door so that he could see out into the office and saw Scott and Cass laughing and joking with his team, "I'm so glad I don't have to go through someone else to get to you guys, it would have just slowed things down so much."

Clay walked into the office, "just as soon as you've all finished can I have all members of the new team in the briefing room."

Danny followed Clay to the briefing room and within minutes everyone was sitting down, "some of you may have already worked with these three in which case they need no introductions. For those that haven't they're civilians and aren't in anyway linked to the Marshall Service. Having said that you need to listen to what they have to say and if they ask us to do something we do it and when I say we that includes me." A few people around the table looked shocked at the last remark

Scott took over, "for those of you round the table that don't know who we are I'll explain. We're a team comprised from multiple agencies across the globe, created to enable us to work outside of the normal political restraints. Cass is a serving FBI agent and I'm a Navy Seal, Danny here, well Danny is an annoying kid but he does supply the pizza so be nice to him." A number of people laughed "All joking aside he shouldn't be underestimated" Scott paused to look at Cass who instantly closed her eyes in expectation of the immediate ridicule as the shooting story was relived once more, "you'll all probably be aware of the recent warehouse raid that went wrong resulting in an FBI agent being shot," Scott looked round the table to see a number of people nodding, "well Danny was the one that firstly pulled the FBI agent out of the line of fire and then shot the gang member. Taking into account he wasn't carrying at the time, he used the agents weapon and add that to the fact that he has no military or agency training in my book he's earned the right to be sitting here with us."

The room was silent, Clay broke the silence, "just so that you're all aware and fully understand my feelings. If Danny asks me to do anything at all I'll be doing it immediately and without question," Clay looked round the table, "does anyone have any questions?" Nobody said anything.

Cass took over, "if there aren't any questions then we'll move forward."

One of the Deputy Marshalls that they had previously worked with raised his hand and spoke, "you know it's funny Cass but I was actually expecting Scott to use the fact that Danny outscored you on the range rather than the warehouse shooting to demonstrate his right to be here."

Scott and Danny laughed and Cass rolled her eyes, "bloody hell," she slumped back in the chair, "I'm getting a coffee, you've got five minutes and I don't want to be the topic of conversation when I get back." With that she got up and left the briefing room to get a coffee. When she returned things were back to normal and although almost everyone looked at her as she sat down nobody was brave enough to say anything.

Scott carried on, "Danny and I have managed to find out the following," Scott passed round some folders that contained the bullet points of what they knew so far about the gang member "We've got less than twenty four hours to find the missing pieces and build a full background on this guy, we need every scrap of information we can find. We need his financial records scrutinized, his phone records gone through, a full background check and a search of his home. Now some of you have worked together before and you know each other's strengths and weaknesses. I don't have time to go through it all so please split yourselves up into four teams basing the strength of that team on the task in hand."

Within minutes there were four clear teams, two teams of three each dealing with the financial and phone records. A team of six dealing with the background checks and a team of six to carry out the search. As three of the teams were going to be office based Clay elected to stay back and oversee that part which left Scott, Cass, Danny and three of Clay's team to conduct the search. Not knowing what they'd find they took two cars to the address they had, not every house belonging to the gang members had been searched yet and this was one of the ones that still needed to be done. A search warrant had already been arranged and when they arrived the three members of Clay's team affected entry into the property. It was a two story house and as soon as the Marshalls declared the building clear Scott, Cass and Danny entered the building. As the team had cameras in their go bags they split into three groups taking a room each.

They took their time making sure that they checked everything, they eventually found several notebooks, bank statements, weapons, drugs, phones and a significant amount of cash. It had taken them three hours but everything had been images and placed into evidence bags, they loaded the cars up and took it all back to the office. Once back there they gave the bank statements and phones to the two teams dealing with that side of things. For the moment they ignored the weapons drugs and cash. They all felt that all of those items were straight forward and didn't really relate to what they were currently focusing on so they made a start on the notebooks.

Just over two hours later they had a list of five names that they'd found in various notebooks with a broad physical description underneath. They'd also found an entry that just said 'Paid back D the 4k I owed him today which felt good' checking the bank statements for the date mentioned they found a payment of 4k, they contacted the bank for details of the account it was paid into and after several phone calls backwards and forwards they got the information they wanted. The payment was made to a Damian Stevens and along with the name

382

came the account details. There was suddenly a noticeable ripple of excitement throughout the office, this could well be a major step forward. Cass and Scott had been here before though and wouldn't get excited until it had been confirmed that this was in fact someone of interest. Suddenly they now had six extra people that now needed looking into. The two larger teams split themselves down even further so that they could start looking into all six people simultaneously.

Before he started Danny quickly ordered two dozen pizzas with some extras and drinks. Things were moving fast now and while everyone was busy he thought it would make sense to supply some food and drink in order to keep the workflow going. True to form several of the staff in the outer office not currently working on the case had made it known to Clay that they have the capacity to help if he wanted them to. Clay didn't hesitate and suddenly they had an extra six people jumping in to help. Danny called Grace to see if anyone had managed to look at the laptop they'd found. As luck would have it Grace had already started work on it and had sent a number of encrypted emails across to Nick as he was already working on the emails they had from Joseph. Danny called Nick who was able to confirm that the two sets of emails carried the exact same encryption and so far from what he had managed to ascertain they had been sent via the same route at various points. He told Danny the file to look at to get the transcript from the emails, Danny thanked Nick and ended the call.

"Cass can you jump on the server and bring up the files that Nick has put in the encrypted email folder."

"Yep I'm in."

"Good, there's a folder called Grace that contains a series of un-encrypted emails from the laptop."

"I'm in and there are a couple of dozen at least, Nick has put them into groups."

"In groups?" Danny sounded confused, "I'm only expecting one group of emails."

Cass expanded the folder view, "hang on Nick has added some notes. After tracking the email he found one going to a courier and from that he was able to track several emails going from courier to courier. It seems like he's managed to add a bit of an email chain which is something we certainly didn't have before."

Danny sat down next to Cass and they started to read the new and somewhat unexpected chain of emails, "can you print them all out please Cass, it'll be easier to create a timeline with them in front of me."

Cass went into each email and clicked on print, a couple of minutes later Danny had a pile of paper in front of him and started to create a timeline. Almost twenty minutes later he had them all in order and had created an accurate track of the conversation between the couriers, he was half way through reading one of them for a second time when he put it down and grabbed one of the others he'd already read. At first it didn't make sense then all of a sudden the penny dropped. "Cass I think we've missed something, well not so much missed as didn't have the full picture." He picked up two of the emails and went back over to sit next to her. "So here are two emails one from the courier we know that picked up Phoebe and a reply from another. Almost three quarters of the way through the other courier mentions that they've dropped one off at the plane which will shortly be on the way to meet them. The way I read it that implies that there was another kidnapped girl on the plane apart from Phoebe."

Cass read through both emails a couple of times, "I think you're right, hang on let's look at the planes itinerary," she worked her way through the files on the server to find the one she was looking for, "so the stop before they picked up Phoebe has them loading an authorised patient on a transfer to Europe and hang on a sec," Cass clicked on a different folder, "here's the confirmation that the patient was dropped off." She read through it all once more, "we need to get the CCTV rechecked at the airport because looking at this you're right they loaded two people, one legitimate and then the one that the courier dropped off."

Danny paused for a second before speaking, "that could mean that the drop off that Katie is looking into may not be Phoebe. She could have been dropped somewhere else. I'll call her and get her to look into where else that plane went to in Europe." Danny called Katie and updated her, telling her where the emails were on the server so that she could go through them as well to see if she came up with the same conclusion.

Chapter 42 (North America)

Although Damian had slept fairly well though the night he'd had some vivid dreams and when he woke he knew that despite the current distraction he was still struggling with the events of the last few days. He was back in his motel room after having had a quick coffee with Stella and making an excuse to leave to get a few urgent emails dealt with. On the way back to his hotel he had looked over his shoulder a couple of times. Not for any specific reason but in one of the dreams he'd been followed and the thought had resurfaced as he was walking along the sidewalk. There wasn't anyone there obviously but he couldn't shake off the feeling that he'd need to be extra careful and vigilant over the next few days. Even if it was just to convince himself that there wasn't anything to be worried about.

When he got back to his room despite the knowledge that he was being paranoid the first thing he did was check his pistol. He removed the Glock from its holster and ejected the magazine, he didn't really need to as he knew it was loaded but it was a habit that was very hard to stop. Sliding the magazine back into the pistol grip he replaced the Glock back into the holster. He had a concealed carry permit but very rarely used it. Feeling a bit more secure he put the pistol back into his bag trying to convince himself that he was worrying about nothing.

He threw his Mac into a backpack along with a book he'd found in the motel reception area. He'd learnt that reading a book, or at least to be pretending to be reading a book, was a perfect cover for being able to be in one spot for some time whilst observing what was going on around. He had some legwork to do today and wanted to check out some of the places that he'd listed that appeared in the social media searches he'd conducted on his possible targets. He didn't necessarily expect to see any of the girls but at least he'd be able to check out the lay of the land especially as he may well be using one of the places to accidently bump into one of them.

On the way to the first coffee shop he found that his subconscious was still getting the better of him and before he could stop himself he was looking over his shoulder every so often. He shook his head and tried to focus on what he was doing rather than let his mind drift. Once he settled down in the coffee shop he relaxed a little and got his Mac out to carry on scouring through various social media accounts to see what other information he could get on the girls. He didn't lose site of the fact that he was in a potentially target rich environment and kept an eye out on the various customers as they came and went. He'd found in the past that sometimes circumstances just work out and present you with the unexpected.

He didn't really expect to be that lucky but after a refill he had amassed quite a few more facts and now two of the girls he was targeting appeared to be very good prospects indeed. He'd managed to get home addresses, the colleges they were at, part time work addresses and several key locations they frequented. One of which was the very coffee shop he was currently sat in. After a couple of hours he'd regained his focus and was eager to try the local library especially as both girls had posted on Instagram from there at around lunchtime. On different days admittedly but that didn't matter to Damian, the important this was that it was a second location that they both frequented so it increased the chance of him being able to orchestrate a seemingly chance meeting.

He spent the first couple of hours trawling social media for more facts. It never ceased to amaze him as to how much information could be easily pieced together if you looked hard enough. He was beginning to get a really good bit of background on the two possible girls. He paused and looked up, looking round the coffee shop and gazed out of the window. He found himself looking straight at a man sitting in a parked car holding a coffee, nothing really strange about that on the surface except for the fact that he was looking straight at Damian.

Damian paused a second before looking away, his heart was pounding. Questions racing through his mind, he forced himself to calm down and take a deep breath. He closed the lid on his Mac and leant forward to pick his backpack up. Placing the Mac inside he stood

386

up, trying to remain casual he glanced out of the window to see that the vehicle was still there but the driver was no longer sat inside. He left the coffee shop and knew that he needed to take a very indirect route back to the motel. He was annoyed with himself for not having packed the Glock in the backpack. As he turned the first corner he risked a quick look to see the driver returning to the car carrying several bags being followed by a woman carrying just as many as he was.

He let out a big sigh and instantly relaxed, he walked a couple of blocks before deciding to take a direct route back to the motel to collect the Glock. The incident had rattled him enough to warrant the need for him to be prepared. Whilst walking back he tried to convince himself that he was being stupid and that the fact that the driver was looking straight at him as purely a coincidence. In truth he probably couldn't have seen inside the coffee shop so in reality wasn't even actually looking at him. The issue was that he was on edge and no matter how he played things out he needed to know that he had a little security. He was fairly confident that Goodbanks wouldn't want him killed but the world that Miguel moved in didn't really take into account what other people may or may not want.

Once back in the room the first thing he did was remove the pistol from his bag and clip the holster to the back of his jeans. With that in place he removed the pistol and once again checked the magazine, this time racking the slide to put a round in the chamber. Placing the pistol back in the holster he changed his jacket for one that was slightly longer and baggier. He slid a notebook into the inside pocket and go the book out of his backpack. He wanted a little more freedom and carrying the book in his left hand he left the motel and made his way towards the second coffee shop that he'd decided would be a good place to continue his research.

He was now very conscious that he needed to pay real attention to what was going on around him and as he made his way along the sidewalk he carried out every surveillance check that he knew. Even though nobody would actually know where he was heading he took an indirect route to the coffee shop. Feeling a little more confident he started to relax in himself and although he was still paying attention he felt much better and even started to consider the fact that he may have overreacted and needn't have gone back to the motel. What he failed to take into account however was that he'd completely missed the two vehicles parked up a short distance from his motel. Each contacting two people that were, unlike the previous guy sitting in a car, very much indeed interested in him. They watched him enter the motel and were still there when he left.

Still completely oblivious Damian carried on towards the second coffee shop. When he arrived he ordered a large coffee and found himself a table that gave him an unrestricted view of the front door. Despite feeling a little more at ease he still wanted to play safe and the table he chose gave him that ability. He got the notebook out of his inside pocket and placed it on the table. Getting his phone out he carried on with his research. Every so often taking the time to look up to see what was happening around him. After an hour or so he ordered another coffee, far more relaxed and almost feeling normal once again he once again picked up his phone and began another search.

Half an hour had gone by and he was beginning to struggle, he'd followed several dead ends and hadn't added anything new to the notebook at all. Looking up he couldn't help himself as a look of shock appeared on his face. Waiting for a coffee to be prepared was Kayla, one of the two girls he was researching. He quickly regained his composure, putting his phone down he picked the book up and opened it in such a way that he could watch her out of the corner of his eye whilst, to anyone looking at him, appear to be reading.

He now had a quick decision to make, if she didn't sit down should he follow her. He thought about it quickly knowing that he only had a minute or two before her drink was ready. Holding back the need to smile he took a deep breath as the barista placed a large cup of coffee down in front of Kayla rather than a takeaway cup. Kayla picked the coffee up and made her way over to a table that was just about in view of where Damian was sitting.

Putting the book down he picked his phone up once again and scrolled through to the drop box app. Opening it up, he selected the document that had all of the research he'd found on Kayla and started to refresh his memory. Of the two she would be his second choice as she had what seemed to be a slightly larger circle of friends on social media. Having said that, a few likes and the odd comment every now and then wasn't exactly anything to worry about from his perspective and she still remained a very strong target. Even more so now that he could actually follow her when she left. Having finished reading his notes he closed the file and put the phone back in his pocket. He now needed to be ready to leave almost immediately so reading the book was the best thing he could do because he could stand up almost straight away after she'd gone out of the door and only be a couple of seconds behind her.

He allowed himself a slight smile as he aimlessly read the page in front of him, he wasn't really focusing on the words at all but realised that he had to make it look as though he was actually reading. Inwardly he was annoyed with himself for allowing things to get on top of him earlier. Still he considered the fact that if he hadn't reacted in the way he did when he saw the driver of the car seemingly looking at him he probably wouldn't be sat here now looking at Kayla every now and then over the top of his book.

He could see that she was also reading a book and occasionally checking her phone, she wasn't spending long looking so he assumed she was just checking on the time and about ten minutes later she stood up. Putting her phone in her pocket and the book into the small bag she had on the table in front of her. Standing up she put the bag over her shoulder and made her way to the exit. Damian closed the book in front of him and paused for a second before standing up. Luckily the coffee shop was busy enough that people were almost constantly entering and leaving so it didn't at all seem strange that he'd chosen that moment to leave. He was just another customer going about their business, well almost.

Kayla had turned left and so Damian did the same, for the moment he could follow her without concern as the sidewalk was busy and he wouldn't really be noticed. He kept his distance and was grateful that she seemed to be walking with purpose so he didn't need to really worry about having to walk slowly to remain behind her. He was focused on running through the options of what to do if she did certain things. The challenge he faced was he actually had no idea whatsoever as to where she was heading and although he was following her now he may have to simply let her go depending on where she went and what she did. He didn't really care at the moment, the fact that he'd been fortunate enough to be in the right place at the right time was good enough for him. Maybe, just maybe if he'd been caring a little more he would have noticed that he was being followed. As he'd moved away from the cafe four people began to follow him, two on each side of the road. Adopting what was obviously a very professional approach and as a result of Damian being far too engrossed in what was going on in front of him they were able to follow him with ease.

Damian followed Kayla for about twenty minutes when she crossed the road and entered a large office block. Damian stayed on his side of the road and leaning against a wall he took his phone out and did a quick search on the address. Two companies were listed, one a financial business the other a private medical practice specialising is beauty treatments and procedures. Happy that there wasn't anything for him to be concerned about he put his phone away and walked a little further down the road to a bus stop. He sat on the bench and opened the book once more. He was able to easily watch the entrance to the building and decided he'd wait for half an hour or so.

Pausing he lowered the book to have a casual glance around, his heart stopped and he became instantly alert. On the opposite side of the street were a couple that just didn't seem to look as though they should be there. The man was looking over the woman's shoulder and had glanced straight at Damian at the same time his eyes came to rest on them. Damian controlled himself and continued to look past them but not that far that he couldn't keep them in his peripheral vision.

Alarm bells started to chime in Damian's head, this didn't feel right. Trying to remain calm he stood up as naturally as he could. This time he had a feeling that this wasn't a chance encounter and his earlier apprehension had been well placed even if it was a false alarm. Forgetting Kayla he started walking away from the couple trying to put a bit of distance between himself and them without hopefully letting on that he'd spotted them. His first thought was that Miguel had put a hit out on him. Something he knew very well could be a very real possibility. In order to get another look at them he decided to cross the road so that he could use the pretext of checking for oncoming traffic to get eyes on them again.

As he turned to look, he could see that they'd given up any pretence and were purposefully following him. That was made worse as he was looking to see if any cars were coming, he noticed a second pair on his side of the road. He knew he was now in trouble and he had absolutely no chance of losing four of them. His mind was in turmoil as he struggled to come up with a plan. Face them or run seemed to be the only two options and knowing Miguel the people he'd hire wouldn't care what he did they'd still carry out their assignment.

Making a decision he stayed on the same side of the road he was on and started to walk faster. He wasn't going to start running just yet he needed a few seconds to gather his thoughts, he realised almost instantly that the situation was hopeless and at that point decided he wasn't going down without a fight. He had nowhere to go and no way out so he started to run, his plan was to run a short distance stop and turn around to face his pursuers and then let things play out. As he ran he heard someone shout out "Damian Stevens FBI stop," He laughed out loud, FBI is that the best approach they could come up with.

Stopping suddenly, he span round, his right hand reaching behind him pulling the Glock out he faced the couple on the other side of the road. They'd both drawn pistols and were in a shooting stance. Damian didn't hesitate and fired two shots, that was all he managed. If he'd been a casual observer he would have seen several bullets hit his body. Almost every single one a fatal shot, he was dead long before his body hit the ground.

Chapter 43 (Europe)

"He called her Phoebe and as far as I am aware that is her real name."

Alek tried not to give away his relief, he had been hoping that this was Phoebe but didn't want to get his hopes up too high. Charlie arrived with the spare mag and gave it to him. Alek turned back to Peter, "I'm ready let's do this."

Emile held his hand up to the access panel and there was a soft barely audible click and the light turned green. Peter opened the door and the first of his two man teams entered and went right. The second pair went left and then the four man team entered and went straight up the central corridor. Alek made his way up the corridor with the G36 firmly in a firing position, moving the barrel at the same time as he scanned with his eyes. They got to the intersection and the four of them split into two groups of two. Alek stopped at the door to the control room and felt a tap on his shoulder letting him know that Peter was ready for him to enter the room.

Alek paused for a split second then removed his left hand from the rifle and placed it on the door handle. Twisting the handle he pushed the door open and advanced through the door sweeping left and right with the rifle as he stepped forward. Peter was right on his shoulder but the room was empty. Alek called the room clear and lowered his rifle, Peter did the same, "Emile was possibly telling the truth then?"

"It seems so," as Peter answered he stepped forward to the central console that dominated the room. Several large blank monitors were on the wall in front of them. On the long desk were a couple of keyboards, a microphone and a couple of joysticks. Two monitors were mounted in a panel along with several displays containing multiple buttons. After a quick look Alek realised that this room seemed to control the whole complex. Alek pushed a button marked Guest Bedroom and one of the large monitors in front of them came to life showing a girl sitting on a bed reading.

Peter and Alek looked at each other, Alek spoke first, "she seems to be perfectly all right but I don't want to go bursting in there. I'd like to bring Charlie and Emile up here. I want to find out how they communicated with Phoebe so that we can hopefully reassure her before we open the door."

Peter spoke on his radio and confirmed that all three other teams had cleared the complex and there wasn't anyone else here. He spoke into his mike and less than two minutes later Charlie and Emile came into the control room. Emile was flanked by two members of Peter's team and back in plasti cuffs.

Alek turned to Emile, "how do we talk to her?"

"It's indirect, you type into the left hand keyboard and it appears on the screen next to her bed. She'll know you're typing because the music volume will drop as you send a message. She'll then speak and we'll hear her in here."

Alek turned to Charlie, "I'm going to send you in first, Peter will be right behind you but won't go in the room with you. If you need him he'll be straight in. I'll be watching on the screen but it's going to be down to you to make the decision as to if he needs to assist you."

Charlie looked away from Alek and up to the screen, "first impression is that she seems to be absolutely fine. Her body language tells me she's comfortable and the fact that she's reading and listening to music would indicate that she's okay with her surroundings. I'll take it nice and slow and see how we progress."

"Okay," Alek turned to Emile, "how do we enter the room?"

"On the right hand keyboard push the number three to bring up the dining area on the monitor next to the one you can see Phoebe on. Then on the smaller panel to the left of the keyboard button one opens the outer door to the dining area to let you in and button two opens the door from the dining room to the bedroom." Emile didn't say anymore, he'd realised that he wasn't in a good position at all and he quickly realised that right now cooperating was the only thing he could do to possibly help him reduce the trouble he was in.

Charlie sat down at the desk and tapping the button on the keyboard looked up at the display of monitors. Sure enough just as Emile had said the dining room area suddenly appeared, turning to Emile she asked. "Will she hear if I open the dining room door now?"

He shook his head, "no, the room she's in is soundproof and she won't hear anything until you open the interconnecting door between the dining room and her room."

Charlie turned back round to face the desk and pushed a button on the panel Emile had mentioned. Looking back up at the screen she could now see that a door had opened on the left hand side of the dining room, "I hope this works," she typed 'Hello Phoebe.' she moved the mouse pointer over the send icon and then taking a deep breath clicked send. Looking up at the screen she saw that Phoebe had lowered the book and was now looking at the screen, suddenly Phoebes voice filled the room.

"Hello."

Charlie quickly typed 'How are you feeling' and clicked send once more.

"I'm okay, feeling a bit hungry actually but other than that okay, do you want me to do something for you?"

Charlie replied 'No that's okay'

Phoebe paused for a second, "oh, okay if you're sure, I don't mind. I'm nice and relaxed so it wouldn't take me long."

Charlie replied 'No that's okay' and turned to look at Emile, "what does she mean?"

Emile hesitated, suddenly he didn't want to be in the room, "erm, well he would have her perform for him and she'd be rewarded with food or gifts."

Alek took a step towards Emile, "what do you mean perform?" There was a noticeable tone to Aleks voice.

Emile swallowed, "I ..... I need you to understand that I didn't have anything to do with this."

"Other than willingly help him to imprison someone you mean. Now tell me what you mean?" Alek slowed down the last part of the sentence and emphasised each word.

Emile was now visibly shaking, "he would get her to play with herself while she was taking a shower or in bed."

Before Alek could say anything Charlie jumped in, "Peter can you get one of your medics in here so that I've got some equipment to hand in case I need it."

"Yes that's not a problem."

Emile spoke, his voice lacking confidence and much quieter now, "we've got equipment here, I've got a full trauma kit and oxygen."

Alek turned to Peter, "take him to get it but if he tries anything at all please feel free to subdue him however you see fit."

Peter smiled, "he won't try anything, but if he does don't worry he'll be thoroughly subdued," with that Peter followed Emile who was now virtually being carried by the team members either side of him.

Charlie carried on typing 'Phoebe I need you to focus on what you're reading'

"Okay." Phoebe's voice once again filled the room.

Charlie looked up at the monitor to see that Phoebe had now put the book down and had turned on the bed to face the screen 'In a moment the door to the dining room will open'

"Oh that's good, I was wondering when lunch would be ready."

'It's not for lunch Phoebe, I need you to understand what I'm writing and to concentrate'

"Oh, well I promise I'll do whatever you ask."

Peter returned with an oxygen bottle and mask in one hand and a decent sized medical kit slung over his shoulder. "It's a full size trauma kit Charlie just like he said and should have everything you may need. I'm hoping it'll just be the oxygen that you need though."

Charlie turned back to the keyboard 'When the door opens I want you to wait where you are until I tell you it's ok to go through the door'

"Sure." Phoebe said it with a matter of fact tone to her voice almost as if anything Charlie requested would have been okay.

Charlie turned to Alek and Peter, "I have no idea how she's actually going to react so Alek can you stay here and watch the screen. Peter can you come with me and bring the medical kit," with that Charlie stood up and as she did Alek slipped into the seat in her place.

Charlie walked out of the control room with Peter following her, she got to the now open doors that lead into the dining area, "Peter if you can wait here out of sight and if I need you I'll call you."

Peter lowered the trauma kit off his shoulder onto the floor beside him and placed the oxygen tank and mask next to it, "good luck."

"I think we may need it." Charlie walked through the door and sat down at the table. She sat in the seat facing the door, looking up at the camera she put her thumb up and nodded to Alek.

In the control room Alek pushed the relevant button, looking up at the screen he saw the door open and he watched as Phoebe turned her head to look at the now open door.

Charlie paused for a second before she spoke, "Phoebe can you hear me?"

"Yes I can." Phoebe's voice didn't have the same confident tone it did a short while ago.

"I need you to listen carefully to me Phoebe, can you do that."

"Yes."

"My name is Charlie and I'm an officer with the British Army. I'm here along with a specialist team from the Police and we're here to take you home. Do you understand what I'm saying?"

There was a long pause before Phoebe spoke, "yes, but I don't know if I believe you."

"That's understandable Phoebe, come to the door and you'll see my ID on the table." Charlie slid her ID card across the table. Charlie heard Phoebe get up off the bed and suddenly she came into view but stopped at the end of the bed and didn't approach the door.

Phoebe looked at Charlie, "you're not in uniform how do I know you're real?"

"I don't always have my uniform on Phoebe," Charlie thought for a second, "would you feel better if a uniformed police officer came in with me?"

"Yes I would," Phoebe still didn't move from where she was, she looked around nervously.

"That's okay, he's just outside the door but please realise that he's part of a special team so he looks more like a soldier than a policeman. His name's Peter and I'll ask him to step into the room and stand behind me in clear view with his hands up if that's okay?"

"Yes that's fine."

Peter stepped into the room, his assault rifle was slung across his back and he kept his hands held up where Phoebe could see them, "hello

Phoebe my name is Peter and I'm in charge of the team that have been sent here to assist in your rescue."

Phoebe tilted her head slightly and looked at Charlie, "are you really here to help me?" Her voice now had a certain amount of desperation to it.

Charlie smiled, "yes we are."

Phoebe bit her lip and didn't respond, it seemed as if she was weighing up what Charlie had said, "I'm not sure if I can believe you."

"Well that's understandable, what can we do to help you?"

"How many of you are there?"

"I've got a colleague that's part of my team and Peter has over twenty members of his team in the area. Outside are local Police and Military Police and we're all here to help." Charlie had kept her voice as soft as she could in the hope that it would help.

Suddenly Charlie could hear movement behind her and she saw Phoebes eyes widen, Charlie turned to see Alek entering the room, he had a big smile on his face and his arms were full of food and drink.

"Hi Phoebe, my name's Alek and I work with Charlie. I know you're hungry so I grabbed whatever food I could find in the kitchen." Alek stepped forward and placed all the food on the table as close to Phoebe as he could. He then stepped back, as he did he pulled a chair with him and sat down next to Charlie. He sat slightly away from Charlie and the table so that there wasn't anything between him and Phoebe.

"Now I can totally understand your lack of trust. I was once held captive and I can completely relate to where you're coming from so we'll do this any way you want," he paused for a second, looked at Charlie and then looked back at Phoebe, "we can do several things for you, we can sit here and answer any questions you have. We can leave the room and let you eat and call us when you're ready, you can take some food back into your room and we'll close the door until you tell us you're ready. It really is up to you"

"Don't leave me," there was noticeable panic in her voice.

Charlie spoke again, "we're not going anywhere Phoebe but Alek is right we'll do this any way that you want."

Alek took his jacket off and turning slightly put it on the back of the chair he was sitting on. Pulling his sleeves up he leant forward and placed his elbows on his knees and put his hands together, "so, trust is going to be important here Phoebe. I get why you wouldn't trust us at all so here's my first thoughts. We know you're hungry because you mentioned lunch earlier. The food in front of you is safe to eat and to prove it take a look at what's there and tell me what you want me to eat. I can't second guess what you're going to choose so if I'd drugged any of it I'd have to drug the whole lot. The sandwiches are fresh, although they don't look great I didn't really have a great deal of time to prepare them."

Phoebe looked at Alek and then looked at the pile of food, Alek watched as her eyes went from item to item, "I don't know what to do, I want to believe you but I don't know if I can," She looked at Alek.

He smiled back, "that's okay, you tell me what you want and I'll do what I can to make this as easy as possible."

Phoebe was biting her lip once again, "I'd like a phone so that I can call someone outside of this place," Phoebe looked at Charlie and then back to Alek, "eat one of the sandwiches in the second pile and an apple."

Alek got up slowly and moved forward slightly so that he could reach the pile of sandwiches Phoebe was talking about, "which one would you like me to eat, it's important that you choose exactly which one." His hand hovered above the four sandwiches.

Phoebe thought for a second, "the bottom one closest to you and the apple closest to me."

Alek picked up the sandwich and the apple that Phoebe had chosen and sat back down. Without any hesitation he took a bite of the sandwich noticing that Phoebe hadn't taken her eyes off him for a second.

Charlie took her phone out of her pocket, "here's my phone Phoebe, the unlock code is 8232. If you look at the recent calls there are three particular names that you could call. They're all members of our team and they'll do whatever they can to put your mind at rest. Katie is with Interpol and is heading the team that Alek and I are part of. Cass and Joss are with the FBI and CIA and are in charge of two teams that are doing their very best to find you and others like you," Charlie stood up and took a couple of slow steps forward and placed the phone as close as she could to Phoebe.

Alek had finished the sandwich and had taken a bite of the apple, "I'm also going to give you my phone as well Phoebe, the code is 3495. If you go into the address book you'll see a contact listed as big boss.

Call that number and you'll find yourself speaking to a five star general in the United States Army. He's our ultimate boss and he's very aware of the current situation as we brief him daily. He's very direct and deals with facts so ask him anything at all and I can assure you he'll tell you what you want to know." Alek moved forward and slid his phone towards Phoebe, "tell you what, take both phones and go sit on your bed and make a call to anyone you want. We'll move back out of the room but we'll leave the door open."

Phoebe looked at Alek and then at Charlie, "I ..... I don't know what to do."

"Well we aren't going to force you to do anything at all Phoebe," Alek kept his voice soft and calm, "it's really up to you as to what you do next."

As if she'd suddenly made her mind up Phoebe stepped forward and picked up the phone Alek had put in front of her, she pushed the button and the display came up asking for the unlock code.

"3495." Alek knew she wouldn't have remembered what he had said.

Phoebe put the code in and the display came up, she touched the phone Icon and selected recent calls. Scrolling down to the one marked big boss she pressed the call button and put the phone to her ear, after three rings a voice answered, "Mr Lyashev this had better be good as I'm about to go into a meeting with the joint chiefs."

Phoebe paused before saying anything, "who is this," she looked at Alek with a look of fear and concern.

"This is General Leverson, more importantly who's this?

Phoebe didn't know what to say so she just blurted out, "Phoebe."

"Phoebe," there was a pause, "the Phoebe that my team are trying to find?"

"Yes." Phoebe said quietly.

"Am I glad to hear your voice young lady," the Generals voice suddenly softened, "is Alek with you?"

Phoebe managed to mumble, "yes," before bursting into tears and collapsing on the floor.

Charlie and Alek rushed forward, Alek picked up the phone which was now on the floor as Phoebe had let go of it as she fell.

"General it's Alek, we've got her and she'll be fine. I'm with Charlie and we're in a safe location."

"Well done Alek, take good care of her and I expect to see you all shortly."

"Will do General," with that Alek disconnected the call and put the phone in his pocket.

Phoebe was still on the floor but her head was now buried in Charlie's shoulder and she was sobbing uncontrollably.

Alek looked at Charlie, "you okay?" Charlie looked at him and nodded. Alek looked over at the door, "Peter."

Peter appeared at the doorway, "what can I do?" He'd been listening to the conversation so despite the fact that Phoebe was now on the floor with Charlie attending to her he wasn't worried.

"Can you get the rest of our team in here. I need them to start imaging everything and downloading data etc."

"Will do, I've got a few members of my team forensically trained if you want to use them as well."

"Yes please Peter that would be great," Alek turned back to Charlie, "let's get her up and onto the bed."

Phoebe lifted her head away from Charlie's shoulder, "no, I don't want to go back in there" Her sobbing was a bit more under control now "I don't ever want to go back in there."

Charlie looked at Phoebe with a smile, "you don't need to, as soon as you feel up to it we'll get you outside and away from here."

Phoebe nodded and didn't say anything more, Charlie turned to Alek. "Let's get her up and on the chair." Alek help Charlie and they lifted Phoebe up to her feet and walked her over to the chair. Once Phoebe was sat down Charlie made her way to the door to collect the trauma kit that Peter had left outside. Phoebe looked suddenly startled, "don't leave me," her voice sounded desperate.

Charlie stopped and tuned round, "don't worry Phoebe, just outside the door is a medical kit and I want to give you a quick check over before we take you out of here, is that okay?"

Phoebe looked at Charlie and then turned to Alek who nodded gently to her. Phoebe looked back at Charlie again. "Yes."

"So I'll keep talking to you as I go so that you know I haven't gone anywhere other than outside the door," Charlie turned and walked out of the room, "I just want to check your blood pressure and carry out a few simple checks" Charlie was back in the room with the kit. She placed it on the table "I want to listen to your heart and then if

400

everything is okay and you're comfortable enough we'll get you away from here." Charlie removed a stethoscope and blood pressure cuff from the kit

Phoebe looked at Alek and then at Charlie, "I feel fine."

Alek dropped down to one knee so that he was at roughly the same height as Phoebe, "we don't doubt that but it's better to be safe than sorry and to be honest it'll only take Charlie a couple of minutes and then we can get going."

Phoebe nodded, "where are we going?" Her voice had gained a little confidence now and she didn't sound as frightened when she spoke.

"Well that's actually a good question, we're actually staying at a military base currently but we can book a hotel if you'd rather." Alek looked at Charlie, "I'll book us back into the hotel we were at."

"I don't want to be left on my own." The panic was back in Phoebe's voice and her eyes darted from Charlie to Alek and back again.

Pausing before he spoke he made sure that Phoebe was looking directly at him. "I'll make sure that one of the rooms is a double room and Charlie will stay with you."

Phoebe just nodded.

Charlie picked up the blood pressure cuff, "Phoebe all I'm going to do is take your blood pressure and then have a quick listen to your heart okay?"

"Yes that's fine," she lifted her arm so that Charlie could apply the cuff, once in place she inflated it. Picking up the stethoscope she checked Phoebe's blood pressure slowly deflating the cuff as she went. "That's perfect now I just need you to take a few deep breaths for me." As soon as Phoebe had done that Charlie moved behind her, "can you lean forward a little for me and take another couple of deep breaths." Phoebe obliged and Charlie stood back up placing the stethoscope on the opened trauma kit. "Everything is absolutely fine so as far as I'm concerned we can get out of here."

Alek went down on one knee so that Phoebe didn't have to look at up him as he spoke. "I know that you don't want to go back in the bedroom but you're going to need a change of clothes and something for your feet so I'll go in and get you a few bits, what would you like?"

Phoebe stared at him for a second, "I don't want any of it. I just want to get out of here."

"I understand," he paused for a second, "I'll bring the car down as close to the door as I can get it and on the way to the hotel we'll stop and get you some clothes and some other bits and pieces. Does that sound okay?"

Phoebe looked at him for a second then bursting into tears and launched herself forward throwing her arms around his neck. Alek almost fell backwards but managed to stabilise himself. He put his arms around her and held her tight "It's all right." Phoebe was sobbing uncontrollably now and Alek waited until she stopped before pulling himself away, "Let's get you out of here," as he went to stand up he took hold of Phoebes hand and she stood up with him, he looked at her. "You stay here with Charlie and I'll go and get the car sorted out."

Phoebe nodded without saying anything and Charlie put an arm round her shoulder, "why don't we sit down for a minute while Alek goes and sorts that out?"

Phoebe had gained a little more control and replied, "okay....... sorry for crying."

Charlie smiled, "you don't have to be sorry for anything at all Phoebe, it's perfectly natural and please don't worry."

"I just can't believe you're here, I tried so hard to not worry but I was beginning to come undone .... how could someone do this?"

Charlie sighed, "I don't know Phoebe but try not to think about it. I know it's not going to be easy but you're safe now."

Alek made his way out of the complex which was now alive with activity. He could hear numerous voices and as he walked along the corridor he saw multiple flashes of light as various cameras took images. He smiled to himself happy that they'd finally managed to get somewhere. Stepping out of the complex into the barn he took his phone out of his pocket he called Erica. "I'm going to get you to drive Phoebe, Charlie and I to the hotel, we'll keep her there for a few days until the American Embassy take over, which I'm sure they will just as soon as they get their act together." He paused listening as Erica responded to him "Okay well I'm outside now and I'm going up to the MPs to give them their weapons back.

He walked out of the barn to find that the MPs had moved their vehicles and they were parked just outside along with a multitude of other vehicles. Peters team had moved some of their vehicles down to the barn and the local Police also had a fair few parked up as well. Alek made his way over to the MPs "Hi guys, thanks for these." He handed back the two G36cs that he and Charlie had used. He gave the two MPs a quick rundown on what had happened and what their plans were and agreed with the MPs when they said they may as well head back to base. Alek thanked them and turned round as he heard someone approaching from behind.

Erika had been working with Ralf in one of the rooms photographing various bits of evidence and after telling Ralf what was going on had left him to it and made her way outside to find Alek. The two cars had already been moved and Erica jumped into one of them and reversed it into the barn. While she was doing that Alek went to find Peter to thank him and his team for their help. He found him in the control room assisting Karl. They were busy downloading the various hard drives on the computer system. Alek explained to both of them what he was going to do and thanked Peter for his help. Making his way back to the dining area he asked Phoebe if she was ready, she simply nodded and he told her to follow him.

They moved swiftly through the complex and out into the barn. Erica had managed to get the car almost down to the door so Phoebe only needed to take a few steps before she was safely seated in the back. Charlie got in next to her and Alek made his way round to the passenger seat and got in. Charlie introduced Phoebe to Erica and two minutes later Erica was carefully negotiating her way round the various vehicles and making her way back to the main road. Phoebe looked vacantly out of the window as the scenery flashed past tears streaming down her face, she closed her eyes to try and shut it all out, she was struggling to take it all in.

Chapter 44 (North America)

The following morning there was a noticeable level of excitement as Clay came into the room. He looked around the room at the smiling faces. "Well you all seem happy with yourselves."

Danny looked round the room then looked at Clay. "They should be, all their hard work has possibly paid off. One of your team found a college photo in the evidence and did some digging. D could well be Damian Stevens who went to college and was best friends with Rick Cairns. A little more digging and there's some email correspondence between them so at this stage we're definitely going to assume that Damian Stevens is now a person of interest."

Clay sat down, "well that's a huge step forward."

"Yes it is and he works for Steven Goodbanks so would definitely have access to some very high level contacts."

Clay looked shocked, "Goodbanks, he's rather high flying and certainly not someone I'd connect to this kind of thing."

"Well at this stage we don't think he probably has any idea. It seems that Damian has kept up his friendship with Rick and we can only guess has decided to make some extra money on the side," Danny paused, "quite a bit of extra money it would seem."

Clay nodded, "so what do we do now?"

Cass took over, "I've already spoken to Barney and he's forming a plan as we speak. I think due to the nature of his connections we'll probably leave you guys out of any initial research in case it goes wrong, that way it'll be the FBI that Goodbanks comes after rather than the Marshall Service."

"Well that makes sense and I've got to be honest and say thank you. The last thing we'd need right now is some negative publicity especially as we seem to be doing rather well with this investigation at the moment."

"You guys can carry on with what you're doing. There's still so much to go through and now we have another lead there's no reason why you can't do the background work on that." Cass looked down at her phone as it stared vibrating, "It's Barney, Danny can you take over." Cass picked the phone up and left the room.

"So as Cass said we'll keep doing what we're doing and let someone else worry about treading on peoples toes." For the next ten minutes or so they discussed various bits that they'd pieced together and split back up into the smaller groups they'd been working in. Danny, Scott followed Clay into his office as the table they were all sting around had suddenly been covered in various boxes and evidence bags once again.

Cass joined them a few minutes later, "Barney has already got Jess in the air on her way down here with Jake and Boyd, he wants Danny to work here with you Clay and for Scott, Jake, Boyd and I to follow up on Damian. The stakes have just got higher. Katie and her team have just found Phoebe alive and in seemingly good health and she's on her way to a place of safety right now which means we'll be moving in on everyone we suspect of being involved. The thinking is that we've got lucky with Phoebe and although there may be an unknown number of other victims we need to stop this straight away. It's believed that Damian may well be at the top of the food chain so we've been given the go ahead to pick everyone up."

Clay arranged for one of his team to drop the four of them at the airport and less than an hour after being dropped off they were on board the plane and Jess was taking off once more. The flight was quite short and leaving Jess to fly back to Luke they made their way outside the terminal building to meet an agent form the local field office that was waiting with two surveillance vehicles that had been made available to them. They didn't want to use rentals from the airport as they wanted the ability to blend in and a sparkly shiny rental car didn't exactly give them that sort of flexibility.

They paired up and took a car each, Jake and Scott took the lead with Cass and Boyd following. On the flight they'd discussed the best approach and had agreed that they'd start with some straight forward reconnaissance for the motel that Damian had last used his credit card at. They also had a few local bars and restaurants on the financial report they'd received back for Damien's cards.

Pulling up just short of the motel they parked the cars on opposite sides of the road some way from the entrance. It gave them the ability to watch the motel and the approaches without being too close to anyone going in or leaving. In order to get a better idea of the motel layout Cass and Boyd went into the reception posing as a couple looking to possibly rent a room for a couple of days while they were in town. Having got what they needed they made their way back to the car and Cass called Scott, "the layout is pretty standard but I think we'll have a problem picking him up in the motel. It doesn't really have a large enough reception area for us to blend in, we'd stand out too much so I think we'll have to have a plan B."

"Well there was always going to be a chance that would be the case," Scott paused, "I suggest that if he does turn up here we follow him to a suitable point and then detain him."

"It's not an ideal plan but under the circumstances it's the best we're going to get as we have absolutely no idea where he may be or where we could wait for him."

Cass thought for a second, "we'll have to wing it and play it by ear. If he does come back here then we'll follow him for a short while to see where he goes and if we find ourselves in a favourable situation then we'll move in."

"Sounds like a plan, I suggest we don't simply stay in the cars so Jake and I will take a walk for a couple of blocks to get the lay of the land. Once we're back you and Boyd can do the same." Cass agreed with his idea so Scott finished the call. They were dressed in a fairly casual manner so they wouldn't look too out of place walking about. Scott and Jake left the car and started walking. They covered several blocks making mental notes of key things they may need to remember. They grabbed a couple of coffees before getting back to the car. Scott called Cass to give her a quick update and to let her know the ground they'd covered. Cass let him know that she would cover the other direction with Boyd.

Within forty minutes they were both back in the car and like Scott and Jake they were making some notes for reference. They were just running through what they'd written when Scott called. "Cass he's just crossing the street heading for the entrance to the motel."

Without making it too obvious Cass moved her head slightly so that she could see him in her peripheral vision, "I've got him, he seems to be in a bit of a hurry, that's certainly not a casual pace he's moving at."

"So normal process then, two of us watching out for him at all times and the other, we'll do one hour on one off and reassess in a few hours' time."

Cass nodded without realising it, "sounds like a plan to me, if he does come back out we'll all follow leapfrogging as we go."

Less than twenty minutes later Damian came back out of the motel. Cass noticed that he was walking with far less determination this time. Something had changed. Cass and Boyd waited until Damian had gone out of view before getting out of the car closing the door she looked up the street and saw that Scott and Jake had done the same. Cass and Boyd were on the same side of the street as Damian. Cass didn't need to look over her should to see where Jake and Scott were. She just knew that they would be following on the other side of the street.

They hadn't been following for long before Damian entered a coffee shop. Cass and Boyd were lucky as there was a bench close to them so they sat down and made it look as though they were talking. Jake and Scott weren't so lucky so they carried on past the coffee shop and entered a sandwich shop with was still just in sight of the coffee shop. Jake sat down while Scott went and ordered two coffees. While he was waiting Jake called Cass, "how do you want to play this?"

"Well I think we follow him for a bit and when we feel he's in an open enough area we move in and detain him."

"Scott and I will stay on this side. I'm not sure what he's doing but from what I've seen so far this should be fairly straight forward."

Cass laughed, "we've thought that a fair few times in the past and things haven't always gone the way we thought they would. Having said that I'm hoping this will be a simple arrest."

"Okay, Scott's back so I'll update him." Jake finished the call and put the phone down next to the coffee that Scott has just put in front of him, "Cass said we'll follow him for a while till he's in an open area and then we'll move in and arrest him."

Scott nodded, "seems straight forward enough although in the past we've often found that not to be the case."

Jake laughed, "That's what Cass said."

"Well we've learnt to accept that things just simply don't go the way we want them to and try to plan accordingly," Scott shook his head, "sadly despite all the plans and training you just can't allow for the unexpected."

Jake looked away from the coffee shop and looked at Scott. "Hopefully with four of us we should be able to keep this under control and detain him without any fuss."

Scott smiled, "I'd like to think so."

They both shifted their attention to the coffee shop that Damian was sitting in. This was the part of any surveillance that tested your patience, just waiting for something to happen. Jake and Scott engaged in idle chat every so often making sure that at least one of them was watching the coffee shop at any given time. The minutes dragged on and Jake got up and ordered another coffee. Whilst up he used the rest room knowing that there was no telling when they'd next be able to stop.

Putting the two coffees down on the table and sitting back down he knew he didn't need to ask if anything had happened. He'd spent enough time with Scott to know that if there was anything he needed to know he would have been told. Now that Jake was back it was Scott's turn to use the facilities and less than five minutes later he was once again sat down next to Jake.

Cass and Boyd didn't have the luxury of having use of a restroom or indeed the ability to get a coffee. They had discussed one of them getting a couple of coffees but had decided against it just in case Damian suddenly appeared. The minutes dragged on and on. Cass was watching the coffee shop and as Boyd had his back to it she was relaying what was happening. To anyone observing them it looked as though they were simply having a conversation, which was exactly what they wanted.

Ten minutes later Damian stepped out of the coffee shop and stated walking away from them. Cass and Boyd got up and started to follow. Damian turned left and whilst now he was out of sight Cass and Boyd upped their speed. Reaching the corner they crossed the road so that they were now on the opposite side of the street to Damian. Cass had seen Jake and Scott cross in front of them and Cass instinctively knew that Scott would now follow on the same side as Damian as he was part of the leading pair.

Cass was thankful that Damian didn't seem to be paying any attention at all to what was going on behind him, which made their job so much easier. Cass saw Damian stop and he appeared to be looking at a building on the opposite side of the street. Cass and Boyd stopped and Cass took her phone out of her pocket to make it look as though she and Boyd were checking something. She saw out of the corner of her eye that Scott and Jake had done the same. She could see that Jake was pointing back down the street the way they'd just come in an attempt to make things look as natural and realistic as possible.

This was always a difficult situation and not easy to deal with when following someone on foot. Thankfully Damian started moving again and Cass and Boyd once again started to follow him. Much to their frustration he stopped a short while later and sat down on a bench. Cass decided to move as close as she felt was safe and taking out her phone once again called Scott, "this doesn't look great and I have a feeling we're not going to find anywhere really suitable to take him."

"I agree, let's get closer and give him a chance to settle down and then we'll move in."

"Okay," Cass put her phone back in her pocket, "let's get a bit closer and stop just short of him. Once Scott and Jake are in position we'll give it a few minutes and then move in on him."

Boyd nodded in agreement and they carried on walking, they stopped a short distance away from Damian, Cass had her back to him and Boyd was watching him over her shoulder. Cass could see Jake and Scott on the other side of the road in a similar position. She was about to take her phone out to tell Scott to get ready to move when she saw the look on Boyd's face change.

"What is it?"

"I think he's on to us."

"Damn, are you sure?"

"He's running."

Cass span round and started running a fraction of a second behind Boyd, she could see Jake and Scott slightly ahead of her and she heard Jake shout "Damian Stevens FBI stop," she saw Damian suddenly stop and draw a pistol from behind his back. Cass and Boyd drew there's at almost the same moment and they saw Damian fire. They both fired off two shots and the noise from just to the right of them told her that Jake and Scott had done the same. Damian went down straight away.

Suddenly people were screaming and running away from them. As they moved forward they kept their guns trained on the now inert form on the ground.

Cass kicked the pistol away from Damian's hand and knelt down to check for a pulse. She didn't really need to do that as he was laying on his back with several well placed bullet holes in him and his eyes were wide open. Boyd had holstered his pistol and now had his ID in his hand and was informing on lookers that he was FBI and they needed to move back. Cass stood up and took her phone out of her pocket. She called 911 and reported their location and that shots had been fired by federal agents. She turned to check on how the others were dealing with the crowd only to see Boyd on his own. She put the phone in her pocket and holstered her pistol.

She saw a crowd gathered on the opposite side of the street. She looked at Boyd, "shit the shots Damian fired must have hit a passer-by."

Boyd looked worried, "go and help them, there's nothing we can do here and I can keep the crowd back till help arrives."

Cass crossed the road and taking out her ID she held it up, "FBI move back please," as the crowd parted she saw Jake on his knees blood spreading from a wound on his shoulder, "Jake you've been hit."

Jake ignored her at first, he was frantically doing chest compressions. He looked up at Cass with a look of total desperation. His hands covered in blood which was obviously the victims and not his own. Cass heard the first of the sirens approaching and naturally looked up, looking back down the colour drained from her face as she stared straight into the open and now sightless eyes of Scott.

Epilogue

It had been four weeks since Scott had been killed and some of the team were still struggling to come to terms with the loss. They'd lost people in past operations but it had been a while since that had happened. The investigation into the shooting showed that Damian had managed to get two shots off. One hitting Scott in the shoulder and the other in the chest, clipping his heart. According to the autopsy results death was instantaneous. Scott had been the closest person to Damian at the time of the shooting and the assumption was that he presented the greatest threat which is why Damian had targeted him.

The scene at the time of the shooting was absolute chaos, people running for their lives as numerous shots were fired. Cass and Boyd had run forward still adopting a firing stance even though they could see that Damian was well and truly down. They'd checked for signs of life but Damian was dead. Putting their pistols back in their holsters they'd turned round to survey the scene. Cass could see several people looking from various places of safety, she saw Jake down on his knees and after telling Boyd to call it in she'd made her way over to Jake.

The horrifying sight of seeing Scott lying there rooted her to the spot. She could see Jakes mouth moving but she couldn't hear anything he was saying. The shock of seeing Jakes hands covered in Scott's blood as he tried to administer CPR was just too much for her and for several seconds everything was blanked out. Suddenly she came to her senses and could hear Jake pleading for help, she knelt down and checked for a pulse. She looked at Jake with a tear running down her cheek. Unable to speak all she could do was shake her head to indicate she couldn't find one. Jake kept up the chest compressions as Cass heard the first of the approaching sirens. Boyd had call 911 and requested both Police and paramedics, after that call he phoned Barney straight away.

Barney took a few minutes to absorb the news before making several calls. The first was to Jess asking her to fly straight back to Luke as he had an assignment for her. He knew that she wouldn't be in a fit state to fly as soon as she heard the news and wanted her to be with other members of the team when she found out. The next call was to the General, after giving him the bad news he asked for a favour. The General had understood the request straight away and dealt with it without question. As a result within an hour and a half of the General finding out, Charlie was on a flight to Luke Air Force Base. Luckily she was on an American Air Force Base and the General had enough clout and was owed enough favours to be able to get her straight on a military jet.

The next call was to Clay, he didn't want to tell Danny over the phone and had already told Jess to collect Danny on her way back to Luke. Barney asked Clay to keep the news from Danny but to get him to the airport as quickly as he could making up any excuse, he wanted to make it easier. He wanted Danny in the air with Jess so that they wouldn't find out until he could tell them both personally. Clay understood straight away and offered his condolences.

Next Barney set up a video call with the team in Hove and the Team in Europe. It wasn't an easy call and he would have rather been able to have done it in person but the logistics simply just didn't allow for that. The two groups took the information well. Barney had expected that as most of them had military backgrounds and had experienced the loss of teammates before, not that it made things any easier.

Barney still had a few of the team with him at Luke and he called them all in and sat them down giving them as much information as he could. Once he'd briefed them he grabbed a Humvee and drove to the far side of the airbase. Cole was still on base attached to a unit and Barney only felt it fair that it should be him that broke the news. He found Cole filling out an after action report in one of the squad rooms and once again recounted what had happened. Without hesitating Cole told Barney he'd like to go back with him to help with the team as they dealt with the shock, Barney smiled and nodded. While Cole cleared things with the Major he was working with Barney called the general to update him on what was happening.

Jess had just landed with Danny and they were both walking down the steps of the plane when an F15 taxied in and stopped next to them. They were both surprised as the fighters didn't usually use the hanger they'd been using. The ground crew carried out their duties and within minutes the Pilot and Co-pilot were stepping out of the plane, once on the ground the Co-pilot shook the Pilots hand and started to walk towards them. Danny looked at Jess and shrugged his shoulders only to find himself a few seconds later looking at Charlie as she took her helmet off. Once they'd finished hugging each other they made their way to meet Barney who was now back in the office with Grace and Cole.

Charlie, still in her flight suit, smiled at Barney, there was obvious strain in his voice when he replied and she knew instantly that something was wrong. They all sat down and Barney gave them the news, as expected Jess and Danny didn't take it too well. Leaving Cole to talk to them both he motioned Charlie to follow him as he left the room. Once outside he smiled at her. Not the usual smile full of warmth and under the circumstances that wasn't a surprise. "It's obvious why I've got you all the way over here and I just want to apologise. I know you don't like leaving things half done but right now I need help keeping things on track. This'll hit them all really hard and we've still got a fair bit of work to and I need them all focused and there simply isn't anyone better at that than you."

Charlie smiled, "Come on let's go and get things started."

Over the next few days Charlie drove them hard, mindful of how it would affect various members of the team she kept them busy and focused on the task at hand. She worked with Cole to ensure that a close eye was kept on Danny without him really knowing about it. By the end of the third day she'd managed to get everything buttoned up so that the whole Stateside team were back at Luke and two days after that they were all on their way back to the UK. As always at the end of any of their operations they completed various reports and everything was handed over to the relevant authorities and in this case it was the FBI, CIA and the US Marshalls.

Before leaving the States the team had attended Scott's funeral. For many of the team it was a stark reminder of the everyday dangers that they faced and for others it was a harrowing affair and incredibly difficult to deal with. The General had been present and had made sure that the team had everything they needed to help them deal with the loss. Once back at Luke Barney and James had been tasked by the General to find a replacement for Scott as quickly as possible. They both knew that the request was a simple matter of practicalities and needed to be dealt with as soon as possible. They didn't let the rest of the team know what they were doing as they felt it would make things harder than they already were.

The team in Europe had done exactly the same and they were all back in the office in Hove within a day of each other. Almost immediately James set up the task list of things to do and as always without question the team got on with their allotted assignments. There had been multiple arrests both sides of the Atlantic, where possible they'd managed to keep the majority of them low profile. In the end they'd managed to link eight couriers, six medical staff and fourteen men who had made use of the services provided. The arrests themselves then gave them a whole new amount of data to follow up on and the team were busy collating things with various agencies.

In the States the FBI and CIA had been given the lead and they were busy sifting through the vast and endless emails and follow up investigations. In Europe Interpol had followed up on several leads and had found three further victims still alive and had arranged for their safe return to the States. The US Marshall Service oversaw the necessary arrangements for all of the victims and worked with them gathering statements and detailing everything that could be remembered. That included Phoebe who Clay personally took care of. She was still struggling to come to terms with what had happened and Clay did whatever he could to make it easier for her.

Frederik's trial wasn't advertised and didn't take very long, the evidence against him was overwhelming. Despite paying for the best lawyers once some of the videos had been played to the jury his fate was sealed. His lawyers had tried to plea bargain but the judge ruled that they simply didn't have and strength behind their request or in fact anything to bargain with. One of the videos shown was of the girl before Phoebe and it was clear to see that he murdered her. The jury came back with a unanimous guilty verdict on all counts and very shortly after he was sentenced to life. Every person that had been involved had been given custodial sentences. Some were able to achieve a reduction in their sentence by divulging further information which in turn led to more arrests.

Within two days of being the UK a further eleven arrests were made as more evidence and names came to light. The team were now completing their final reports and handing the last few bits of information over. Barney called them all into the office for a final debrief before they closed the assignment. He looked round the table and took a deep breath. "I've just come off the phone with the General and he passes on his congratulations. Now I know that this assignment has cost us dearly but as hard as it is we have to look at the bigger picture and focus on the good that we've achieved. Our hard work has saved a number of people and has made a huge dent in what was a very profitable and high level trafficking ring"

James lent forward in his chair. "We've just found out from the FBI that as far as they're concerned Damian Stevens was acting on his own and it seems that Steven Goodbanks had no idea about the trafficking network that had been created. What we've managed to uncover is huge and we really mustn't lose sight of that. Now we've got at least a week off, assuming that we don't get a priority call from the General. So make the most of it and go and enjoy yourselves."

Barney took over once more, "we've got two non urgent jobs for when you all get back. Katie you'll take the lead on one and Cass you'll run the other. Cass you'll be stateside for yours and you'll need a team of six so I'll leave you and Katie to work out who's working in which team. Right, I'm taking Bruce for a walk along the seafront so if any of you have left before I get back enjoy yourselves. Take it easy and I'll catch up with each of you soon."

Half an hour later Barney was sat on the beach between Brighton Pier and the remains of the West Pier, Bruce was sat next to them eying up the nearest seagull. Barney knew that the loss of Scott was a terrible price for the team to pay for success. He also knew that sadly the outcome although overall positive sometimes had devastating side effects.

On the other side of the Atlantic Jake and Boyd were sat at the bar enjoying their second drink, they'd just completed the last report and sent it to their superiors. Boyd downed the rest of his beer, "well Jake that's my lot, I'm going to go to the store and get Janey to pick me up."

"Okay, I'm going to have one more then grab something to eat, see you tomorrow."

Jake picked up his glass and watched Boyd leave. As he swivelled back round to the bar his eyes fell on a very attractive woman that was looking directly at him, he smiled and she smiled back. He motioned to the bartender for another drink. Seconds later another Jack Daniels was in front of him, he picked it up and let his mind wander. The last few weeks had been tough, he'd taken the lead on the case and had been under constant pressure to deliver results. His superiors wanted to achieve a better result than the CIA and had simply dropped all of that pressure squarely onto Jake and thankfully he'd managed to deliver.

He suddenly became aware of a presence by his side, he turned his head to find himself looking straight into the eyes of the woman he'd smiled at moments before.

"Mind if I join you?" She had a soft but direct tine to her voice.

Jake smiled again, "no, please feel free, can I get you a drink?"

"What are you drinking?"

"Jake Daniels."

"That'll do nicely."

Jake motioned the bar tender once more, "one for the lady please."

Jake turned to face her, "what brings you here?"

"I was supposed to meet a girlfriend but she stood me up. I was about to leave when I saw your friend go so I thought I'd try my luck." She laughed

The barman put the drink down next to her and she picked it up knocking it back in one, "Two more please," she smiled at Jake, "I needed that."

Jake laughed, "I'm Jake," he held out his hand.

She took it and looking directly into his eyes replied, "hi Jake, I'm Angie."

Printed in Great Britain
by Amazon

24396034R00239